Sisters of Sword & Song

ALSO BY REBECCA ROSS

The Queen's Rising
The Queen's Resistance
Dreams Lie Beneath

REBECCA
ROSS

Sisters of Sword & Song

Quill Tree Books
An Imprint of HarperCollinsPublishers

Quill Tree Books is an imprint of HarperCollins Publishers.

Library of Congress Cataloging-in-Publication Data

Names: Ross, Rebecca (Rebecca J.), author.
Title: Sisters of sword and song / Rebecca Ross.
Description: First edition. | New York, NY : HarperTeen, an imprint of
    HarperCollins Publishers, [2020] | Audience: Ages 14 up. | Audience:
    Grades 10-12. | Summary: "Halcyon faces a fifteen-year sentence after
    being charged with murder, so her younger sister Evadne offers to carry
    part of her sentence and tries to uncover the truth behind the supposed
    crime along the way"— Provided by publisher.
Identifiers: LCCN 2020000849 | ISBN 978-0-06-247142-0 (paperback)
Subjects: CYAC: Sisters—Fiction. | Relics—Fiction. | Gods—Fiction. |
    Magic—Fiction. | Fantasy.
Classification: LCC PZ7.1.R728 Si 2020 | DDC [Fic]—dc23
LC record available at https://lccn.loc.gov/2020000849

Typography by Molly Fehr
21 22 23 24 25   PC/LSCH   10 9 8 7 6 5 4 3 2 1

First trade paperback edition, 2021

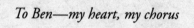

To Ben—my heart, my chorus

The Nine Divines
and their Earthly Relics

Magda, mother goddess of the sun:
The Sunstone Ring of Healing—grants enchanted healing to its bearer*

Irix, father god of the sky:
The Sky Cloak—grants power over weather and elements*

Ari, goddess of the moon and dreams:
The Shawl of Stars—grants protection to its bearer; is impenetrable and rebounds weapons

Nikomides, god of war:
The Devouring Sword—grants dominion over enemy weapons, turning them into dust; also cuts down enchantments

Euthymius, god of earth and beasts:
The Golden Belt—grants animal allegiance to its bearer

Acantha, goddess of fate and knowledge:
The All-Seeing Crown—grants its bearer protection from enchantments and enables them to see the past, present, or future of the one they look upon*

Loris, goddess of water and sea:
The Pearl Earrings—grants the power to breathe underwater*

Pyrrhus, god of fire (trapped beneath the earth):
The Ember Stone—grants fire effortlessly when the stone is breathed upon

Kirkos, god of the wind (fallen):
The Winged Necklace—grants flight to its bearer*

Denotes relics that are unaccounted for

THE FIRST SCROLL

A Necklace
Made of Wind

Evadne

Evadne stood beneath the olive tree watching Maia climb with a knife clenched in her teeth. The sun was setting, but the breeze was warm, sighing from the west, where the Origenes Sea churned just beyond the grove. It would storm by evening; Evadne could sense it coming on the wind. And then tomorrow would arrive, the day her family had been anticipating for eight long years.

One more sleep until I see her, Evadne thought, hardly remembering why she was standing in the grove until she heard Maia slip and catch herself on a limb. The tree shuddered in protest although Maia was the smallest of their family, hardly reaching Evadne's shoulder in height. She had insisted she be the one to climb.

"Can anyone see us?" Maia asked once she had regained her balance, her words blurred by the blade still held by her teeth.

Evadne glanced around the grove. They were at the thick heart of it; the grass was spangled with light, and the branches rustled with the breeze. She could hear sounds of the villa—voices and laughter—echoing in the distance. Both of their fathers should be together, working at the oil press on the far side of the property.

"We are alone, Maia."

Maia cut the branch and let it drop to the ground, right at Evadne's feet. She cut another, her knife ticking against the bark.

"Do you think your father will know, Eva?"

"That we cut from the god tree?" Evadne gathered the green-and-silver leaves, staring up as Maia balanced on the tree's warped limbs. She imagined a god tumbling through such branches, breaking his wings, and said, "Well, if my father realizes it, I will simply tell him it was all for Halcyon, and what can he say to that?"

Maia swiftly traded one worry for another. "Do you think Halcyon will recognize me tomorrow?"

"You are her cousin. Of course she will recognize you." But despite her confidence, Evadne had gnawed on this same worry for days. She had not seen Halcyon in eight years.

Evadne remembered the morning Halcyon had departed, had traced it so many times in her memory that she often dreamt about it at night. Evadne, nine years old, propped on a crutch, her ankle bandaged as she stood in the courtyard. Halcyon, twelve years old, hair bound back in braids, her belongings packed in a satchel, waiting to ride with their father to the city of Abacus.

"Don't go, don't go." Evadne had wept, clinging to her sister.

But Halcyon had smiled and said, "I must, Eva. The gods will it."

"Do not tell her this," Maia said, shifting to another branch, "but I was once jealous of your sister."

"So was I," Evadne confessed and with a shock discovered that the flame was still there, burning within her. *So am I,* her mind amended. *I am jealous of Halcyon, although I do not want to be.*

Maia stopped cutting to look at her, and for a moment, Evadne feared she had spoken her secret aloud.

"Do not mistake me," Maia rushed to say. "I was relieved *someone* in our family finally inherited *something* good. Halcyon deserved to make a name for herself. But . . . I do wish you and I could have something, too."

"Yes," Evadne agreed.

She and Maia were like the other members in their family. Void of magic, all because of their ancestor, a disgraced god who had fallen into this very olive tree centuries ago to break his wings. Or so the legend stated. That was why Evadne's father disliked anyone touching it, or climbing it, or harvesting from it. The tree had been the end of Kirkos, god of the wind. But it had also been a beginning. The beginning of this grove, of their family.

"Why would a god be so *foolish*?" Evadne had often ranted to her mother when they worked at the loom. "He had everything. Why give it all up?"

Truly, her anger stemmed from the fact that she was magicless and common and bound to live the same dull life every day until she returned to the dust. All because of Kirkos's choice to fall.

And her mother would only smile, a gentle but shrewd smile. "One day you will understand, Eva."

Well, Evadne believed she already understood. The truth was Kirkos had flown over this piece of land, a grove that was called Isaura, and had seen a mortal woman harvesting olives. He had come to love her so ardently that he had surrendered his immortality and power to remain on Earth with her, living as a mortal man, to tend the grove at her side, to give her children, to be buried beside her when he died.

If any of his descendants aspired to ascend within their court, it would not be by inherited magic but by some other gift or strength.

Which Halcyon had done.

"Do you think we have gathered enough?"

Maia's inquiry brought Evadne back to the present. She glanced at her armload of olive clippings. "Yes, more than enough. We should get back. Our mothers will be wondering what has taken us so long."

"Perhaps they will think one of the gods flew over the grove and—literally—fell in love with us," Maia said brightly as she dropped from the tree. It was a frequent quip of their family, but Evadne still laughed.

"Lightning never strikes in the same place twice, Maia. Sorry to disappoint you."

The cousins walked through the trees, finding the main path that wound up the hill to the villa. Most of the time, Evadne's right ankle ached only in the cold seasons. But it ached today, despite the sultry weather of a storm about to break, and every step through the grove was unpleasant. And when she noticed Maia glancing at the hem of Evadne's chiton, whisking over the grass and stained with dirt, she realized why Maia had volunteered to climb the tree.

"Am I limping *that* much, Maia?"

"No. I was just thinking about how hard it is going to be to get all that dirt washed out of your clothes."

Evadne shook her head but couldn't resist a smile. Their chitons were simple, made from white linen and cut into sleeveless tunics that they wore long. The garments were fastened at the shoulders with brooches and cinched at the waist with woven leather belts. In the cold seasons, they traded linen for woolen chitons and cloaks the color of the earth: umbers and greens and grays. Colors that blended into nature and quietly proclaimed their status in society, which was the lowest in their court.

How many times had Maia and Evadne and their mothers lamented over the stains that the grove gave their raiment on a daily basis? Laundry days were detested.

But just once, Maia swore, most likely when she was an old woman and held no more fear of what other people thought, she would wear the esteemed purple, as if she were Queen Nerine herself.

The girls walked the rest of the path in silence. Evadne was distracted by the ache in her stride, an ache sparked by the recent labor she and her family had undertaken, preparing for Halcyon's return. The past two weeks, they all had been stricken with work, eager to make the villa shine like a new coin, a place worthy of a girl who had ascended in the Common Court.

They had harvested the best of the fruit and gathered the first pressing of olives, oil so rich it was deemed sacred. They had aired the blankets so they would smell of summer winds and scrubbed the tiles and frescoes until they gleamed. They had filled all the lamps with oil and prepared their finest garments. Halcyon's name had been spoken frequently, reverently, like she was a goddess, and Evadne and her family had let the promise of her fill every corner and corridor of the villa.

By sundown tomorrow, Halcyon of Isaura would be home.

And what stories might she tell Evadne and Maia? Stories of the world outside the grove, one that glittered of the upper class and cities and chitons so fine they were iridescent in the light. It would be like opening a box of treasure, like a divine relic that Evadne could only admire, not touch and claim.

She dreamt of ascending rank in her court, too. Of leaving the dirt-stained chitons and windblown hair and seasonal strain of a land steward. To no longer be looked down upon by others, simply because she worked in the grove.

Evadne cast the ascension desire aside; it would never happen, so why did she keep entertaining it? She dwelled on her sister again and tried to imagine what it would be like to reunite with Halcyon, hugging her after all those years separated, and a jolting mix of joy and nerves shot through Evadne. Which would Halcyon sense more? The overflowing delight or the pinch of envy?

The girls reached the courtyard of the villa, where a herald waited beyond the gates, ringing the bell for admittance.

"What news could he possibly bring now?" Maia growled beneath her breath. "A higher tax on oil for us to pay?"

Indeed, that had been the most recent news—higher land and production taxes. The tax on a jar of second-pressed oil would soon be almost as much as its cost was, due to be paid at the end of the season.

"Here," Evadne said, dumping her olive clippings into her cousin's arms. "Take these inside. I will see what he wants." She walked across the warm flagstones and opened the gates.

The herald sighed, annoyed. He brushed the dust from his tunic and said, "I have been ringing this bell for close to half an hour!"

"Forgive us, herald. My family is preparing the villa for a visitor tomorrow." *Visitor*, as if Halcyon were a stranger. Evadne raised her brows, expectant. "What news do you bring us?"

The herald withdrew a roll of papyrus, bound by a wax seal. It was crushed, a testament of its long journey from the royal city of Mithra. "A new decree, by order of Queen Nerine."

Once, the mere sound of the queen's name had conjured wonder and hope in Evadne. Queen Nerine ruled Corisande with honor and equality and justice. Her profile had been etched upon the silver Akkia coins, and Evadne had often held that coin in her palm, trying to memorize the queen's features, as if Evadne could become her someday.

But that had been years ago. Before the laws and taxes had

begun to creep heavier and heavier upon common people.

She broke the seal and unrolled the papyrus, knowing the herald would not leave until he watched her read it.

By Order of Nerine, Queen of Corisande, Descendant of the Divine Acantha, Ruler of the Common Court and the Magical Court, Lady of the Origenes Sea:

From this day forth, the seventeenth day of the Archer's Moon, it is now recorded in the annals that any common person, should they come into the possession of a divine relic, is no longer considered a member of the Magical Court. A heavy fine will be imposed upon relic possessors who do not surrender their discoveries to the Mages' Council at the School of Destry.

Evadne rolled up the decree, her face guarded as the herald turned to mount his horse, and ride to the next village. She closed the gates with a clang, her mind consumed with thoughts of the gods and their relics.

There were nine divines. Well, eight now, since Kirkos was no longer considered a deity with his fall. Magda, mother goddess of the sun; Irix, father god of the sky; and their seven divine offspring: Ari, goddess of the moon and dreams; Nikomides, god of war; Acantha, goddess of fate and knowledge; Euthymius, god of earth and beasts; Loris, goddess of water and sea; Pyrrhus, god of fire; and Kirkos, god of the wind.

Centuries ago, when the kingdom of Corisande had just begun, the nine gods and goddesses came down to live among the mortals. They ate mortals' food, drank their wine, slept in their beds. And so their magic had trickled into mortal blood, and magical children had been born.

But not every child born inherited the magical gift of the gods. It was a fickle thing, skipping a son or a daughter, and then skipping entire generations. Keeping track of a family's lineage soon became an obsessive hobby for the upper class, who would arrange marriages and count generational gaps, trying in vain to predict when the next mage would be born in the family.

When the gods and goddesses realized the clamor they had inspired, they left the mortal kingdom, returning to their villas in the sky to be worshipped at a distance. But they each left behind a possession, a relic of theirs that was infused with magic. The divines hid them throughout Corisande, hoping the relics would be claimed by common-blooded people, those who were magicless. So the era of relic hunters had begun. To find and possess a relic meant one could wield a tiny source of magic, no matter their common blood. They could join the prestigious Magical Court. *Until now*, Evadne thought with a frustrated sigh.

"What does it say?" Maia called, leaning out one of the villa windows.

Evadne walked it to her cousin, watching Maia scowl as she read the edict.

"How ridiculous! Why would the queen even decree this?"

"It sounds as if the Magical Court is tired of common people joining their ranks," Evadne said. "And they complained so much about it that the queen had no other choice but to cast it into law."

Maia crinkled it in her fingers. "My brother is going to be upset."

"As if he were ever going to discover a divine relic."

"True," Maia said. "Lysander can hardly tell east from west. I wonder if Uncle Ozias ever found a relic, though."

Ozias had left the grove when the girls were little to become a relic hunter, to both of their fathers' great dismay and anger. There had been a falling-out among the three brothers, hinging on the fact that Kirkos's relic was unaccounted for. Ozias had believed the fallen god's necklace had been buried with him in the grove, and they should dig up the god's bones to claim it. Gregor and Nico had refused to allow it, and Ozias had left, disowning his family.

They did not expect to see Uncle Ozias again.

"Unlikely," Evadne said. "My father thinks Uncle Ozias ended up in the quarry at Mithra."

Maia scrunched her nose. "Gods, I hope Uncle Ozias is not there! That is where all the common murderers are sent."

"Relic hunters often kill to get what they want."

"Such morbid thoughts, Eva. Come, forget about the decree and help me weave crowns for Halcyon."

The anxious butterflies returned to Evadne's stomach as her family gathered in the common room to eat supper. Talk centered on the new edict at first—Lysander was, predictably, upset by it—but that conversation soon faded; there were far more important things to discuss. Like Halcyon.

Evadne and Maia sat on the floor and wove their olive branches into crowns—one for every member of their family to wear tomorrow to honor Halcyon. The weaving motions gave Evadne purpose, a comfort, until Lysander sprawled on the floor near them, picking the leaves off the branches.

"Lysander, *stop*!" Maia squawked.

Lysander ignored his sister as he tore another leaf. He was still indignant about the new decree; everyone knew he wanted to chase after relics, with or without his parents' blessing. He wanted to be the first of their family to join the Magical Court.

"I wonder how many scars Halcyon has now," he said.

The room fell silent. Evadne's father, Gregor, froze on his bench, a piece of stew-drenched bread halfway to his mouth. And Evadne's mother, Phaedra, who was mending a torn cloak, also went still, as if her hands had forgotten what to do with the needle and thread.

Aunt Lydia, Maia and Lysander's mother, had been lighting the oil lamps because the last of the sunlight had drifted out the open window, and she appeared shocked at her son's words. But it was Uncle Nico who was the first to respond, his bearded face wrinkled from squinting hours in the sunlight, his curly hair limned with gray as he continued to mend a pair of sandals on his lap.

"She will not have any, Lysander. You remember how swift Halcyon is. She was impossible to champion. And should she have scars . . . well, they would be marks of achievement."

The pressure in the room eased as they began to reminisce about Halcyon.

"Remember how she beat all the village boys in a race?" Aunt Lydia said, voice thick with pride as she finished lighting the lamps. The firelight flickered through the room, a dance of gold and shadows.

"No one could best her," Maia agreed. "There was that vile boy from Dree. Remember him, Eva? He thought he could beat her in a fighting match, but she proved him wrong *twice*. Laid him out cold on the ground in one punch. Glorious."

Yes, Evadne thought, remembering. She spun two more crowns, and when the storm finally broke, she rose, ready to dismiss herself for bed.

"But, Pupa!" her father cried. "We have not sung tonight! You cannot go to bed yet."

Her father would sing every night if he could convince Evadne to join him. He was also fond of nicknames. Long ago, he had dubbed both of his daughters: Halcyon was "Sprout," and Evadne was "Pupa." Pupa, as in insect larvae. When Evadne had learned what it meant, she'd been angry until he had told her it was the stage of transformation, when a butterfly was spinning her wings. Since then, they had made a game of finding cocoons in the grove.

"Sorry, Father," Evadne said. "But I am too tired. Maia will sing with you tonight."

Maia ceased her weaving, mouth agape. "Who, *me*? I can't sing!"

Lysander huffed his agreement, only to earn a swat from Maia.

"We shall *all* sing tonight," Phaedra said, setting aside her mending. "Save for you, Eva. I know you need rest."

Her family began to sing the Harvest Song as Evadne slipped away. She slowly ascended the stairs to the upper floor, following the corridor to her bedroom.

She entered her chamber, closing the door behind her. It was dark; her oil lamp must have burned out. Evadne crossed the room to reach her lamp stand, feeling her way with her bare feet until she discovered the floor was damp. She halted, staring at the window, the shutters drifting back and forth in a gust of storm, and she knew that she had bolted them before supper.

She sensed it then. Someone in the room, watching her in the darkness. She could hear them breathe, a rasp trying to hide in the patter of rain.

Her dagger was on the shelf, a few paces away, and Evadne lunged to it, her right ankle smarting with the sudden movement. But a shadow peeled itself free from the darkness, intercepting her. A cold hand gripped Evadne's wrist, drawing her about to face them. Evadne gasped, filling her lungs to scream, but the hand flickered to cover her mouth like a seal. There was a gentle strength in their grip, a hesitation that made Evadne realize . . . the stranger was not going to harm her but wanted her quiet.

"Evadne." A girl spoke, her voice breaking on the sound, like a wave on a rock.

Evadne did not move, not even as the hand lowered from her mouth. She could not see the intruder's face, but she suddenly sensed her presence . . . tall and lean, the scent of metal and rain on her skin, the familiar cadence of her voice, one that had lived only in Evadne's dreams and memories the past eight years.

"Evadne," the girl whispered again. "It is me. Your sister, Halcyon."

— II —

Evadne

Halcyon?" Evadne tentatively reached out, her fingertips meeting an array of cold scales. Scales like a serpent. A monster. Startled, she brought her hands back, and then she realized it was only Halcyon's armor. She yearned to see her sister's face, but the darkness shielded her. "What are you doing here? When did you arrive? We were expecting you tomorrow night!"

"Evadne," Halcyon said again, and the sound was heavy, reluctant.

Evadne's excitement waned.

Something was wrong.

"I realize I have come a day early," Halcyon began. "And I am sorry to have surprised you tonight, but I wanted to see you first."

"Let me light the lamp," Evadne said, reaching for Halcyon's hand. "Come, sit on the bed."

This room had once belonged to them both. And Halcyon still

had it memorized, Evadne realized, as she effortlessly located the bed in the darkness. Evadne fumbled to find her lamp stand, lighting it with her ember stone. She was trembling when she finally turned to behold her sister.

Halcyon was beautiful.

Her skin was tanned from her days training in the sun, and her raven hair brushed the tops of her shoulders, glistening from the rain. Her face was still perfect, her cheekbones more pronounced now, but her eyes were the same shade of honey, framed by long lashes, and her brows were still arched and elegant. Her arms were corded with muscle and speckled with little scars, but the scars were not unsightly. They were as Uncle Nico had said: marks of her achievement, a testament to her training and her prowess with sword and spear and shield. She was a hoplite in the Queen's Army, a member of the Bronze Legion now.

And if the scars on her arms were not enough, her raiment proclaimed exactly who she was.

Her chiton was dyed bright red, the color of the army, and was tailored the length of her thighs, resting beneath her armor's hard linen pleats. Her cuirass was made of bronze scales, its two yokes coming over her shoulders to tie at the front. The straps were painted with the entwined serpents that represented Nikomides, the god of war, symbols to guard Halcyon's front and back in battle. Her sandal straps crosshatched their way up her calves, knotting just beneath her knees.

Halcyon was foreign to Evadne in this armor, in these clothes. A stranger.

And Evadne knelt before her, awed and proud of who Halcyon had become. Halcyon, her sister, the girl who was swift and strong. The girl who had ascended.

Halcyon smiled and leaned forward to frame Evadne's face in her hands.

"Ah, look at you, Sister," Halcyon whispered. "You are so beautiful. And this hair! Just like father's." She touched the unruly brown waves. "How I have missed you, Eva. I have missed you every day since I left."

"As I have missed you, Hal."

"Why are you kneeling? Come sit next to me!" Halcyon tugged her upward, and Evadne settled beside her on the bed.

They were quiet for a moment. Evadne didn't know what to say, even though she had been hoarding questions for years.

Halcyon, at last, ended the silence. "Tell me what adventures you have had while I was away! I trust our parents have been well? And Maia? And that Lysander is still as pleasant as ever?"

Evadne laughed, thinking not much had changed since Halcyon had left. She began to tell Halcyon news of their family, of the grove. It was their common ground, and Halcyon listened intently, asking after the crops and harvest and the pressing. She asked about the seasons that had continued to cycle in her absence. Rain and storms and drought and lean and plenty.

"But enough about the grove," Evadne eventually said, her focus drifting to the formidable gleam of Halcyon's armor. "I want to hear about the legion."

Halcyon looked down at her hands. Evadne realized there was

something dark beneath her sister's nails. At first, she had believed it to be dirt, but it was something else. Like old blood.

"The legion," Halcyon said, and she sounded exhausted. "Where do I even begin?"

Begin at the beginning, Evadne wanted to beg her. *Begin at the day you arrived at Abacus.*

A knock sounded on the door, and the moment broke. Halcyon soundlessly shot to her feet; her entire body went rigid, her hand moving to the bone hilt of her kopis, a small scythe, sheathed in leather at her side.

Evadne gaped up at her sister, startled by her defensive reaction. It was as if Halcyon expected an enemy to lurk on the other side of the door, and not their father, who gently called, "Pupa? Pupa, are you still awake?"

A beat of silence. Halcyon stared at the door, eyes wide, and Evadne stared at Halcyon, heart skipping in alarm. Something was off about her sister.

Another knock. "Eva?"

Halcyon pivoted, casting her desperation on Evadne. "Please, Eva. *Please*, do not tell him I am here."

But why? Evadne almost demanded until she saw worry mar her sister's brow, and she feared Halcyon would flee, back out the window.

Evadne stood and motioned for Halcyon to stand against the same wall as the door, so if their father peered into the room, he would not see her.

Halcyon obeyed, and Evadne cracked open the door to find

her father waiting with a sleepy smile.

"Ah, good. I thought I had woken you."

"No, Father. Do you need something?" Evadne stood firmly on the threshold, like a barrier, to keep him from catching a glimpse of Halcyon.

"I was thinking about tomorrow night. About Halcyon's return," Gregor said around a yawn.

"Oh?"

"What should we sing for her? Your mother suggested the Song of Eternal Night, because that was once Halcyon's favorite. But perhaps we should sing something different? Should we sing a war song? Would she prefer that now, do you think?"

Evadne swallowed. From the corner of her eye, she could see Halcyon hiding against the wall, her armor reflecting the firelight, her hair still dripping rain, her chest rising and falling as she fought to breathe quietly.

Evadne's hesitation made Gregor worry.

"You are still planning to sing with me, aren't you, Eva?"

She flushed with guilt. "Of course, Father. I am happy to sing with you tomorrow night, and I think Halcyon would like the Song of Eternal Night."

Gregor's smile returned, and he glanced over Evadne's shoulder, where Halcyon's bed rested against the wall, blankets freshly laundered and folded in wait for her. The joy was written on his face; his firstborn daughter would soon be home, and Halcyon was going to fill the empty space that had been haunting the villa and grove since she had departed.

"Anything else, Father?"

Gregor kissed Evadne's brow and said, "Close your shutters, Pupa. You are letting the storm in."

Evadne laughed, a wispy, nervous sound. But her father did not notice, disappearing down the corridor.

She closed the door and looked to Halcyon, riddled with questions. Her sister slowly sank to the floor, her face ashen. She was no longer the fierce hoplite, the unbeatable girl. Halcyon looked afraid, and that made Evadne afraid.

"Halcyon? What has happened?"

Her sister shut her eyes, as if the question were a punch.

"Hal?" Evadne took hold of her shoulder, soft but insistent.

Halcyon looked at her, dazed.

"You must tell me what has happened," Evadne whispered.

"Eva . . . do you think you can find me something to eat and drink? I cannot remember the last time I ate."

Evadne was shocked by that admission, but then she realized that the only possessions Halcyon carried were the kopis sheathed at her side and a canteen slung across her shoulder.

"Yes. But first, let us undress you from this armor. You can lie on your bed and rest, and I will fetch you something from the storerooms." Evadne helped her rise, guiding Halcyon to her bed. She sat but made no effort to undress herself.

Uncertain of what else to do, Evadne hurried to close the shutters before their banging could draw Gregor back. When she glanced once more at Halcyon, she saw that her sister had finally lain down.

Evadne slipped from the room, moving as quietly as she could through the villa, down to the storerooms. But her heart was churning, pounding in her ears like a chorus . . .

What are you running from, Sister?

What have you done?

— III —

Halcyon

I *t was not supposed to be like this*, Halcyon thought as she listened to Evadne quietly leave the room. Halcyon was to return home with joy and honor. It was not supposed to be as a fugitive, creeping in through her little sister's bedroom window.

Although this had once been Halcyon's chamber, too. In another life.

She lay on her childhood bed, pressed her face into the blankets. She breathed in the fragrance of the old days, a medley of sun and salt wind and the green enchantment of the grove, until she could not bear it and made herself stand.

This room was exactly how she remembered it. Evadne's side cluttered with trinkets and scrolls. Halcyon's side bare and minimal, save for the wall aligned with her bed, where the fresco of a basilisk had been painted over. This had once been Uncle Ozias's room, but when he'd departed years ago, it had been given to the girls. Evadne had been frightened of the ancient serpent on the wall, and Gregor had had no choice but to paint over it. The basilisk had never bothered Halcyon, though, and she studied the cracks in the paint, where flashes of the beast could still be seen.

Nausea crept over her, and Halcyon reached out to steady herself on the wall, on the fading basilisk, cold sweat trickling down her back. It had taken the last of her strength to act normal, to hide her weariness from Evadne. But this was a skill the hoplites learned in their first year of training: how to push themselves, and then push themselves even more, when it felt like there was nothing left in them. There was always more, the commander had told her when Halcyon, twelve years old, had collapsed on the ground, ill from exertion. He had stood beside her, his shadow granting her some relief from the scorching sun, and he had watched her vomit. She had thought she would die, but she did not curl up into a ball, not with him watching.

"Get up," he had said. "There is always more strength to draw from. You must find where it hides and wield it."

And she had not whimpered, *I cannot*, as did the other first-year hoplites. Although she had questioned why she had chosen the hoplite legion in that moment of pain; she could have easily been accepted into the charioteers or the archers or the oarswomen of the fleet. But no . . . Halcyon had wanted to be a foot solider. It was the hardest, the most demanding. The most glorious in her mind.

Halcyon straightened, her hand slipping from the wall, her nausea subsiding. She cast away thoughts of the commander and of the last eight days. She walked to Evadne's side of the room, where the color and life dwelled, her attention focusing on the wax tablet that sat on her little sister's oaken chest.

Halcyon's handwriting still marked the wax. Amazed, she reached for the tablet and studied it, her heart softening with the memory.

It was the cipher she and Evadne had created together, a language only the two of them knew. A language inspired by nature—trees and flowers, birds and dragonflies, mountains and rain clouds.

It had been Halcyon's idea. The secret language of "Haleva" had emerged as an effort to cheer Evadne.

Evadne had just learned how to read and write in the Common Speech and in the God Tongue. She had fervently believed that she would inherit magic, despite her being a descendant of Kirkos. And no one had tried to douse that innocent hope. Not even Halcyon, who watched Evadne take a quill in her hand, learning her letters and words, expectantly waiting for the magic to wake in them.

Magic, for all of its mysteries, was forthright in its choosing. If a child had inherited it, magic would make itself known in literacy. There was never any doubt to its manifestation. Halcyon did not fully understand the phenomenon, but she had heard it explained like this: A mage cast magic with their dominant hand, be it right or left. And when they wrote with that hand, their words would refuse to stick to the papyrus. The words would fade, or slip off the edge, or turn into something else, as if they had a will of their own. But truly, it was the magic, humming in their handwriting.

As Evadne had become literate, it had become apparent to her family that she was common as they all were. And yet Evadne refused to believe it. Not even as her inked letters remained married to the papyrus, immobile and magicless.

"I am certain the magic will appear tomorrow in my letters," Evadne would tell Halcyon every night when they climbed into bed. "I wonder what the Destry is like. Do you think Mother and Father will send me to the school right away?"

The Destry was the school for mages. Any child who exhibited magic in their writing was to be sent to the Destry, located in the royal city of Mithra, to be properly instructed in magic until they came of age. It was a requirement by law.

And Halcyon had lain in her bed, listening to Evadne talk her wonders about magic and the Destry, as if she were bound to attend.

"You must help her understand, Halcyon," their mother had finally said to her. "Evadne does not have magic, and you must help her bear this disappointment."

That was when the cipher, Haleva, had been born. Halcyon had helped Evadne create her own magical language, and it had eased the sting in Evadne's common heart. It had also made for hours of vast amusement as the sisters sent messages to one another, drawing fury from Lysander and fascination from Maia.

The door creaked.

Halcyon snapped her attention to the threshold, tense, but it was Evadne, returning with a food sack and a flask tucked beneath her arm.

"It is only me," Evadne reassured her, and Halcyon relaxed. "I see you found the old Haleva cipher."

Halcyon glanced down to the wax tablet. "You never erased it, even after all these years?"

"How could I erase the only magic I have ever known?" Evadne smiled and began to walk across the floor. That was when Halcyon noticed it. The limp in her sister's gait.

"Evadne," Halcyon breathed, looking to where Evadne's right foot peeked out from her hem. "Your ankle still troubles you?"

Evadne froze for a beat. It almost seemed like she was embarrassed, ashamed of it.

"Oh. No, not usually. Only in the cold seasons."

Evadne resumed walking—she was trying to conceal her limp, and that vexed Halcyon—but she handed over the food and ale, and Halcyon sensed she did not want to talk about it.

They sat side by side on Evadne's bed, the wax tablet resting between them, and Halcyon began to search the sack. She had been surviving on berries and nuts and stolen chickpeas the past week, and occasionally a fish or a hare if she had the time to hunt, which was slim with the commander pursuing her. Her mouth watered when she drew out a honey cake. One of her favorites. She ate slowly, savoring it, listening to the rain tap against the shutters, knowing she should ration the food. But she drew out a pair of figs next and devoured them both without a second thought.

Evadne was quiet. She traced the wax symbols of Haleva and

then asked, "Why did you arrive early, Hal? Why did you crawl through my window?"

Halcyon swallowed the last of the figs and knotted the sack. It was time, she knew. She drank a few sips of ale from the flask, remembering the speech she had practiced.

"I'm in trouble, Eva."

Evadne patiently waited for an explanation. When it failed to come, she said, "Yes, I gathered that much. What kind of trouble?"

Halcyon let out a breath. "I cannot tell you the details. No matter how much I want to."

"You do not trust me?"

The words cut, but Halcyon parried them quickly. "I trust you with my life, Evadne. That is why I chose *your* window to climb through."

Evadne glanced away, distressed.

Halcyon sighed and reached for her hand. "I do not tell you because I want to protect you."

"And what are you protecting me from?"

"Look at me, Eva."

It took her a moment, but Evadne brought her eyes to Halcyon's.

"Tomorrow he will arrive here," Halcyon whispered and felt the corresponding tightness in Evadne's grip.

"'He'? Who do you speak of?"

"The commander of my legion. Lord Straton." Halcyon hesitated for a beat. "Eight days ago, I committed a crime. I did not intend for it to happen, but it did, and my hand bears the guilt of it."

"What—"

"I am not going to tell you the crime, Eva. And it is not because I mistrust you, but because he must not know you aided me. When Lord Straton arrives, he will tell you what I have done, and why he is hunting me, and you must be surprised, as our parents will be. Or else he will know you helped me. Do you understand?"

Evadne was silent, but Halcyon could hear her breaths quicken. "You have been running from him. For *eight* days?"

Halcyon nodded. It was an astounding feat that she had outwitted and outrun Lord Straton with only her canteen and her kopis. Again, she imagined him camped somewhere near, scowling at the storm, asking himself, *Where would she run?*

By dawn, he would know. He would realize how close he was to Isaura, and he would come.

"What if you remained here, Hal? To speak with your commander when he comes tomorrow? If the crime was an accident, as you said, surely your commander will understand."

"No. He will not, Eva. If he catches me . . ." She could not finish it. Partly because the image truly terrified her, and partly because she had no inkling what Straton would do.

Evadne's face went blank, like she was drifting into shock. "He would not kill you, would he?"

And Halcyon, as much as she wanted to, could not lie. "I do not know, Eva. That is why he must not catch me."

Evadne stood and paced in a circle. But she finally came to a stop before Halcyon, her voice husky as she whispered, "I can hide you, Halcyon. You remember the sea caves on the coast? Where Lysander slipped and broke his arm? I can take you there now."

Gently, Halcyon answered, "That is a generous offer, Eva. But you must not hide me. Lord Straton will know if you do, and he will not be kind in prying the truth from you. I must run, and you cannot know where I go."

She expected Evadne to object. But her sister surprised her again. "What more do you need? Food? A different set of clothes? We can disguise you."

Halcyon almost took the offer, her hand going to the anchor of her cuirass, eager to shed it. "But my armor . . . Where could you hide it, Eva?"

Evadne bit her lip, glancing around their room. There was nowhere to hide it. Halcyon could not leave a trace.

"I should keep it with me," she said, standing. "And you have brought me more than enough food, Sister. Thank you."

Evadne did not look convinced. The food would last another day, maybe. Halcyon could tell by the weight of the sack. But she could not risk Evadne pilfering more from the storeroom. Their mother might notice.

Evadne walked to the window to open the shutters. The wind and rain blew in, tangling her long hair.

Halcyon followed, her sandals leaving dirty tracks on the wet floor.

"Will I see you again?" Evadne whispered, fearful, as they stood shoulder to shoulder, facing the night.

"Yes. When it is safe for me to return home, I will. I swear it."

Evadne stared into the storm, unable to say goodbye.

Halcyon crawled up to the windowsill. But she glanced back to Evadne and whispered, "Do not be afraid, Little Sister."

Evadne drew in a sharp breath, but if she was intending to speak again, Halcyon would never know.

She dropped from the ledge, catching herself on the vine that grew up the villa wall. Down she went, scaling and slipping against the wet stones, but she soon found the ground and stood in the downpour, gaining her bearings.

Lightning forked across the sky, illuminating the mountains that rose on Isaura's northern border.

Halcyon began to walk to them, thunder shaking the ground. She could hear the groaning of the grove, branches swaying and leaves rustling in the storm, and when she sensed that Evadne could no longer see her, she fell to her knees in the mud and sobbed.

She had been holding it in her chest for days, ever since the accident happened. Suppressing it, as if the emotion would fade. Weeping now gave her some relief, but not enough to dull the ache in her heart.

Do not look back, Halcyon told herself, dashing rain and tears from her face. She knew she would see Evadne's shutters still open, her sister framed in golden firelight. She knew she would crawl back to her.

So Halcyon rose, set her eyes on the dark ridge of the northern mountains, and ran.

⤛ IV ⤜

Evadne

Straton arrived as Halcyon said he would, just as the sun began its descending arc in the sky. Evadne was in the garden with Maia, harvesting herbs in the shade of the villa, when they heard the distant clattering of hooves on the road. Evadne stopped working, her fingers lost in a tangle of oregano. She could feel the tremble in the earth as the commander approached their home. A steady, angry rhythm.

She tilted her face away from Maia to hide the fear that furrowed her brow.

"That must be Halcyon!" Maia cried, jumping to her feet with a broad smile. "Come, Eva!" She hurried down the stone walkway that curved to the courtyard. Evadne slowly rose.

The villa was suddenly a whirl of shouts and excited pattering of sandaled feet. Gregor and Uncle Nico came running from the grove; Phaedra and Aunt Lydia flew down the path from the press. Even Lysander darted from the barn, straw clinging to his clothes.

Evadne was the last to arrive to the courtyard.

The gates were open, anticipating Halcyon's return. Gregor and Phaedra stood at the forefront, arms wound about one another, eagerly awaiting something that would never come.

Just when Evadne thought the suspense would break her, the commander arrived, trotting through the gates into Isaura's courtyard, mounted on the greatest horse Evadne had ever seen. In his shadow were ten other hoplites, their horses lathered like foam from the sea. The warriors were heavily armored; it was painful to look upon them as the sunlight reflected off their bronze greaves, breastplates, and helms. They bore swords, kopises, quivers of arrows, bows, axes, and spears among their traveling supplies.

What had Halcyon done to warrant such a hunt?

"Is my daughter with you, Lord?" Gregor asked, studying the faces of the hoplites that had encircled them. "We are eager to see her again."

Straton was silent. He took his gaze from Gregor, his eyes examining the family, one by one. He was, likewise, searching for Halcyon. His helm was crested with black-and-white horsehair; the wind teased it when his gaze finally settled on Evadne. And there it lingered, measuring her face.

Evadne went cold with dread.

"I was about to ask the very same of you, Gregor of Isaura," the commander said, removing his scrutiny from Evadne. "Halcyon is not among us, but perhaps one of you or your kin has seen her this morning, or the night before?"

"No, we have not seen her yet, Lord. She is expected to arrive this evening."

"Indeed," Straton said wryly. "As we are both waiting for her, perhaps my warriors and I may sup with you tonight, to celebrate Halcyon's homecoming."

Gregor and Phaedra exchanged a furtive glance. They finally sensed something was amiss.

"Of course, Lord," Phaedra said, her voice pleasant despite the sudden strain in the air. "Come inside and refresh yourselves."

Straton dismounted, and Lysander stumbled forward to take his horse to the barn. The commander looked at Evadne again. He knew she was Halcyon's sister. That was why he continued to scrutinize her. He lifted his hand, giving a signal to his warriors.

The hoplites paired into five groups and turned their horses back to the gates, cantering to the south, the north, the east, and the west of Isaura. Evadne knew they were riding to search the hillsides and the grove.

Run, Halcyon, Evadne prayed. *Run swiftly, Sister.*

"What are they doing?" Maia mused aloud.

Lydia pivoted and grasped the girls' arms, guiding them to the villa door. "Make haste, the two of you. Go wash and don your celebration clothes and then come to the kitchen and help us prepare Halcyon's feast."

"But Halcyon is not here yet," Maia objected.

"Do as I say," Lydia replied firmly, but she was not looking at Maia; she was looking at Evadne.

And all Evadne could think was her aunt had noticed the missing food.

Evadne entered the villa, going directly to the wash bucket. She was filthy from the gardens and scrubbed her hands, anxious to feel something other than dread.

"Do you think Halcyon is in trouble?" Maia whispered as she stood beside Evadne, their elbows bumping.

Evadne avoided Maia's gaze. "I do not know."

She left her cousin to wash, moving as fast as she could up the stairs to her bedchamber.

Halcyon's blankets were wrinkled from when she had briefly lain down on her bed. Evadne rushed to refold and straighten them. And then she noticed the floor. Sunlight poured in through the open window, illuminating Halcyon's footprints on the tiles.

Evadne stripped off her chiton and dipped it into her pot of water, falling to her knees to scrub the prints away, angry and heartsick. This was not how this day was to unfold.

Once the floor was clean, Evadne opened her oaken chest and found her best chiton, the one she had been saving for tonight. It was white, its hem patterned with a green vine. The most adorned of all her garments. She donned it, cinching it with her leather belt before reaching for the two brass brooches her mother had bought her as a gift. They were fashioned as olive wreaths, and Evadne fastened her chiton at the shoulders with the pins, her hands trembling.

Do not be afraid, Little Sister.

She looked out the window. In the distance, the Dacia Mountains rose like the knuckles of a god's hand. Evadne wondered if Halcyon had fled to those mountains to hide, but then she thought how foolish that would be, because of Mount Euthymius.

Mount Euthymius was the tallest summit in the kingdom, and even though Evadne could not see it from her window in Isaura, she knew the Dacia ridge answered to it. No one wanted to live in the shadow of Euthymius, where fears manifested and had the power to roam the land as phantoms, where the door to the Underworld could be found in the mountain's vast heart.

As a girl, Evadne had been terrified of the summit, as all the children of Corisande were taught to be. Euthymius, god of earth and beasts, had laid claim to it centuries ago, during the era when the nine divines dwelled among mortals. Euthymius's brother, Pyrrhus, god of fire, had foolishly taken stones from the mountains and breathed his fire into them, leaving the "ember stones" as relics throughout the kingdom, much to the adoration of common people, who could now spark fire effortlessly. Soon, more people worshipped Pyrrhus than they did Euthymius, and Euthymius grew jealous and irate that his brother had used pieces of the earth for his magical fire. He began to devise a way to make Pyrrhus pay.

It did not take long.

Pyrrhus wanted a passage forged below the earth, so he could create his dream of an Underworld. Euthymius and his sister Loris, goddess of water, made an agreement with Pyrrhus, that they would carve into the mountain's heart and create a door for him. But in order for Pyrrhus to reach the door, he had to pass through layers of earth and water, and it swallowed all his fire. He was the only god still earthbound, trapped behind his own door in the mountain ironically named after his brother. As such, his rage could still be felt from time to time, in the trembling of the earth. And all the temples throughout the kingdom—even those where Euthymius was worshipped—never let their fire burn out like Pyrrhus had.

Evadne closed her shutters. She shivered, as she always did when she thought of Mount Euthymius and the god of fire trapped beneath the ground.

No, Halcyon would not run to the mountains. Even she had been afraid of Mount Euthymius, Evadne thought as she returned to the main floor of the villa.

She could feel Straton's presence like a shadow had fallen over them. Evadne began to walk the corridor to the kitchen until she heard her father speaking.

"I must ask, Lord Straton. Why have you come here for Halcyon? Has my daughter done something to merit this visit?"

The men were in the common room. The doors were ajar; Evadne paused in the shadow of the threshold, listening.

"I think we should wait and let Halcyon answer that herself, when she arrives," the commander said.

He had no doubt his warriors would find her, would drag her home in shame.

Evadne gritted her teeth, hating him in that moment.

She went to the kitchen where her mother, Aunt Lydia, and Maia were already at work bringing out bowls of fruit and warming flatbread on the cooking brazier.

No one spoke.

Evadne opened the cellar door to bring up two jugs of ale. When she returned to the kitchen, Gregor was waiting for her.

"Pupa." Her father sounded terribly calm. "Lord Straton wants to speak to you. Serve him a cup of ale, answer his questions, and then return here at once. This is nothing to fret over. You are blameless."

But she was not blameless.

Evadne found the nicest goblet from the cupboard and filled it with ale. Her family watched, frozen as statues in a temple, and perhaps that was why she was able to move with grace, because she knew what was about to happen.

She entered the common room.

The commander sat on her father's bench, his legs outstretched, crossed at the ankles. Mud freckled his armor, and his weapons were laid out around him. He had finally removed his helm, and Evadne could see his face.

Straton's brow was heavy, his cheeks pronounced. His skin was weathered from the sun and scarred from blades. His dark hair was cropped short, shot through with silver. Even motionless and quiet, his presence commanded the room.

Evadne brought him the refreshment. In her sudden anxiousness, the ale sloshed over the side of the cup. The amber drops gathered on the commander's scar-flecked hand—and his hand was huge, one that could effortlessly squeeze life from a throat.

Evadne envisioned it gripping Halcyon's neck, and she froze before him.

"Sit, child." His voice was surprisingly gentle.

He took the cup, and Evadne sat directly across from him. She tried to relax, but with Straton watching her . . . she felt like a mouse beneath the gaze of a hawk.

"Halcyon spoke of you often at the camp," the commander said.

"She did?"

"Yes. Her little sister, Evadne. The two of you were very close, before she left to train in Abacus."

Evadne swallowed. What had Halcyon told him?

He was waiting for her to respond.

So she nodded, words caught in her throat as she tried to antic-ipate what he would say next. She noticed his gaze flickered to her right foot, nearly hidden beneath the tumble of vine-laden hem.

"She told me how she saved your life that day, long ago. It was right before she joined my legion, so she would have been twelve, which made you what? Nine years old, Evadne?" Straton raised his eyes to hers again; they were a shade of blue, and they burned. It was like staring at the sky that ringed the sun, and it was difficult to hold his gaze, but Evadne did, refusing to look away from him.

And he pitched her back in time.

Halcyon had just beaten the vile boy of Dree in a fighting match, and she and Evadne and Maia and Lysander were walk-ing the road home with the swagger of champions. They passed a shepherd and his dog, and the dog had not seemed right, relent-lessly barking at the children, straining at his leash. Evadne had been afraid, but the dog was bound and the shepherd apologized and the children had continued onward.

But the dog had gotten loose and chased after them.

Lysander and Maia had crouched down, huddled beside a tree, but Evadne had run, despite Halcyon shouting at her not to. The dog had gone for her ankle, and she could still feel its teeth sinking into her skin, the way it had jerked and snapped her around, as if she was weightless.

As Evadne sprawled on her back, the dog lunged for her face, but something had come between them. A branch, swinging with incredible force, catching the dog in the mouth.

It was Halcyon, and Evadne had watched, stunned, as her sister beat back the dog, beginning a dangerous dance with it, wielding nothing more than a branch she had picked up from the roadside. And when the dog had snapped her branch in two, Halcyon had still not been afraid. She had taken the animal to the ground.

"I cannot seem to remember now," the commander said, and Evadne drew her right foot farther back. "Did Halcyon kill the dog?"

Evadne flushed. Her fingers clenched in her lap—she could hear her pulse beat in her ears—but she was calm, collected as she countered him. "What do you think, Lord?"

Straton smiled, but it was a bitter one. It cast a sinister expression on his face, and Evadne finally glanced away.

"I imagine she did," he drawled. "It was, after all, why your parents decided to bring her to me. It was the moment, Halcyon claims, when she knew she was not destined for the grove but for something else."

As much as it irked her, the commander was right. Halcyon was gifted. Killing the dog to save Evadne from a mauling had been the final sign Gregor and Phaedra needed.

Halcyon was not made for the grove. She did not belong there.

"Is she surprised to see that you limp?" Straton asked. His audacity brought Evadne's gaze back to his. And he seemed to be waiting for it, to see what her eyes held, because he continued, "Your foot would have been healing when she departed for Abacus years ago. She must hate to see that your old pains still give you grief."

"I imagine she will be surprised," Evadne replied in a near hiss. "When she finally sees me again tonight."

The commander set aside his ale. "You and I can cease with the pretense, Evadne."

"I do not know what you—"

"Where are you hiding her? I know she came to you for aid last night. Where are you keeping her?"

Evadne drew in a deep breath. She saw his game, how he had provoked her, hoping her anger would loosen her tongue. Her voice emerged flat. "I do not know what you speak of, Lord Straton. I do not know why you have come here, asking after Halcyon. We have not seen her, but we expect her to arrive tonight. You can wait to talk to her then."

"She did not tell you," he stated softly with realization. "Although how can I blame her? I would not want to tell my sister such a crime, either."

"Lord Straton—"

"Do you want me to tell you, then, Evadne? Do you want me to tell you what Halcyon has done and why she is running from me?"

Evadne could not breathe. Her heart was pounding so hard she worried that she would be sick at the commander's feet.

He continued to wait for her to answer, but when Evadne remained silent, he sighed and sat back in his chair.

She thought he would withhold the knowledge, and she began to rise, even though he had not dismissed her. And his voice rose with her, honed to cut.

"Your sister has committed murder."

The words hit her like a stone. She stood before Straton, her mind trying to reconcile what he had just uttered with what Evadne knew of her sister.

Halcyon was good. She was loyal. Courageous. Respectful. She was nigh perfect.

How could she have *murdered* someone?

Evadne sat back down, her legs quivering.

But Halcyon had also been away for eight years. Did Evadne even truly know her sister now? She had snuck home, blood beneath her nails, uncertain what the commander would do if he caught her. And what had she said to Evadne?

"It was an accident."

Straton laughed, a hacking sound that made the hair stand on Evadne's arms. "Is that what she told you? That it was an *accident*?"

His scorn was blistering. Evadne covered her mouth, her composure beginning to crack.

"Halcyon slayed a fellow hoplite," the commander said. "And then she ran. She is a murderer and a coward, and if you do not tell me where you are concealing her, I will punish her tenfold when I drag her to—"

"Get out."

Gregor's voice sliced through the air. He walked deeper into the chamber, to stand behind Evadne, his stare fixed upon the commander.

Straton quieted, surprised that Gregor had interrupted him.

"You cannot come into my home and speak to my daughter in such a way," Gregor stated coldly. "Leave. *Now.*"

Straton took his time gathering his weapons. But he kept his eyes on Gregor, who returned the bold stare, and they spoke a silent language Evadne could not understand but all the same felt like a kopis grazing her skin.

The commander departed, slamming the door.

Once he was gone, Evadne could breathe again, and she drew a shaky gasp. She felt her father's hand on her shoulder; his touch was gentle until she tried to stand.

"Not yet, Pupa."

He moved to kneel before her. His eyes searched hers.

"Gregor," Phaedra warned. She appeared at the edge of Evadne's vision, as did her aunt and uncle and her cousins. "Wait until he has ridden away."

Evadne should not have been surprised that her entire family had eavesdropped. They must have heard the exchange between her and Straton. And Gregor continued to stare at her. She saw the twitch in his cheek.

Maia hurried to the window, peering out into the courtyard. It felt like an hour had passed before she announced, "He's gone."

Gregor rushed a hand over his beard, deliberating. "Is it true,

Evadne?" he asked. "Did Halcyon come to you last night?"

"Father . . ."

"Answer me!"

Evadne flinched. Her father rarely raised his voice, and when he did, it had never been directed at her. She sat deeper in the chair.

"Do not lie to me, Daughter. Did that man speak truth? Did you aid your sister?"

If she spoke, she would break. Evadne nodded, her throat narrow.

"When did this happen?"

Evadne made no reply, struggling to hide her tears. But she watched the revelation unfurl in his eyes. He was thinking of last night, when he had come to Evadne's room. The window had been open to the wind and the rain . . .

"Where is she, Evadne? I hope you hid her well, because Lord Straton is going to kill her when he finds her."

"I-I did not hide her, Father!" Evadne stammered. "I gave her food and drink. She refused to tell me what she had done, why she was running, or where she planned to go."

Again, that terrible expression overcame Gregor's face. He rose and glanced at his brother and nephew. "Nico, Lysander, come with me."

Evadne knew the men were going to search for Halcyon. And Evadne would not sit idly, waiting for them to come home. She stood and breathed, "Father, wait."

Gregor paused, but he did not look at her. "I want you to stay here, Evadne. Do not leave these villa walls, do you understand?"

Was he punishing or protecting her? She could not tell, but nor would she stay here. She walked to him, and Gregor had no choice but to lift his eyes, to look at her. There was such fear, such bloodshot agony within him.

Evadne whispered, "I think I know where to find Halcyon."

Halcyon

Halcyon had set her hope on the mountains. It was the only place she could think of where the commander might not follow. The mountains of Corisande, especially the western ridge that was called Dacia, were known to be harsh. Not many mortals lived at such heights due to the foul weather but also because of the proximity to the dreaded Mount Euthymius.

Halcyon, however, no longer feared that summit.

And as she departed Isaura in the storm, she knew she was ill-prepared for the hike. She would need to stop somewhere to pilfer, somewhere like the village of Dree.

Halcyon set her pace, risking the road because it was faster. But soon she had to slow to a walk, so exhausted she could hardly feel her legs. She had been catching sleep hours at a time, whenever she felt safe. And while she wanted to keep pushing herself, her mind was becoming foggy.

She had time. The storm would slow Straton. And the grove of Isaura was difficult to find, one of the last magical enchantments Kirkos had cast before he fell.

Halcyon veered from the road. She knew there was a grotto nearby, a place where she and Evadne and the cousins had often explored. It was also a place where travelers could find shelter, and she searched it warily.

It was empty, and Halcyon lay down on the ground and rubbed her calves, groaning. She closed her eyes, setting her mind to wake in an hour. Even here, in the deepest pit of slumber, no dreams could reach her. She did not see Xander, like she had the other times she had slept. Xander with blood cascading down his body, reaching for her, haunting her nearly every time she closed her eyes.

When Halcyon woke it was almost dawn.

Cursing, she stumbled up and gathered her food sack, eating a few more figs and a soggy honey cake as she ran alongside the road. The storm had passed, and her mind felt sharper now; she was able to push herself faster.

She and Xander had traveled this very course only weeks ago. They had come in the night to meet with Bacchus, the priest of Dree. No one had seen the two hoplites slip into the village, into the temple. No one had seen them leave. It had been difficult for Halcyon at the time, to be so close to home and not be able to stop and see her sister, her parents. But she had told herself that her eight years of training were about to end, and her reward—a visit with her family—was imminent. She only needed to remain focused on the task before her.

But how things had now changed.

She crested the summit and stood in the golden hue of dawn. The valley between her and Dree was deep with wildflowers, their purple blooms bending in the breeze. Goats grazed nearby, drifting like a cloud. The scene was idyllic. Halcyon continued to regard it, surprised. The village had appeared different in the night, when she had last been here with Xander. But in the light, she discovered it was just as she remembered from childhood. The village was built at the footstool of a craggy slope, the houses crafted from the pale rocks harvested from the mountains. The roofs were thatched in straw. And at the crown of Dree sat the Temple of Euthymius, the god of the earth, their patron. Within those pillars, fire always burned, and offerings of grain and oil were given.

Humble people dwelled here, people like Halcyon's family. They worked to survive; they were diligent and productive. Potters and sandal makers, goatherds and bakers, weavers and blacksmiths.

How was she to steal from them?

Again, she considered going directly to Bacchus for aid, but Bacchus was a priest. He would sense the bloodshed on her, and there was a good chance he would hold her until Straton arrived.

I will repay it all, she swore as she began to approach. *I will give back everything that I take as soon as I can.*

The village was just beginning to stir. Halcyon chose the outermost abode, hiding behind a stack of hay. There was a garden to her left, a rectangle filled with lettuces and radishes and herbs.

She harvested a few, lightning swift. She then snuck to the storehouse, a small, lopsided building just behind the main dwelling. It was warm and musky within, but there were shelves crowded with provisions. Pots of millet seed and barley, jars of preserved fruits and honey and oil, fillets of smoked fish and dried strings of goat meat.

Halcyon began to fill her sack. Her hands trembled. The exhaustion began to tug on her again.

The door swung open. Sunlight flooded in, limning her thievery.

Halcyon spun, raising her hands. And she froze, just as the man on the threshold did, gaping at her.

He looked vaguely familiar. Sandy-brown hair that dragged into his eyes, huge uneven shoulders, a patchy beard and mole on his chin.

"*Halcyon?*" the vile boy of Dree cried, only he was not a boy anymore. He was a man, and he dwarfed her, now. *Laneus*. His name rushed back to her in a shiver.

Once, she had knocked him out cold with a perfect punch.

Once, he had despised her, because she was faster than him.

Once, he had wanted to be accepted into Straton's legion but had been denied. Because the truth was he was lazy and cruel, and boys like that made for twisted warriors.

It seemed his hatred for her still thrived.

"Is the legion not good enough for you, then?" he sneered, stepping closer. Halcyon was trapped. There was only one door, and his girth was blocking it. "You had to slink home and steal from us now? You remember what we do to thieves?"

Halcyon struck first. Her fist moved faster than light, crunching his nose.

He howled and spun to the right, taking out a shelf, and Halcyon darted past him as he thrashed.

She flew back to the garden, rounding the haystack only to slam into another man. Laneus's brother. The impact nearly bowled him over, but he snatched her, regaining his balance. He had her arms twisted behind her before she could rally, and her sack of goods dropped with a sad plop between them.

"Who is this, Laneus?" his brother called. "Was she stealing?"

Laneus emerged from the storehouse, his nose crooked, his face coated in blood.

For a moment, Laneus evaporated, and Xander stood in his place, face pale with the sting of death, his blood a river that crept across the ground to touch her toes. . . .

Halcyon closed her eyes, struggling to hold her spirit together. She heard a snicker, a gloat.

"You do not recognize her, Aedus?"

She felt fingers in her hair, yanking her head back. She opened her eyes to see Aedus staring down at her, mouth slack.

"No . . . It cannot be her."

"It is. Hold her now. I want to give her a proper greeting."

Halcyon watched, impassive, as Laneus prepared to strike her. She let her mind slip far away, preparing for the pain. She was in the grove; she was a girl, again. She was writing Haleva messages in the soil for Evadne to find . . .

"Enough of this," a man snarled, and Laneus's fist froze before it could smash her teeth.

Halcyon sharpened her focus, looking to where an old man stood a stone's throw away, leaning on a staff, glaring at the three of them.

"Your mother taught you better than this," he rasped, his gray hair long and unkempt. "You shame her memory, Laneus. As do you, Aedus."

"But, Papa!" Laneus said, gesturing to his bloody nose. "Look what she did! And this is—"

"I know very well who she is," the old man responded. He stared at Halcyon a long moment, but she could not read the lines on his face. "Take her to Bacchus. Now."

The brothers obeyed, grumbling. They waited until they had dragged Halcyon out of their father's sight, up the road that wound to Euthymius's temple.

Halcyon never saw it coming. Although she should have expected it.

Laneus struck her, as he had always wanted, along the curve of her jaw. It was the only time he would ever beat her: when she was overtaxed, when she had not eaten a proper meal in days, when she was held prisoner.

And Halcyon folded into the darkness.

When Halcyon stirred, the world had changed. Or so it felt to her. She was bound to a thick post in the center of Dree's market by her wrists and ankles. It forced her to remain on her knees with her chest and face defenseless, the plank aligning with her spine. She knew exactly what this was, even before she fully opened her eyes, quietly testing the ropes that bit into her. She was fastened to the Thief's Stave, a public place of shame that she had passed many times as a girl, never imagining she would one day wake to find herself tied to it.

The stave was the mildest of punishments for thievery. The thief would be knotted to the wood and would wait in shame for another to come and pay their debt. Some thieves, such as those who stole jewels or horses might find themselves bound for days.

She was fortunate Laneus had not pressed the heavier charge upon her, one that would result in losing a hand.

The sun was hot on Halcyon's hair, and her head felt as if it had split open. She cracked her eyes to see the blur of people moving about the market, and then one particularly ugly face came into focus. Laneus.

"I caught her, I did," he was saying to anyone who passed by. "Stealing my winter goods. I caught her before she could take one morsel from me."

"Looks like she got a little swing at you," a man said mirthfully, indicating Laneus's nose, which still sat crooked on his face.

Laneus sputtered some indignant response, and Halcyon closed her eyes once more, struggling to swallow. Her throat was dry; her lips were peeling. How long had she been bound here?

"You thirsty, Halcyon?"

She kept her eyes shut, even as she felt Laneus's presence draw close. He was pouring water out on the ground; the trickle was like music to her, and Halcyon inadvertently strained toward it.

"Come now, Hoplite. Show us your illustrious strength," he goaded. "Break your binds, like the goddess everyone believes you to be."

"If water means so little to you, Laneus, then perhaps you could do without it," a deep voice spoke, and at once the water trickle ceased. "The same could be said of your food stores. If you have plenty, it would not harm you to share."

Halcyon looked up and saw Bacchus standing nearby, the breeze stirring his brown robes. He was an old man of mysterious age, his hair a thin crown of white on his head, but his voice was strong and resonant.

Bacchus was the only priest of Euthymius in the kingdom. The only mortal who could speak with and hear the god of earth and beasts. He also possessed the relic of Euthymius, and he wore it openly, fearlessly. The Golden Belt was cinched at the priest's waist now, etched with mountains and fauna. Bacchus was common-blooded, but wearing the belt gave him the ability to command animals.

Halcyon wondered if he would be required to return the relic to the Mages' Council, as the new decree stated. Or if he would defy the edict.

Bacchus stared at Laneus until he slunk away. Only then did the old priest look at Halcyon, and she felt a flare of shame.

"I take it your parents do not know you are here, Halcyon of Isaura," Bacchus said, voice pitched low. "Or Lord Straton."

"No, Lord." Her jaw throbbed with the movement.

"Laneus wanted to take your hand in punishment. I would not allow it."

She tried to swallow. Her tongue stuck to her teeth as she whispered, "Thank you."

Bacchus knelt and tilted a jar of water to her lips. Halcyon drank, the ache in her temples easing. She could smell the smoke and cassia spice in the priest's robes. He wore a pendant of Euthymius around his neck, a circle of clay pressed with a mountain.

When their gazes met, her heart trembled like a lyre string. Because she knew he saw the divide in her, the fracture.

"I suspect that the very worst has happened," he said. "To see you are alone. Without Osprey."

Osprey, Xander's code name.

"Yes, Lord."

Bacchus was quiet for a beat, and then murmured, "And where is the map?"

"With Lord Straton. I have failed."

"Failure is never final unless you choose it to be," Bacchus said. "Where there is life, hope can be found. Do not give up, Halcyon."

He left her fastened to the stave. There was no sense in trying to escape. Her kopis was gone. Countless eyes studied her; countless voices whispered about her. Some of them recognized her.

It would not be long before word of her thievery spread. Her parents would hear of it and be further shamed by her.

She bowed her head in the sunlight, sweating, shivering. Waiting.

And she knew the moment he saw her.

The market fell silent; there was only the clucking of a few hens, the rush of mountain wind, and hoofbeats coming to a slow halt on the dirt road.

Halcyon raised her chin, opened her eyes. And looked directly at the commander.

— VI —

Halcyon

Straton sat on his stallion a few paces away, staring at her, the sun setting his bronze armor aflame. It seemed that was all he could do: sit on his horse and stare at her.

She thought she would be eaten by fear in this moment of their reunion. But Halcyon exhaled, relieved. *It will soon be over*, she thought.

She watched him dismount. She refused to meet the gazes of the other hoplites in his company, hoplites she knew well. She had been part of their squad; they had trained together. They had been like brothers and sisters. Once they had been her pride, and she theirs.

No more.

The hoplites remained in a tightly knit group, mounted and awaiting orders, with shields depicting a scorpion on their arms. Straton approached her alone. He came to a stop before her, tall and immovable as a pillar.

His eyes burned through her, but Halcyon did not appear afraid, not even when he unsheathed his sword.

But she heard gasps from the people of Dree who had crowded the market.

Even Halcyon felt a spasm of surprise. She had thought that he would take her back to Abacus. That he would want to speak with her before he executed her. She had thought she would have a moment to explain.

The commander was renowned for his justice, his sense of honor. Years ago, he had been selected by the queen to become her war advisor. He often supped at the royal palace at Queen Nerine's side, granting her counsel.

He never broke rules, and it had taken Halcyon a few years to truly understand him, to learn how to gain his respect. But looking at his face now . . . his fury was tangible, and that lawfulness was unbalanced. All due to her.

Straton stepped behind her, his sword ready to cut.

And Halcyon's thoughts tangled as she watched his shadow, his arm lifting the sword. She closed her eyes at last, waiting to feel the sting of his blade in her throat.

Do not be afraid, do not be afraid, do not be afraid—

There was a thunk, a vibration in the stave, and then Halcyon found herself falling forward, her binds cut loose. She rushed to bring her arms around, shoulders sore, and caught herself a moment before she would have smashed her face into the dirt.

She was still sprawled on her belly when she heard a heated voice.

"She is mine to set free! She owes me a debt!"

Halcyon eased herself up to see Laneus rushing across the market. But the moment Straton turned to look down at him, Laneus halted, his face wrinkling with fear.

"And what debt is that?" Straton said.

"She, um, well, she broke into my storehouse and stole my provisions."

Halcyon sat back on her heels. She felt the commander look at her, but this time she kept her eyes on the sky. *Yes, I have added to my list of crimes, Lord.*

"What did she steal, then?" The commander sounded extremely impatient. He was sheathing his sword, moving to where Halcyon knelt.

"She stole a few radishes. Three fillets of fish. A pot of honey. A bowl of plums . . ."

Straton opened the leather satchel hooked on his belt. He procured a silver Akkia and flicked the coin at Laneus with apparent disgust. The silver tumbled to the ground, and Laneus scrambled to recover it.

"Get up," the commander now spoke to her, rough-hewn.

Halcyon struggled to rise. He took hold of her arm, his grip like iron, and dragged her across the market, the crowd parting for them. Eventually, Halcyon got her feet beneath her, and he shoved her forward to walk before him up the hill to where the temple sat. The white pillars gleamed in the light, and smoke plumed upward to the clouds in lazy strokes. And there stood Bacchus on the stairs, watching them come.

"Lord Commander," the priest greeted.

"Lord Priest," the commander returned as Halcyon struggled to ascend the stone steps.

She finally reached the top, panting. She could feel the men's gazes flicker to her; both sets of eyes were inscrutable.

"A private chamber?" Straton requested.

"This way, my lord," Bacchus said, motioning for them to follow him into a narrow atrium. It led to an arched door, the ash-wood carved with fauns and laurel trees, and within was a small chamber. The priest's bedroom, sparsely furnished. There was a hay mattress in one corner, a stool, a table covered in scrolls, a brazier whose embers still flared warm.

The same chamber where Halcyon and Xander had met with the priest, weeks ago. The memory was sharper than a blade in her side as Bacchus left them, closing the door in his wake.

Straton refused to look at her. She felt as if she had turned into a shadow; she slid to the ground and sat in a heap, the last of her strength zapped.

She could hear him breathing. He sounded just as ragged as her, as if he could finally drop his appearance and reveal how exhausted he truly was. He was no longer hiding his devastation. His heart was broken, had been broken for days, and his face exposed his anguish.

If she was to ever have a moment to try to explain what had happened, why she had run . . . it was now.

"Lord Commander . . . I am sorry."

He stiffened. Still, he did not look at her. "You are sorry it happened or sorry you could not get away?"

His words cut deep. Halcyon wondered if he truly thought she was unrepentant for killing Xander.

"Do you know me so little, Commander?"

He ignored her.

And she pushed herself to her feet, armor creaking. "You have only trained me the past eight years. You chose me for this, Commander. *You chose me,* and you chose Xander, and if you think I have changed overnight, that I have morphed into a creature that holds no morals, no feelings, then you are not the man I believed you to be, either."

He turned and glared at her. But a small gleam of respect had returned. Her words forced him to dwell on that which he did not want to: he had hand-chosen her, out of a thousand other possibilities. And he had chosen Xander. In a way, he had brought this upon them all.

"Xander and I were doing just as you asked." She reached out to steady herself on the table. "We were preparing to fight without our sight. I was blindfolded, and I was sparring with him, and I . . ." She stopped abruptly, because Straton's face was suddenly terrible to behold.

"And what then, Halcyon?"

"Do you really believe it, Commander? That I would murder Xander?"

He cast his eyes away. "It would be an easy out for you. If Xander was dead, you would be absolved from fulfilling the mission. If you had been afraid—"

"But I was not afraid!" she cried. "I told you from the very beginning. I would go. And what is *easy* about turning my back on what I vowed I would do, Lord Straton? You cast me into a mold that I do not fit, and you know it and should be ashamed of such lies!"

"*I* should be ashamed?" he snarled, stepping closer to her. "I think that is *you*, Halcyon. Coward of Isaura, who ran when she should have remained."

There it was. The word she was waiting for. *Coward.* It split her open, and she staggered, because she believed it.

She should have remained with Xander. She should have waited beside his body, waited for the commander to come.

But even now . . . she knew that she would do it all again. She would still run, frantic from terror, his blood glistening on her hands.

"For eight years I have trained you," Straton said. "Eight years I have prepared you for battle, for the unknown. I have taught you everything I know. And in the past when I saw fear in you . . . you did not allow it to snare you." He scrutinized her. Halcyon felt bruised. "Why have you proven me a fool? Why did you run from me, Halcyon?"

"I feared you would kill me, Lord," she answered honestly. "That you would not believe me when I said it was an accident. I ran to save myself."

"Cowards run," he snapped. "You should have remained. You should not have fled."

She was silent, thinking of the mission that had been given to her. How in just one breath, everything had fallen apart.

"I was blindfolded," she said, knowing these words would smolder in her if she didn't release them. "We had a chosen word, as you suggested, to indicate the yield. And I did not hear Xander's yield. And I knew it, the moment my sword nicked him. I knew I had given him a mortal blow, and I . . ." Halcyon could not breathe as she remembered it. The gurgle, the sound of a sword dropping. She had ripped away her blindfold to behold Xander's sliced throat. A seemingly small nick but one that would drain him in a matter of moments.

His blood had been a torrent, a flood.

Halcyon covered her face with her hands. The commander hated tears. She wrestled them away, her fingers dragging down her face.

"Xander was the brother I always wanted. I loved him. And I know that I have compromised the mission. I stole a life that I never intended to harm, and then I ran from you. I am a coward, as you say, and you should kill me. It is the justice I deserve."

Straton was silent. He was breathing heavily again, as if Halcyon's words had pierced him. He walked to the lone window in the chamber and stared at the outer world, the silver in his hair catching the light.

"Have you told anyone else?" he asked. "Have you told your sister about the mission?"

"I have not broken my oath to you, Lord."

The commander turned to look at her. "Then you know what I must do, Halcyon."

He had warned her and Xander both at the beginning, before he had divulged any details of the mission, that it might come to something like this, if the worst befell them. They had agreed to it as they had taken their code names, Xander and her, believing they were invincible.

But the worst had happened. And only Halcyon remained to carry the burden, to keep the mission hidden. Hemlock had been watching the commander for moons. Hemlock, a person who was still unknown to them but was proving to be their greatest obstacle, scheming to impede them.

She bowed her head and whispered, "Yes, Lord. Do what you must."

She wondered if the commander would try to press onward with his plans. Would he dare to ask his other son to complete what Xander and Halcyon started?

They were running out of time.

Straton walked to the door and opened it. He waited for her to come forward, allowing her to lead him back through the temple, down the road to the market, where the crowd still teemed and the hoplites continued to wait.

Halcyon stood by the stave, watching as the commander approached one of the hoplites. She knew who the warrior was by the mere crest on her helm, the long horsehair stained white and red. It was Narcissa, the leader of the Scorpion Squad. Halcyon's captain.

Narcissa listened to Straton's order, her green eyes flickering to Halcyon. She dismounted and removed her helm, her long brown hair bound back in braids. There was no emotion in her face as she procured her whip from her saddle, no hesitation in her stance as she walked to Halcyon. She stopped an arm's length away, and the two women stared at each other.

"Halcyon of Isaura," Narcissa said. "You have slayed a fellow hoplite, your own shield mate, Xander of Mithra. You have fled from your commander. You have broken the most sacred of our laws." She paused, letting her whip unwind in her hands. Its long tail lay coiled like a serpent. "You shall receive twenty lashes for your cowardice. Remove your armor and kneel before the stave."

Halcyon began to unyoke her cuirass. It felt as if she was underwater; the sound was muffled, and her arms were heavy. But she lifted her armor and let it go; the bronze clanged on the ground beside her. All she wore now were her sandals and her red chiton, damp with her perspiration.

"On your knees," Narcissa said.

Halcyon turned to the stave and wrapped her arms about it. Another hoplite came forward. Iason. He bound her hands to the wood, and she knew it was not to hold her here but to hold her up when she lost consciousness.

Iason did not meet her gaze. He looked stricken as he backed away.

Halcyon felt the commander's presence to her right; he divided the wind, and his shadow reached for her across the ground.

The sound of footsteps. Narcissa approaching, unsheathing her kopis. She tore Halcyon's chiton to expose her back.

There was a moment of silence. Of trembling peace. And then came the first lash.

VII

Evadne

E vadne stood in Dree's market, her eyes vacant as she stared at the bloodstain on the ground. It had taken her and her family a few hours to arrive at the village. And she would have thought this was all some nightmare, that she would wake if she could only rouse herself. Save for the blood. The blood was real. It still glistened in the evening light, as if the dirt would not drink it.

She wondered how long it would take for it to fade.

The commander and his hoplites were gone, journeying back to Abacus, Halcyon with them. Evadne had caught a glimpse of her, through the gaps between armor and spears and horses. Halcyon was like a fallen goddess, dark hair draped over her face, the wounds on her back dressed and covered with white linen.

Her father had pushed a path through the hoplites, utterly reckless. He had finally been granted a moment with Halcyon, a moment where he touched his daughter's unconscious face and breathed her name, as if she would awaken. Gregor only stumbled away when the commander said something to him, words that Evadne could not hear.

And then Halcyon and her people were gone.

Gregor knelt in the dirt between the tracks of the wagon wheels, just as numb as Evadne. The people of Dree began to drift from the market, the entertainment waning. A few remained, staring at Gregor. But none of them offered to help him, to comfort him.

And then Evadne saw the vile boy of Dree, the one Halcyon had beaten all those years ago. He was standing nearby, laughing with another young man. Something familiar was hooked to his belt. Halcyon's kopis, sheathed in leather.

Evadne was striding toward him before she knew what she was doing, that anger kindling, burning away the last of her shock. She walked right up to him, and he broke his conversation off midword, arching his brows at her.

"And who are you?" he asked.

Of course he would not remember her. Not many people did, for who recalled the quiet sister when there was Halcyon?

"That does not belong to you," she said, indicating the kopis.

He glanced down at his belt. "Well, I do not think Halcyon will be needing it anymore. Do you?" And he laughed.

She wanted to strike him. Gods, how her fists curled, and she wished that she had asked Halcyon to teach her how to fight.

But the moment never came. Another voice joined the conversation, one that Evadne knew and respected. Bacchus, the priest of Dree.

"And have you become a thief now, Laneus?"

The glee on Laneus's face froze as he stared at the priest.

Bacchus continued, "Because I do not recall Halcyon bestowing her kopis to you. You should give it to her sister for safekeeping, or perhaps you would prefer to spend a few days tied to the stave?"

Laneus's lips curled, but he unfastened the kopis and dropped it at Evadne's feet. She heard him growl an obscenity at her, one that made her blood boil, but she had the kopis now.

She bent to retrieve it, holding Halcyon's small scythe in her hands. And it almost made her weep, to have a remnant of her sister.

"You should help your father home, Evadne," Bacchus said gently. "His soul is grieved."

She turned to see her father still kneeling in the dirt. Uncle Nico and Lysander also watched him, eventually having no choice but to draw him upward. The sun was setting. It was time to return home and bear the news to the others who had remained behind in the villa for appearances' sake. Evadne could not even begin to imagine breaking such news to her mother.

"What did Lord Straton say to you, Gregor?" Nico asked, holding his brother up.

Evadne thought she had never seen her father look so frail. He looked like he might die; his skin was gray, his eyes unfocused. She realized he was in shock.

"Father? Uncle Nico asked you a question." She exchanged a worried glance with her uncle when Gregor remained silent.

"Halcyon's trial will be in six days," Gregor finally said in a hoarse voice. "It will be held at the agora in Abacus."

The moon had risen by the time they reached Isaura. Phaedra, Lydia, and Maia bolted into the courtyard, eager for news of Halcyon.

Evadne did not linger to witness Nico telling them what had befallen her sister. She was almost to her bedchamber when she heard the echo of her mother's sobs, closely followed by Maia's wails. Lydia was silent, but she would cry later, when she was alone.

Evadne's room was dark. She moved through that darkness and lay down on Halcyon's bed.

For a moment she did not think; she only breathed, her eyes open to the night.

She had guided her father and her uncle to the sea caves earlier that day, thinking Halcyon had gone there to hide. They had wasted time searching the coast. Of course, Halcyon would go to the mountains, unafraid of Mount Euthymius. Evadne had even stared out her window at the Dacia Mountains, convinced Halcyon would not go that path. How wrong she had been.

If only Evadne had thought of Dree sooner; if only they could have reached Halcyon before the commander. How different this day would have been.

Carefully, Evadne reached for Halcyon's kopis. She unsheathed it to watch the moonlight dance upon the blade.

If I had magic, I could save you, she thought. *I would raise my hand in the agora and cast a charm to set you free, Halcyon.*

But Evadne had not been born with magic in her blood. If she was ever to taste it, she would have to possess one of the divine relics. It was an enticing thought, and she wondered about the relics that were lost. Irix's Sky Cloak, Magda's Sunstone Ring of Healing, Acantha's All-Seeing Crown, Loris's Pearl Earrings, and Kirkos's Winged Necklace were all deemed missing.

If she had Irix's Sky Cloak, she could control the skies, the weather. She could summon a drought. She could bargain for Halcyon's freedom in exchange for rain. Or if she had Kirkos's Winged Necklace, she could descend from the clouds and take Halcyon in her arms. She could fly them far away from Abacus, from Corisande. But where would they go after that?

No, these whimsies were unfeasible, ridiculous. Evadne was a common girl from a common family, and she would never possess a divine relic.

If she wanted to save Halcyon, she would have to do it another way.

Evadne and her parents set out early the following morning. It would be a three-day journey east to Abacus if the weather held. Evadne had never ventured so far from home before, and she watched from the wagon as Isaura began to grow distant, until it was swallowed by the hills.

The bluffs and valleys soon became flat, open fields, where millet and barley flourished. Falcons and goldcrests soared overhead, wings outstretched to glide on the breeze, and Evadne thought of her sister, how she had always imagined Halcyon with wings.

She wondered how Halcyon was faring, if she was in pain, if her commander was ensuring her wounds were looked after. She tried to predict what might happen at her sister's trial. And the desire to redeem Halcyon flared in her again. The sister she had sometimes envied but had always admired and loved.

She did not envy her now.

They camped beneath the stars that night, a good distance from the road. Evadne helped her mother set out a small repast of flatbread and smoked fish, and her father sparked a fire with his ember stone. They sat quietly and ate as evening arrived; they had hardly spoken the entire day, each of them lost in their own thoughts.

Evadne struggled to eat her dinner, conceding to unwind her bedroll on the grass, folding herself into the blankets. She was on the verge of sleep when Gregor finally spoke, low with remorse.

"I should never have let her go to the legion. I should have kept her where it was safe, in the grove."

Phaedra was silent for a moment. "You cannot blame yourself for this, Gregor."

She spoke with confidence, because she believed Halcyon would be pardoned, that Halcyon would live. But it was evident Gregor was preparing for his firstborn daughter to die.

And Evadne did not know what she thought, but she felt strung between her parents.

She fell asleep thinking of Halcyon, and her sister followed her into her dreams. They were in the grove, and Evadne was writing in the Haleva cipher. She drew the symbols into her wax tablet with a stylus, eager for Halcyon to read the message. But when she handed it to her older sister, Halcyon frowned.

"I do not know these symbols, Eva."

A shock went through Evadne. "What? Yes, you do, Hal. It is our language."

Halcyon shrugged, hopeless. "I have never seen this before."

Evadne stared at the wax tablet. She watched as her letters began to tremble, growing wings and scales, morphing into creatures that moved off the wax, vanishing into golden dust.

Magic. Evadne's hand had just wrought magic.

"Did you see that?" she breathed, eyes wide in wonder. And she was not imagining it. Halcyon also saw the words awaken, metamorphose. "Do you know what this means, Hal? I can save you now."

"Save me from what?" Halcyon asked.

Evadne never answered. She was woken by a thread of laughter. Men's voices, and they were growing louder.

"Phaedra!" Gregor hissed.

Evadne sat upright, startled into lucidity. She turned to see her father standing nearby, a dagger glinting in his hand. The fire cast an eeire light about their camp.

"What is it, Gregor?" Phaedra whispered.

"Grab your dagger. Someone is coming."

Evadne listened to her mother fumble through her pack to find her blade. She did not move, her heart skipping as the voices drew closer. They had seen the fire. They could see Evadne and her parents, but Evadne, Gregor, and Phaedra could not see them.

The gooseflesh rose on her arms.

"May we join your fire, humble friends?" a man called out, his body still hidden in night. He spoke with a strange yet pleasing lilt.

Gregor was silent, but Evadne could tell his eyes were desperately searching the darkness, to catch a glimpse of the stranger.

"Come now. We mean no harm to you and your wife and daughter. We just want to warm ourselves by your fire."

"Show yourselves," Gregor demanded.

There seemed to be a deliberation. Evadne heard murmurs, and then, at last, the speaker stepped into the firelight. Two more people were with him, a young man and a woman, trailing at his sides.

Evadne warily studied the speaker. He was dressed in a white chiton with gilded trim so rich it looked as if the linen had been dipped in molten gold. A blue mantle was wrapped across his chest, clasped at his shoulder by a pin fashioned as a storm cloud. A symbol of the sky god, Irix, who he must claim as his ancestor. His raiment alone proclaimed what he was. A mage.

Evadne's gaze dropped to his hands. Every mage wore a silver ring after they graduated the Destry. Which finger they wore the ring on corresponded to how powerful their magic was. A ring on the pinky revealed a very shallow well of magic, but as the fingers progressed across the hand, the deeper the magical well ran. A ring on the thumb signified the greatest depth of magic.

This stranger wore the silver ring on his forefinger.

Gregor lowered his dagger, and Evadne felt her father's dread. For what could a man with a blade do against a man with magic?

"Ah, thank you, friend," the mage said. Again, his voice drawled with languorous power. It sent a shiver down Evadne's back. "I am Macarius, and this is my scribe, Beryl, and my friend Cyrus."

Scribe? Evadne's attention focused on the woman, who was

dressed just as fine as Macarius, in a white chiton cinched with a belt crafted of bejeweled leaves. Golden suns were clasped at her shoulders, and an indigo cloak shielded her back. She returned Evadne's stare, cold and haughty. And then a smile played on her lips, and Evadne cast her eyes away to the other young man, who wore the telltale saffron sash of politicians. His face was ruddy and beaded with sweat, as if they had been wandering for miles, and hanging from his arm was a leather satchel, brimming with ornate scroll handles.

"Shall we toss another stick on the fire?" Macarius suggested.

Gregor obeyed. Evadne watched him toss two more sticks on the flames, the sparks swarming. And then her father moved to sit close beside her, so that Evadne was hemmed in by both of her parents.

The mage and his scribe sat first, directly across the fire. The politician dropped the satchel with a groan, rubbing his shoulder before he ungracefully collapsed on the ground.

"You do remember what you carry, Cyrus?" the scribe, Beryl, said in a sharp tone, looking at the politician with heavy-lidded eyes.

"Yes, and I don't know why I ever agreed to it!" Cyrus countered.

"Peace, my friends," Macarius said. "We have yet to meet our new acquaintances." He looked at Gregor, and when Gregor remained taciturn, his eyes shifted to Evadne. "And you are . . . ?"

"Our names are not important," Phaedra responded.

"But names are how we measure ourselves, are they not?"

Macarius tilted his head to the side. His hair was long and fine, the shade of the moon. But his brows were dark, a contrasting beauty that was difficult to look away from. His eyes remained on Evadne, and he said, "What is your name?"

"Evadne." She spoke before she realized it, her name escaping like smoke. She half wondered if he had enchanted her to speak, and her throat narrowed.

"Evadne," he echoed, as if he wanted to taste her name. "Where are you and your parents traveling to, Evadne?"

This time she held her tongue.

Macarius's smile widened. It made his face appear skewed. "We could be journeying to the same destination. We could join traveling parties."

"We are heading to Abacus," Gregor answered.

"Ah, the splendid Abacus! Such a beautiful, ancient city. It is a shame that we are not traveling the same path, then. Although, I will say, the nightlife of Abacus is rather dull."

Another beat of awkward silence. What did Macarius want? Evadne wondered, avoiding his gaze.

"Well, then," the mage said, his hand drifting upward in elegant offering. "Perhaps I could sing a little song for you, Evadne and your nameless parents, as a way to express my gratitude for the fire?"

"That will not be necessary," Gregor said. He sounded afraid; his hand found Evadne's, and he entwined their fingers. It almost seemed like he was worried that Evadne would leave her parents to go with the mage, bewitched.

But that sort of magic was illegal, Evadne thought, her pulse quickening. Mages were never to cast their magic to cause harm, to bewitch another. And she looked to the politician for reassurance, but Cyrus was yawning, completely disregarding the conversation unfolding around him.

"It is the least I can do," Macarius said, glancing to his scribe. "What should I sing for our new friends, Beryl?"

Beryl grinned. Her teeth gleamed like a scythe in the firelight. "Perhaps the Song of Sustenance?"

"Excellent choice."

Evadne did not have vast knowledge of magic, only bits and pieces she had gleaned from reading myths and listening to gossip that trickled through places like Dree. But she did know that magic could be spoken, and then it could be sung. And sung enchantments were always more potent, more dangerous.

Her eyes darted from Beryl to Macarius to the mysterious satchel of scrolls sitting in the grass at Cyrus's feet. Evadne was still trying to understand the dynamic among the trio, how Beryl seemed to intimately know the mage's spells, and then Macarius started to sing.

His voice was smooth as river rock. He sang in the God Tongue, the ancient language where magic burned its brightest.

Evadne did not want to admire or yearn after it, but his song, his enchantment, stirred longings within her, and she realized she was hungry, that there seemed to be a hole within her and she did not know how to satisfy it.

She listened closely to his words, knowing he had carefully

chosen them for his charm. Her mind was slow to translate at first; it had been years since she had read and written in God Tongue. But soon his words began to click in her mind.

Macarius sang of bread and wine, blood and meat. He sang of olives and cheese and fruits that grow heavy on vines. He sang of plenty; he sang of satiety. He sang of long journeys that come to an end by slaking thirst in cupped hands full of ale.

The song brimmed with joy.

But it did not make Evadne feel that way. Again, she felt a pang of emptiness, as if she had been scraped clean.

She was wary when Macarius finally reached the end of the song. And yet he had not hurt them or enchanted them. Her mother was still holding her dagger in her lap, her jaw clenched. And her father was still gripping Evadne's hand, so tightly it ached.

"I believe that is payment enough for the fire," Macarius said. "Unless you would like another song?"

Gregor declined.

"Very well, then. We shall be on our way."

Evadne watched as Macarius rose. He extended his hand for Beryl, to assist her to her feet. Cyrus had to help himself up, and he moaned as he rose, scowling at the satchel of scrolls he had been delegated to tote.

They disappeared back into the night, laughing just as they had come. And when the quiet returned, and there was no sound but the wind and the fire crackling, Evadne wondered if she had dreamt the entire encounter.

Gregor let out a shaky sigh. He released Evadne's hand, but he remained close to her side, stiff as a plank.

"Go back to sleep, Pupa."

How was she to sleep after that? How could she sleep with the mage's happy yet terribly empty song echoing in her head?

She lay down, her blankets cold. Evadne closed her eyes and pretended to sleep until dawn finally came.

Phaedra was the one who discovered it. She was sifting through their travel sacks to set out breakfast when she gasped.

"Gregor! It's gone. All of it."

Evadne watched in disbelief as her mother turned the food sack inside out. It had been brimming with provisions. And now it was nothing but empty linen.

"What of the others?" Gregor lunged to his feet, joining her at the wagon bed.

They went through the other sacks, all of them limp. They opened the jars of ale, the water flasks. All of them bone-dry. Gregor's money pouch, which he kept belted at his side, was also empty. Even the oats they had packed for the donkeys were gone.

Gregor knelt, the sacks strewn about him on the ground. His fingers tore through his hair, his eyes bloodshot.

"Should we turn back?" Phaedra asked. "We are only a day from Isaura."

"We cannot turn back," Gregor said, his voice hollow. "We would miss the trial."

Slowly, Evadne moved toward him to take one of the sacks in her hands. She searched it, even though she knew it was empty. She pressed her face to it, smelling the memory of figs and cheese.

Her stomach growled in response, and she remembered how Macarius's song had made her feel.

Empty.

The mage had not touched the wagon. He had not approached it at all. She had not even noticed him studying it. But he had sung his enchantment, and in a single chorus he had stolen nearly everything they owned.

"Father," she whispered.

Gregor's face softened. He reached out to touch her hair, to quietly reassure her. She leaned into him, shaken.

Once she had been a young girl, dreaming of magic, believing it to be something good and honorable and worthy. Now she realized how naïve she had been, how uneducated.

Magic was not at all what she had thought it to be.

And Evadne realized there was still much of the world she needed to learn.

When they finally reached Abacus, Evadne and her parents were bedraggled, their hunger and thirst a constant ache. Phaedra had found a patch of wild berries growing in a thorn patch, which had sustained them, and Gregor had speared two fish from a river, but that was all they had eaten.

Evadne was so ravenous she could hardly take in the splendor of Abacus, the city of warriors, where Halcyon had spent a portion of her life.

It was a bright, sprawling place, the terra-cotta roofs smoldering in the sunlight. The buildings were made of white walls, stacked high upon themselves so that the paved streets felt like winding ravines. The doors were all painted red, their lintels carved with the symbols of Nikomides. Snakes and swords and spears. Herbs grew from the window baskets and urns, and there was a constant scent of smoke on the breeze. Evadne could hear shouts from the market mingling with the hammering of forges. Everyone moved quickly, honed with purpose.

They had no coins to purchase a room, so Gregor ended up bargaining for one in addition to two meals a day, on the promise of five jars of first-pressed olive oil.

Evadne ate with her parents, and then they retired to their room to wash the grime from their hands and faces. They combed the tangles from their hair and dressed in fresh clothes—the only possessions that Macarius had not wanted.

They set out on foot toward the agora, to speak to the archon—the judge—of Abacus. Since Halcyon's crime had been committed within Abacus's boundaries, her trial would be overseen by the city's magistrate. Her trial was to take place in this ancient building, a grand structure built of white marble. Its bronze roof was upheld by pillars, each one carved as a hoplite.

Evadne felt small as she ascended the stairs of the agora, her ankle popping. She had never been in a building so vast, and she followed her parents into the cool shadows of a lobby, lost in both wonder and dread.

Halcyon had once explored this city; she had trained and dwelled in the valley beside it. Evadne wondered if she had loved it here, with its constant noise and brightness and bustle. She wondered if Halcyon had walked the same places, through the lobby, into the heart of the agora.

The archon was an old man, his hair white as goose down, his face wrinkled from years of training beneath the sun. He had a private room in the agora, and he sat behind a desk laden with scrolls and maps and dispatches, a jar of quills blooming by his hand, his brow arched as Evadne and her parents approached him.

It was apparent the archon did not want to see them. That he assumed they were about to present a petty case before him. He sighed and motioned them closer. But his eyes sharpened when Gregor introduced them. The parents and sister of Halcyon of Isaura.

"Ah yes. Your daughter is to stand trial for murder tomorrow," the archon said. His eyes were keen as he examined each of them. "If you have come to sway my choice, let me say that it will not work. My jurisdiction does not accept bribes."

Gregor was taken aback. "Lord, we have not come to bribe or persuade you, but to ask permission to see Halcyon."

The archon sighed. "I am sorry, Gregor of Isaura, but that cannot be done. A heavy offense such as murder does not warrant such privileges."

"But, Lord . . . I have not even had the chance to say one word to my daughter. Please."

"It cannot be done."

Gregor looked like he was one breath from falling on his knees and crawling to the archon to further grovel and beg. Phaedra, thankfully, took hold of her husband's arm to steady him.

"My lord," she spoke in a dulcet tone. "We understand that we cannot visit Halcyon. But perhaps we may be granted a quick glance at her? The last time my husband saw her, she had been publicly scourged and was in great agony."

The archon was quiet, assessing Phaedra. Evadne thought she had swayed him—it seemed her mother could sway anyone—but the archon said, "Again, I am sorry. But I cannot allow such. Your daughter has committed two terrible crimes. She killed her shield mate, and then she fled from her commander. She has been labeled a coward, a fate worse than death for a warrior."

"Please, Lord," Gregor pleaded. "We have not spoken to Halcyon in eight years."

The archon's patience finally ebbed. He leaned on the table; the scrolls about him shuddered and the light streaming in from the windows suddenly dimmed.

Evadne had been listening, observing. She stood in that gray light, hardly breathing as she waited.

"It is evident to me that you are unaware of the extent of Halcyon's crime," the archon said, weary. "Who she killed. Is that so?"

Gregor and Phaedra exchanged a glance.

"We were told she killed a fellow hoplite," Phaedra finally replied.

The archon stood. He was still broad and tall in his old age, his arms marked by scars. He wore leather armor and a sword was sheathed at his back, like he could fight at a moment's notice.

And he looked at Evadne, the accused's sister, and the only one of her family who had remained guarded.

"Halcyon of Isaura did not just slay *any* fellow hoplite," the archon said, his pale eyes still fixed on Evadne's. "She killed her commander, Lord Straton's, son."

⇢ VIII ⇠

Evadne

After a restless sleep, Evadne and her parents woke the next morning and made their way to the assembly hall of the agora. A crowd had already gathered, evidence that Halcyon had become one of the most notorious warriors of Corisande's army. When people spoke her name, it was now married to words like *coward*, *fool*, *murderess*.

Evadne tried to ignore those whispers as she sat between her parents on a bench at the front of the assembly. But the murmurs carried, and they made her tremble.

The archon arrived, standing behind a rostrum carved with phases of the moon. A wreath of olive leaves graced his head; the sight only heightened Evadne's anger, even though she knew the wreath was a symbol of insight and knowledge.

The goddess Acantha had worn such a crown when she walked among the mortals centuries ago, an eternal crown her brother

Euthymius had made for her, spun from olive branches. Her crown was the magical relic she had chosen to leave behind on the earth, and it still remained to be discovered. Lysander had been convinced he would be the one to find it one day, whenever he was brave enough to leave the grove. Uncle Ozias had thought the same, but no one had found Acantha's crown, and so the archon wore a common wreath to the trial. As a testament to the goddess, to truth and knowledge.

With his presence, a hush fell upon the hall. He opened a scroll before him, reading quietly for a moment. And then Straton arrived, and in his wake was his family: his wife, a daughter, and another son.

Evadne was too nervous to look at them as they sat on a bench angled adjacent to her family's. But then she felt the heated prompting of a stare. Cautiously, she lifted her gaze.

It was not the commander, who sat so stiff and quiet he could have been carved from stone, or his wife, who was coldly beautiful. It was his children who studied her shamelessly. They were not much older than Evadne, but their faces were drawn as if they had not slept the past week.

The daughter was a reflection of her mother—blond wispy hair, large brown eyes, a pale complexion. She wore a luxurious chiton, so fine it gleamed iridescent when she breathed, and her shoulder brooches winked with emeralds. A silver circlet gleamed across her brow, which denoted her as an accomplished healer, just as her mother was beside her.

The girl glanced away from Evadne first, as if she could not bear the sight of her.

Evadne shifted her gaze to the girl's brother.

His hair was a dark shade of brown, long and loose to brush his shoulder tops. His face was sharp yet balanced, as if a god had taken their time in forming his features. His brows were elegant, even as they slanted over a pair of unusually colored eyes. One eye was brown, but the other appeared to be divided: the top half of the iris was brown, but the bottom half was a light shade of blue. His mismatched gaze pierced Evadne; she responded by dropping hers, noticing his clothes.

He wore a white chiton trimmed with blue squares, and an indigo mantle draped across his chest, buckled at his shoulder with a celestial pin. He was a mage, Evadne realized with alarm, and she looked to his hands, where a silver ring gleamed on his middle finger.

Evadne glanced away from him, focusing her eyes on one of the grand pillars that upheld the ceiling. But she could still feel the mage assessing her, and her skin prickled from his gaze.

Her homespun garments were soon drenched with sweat, and Evadne counted her breaths, trying to tame her wildly beating heart.

Another wave of silence washed over the assembly.

It was a stifling quiet, gradually broken by the faint metallic clang of chains, a sound that grew louder and louder.

At last, Halcyon had arrived.

She was brought in from the back of the assembly, so the crowd could watch her approach the archon. Evadne could not see over the others, not until Halcyon was nearly to the front. Her sister was escorted by two guards, one holding each of her arms. She was draped in chains, to subdue her, because even after being whipped and imprisoned, Halcyon still radiated strength.

With a shock, Evadne saw that Halcyon's hair was gone; they had shaven her, and only a shadow of her dark hair remained on her scalp. The sackcloth she wore was smudged in grime and speckled in old blood, and her feet were bare, dirty.

Evadne could only imagine how painful each step was for her, with her back still torn and healing. And yet Halcyon did not arrive hunched and broken. She arrived with her chin held high, as if she did not feel the pain.

Evadne thought of all the times she had been proud of her older sister, when Halcyon had won the mountain footraces and knocked vile boys to the ground with one punch. But they were eclipsed by this one moment, when her sister maintained her dignity and honor. Gregor began to shake beside her on the bench, and she knew his emotions were fraying.

Evadne reached for his hand, lacing her thin fingers with his broad ones, and they quietly held to one another, their eyes on Halcyon alone.

Halcyon, however, did not turn to look at them. Surely, she felt her family's presence, Evadne thought. But Halcyon refused to acknowledge them, did not spare them a glance. She came to a halt directly before the archon and stared up at him, waiting.

"Halcyon of Isaura," the archon began, his voice carrying like thunder over the assembly. "You have been brought before me today with two charges pressed upon you. You are being accused of the murder of Xander of Mithra, a fellow hoplite and your shield brother. You also stand accused of cowardice: you ran from your crime and evaded your commander. Three witnesses shall testify. You must remain silent during their testimonies, but you, likewise, will have a moment to speak and answer questions I will voice to you. Depending on what is presented today, your sentence will be announced either at the end of the trial, or at midday tomorrow. Do you understand and accept these terms?"

"Yes, Lord," Halcyon said.

"Chain her to the stand."

The guards directed Halcyon to the stand adjoined to the archon's rostrum. She would now face the crowd, and as the chains about her wrists were locked to the wood, Halcyon closed her eyes.

"Be strong, Sprout," Gregor whispered, so low and gentle that Evadne almost missed the words.

And she would always wonder if the gods drew that whisper across the marble floor, up the stand and up the chains to Halcyon's ears. A sightless comfort. Because she opened her eyes and looked directly at Gregor.

The tension in her face eased.

She looked to Phaedra, color returning to her cheeks, and then she looked to Evadne.

The corner of Halcyon's mouth curved, so miniscule that most would not notice. But Evadne saw it and knew Halcyon was trying to wordlessly reassure her.

"Iason of the Eastern Isles, come forward," the archon said.

The summoned hoplite emerged from the crowd and stood directly before the archon. Evadne noticed he refused to look at Halcyon.

"Iason, you were the one to find the body of Xander," the archon began, referring to his scroll. "Tell us what you know of Halcyon and Xander's relationship, as well as what you witnessed that day."

"At dawn, Xander told me he was going to practice spar with Halcyon," Iason said. "This was not surprising. The two of them had been shield mates for only a year. They sparred frequently in the beginning, in the training ring. But then they began to spar in private places. When I asked Xander about this, he would not tell me, but said it was necessary. And I did not press him any further, because it was not my business what he and Halcyon did."

"But Xander was fond of Halcyon?" the archon asked. "Was there any enmity between them?"

Iason shook his head. "Not that I saw. They were well suited."

"Do you have any idea where they were practicing?"

"No, Lord."

"Did you ever suspect that Xander and Halcyon were lovers?"

Iason hesitated. He glanced at the commander before replying in an uncertain tone, "Yes, Lord."

Evadne frowned. Not once had this thought crossed her mind.

She looked at her sister. Halcyon's eyes were dull as she continued to watch Iason testify. Dull, like the last of her light was about to extinguish, and that made Evadne panic.

She had never seen her sister vanquished. But that is what she saw in Halcyon—the deep breath drawn before a surrender.

"Continue with your account of the day Xander died," the archon requested. "How did you find his body?"

"I saw Halcyon . . ." Iason paused again, hesitant. "I saw Halcyon running back to camp at midday. She appeared haggard, frantic. There was blood on her hands, on her face. When I attempted to speak to her, she was incoherent. Eventually, after she had caught her breath, I was able to make sense of her words."

"What did she say?"

"She said, 'I did not mean it. It was a mishap.' Over and over. And then she told me where to find him. I thought she would remain in the camp, that Xander was injured. I left Halcyon to go to the place she had described."

"Which was where?"

"In the Dione Ravine, south of our camp."

"And what did you find, Iason?"

Iason bowed his head, studying his hands. "I found Xander lying in a pool of blood on the ravine floor. His throat cut."

"Was there anything else unusual?" the archon asked, squinting down at the hoplite. "Anything to indicate that Xander and Halcyon had been in a lovers' tryst?"

"I did find something odd. A strip of linen on the ground near Xander."

"A strip of linen?"

"Yes, Lord. I do not know how else to describe it. A tourniquet, perhaps?"

A subtle movement caught Evadne's attention. It was Straton;

he had flexed his fingers and tapped his knee, and it seemed the archon noticed this as well. A wordless signal between the two men. Instantly, the mystery of the linen was forgotten as the archon said, "Very good, Iason. You are dismissed." He wrote on the scroll before him, and it took every ounce of Evadne's control not to raise her voice, to draw attention to the fact that Straton had just swayed the archon. "I now call forth Symeon of Aphra."

Iason melted back into the crowd and another hoplite stepped forward. He also refused to make eye contact with Halcyon.

"Symeon of Aphra, you have known both Halcyon and Xander for seven years now," the archon said. "What can you tell me of their relationship?"

Symeon replied swiftly, without doubt. "They were lovers, Lord."

"And what evidence do you have, Symeon?"

"The two of them were very careful. But one day, I witnessed their affection. Last spring, behind one of the tents, Xander caressed Halcyon's face, as a man does to the one he loves."

"Anything else?"

"Yes, Lord. Xander and I shared a tent, and there were nights when he would steal away. I can only surmise that he went to be with Halcyon. They were also absent from camp for days, a few weeks ago. Some of us believed they had gone to a priest, to be secretly married."

The commander shifted on his bench. Evadne darted a glance at him; his face was emotionless, but there was a gleam in his eyes. It almost looked like a warning, and the archon must have understood, because he promptly dismissed Symeon and called forth the final witness.

"I lastly summon Narcissa of Cantos, captain of the Scorpion Squad."

A third hoplite approached the rostrum. She was tall and lithe, her long brown hair held captive in a braid.

Evadne recognized her. She was the warrior who had whipped Halcyon, and then knelt and cared for the wounds she had wrought.

At last, a flicker of emotion in Halcyon. Her brows pulled close together before she closed her eyes, as if she could not bear to look at her captain.

Narcissa, like the other two warriors preceding her, did not spare Halcyon a glance.

"Narcissa, you have been Halcyon's captain for five years," the archon began. "Tell us what you know of her."

"Halcyon was one of the finest warriors of the legion," Narcissa answered. "There was no one who could outrun her, and only few of us could disarm her."

"So she is very strong?"

"Yes, Lord."

"Is she prone to violence?"

"Yes. On some occasions."

Evadne's heart plummeted. Halcyon was *not* prone to violence. Halcyon was good. Halcyon was loyal.

"How would you describe Halcyon?" the archon pressed.

"Competitive. Private. Conscientious."

"Does it surprise you that Halcyon would make such a grave error, if you believe her claim that killing Xander was 'a mishap'?"

"Yes, it surprises me," Narcissa replied. "As I said, Halcyon is conscientious. She rarely makes mistakes."

"Did you ever suspect that Halcyon and Xander were lovers?"

"I confess the thought crossed my mind from time to time. Particularly when the two of them seemed to become inseparable. But Halcyon had never been one to tell me who she favored. As I said, she was private. She was focused on her training, entirely."

The archon wrote in his scroll and dismissed Narcissa.

Narcissa finally looked at Halcyon, just before she turned away, but Halcyon's eyes remained closed, her long lashes lying flush on her cheeks. Her face had gone pale again.

Evadne's stomach wound in an anxious knot as the archon directed his attention to her sister.

"Halcyon of Isaura, I will now ask you questions, and by the wrath of the gods, you must answer them truthfully. Do you swear it?"

Halcyon opened her eyes. But she focused on nothing; her gaze was distant. "I swear it, Lord."

"How long had you and Xander been shield mates?"

"Four seasons."

"And did you choose Xander?"

"No. Lord Straton chose me for him."

"Were you and Xander lovers at any point in time?"

Halcyon hesitated. "No. He was a brother to me, and I was a

sister to him."

Evadne knew Halcyon was speaking truth, despite her confliction. But whispers spawned in the crowd that stated Halcyon
was lying, that there had been something more between her and
Xander.

"What do you have to say about the affection Symeon claims
he saw between the two of you?"

"That was affection between shield mates, Lord. Xander was
concerned he had hurt me in our spar that day. He was ensuring
that I was well."

"Did he ever anger you?"

"No."

"Did you flee the camp after Xander's death?"

"Yes."

"You did not go to your commander after the incident?"

"No."

"Why?"

"I was afraid, Lord."

"Afraid of what?"

"Of Lord Straton's wrath."

"But why should you fear him?"

"Because I had just killed his son."

"So you confess to the killing?" the archon was swift to say.

Perspiration beaded Halcyon's brow. "It was an accident."

"How could someone as accomplished as you, Halcyon of
Isaura, make such an appalling mistake? The witness Iason said
you slit Xander's throat. I do not understand how this could be a

mishap."

Evadne watched her sister closely; she watched how she breathed, how she spoke, how her eyes had become overcast. *Do not surrender, Halcyon*, Evadne wanted to shout at her. *Do not go down without a fight.*

Halcyon's gaze flickered at last, finding the commander. Straton's eyes were already on her, his expression rigid as a shield.

"Xander let down his guard," Halcyon said, so softly that the archon had to bend closer to hear her. "Xander had yielded, but I did not . . . see it. I was already in motion, and my sword caught him in the throat."

The assembly was quiet. No one seemed to breathe in that moment, the moment of Halcyon's confession, when she stared at the commander and the commander stared at her.

"I have brought pain to your family, Lord Straton," Halcyon continued. "I am sorry, and I know my words will never be enough to atone for it. Not a moment passes when I do not wish it had been different, that I had been the one to fall, and Xander the one to live. I am a coward, and I do not deserve to live."

Shock rippled through the crowd. Evadne felt her father's hand slip away from hers, to cover his face. On her other side, Phaedra was pale, devastated as she stared at Halcyon. Even the archon appeared disarmed by Halcyon's candid words, and he looked at Straton. Evadne noticed it happened again: the commander made a subtle movement with his fingers, tapping his knee.

The archon set down his quill, rising to his feet. Evadne realized he was concluding the trial, that he was about to give the verdict. No one moved or spoke as they waited, breaths suspended, to hear the fate of Halcyon.

"Halcyon of Isaura," the archon began, and her name rang like steel on stone. "By my power and jurisdiction over the city of Abacus, you have been found guilty of accidental manslaughter. For this, you will spend five years working in the common quarry of Mithra. You have also been found guilty of cowardice. For this, you will spend the next five years shackled in Mithra's prison. Last, you will spend the final five years of your sentence serving the house you have wronged, which is the house of your commander, Lord Straton of Mithra. By the gods, this will be done, and should you try to escape this sentence, you will face immediate death."

The assembly became a whirl of noise. Half of the crowd booed at the verdict; half of the crowd applauded. Evadne was silent, unmoving, but her thoughts raged.

Halcyon's sentence was going to devour *fifteen* years of her life. She would be thirty-five years old by the time she would be free.

And Evadne thought of how terrible the common quarry was. How it was mainly composed of relic hunters, vicious men who had murdered to get what they wanted. And she thought of how terrible the prisons of Mithra were. Halcyon would be chained in utter darkness. She would not have company or see daylight for five years. And Evadne thought of Halcyon's service to the commander and his house. Her sister would have to serve a family who resented and despised her.

Halcyon might survive this sentence, but she would be broken by the end of it. Death would have been easier, and Evadne saw the same shock ignite in Halcyon's eyes. Her sister stared at the commander, but now the commander would not meet her gaze. Evadne finally understood Halcyon's meekness and Straton's subtle signals.

Halcyon had come to her trial expecting to be given death.

And Evadne had prepared for this moment. She had believed that Halcyon's sentence would be execution and she had a speech rehearsed; she was planning to pour her words out like precious oil before the archon, to plead for Halcyon's life. But now Evadne had to swiftly weave together a new plan.

The commander was hiding something, and Evadne refused to let it ruin her sister's life.

"Lord Archon?" Evadne was rising, speaking before she could change her mind.

The archon heard her voice, even over the tumult. He scowled, his eyes sweeping the front of the assembly until they found her.

"Lord, may I speak?" she called out to him.

"*Evadne!*" Phaedra hissed, horrified.

"Pupa, sit down," Gregor begged, taking hold of her arm. "Please *sit down*."

Evadne only looked at them, at her father's alarmed eyes, at her mother's barely concealed panic, and said, "Let me speak."

Gregor released her, but he had never appeared so old, so frail.

"Yes, what is it, child?" the archon said to her, holding his hands up so the crowd would hush.

"Evadne . . . *no*." Halcyon's voice arced like an arrow.

Evadne met her sister's gaze, saw Halcyon's mounting distress.

"Speak up, girl," the archon said, impatient.

It had gone deathly quiet in the hall, every eye hooked to Evadne, who was suddenly trembling. In her mind the night before, she had envisioned herself being as brave and strong as Halcyon had always been. She had not pictured herself shrinking, her voice sounding like a poorly plucked kithara string.

"Lord, I am Evadne of Isaura, Halcyon's younger sister. And I would ask to take half of her sentence, to serve it alongside her."

The air teemed with astonishment. It was suffocating; it was difficult to think coherently. But over the noise came Halcyon's cries.

"No, Eva! Lord Archon, I do not accept this arrangement!"

For the second time that day, the archon was shocked. He stared at Evadne as if she had lost her mind.

"Lord Archon," Evadne said, speaking louder, to overpower Halcyon's frantic refusal. "Let me serve at her side. Instead of the fifteen-year sentence, let it be seven and a half years total, split between the two of us. That is two and a half years in the quarry, two and a half years in the prison, and two and a half years in service to Lord Straton of Mithra."

The archon slid his gaze to the commander. So did Evadne.

Straton rose to his feet, his eyes keen as he regarded her. He was the only one who did not appear surprised by Evadne's reckless offer, but she wondered if he ever truly revealed what he felt in his expressions. His gaze dropped to the floor, to her right ankle.

"I am more than capable, Lord Straton," she said. But even as she said the words, her ankle throbbed in disagreement.

"It is admirable of you," Straton said, "but this is Halcyon's sentence, not yours."

"Eva . . . Eva, it is all right," Halcyon said, hoarse. Her chains clanged as she reached out. "Please, Sister. Listen to Lord Straton."

Evadne ignored Halcyon. She continued to hold the commander's stare and dared to say, "I know you once held my sister in high regard, Lord Straton. For you to have chosen her as your son's shield mate expresses that perhaps more than anything. I know justice must be served here today, and my family is grateful that you have spared her life, Lord. But there will be nothing left of my sister come the end of this punishment. If you will not agree to let me serve it alongside her, then give me a portion of it."

"You are naïve, Evadne of Isaura," the archon said, drawing her attention. "You know nothing of justice among warriors. What I have deemed for your sister is the lightest of punishments, considering her crimes."

Again, Evadne had to hold her retort. But her jaw clenched, and her gaze returned to Straton. She was not a fool; she knew it was the commander who had decided Halcyon's fate. The archon had merely enacted it.

Straton, likewise, was not a fool. Evadne could tell he read the trail of her thoughts; she had addressed *him*, not the archon, knowing the commander was the one in power here.

"Lord Archon," Straton said in a placid tone, glancing to where the judge stood behind the rostrum. "I have considered Evadne's pleas and would like to present an altered arrangement for you to consider. Halcyon will serve five years in the quarry and five years in the prison. Evadne will serve five years in my household. And that will complete the sentence for Halcyon's crimes."

The archon furrowed his brow, as if he had to weigh the new arrangement. But Evadne already knew it would be done.

"So be it," the archon announced. "Halcyon, your younger sister will take five years of your sentence by serving the house of Lord Straton. Both of you will begin your sentences at dawn on the morrow. Halcyon, you will be transported to the common quarry, and Evadne, you will travel to Mithra with Lord Straton and his family."

The guards unchained Halcyon from the stand to escort her back to her cell. Evadne stared at her sister, hungry to memorize everything about her before she was dragged away into the shadows.

And Halcyon, who Evadne had never seen cry, who had only ever been strong and courageous before her, covered her face with her hands and bitterly wept.

⇥ IX ⇤

Evadne

Evadne lay on her pallet that night, moonlight pouring in from the open window. The inn was quiet; Gregor and Phaedra had finally escaped into dreams after hours of tossing and turning. Evadne listened to her father's gentle snores, her mind consumed with thoughts of tomorrow, when she was to join Straton and his household. When her life would change.

What have I done?

She was exhausted, and it made her recklessness feel even greater. She was a fool to believe she was capable of exposing a man as powerful as Straton, to believe she could ease a fraction of Halcyon's suffering—and all she wanted was to sleep, to forget about the horror of the day.

She heard a rustle of wings.

Evadne glanced to the window, where a small bird was perched on the sill. It looked like a nightingale, its cream and tawny feathers gilded in starlight.

She held her breath as she watched the bird flutter from the window to the foot of her pallet. It chirped, hopping closer to her. Evadne sat forward and extended her hand in wonder as the bird perched on her finger. It softly trilled, as if it was trying to say something to her. But before Evadne could whisper to it, the bird flew back to the sill and waited.

She rose, following the nightingale to the window.

The bird took flight. She watched as it swooped down to the street, to a boy who stood in the moonlight, his hand outstretched. The nightingale rested on his finger, and Evadne felt her heart stir, awed until she recognized him. Straton's son, Xander's younger brother. The mage.

He continued to stand in the street, waiting. For her, Evadne knew.

She thought about ignoring him, but her curiosity bloomed. What did he want? Why had he come to her in the dead of night when he was bound to see her in the morning?

Her family's room was on the second floor of the inn. Evadne leaned out the window to see if it was possible for her to climb her way down. The mage caught her attention, pointing to the front door of the inn.

She found Halcyon's sheathed kopis and donned her sandals. Her parents continued to slumber, oblivious as she stole across the floor.

The door opened soundlessly. Evadne entered the corridor, edging along the wall to find the stairs. The dining hall was empty, and the main door was unbolted. It was slightly terrifying, she thought as she exited the inn. How effortlessly the mage had charmed a bird and multiple doors. And she could not help but wonder if he was going to harm her.

She stopped on the threshold and stared across the distance at him.

He continued to stand in the middle of the deserted street, the nightingale perched on his hand.

Evadne began to close the space between them. She remembered Macarius's trickery, that hollow emptiness in her stomach, and she stopped a full arm's length away from Straton's son, her wariness evident.

"I intend no harm to you, Evadne," he said, his voice a deep timbre that made him sound far older than he was. He looked as if he could only be a year or two her senior. "I have come tonight out of honor for Halcyon. I spoke with your sister a few hours ago, and she asked to see you. I can sneak you into her cell, but you will have to trust me."

Evadne thought she had misheard him. *"What?"*

The mage whispered to the nightingale, and the bird took flight, vanishing into the shadows.

"We do not have much time," he said. "I am going to cast an enchantment that will render me unseen. Anything that touches me will also be invisible. So you will need to take my hand and hold it until it is safe to let go."

Evadne stared at his hand, the silver ring that gleamed upon his finger. The thought of holding his hand made her hesitate. "Why?

Why are you offering this?" She did not trust him, and made no attempt to hide it.

The mage was silent, studying her. His voice was cold when he said, "Because I would do anything to have the chance to speak to my brother one last time."

She had nothing to say to that. But her cheeks warmed; she felt a tangle of shame, anger.

"Do you want this or not?" he prompted, impatient.

"Yes," she whispered, and the air hummed between them, the magic waiting for him to breathe it in, to speak it out.

The mage turned away from her; it made her anxious until she realized he was singing, and he must want some privacy. Even so, Evadne did not look away from him. She caught bits and pieces of his spell; he sang in the God Tongue, just as Macarius had done, but his voice was not nearly as polished and beautiful as Macarius's had been. His voice was deeper, smokier. There was a bite to it, like gravel under bare feet, and Evadne shivered.

She watched as the edges of him began to glimmer, as he faded into silver dust. And then he was gone, as if he had never been. Evadne stood alone in the street, the night wind whistling through buildings, dragging hair into her disbelieving eyes.

"My hand is before you," she heard him say. "Reach out and you will find it."

Evadne lifted her hand, seeking his. Their fingers bumped, awkwardly weaving together. Evadne's heart beat like a drum as she felt his enchantment steal over her. It was like a veil being drawn against her skin, softer than silk. She watched herself fade into golden dust, succumbing to invisibility.

"We must move quickly," he said. "Do not let go of me until I tell you to."

The mage set a harried pace, guiding her through the maze of streets, past unsuspecting guards. Evadne struggled to keep in stride with him, her ankle flaring in protest by the time they reached the agora.

Up the stairs they went, sightless and quiet as breath. The guards took no note of them as they patrolled the colonnade; they did not hear the doors crack a sliver, and the mage began to lead Evadne through the divide. Her chiton snagged on the handle. She bit her lip, her fingers nearly yanked free from his, but the mage clamped down like a vise, refusing to let their hands come apart.

Carefully, she untethered herself from the brass handle as one of the guards turned, frowning before he shut the doors behind them.

The agora's lobby felt vastly different at night. The air was thick with silence. Oil lamps burned in iron stands, their flames casting rings of light on the polished floors.

The mage guided her forward, past the assembly chamber and down a corridor. A door sat open; firelight spilled into the hall. Evadne felt the mage slow in trepidation as they prepared to pass it, and she didn't understand until she could glance into the open doorway.

Straton was in the chamber. A desk was before him, covered in scrolls and papyri, and the commander sat with his hands covering his face, his armor and weapons hanging behind him on the wall. He was so still he might have been asleep, but then his hands dropped and his face was creased, agonized.

Evadne did not want to feel compassion for him.

But she did, like a pinch in her soul. And his son's fingers tightened on hers, and she could only wonder why he was risking himself like this.

They left the commander behind, passing another set of armed guards as they came to a stone stairwell. The air grew cold as they descended into the prison; torches burned along the wall, awakening stone carvings of beasts and the hoplites who had slain them.

They entered a chamber where two guards sat at a table, playing a game of knucklebones. The entrance to the prison was just beyond them, a huge sliding door latticed in iron, locked. But the mage must have smuggled the key, because he brought Evadne to the door and the keyhole turned until it clicked.

Again, he made the door crack open without sound, and the two of them passed over its threshold before it closed behind them, the guards completely unaware.

And this is why mages are forbidden from common prisons, Evadne thought wryly. The law stated that mages were not allowed in such places. The risk of enchantment was too great—charmed tortures or charmed escapes. But every now and then, it was permitted. If the mage was trustworthy.

The mage must have been here earlier, when he visited Halcyon. For a reason Evadne was anxious to know.

"Grab that torch in your other hand, but take care with it," the mage murmured to her, and she did as he requested. As soon as her fingers had come about its handle, the torch went invisible, and the light vanished.

They moved down the corridor, the mage thankfully knowing the prison's layout, even in the dark.

They passed cell after cell. Evadne could hear mutterings, moans of pains. The sound carried eerily, loud and then faint, like she was trapped in a dream.

Finally, the mage came to a stop. "This is your sister's cell. You can release me now, so the fire will return."

Evadne unwound her fingers from his. The flames in her possession blazed into sight, and she watched as her body returned, taking up space once again. The mage continued to be unseen, but Evadne felt his sleeve brush her arm as he unlocked the door.

"I will stand guard here, but I fear you will not have long," he whispered. "When I open the door, be ready to take my hand to depart."

"Yes, of course," Evadne said. "Thank you."

He made no reply but opened Halcyon's cell door, and Evadne stepped within it.

Halcyon was sitting against the far wall, her eyes closed. Her chest was rising and falling in a frantic pattern, and Evadne's heart twisted to see her sister shaven and in sackcloth, held in a cell that knew only despair.

"Halcyon," she breathed.

Halcyon opened her eyes. The worry in her face melted, and she smiled, as brilliant as if they were home, in their bedroom. As if none of this had happened.

"*Evadne.* My gods, I cannot believe he actually did it!" She struggled to rise, but for once, Evadne moved faster. She set the torch in an iron sconce on the wall and sat before Halcyon, their knees touching. The floor was cold, and Evadne reached for Halcyon's hands, feeling how frigid she was.

"You speak of the mage?" Evadne asked, rubbing Halcyon's icy fingers in her palms. "Lord Straton's other son?"

"Yes. Damon," Halcyon replied. "I asked him if he would bring you to me, but I never imagined he would."

Evadne swallowed her questions, refusing to waste this time she had been given. She brought Halcyon's hands to her lips, to blow warmth into them. "You are like ice, Hal."

Halcyon snorted. "They do not give blankets to murderers."

"You are not a murderer."

Halcyon was quiet, staring intently at Evadne. When she finally spoke, her voice cracked. "Why, Eva? Why did you do it?"

Evadne lowered their entwined hands. "You remember the day you left to join the legion, all those years ago?"

"Of course. I still dream about it some nights."

"As do I. And it took me a long time to get over your absence. I cried every night for an entire season. I hated having our room all to myself. Eventually, the pain faded, but I always missed you. Every day, I wondered what you were doing, what other friends you now had, if you even thought of me anymore."

She paused, her voice wavering. Halcyon's eyes gleamed; her fingers tightened around Evadne's. "At first, I could not understand why you had to go to the legion. But then I did, and I was proud of you. And then I envied you, because you had ascended; you were the joy of our parents. You were destined to do great things, and I was destined to remain in the grove, forgotten. But when I watched you crawl out my window the other night, knowing you were in trouble and yet uncertain as to where you were going . . . I felt it again. The pain of you leaving. I told myself that I would not be left behind this time. That I would follow you, that I would go wherever you went, even if that meant helping you carry a punishment you do not deserve."

Halcyon leaned forward, to touch her brow to Evadne's. They sat like that for a moment, and the coldness, the dankness of the cell seemed to recede.

"You are brave, Eva," Halcyon whispered. "Far braver than me. There is such steel within you, little sister."

"Oh! That reminds me." Evadne leaned away, reaching into her pocket. "I brought this." She laid Halcyon's kopis on her sister's lap.

"Where did you find it?" Halcyon's fingers shook as she traced the leather sheath.

"I took it from Laneus."

Halcyon smiled. "Good." She took the kopis in her grip, but she did not keep it. She set it back in Evadne's palms, curling her fingers over the sheath. "I want you to have it, Eva. But you must keep it hidden, or else he will take it away from you."

"He" being Straton.

Evadne tried to forget about the glimpse of pain she had seen in the commander's face, when he thought he had been alone. But a lump formed in her throat, and it reminded her that there was more happening than she knew of.

"Hal . . ." She drew in a deep breath, tucking the kopis back into her pocket. "Why did the commander choose you to be Xander's shield mate?"

"I do not know," Halcyon replied, too swiftly.

Evadne knew she was lying. She struggled to hide her frustration, that Halcyon would still withhold things from her, even after all the trauma that had happened.

"He must have had a reason, Sister. Lord Straton does not strike me as the sort of man who does things without purpose. Did he ask you and Xander to do something no one else could know about?"

Halcyon's eyes narrowed. The gleam of joy guttered, and she laid her finger over Evadne's lips.

"Why are you asking these things, Eva?"

Evadne drew Halcyon's finger away. "Because I sense there is more to what happened, and he is trying to conceal it by punishing you unjustly."

Halcyon's anger flashed. Evadne had rarely seen her older sister mad; she had always been mild-tempered and patient, even when they were girls. Seeing it now only heightened Evadne's suspicions about the commander.

"Where did such an absurd thought come from, Eva? You must let it go and swear to me that you will keep your head down while you serve Lord Straton. Do not go looking for answers, or you will irritate him, and I cannot bear it, Evadne. If something were to happen to you . . ."

Evadne softened; she heard fear lurking in Halcyon's voice, and she framed her sister's face in her hands to hold her steady. "Nothing is going to happen to me, Hal."

"Swear it to me, Evadne," Halcyon whispered, trembling. "Swear to me you will be wise, you will remain safe."

It was a promise that Evadne did not know she could grant. But she smiled and nodded, and the tension that had been building in Halcyon eased.

The cell door creaked.

"Evadne," Damon spoke, his voice faint yet urgent. "We must go now."

Evadne's heart ached as she reached one last time for Halcyon, wrapping her arms about her. She felt the crinkled back of Halcyon's sackcloth, and when Evadne leaned away, she realized it was dried blood.

"Hal! You've been bleeding!"

"I know," Halcyon whispered. "It will be all right." Now she framed Evadne's face in her hands, holding her steady. "I love you, Evadne. Be safe, be wise, and I will see you again soon. I promise." She kissed her cheeks, and Evadne thought she would weep, the weight of ten years suddenly becoming visceral. "Go now."

Evadne kissed her sister in farewell, and more than anything she wanted to return the words to her. *I love you, Halcyon.* But she knew if she spoke, she would shatter into hundreds of pieces.

She stumbled to her feet, her nose suddenly running, her eyes blurring. But just before she took the torch back from the sconce, Evadne set her eyes on Halcyon. Her sister smiled, and for a breath, it would seem like they were girls again.

How different would they be in ten years?

Evadne found Damon's hand, invisible and waiting. With her other hand she took the torch, and the world plunged back into darkness.

Evadne

E vadne? It is time to wake up."

Phaedra's voice broke Evadne's dream, rousing her. She sat up on her pallet, groggy, until she saw the last thing she'd expected: her mother and father waiting for her, cross-legged on the floor of their room with a spread of breakfast. Her parents had hardly spoken to her after the trial. Evadne knew they were upset, angry at her for striking the new bargain with Straton. But it was evident that they now had something to say to her.

They must have heard me slip out last night, Evadne thought, stifling a groan. She joined Gregor and Phaedra on the floor, careful not to make eye contact with them. How was she to explain what had happened the night before? How would they respond to the fact that she'd snuck off with the son of their enemy? That she alone had been granted a private moment with Halcyon?

"I remember the night you were born, Pupa, like it was

yesterday," her father began in a gentle voice. "You came into the world so quietly, so still that I thought the gods had already taken your breath. But then you reached out and held fast to my finger, and I thought that I would never let you go. Sometimes I forget that we have descended from the god of the wind. A god who broke himself for love of another. But every now and then, a generation will remember what it is like to fly, and they will grow their own wings. Such as Halcyon. Such as you, Eva."

Evadne was shocked. This was the last thing she expected her father to say, and she strove to hide the tears that welled in her eyes.

Gregor reached beneath the collar of his tunic. Evadne watched, confused as he brought forth a silver chain that flashed in the sunlight.

"Hold out your hand, Pupa."

She obeyed with her mouth gaping, her palm upraised. The moment her father set the lapis lazuli pendant into her hand, she knew exactly what this was, even though she had never seen it before. She had only heard legends of it. She had heard her cousin Lysander describe it with near-painful longing in his voice. It had been the crux of Uncle Ozias's falling out with the family. The reason why Ozias had renounced them ten years ago. Because he had wanted it, almost more than anything.

And now it gleamed on Evadne's palm, silver and blue, like a piece of the sky.

Kirkos's relic.

The enchanted object that the god of the wind had given to

the kingdom before he had broken his wings and become mortal. Her ancestor.

"Father . . ." she whispered, overcome. She did not know what pierced her more: The fact that her father had possessed the relic all this time and had kept it hidden and safe—he could have left the Common Court because of it! He could have become a member of the Magical Court years ago—or the realization that he was giving it to her. A small piece of magic. A small piece of home.

"It is time for you to wear it, Daughter," Gregor whispered. "Keep it hidden and secret, or else they will take it from you."

Evadne studied it, traced the charm with her thumb. The lapis stone was carved in the shape of a wing, and the pendant was the length of her pinky. The chain was long enough that she could keep the wing hidden beneath her clothes.

"Does it truly . . ." She could not even speak the question. She met her father's gaze, wide-eyed in wonder.

Gregor smiled. "Yes. When you wear it about your neck, it will answer the command of your heart when you desire to fly. But again, Pupa . . . you must be very shrewd, very careful." He took it from her palm to drape it upon her. Evadne listened to the chain whisper, felt the gentle weight of the wing come to rest over her heart.

"It suits you," Phaedra said.

Both her father and mother, then, had known of the relic and had hidden it.

"Do Uncle Nico and Aunt Lydia know?" Evadne asked, tucking the pendant beneath her clothes.

"No, Eva. It has been our secret for a long time," Gregor replied. And there was a hint of regret in his voice. Evadne wondered if he was thinking of his lost brother, who may or may not be a prisoner in the common quarry, shackled among fellow relic hunters who had let ambition and greed overcome them. The place Halcyon was about to dwell for five years.

They struggled to eat after that, the morning pulsing with anxious energy. But Evadne forced down an orb of flatbread and a few figs before it was time for her to depart. She was to meet Straton at the market well, just across the street from the inn. And yet now that this moment had come, Evadne felt like clinging to her parents.

Gregor rose first, drawing Evadne to her feet. He gave her a fierce hug, one that stole her breath, and pressed a kiss to her brow. And then he turned away to hide his tears, unable to watch her leave.

Evadne gathered her small bag of possessions, Halcyon's kopis safely stored at the very bottom. Her mother walked her down the stairs to the front door of the inn. A door Evadne had slipped through like a shadow earlier.

Phaedra stopped on the threshold. She cupped Evadne's face in her hands and studied her, the rise and fall of her daughter's profile, the darkness of her eyes, the freckles on her cheeks.

"It does not matter that you serve Lord Straton's family now," she whispered. "You are your own self. No one owns your soul or your body or your fate. No one but you, Evadne."

Evadne breathed in those words, let them twine with her blood and her bones, so she would never forget them.

"You have done a courageous thing, one that the gods will see and bless you for. And I am proud of you, Evadne. Use Kirkos's relic *only* in time of dire need, and even then, be wise with it, my love. It is an extraordinary gift, but it can be dangerous if misused," Phaedra whispered and kissed her cheeks. She relinquished her daughter, as she must. Even though it made pain bloom in both of them.

Evadne began to walk toward the market.

She did not look back, even though she felt her mother's gaze.

And each step Evadne took drew her farther from her former life. Fear and doubt warred within her until she thought of Halcyon, who had always been the symbol of valor, a constellation for Evadne to chart her course.

She set her hand over her breast, feeling the lapis wing resting against her heart, thrumming with magic. A promise rose from the earth, from the wind, moving through her like a chorus.

There is steel within me.

I will not bend.

I will not break.

THE SECOND SCROLL

A Crown
Made of Secrets

⋯ XI ⋯

Evadne

S traton waited by the well.

He looked like a god upon first glance, tall and broad and merciless, with the sun blazing down the bronze scales of his armor, as if he were forged from fire. His helm was in the crook of his arm, the black-and-white horsehair blowing in the morning breeze. A small leather satchel was buckled at his belt, and a sword was sheathed at his side, the scabbard trimmed in emeralds.

Evadne wondered how many people he had killed as she arrived to meet him.

His eyes briefly assessed her. She could only hope that she did not look forlorn, afraid.

"Come with me." Straton turned and walked through the market, the vendors, servants, housewives, and hoplites swiftly stepping aside for him. Evadne labored to maintain his pace, drawing the eyes of those she passed. Again, the whispers rose, chasing her heels.

Yes, that is her. The sister of the hoplite who killed Xander.

She's paying a portion of Halcyon's punishment. Fool of a girl.

What possessed her to do such a thing?

Perspiration beaded her brow when the commander finally stopped in the booth of a silversmith. A worn blanket served as a roof, shielding them from the brunt of the rising sun as they waited for assistance. Evadne stood slightly behind Straton, gazing at the array of jewelry set on the craftsman's table.

One tray brimmed with divine tokens. Each of the eight gods and goddesses were represented in silver. Even Pyrrhus, god of fire, had tokens made in his honor, despite the fact that he was still trapped in Mount Euthymius. Kirkos, however, was forgotten, and Evadne felt a pang of sadness, that his decision to become mortal had rendered him insignificant.

"Lord Straton!" the silversmith cried, emerging from an open doorway. "I apologize for the wait. How may I assist you?"

"I need an amulet," the commander said.

The silversmith glanced to Evadne. She read his thoughts, the arch of his brows—he knew exactly who she was. "Yes, of course," he replied, and invited them into his work chamber.

It took a moment for Evadne's eyes to adjust to the dim light, but she soon saw there was a long table set against a wall. Silver ingots and iron instruments were scattered across it. A great scroll was also unrolled among the clutter, inked with designs.

The silversmith fumbled around a few jars, finally displaying an amulet on his palm for Straton to see.

"That will do fine," the commander said.

Evadne remained standing on the outskirts until the silver-smith motioned for her to come closer and stand near the fire. She knew what was about to happen, should have been preparing herself for it. But no one at Isaura was a servant. No one in the grove wore an amulet exposing who they were beholden to. Their arms were bare, sun-kissed, brawny, strong. They were their own masters, knowing they had to labor in order to eat, to survive.

Evadne moved as if she were underwater.

She extended her arm, waiting.

She did not watch as he brought the silver band about her upper arm, welding it snugly in place, Straton's crest dangling from it. She distracted herself with thoughts of Halcyon, wondering where her sister was at the moment. They would be traveling the same direction; the common quarry was on the outskirts of Mithra, Evadne's destination. For the next five years, there would only be a matter of miles between the sisters. Miles that would be impossible to cross.

Although . . . perhaps in time, Evadne could.

Perhaps she might fly there.

As she followed Straton from the silversmith's shop, the amulet glittering on her arm, Evadne plotted how to earn the family's trust. If she appeared humble and honored them, perhaps they would come to trust her just enough to grant her a visit to the quarry.

It was an improbable fancy, but it gave her a burst of hope and energy as she trailed the commander back through the market. She relented to look down at the amulet. Straton's crest was of a sword. One side of the blade boasted a full moon, a tribute to Ari. The other side was etched with a sun, a tribute to Magda. Both sun and moon goddess blood in their family.

No wonder one of Straton's children had inherited magic. The divine ran deep in their blood.

He led Evadne through a second market. Merchants haggled at their stalls, and a long line flowed toward a baker's booth. The sweet aroma of cakes mingled with the stench of fish and donkeys and heated iron, and Evadne's eyes watered. She missed the loamy aura of the grove.

At last, they passed through an iron gate and arrived at a private courtyard, hedged by tall white walls adorned with a flowering vine. A group of people were gathered here, with horses and wagons. Evadne came to a stop when she realized this was the commander's family and their servants, preparing to depart Abacus. Her face flushed when she drew their eyes and felt the pointedness of their stares.

She was not welcome among them.

And she did not know where to go, what she should be doing, so she merely watched as Straton approached his wife the healer, who was regarding Evadne with a cold gaze. He bent to whisper something in the lady's ear, her blond hair stirring with his breath, and Evadne looked away, her eyes settling on their daughter. The girl was dressed in another beautiful chiton with a silver band winking on her brow.

She sat on a gray mare, returning Evadne's stare unflinchingly. Until her brother, Damon, nudged his bay stallion up to her side.

The mage was the only one in the entire courtyard who did not look at Evadne. It was like she did not exist in his world, and it made her feel odd, off-balance. Just hours ago, he had sent a nightingale to her window. He had held her hand and cloaked her with his enchantment.

And now it was as if she were still unseen to him.

She watched him speak to his sister, his conversation drawing the girl's attention.

Evadne, at last, felt like she could breathe, and she looked at the ground, the safest place to gaze.

"This is Evadne of Isaura," Straton announced. "I believe all of us are aware of the arrangement she made with the archon yesterday, to take her sister's place in serving my household for the next five years."

Look up, Evadne told herself. *Do not be afraid. Look up and meet their eyes.*

She did, only to find scowls and disgust imprinted on the other servants' faces. Each of their left arms bore an amulet, the same as hers. And yet she had never felt more alienated and alone.

The longing for Isaura, for her parents, for her family crashed through her, so fiercely that it stole her breath.

Do not think of them, she ordered herself. But the ache in Evadne's chest was almost obliterating.

"She is to be treated as an equal among you," Straton was saying to his servants, who glanced at him with pleading, desperate expressions. "She is beneath my protection, and I do not want to hear of anything ill befalling her while she serves the house and fulfills the sentence." He paused and looked to an older woman, standing beside one of the wagons. "Toula? I would ask that you take Evadne as your novice. See where she could fit best among you, and ensure she has everything she needs. Now, let us return home."

Toula bowed her head to his request, but Evadne saw the aversion in her face when she approached her. Like Evadne was a rodent she was having to corral and deal with.

"What are you good for?" Toula asked, terse. She was not a tall woman, but she was weathered, wiry, as a shrub that defies a mountain and thrives in a rocky crack. She was not one to irritate or anger, Evadne thought.

And yet how was Evadne to answer her? Should she tell Toula of all the days she had labored in the grove, all the days she had pressed olives until they bled gold? Should she tell her of all the mornings she had risen early to till the garden, to plant seeds, to uproot weeds, to watch for locusts, to harvest the fruits when they finally emerged? How she had baked bread and salted fish and gathered nuts, how she had mended holes in her family's garments, how she had scrubbed the floors of the villa until they shone like the burnished floor of Magda's temple?

"I can do anything," Evadne said.

"Good. You can begin your servitude by tending to the chamber pots." Toula turned and walked back to one of the wagons.

Evadne hesitated, uncertain if she should follow her.

The commander had mounted his massive stallion; the horse's hooves clopped over the stones to where Evadne stood.

"I want you to ride in the back of that wagon," he told her, indicating the one Toula was fussing over.

It was then that Evadne understood most of the servants would be walking on foot.

"I can walk, Lord."

"It would be better for you to ride," Straton said, gathering the reins in his hands. And while he did not say it, Evadne felt it in his gaze. *You would slow us down.*

He nudged his horse forward, his wife shadowing him, perched on a chestnut mare.

Evadne moved to the assigned wagon, where Toula waited.

"Sit there," Toula said, pointing to the least inviting spot.

Evadne climbed into the wagon bed and tried to ignore the resentful stares from the other servants. Their traveling party emerged from the courtyard and passed through the gates of Abacus. And Evadne did not realize it, not until they were a caravan on the northern road. But suddenly the hatred directed at her felt justified.

The wagon just behind her was not bearing sacks of food or jars of wine.

It carried Xander's body.

They had been traveling for hours when the sun began to sink beneath the craggy mountaintops. Straton led the caravan off the road into a desolate plain and Evadne struggled to hide her alarm when she realized they were camping in the shadow of Mount Euthymius.

She climbed down from the wagon, stiff from the ride, and tried not to stare at the cursed summit. This was the first time she had ever seen it, but it was exactly how she had imagined it as a girl, when her aunt Lydia had told her and Maia stories about clever Euthymius and Loris, trapping their brother in a mountain. But it was not the trapped god that Evadne feared; it was Ivina, the mage who guarded the mountain. Once a mortal woman, Ivina had been granted eternal life by Euthymius centuries ago to scare away Pyrrhus's worshippers and would-be rescuers. Ivina was the one who spun travelers' fears into phantoms, tormenting those who came too close to the mountain.

Straton's servants did not appear worried about spending the night here, and Evadne surmised they must camp in this spot often when they ventured to and from Abacus and Mithra. But she did notice that the commander personally set a ring of torch stakes about the camp, lighting them before the sun set. And so Pyrrhus's fire crackled and burned, warding off the darkness as night emerged.

Evadne had counted fifteen servants in all, and as soon as the wagons had come to a halt, they bustled to unpack them. All save for Xander's wagon, which was parked just inside the ring of fire and then left at peace. Evadne tried not to look, but her eyes were drawn to it. His coffin was made of wood, carved with Lord Straton's crest. Laurel clippings surrounded it, as did herbs, which were now wilted. Xander's sword rested on top of the coffin, its steel reflected the firelight, the stars, and Evadne tried to imagine the young man whose body rested within the casket, who had once sparred and laughed with her sister.

She felt someone watching her, and Evadne turned to see the commander standing nearby, shadows on his face.

She bowed her head to him and moved away, trying to find her place among the servants. But Evadne seemed to be invisible to them; no one took note of her. No one spoke to her, looked at her. Half of the servants, Toula included, rushed to erect the tents for Straton and his family. The other half scurried to tend to the horses and ready the evening meal.

Eventually, Evadne approached a servant girl not much older than her, who was sorting through a mound of pillows, her flaxen hair bound in a thick braid.

"May I help you?"

The girl startled, dropping the pillows as she gaped up at Evadne. Her face was pale and beaded with sweat. She did not look well.

"You are Toula's charge, not mine," the girl rasped, but then she hunched over, pressing her hand to her belly. "Here, take these pillows and put them in Lord Straton and Lady Cosima's tent. Arrange them so that their heads face east when they lie down, because of Mount Euthymius."

Evadne gathered the heap of pillows, the fragrance of sandalwood wafting up from them, and did just as the girl had instructed, heeding the superstition. One never slept with Mount Euthymius at their head but at their feet. Just in case Ivina sent her phantoms.

Toula had already erected the lord's tent; it was tall and wide, with ample room for a man of the commander's size to move around comfortably. Reed mats were laid over the grass, and oil lamps burned on small wooden tables.

Evadne dumped the pillows at the head of the makeshift bed, her eyes sweeping the tent. Her gaze hung on a small leather satchel—the same one the commander had buckled to his belt that day. It sat on one of the tables, and Evadne hesitated, wondering if she was brave enough to look within it.

She imagined Halcyon would have no qualms about sneaking, and so Evadne reached for the satchel. Her fingers trembled as they sifted through the contents . . . a money pouch, a quill, a small vial of ink . . . two rolls of papyrus the length of her palm, their seals broken. Dispatches, she realized, and she froze, listening to the sounds of camp beyond the tent walls.

She took the risk, swiftly unrolling the first message.

My sincerest apologies about your son. What a loss!

The handwriting was exquisite, feminine, inked in gold. It was signed as *Hemlock*. Evadne quickly rolled it back up, feeling the sinister pulse of the message. Whoever Hemlock was, they were an enemy of the commander's.

Evadne unrolled the second dispatch.

Grant mercy to Kingfisher.

Another cryptic message, she thought with a twinge of disappointment. In place of a signature was the stamp of a great serpent, inked in the bottom right corner. The crest of a fellow legion commander, maybe? But the longer Evadne studied the stamp, the more she realized it looked nothing like the serpents that graced the warriors' armor. This one was greater. A basilisk.

She rushed to replace the dispatches in Straton's satchel, just as she had found them. Evadne's mind was racing when she returned to the girl's wagon, only to find her retching beside it, trying her best to do it quietly.

She straightened, wiping her mouth with the back of her hand, and looked at Evadne with bleary eyes.

"Perhaps you should rest," Evadne suggested.

"No, I cannot," she panted weakly.

"Amara? *Amara*, where is the wine?" Toula's impatient hiss interrupted the girls. "Lord Straton and his family are waiting."

Amara reached for a wine jar but ended up turning her face away, to retch again. Toula jumped back just in time to miss it, a thunderous expression on her face.

"I am sorry, Toula." Amara sank to her knees, clinging to the spokes of the wagon wheel. "My moon flow has come."

"Of course it has. Of all days," Toula stated with a sigh. "I will ask Lyra to make you a brew tonight, after dinner. But I cannot have you sick in the lord's presence." Her gaze flickered to Evadne. "I suppose it will have to be you. Take a jar of wine and that small cup. The cup is yours—you are to take the first sip of wine before Lord Straton, so he can be assured it is not poisoned. Then serve the lord's cup, then the lady's, then Damon's and Lyra's. Do not let their cups go dry, and do not spill a drop of it, you understand?"

"Poisoned?" Evadne echoed, her eyes wide.

"It is merely protocol," Toula said. "Nothing to be afraid of. Amara has been cupbearer for years and has never been poisoned."

Amara, who was currently retching into the grass.

Evadne stood frozen. If she was poisoned and died in her first week of service, what would become of her sister? Would the five years of service be given back to Halcyon?

"Move, girl," Toula said, impatient.

Numb, Evadne chose a jar of wine and grabbed the small tasting cup. She found Straton and his family at the center of camp, reclining on blankets and pillows, oil lamps hanging about them, drenching them in golden firelight. A platter of food was set in the middle of their circle, although no one was eating.

Evadne stood in the commander's line of sight. He watched, a slight frown furrowing his brow as Evadne broke the seal on the jar and poured a small trickle into her cup. A tremor moved through her as she raised the cup to her lips, as she remembered the strange messages hidden in Straton's satchel.

Hemlock.

The stamp of a winding basilisk.

Was she going to die here, drinking poison meant for Straton, miles from home?

Evadne swallowed the wine and waited, heart churning. She waited for what felt like years, but there was no sting of poison. Convinced, the commander motioned her to fill his cup.

She knelt and poured his wine. But when Evadne made to fill his wife's cup, Cosima recoiled from her, guarding her chalice.

"Do you think I want you anywhere near my food and drink?" she asked.

Evadne paused on her knees, jar extended and ready to pour. The wine's sour aftertaste lingered in her mouth as she thought about how ironic Cosima's comment was. Evadne was risking herself, testing the family's drink for poison. She could see Damon and his sister in her peripheral vision, their eyes wide in surprise.

"Mother," Damon whispered.

Cosima paid him no heed. "Where is Amara? *Amara!*"

From the shadows came Toula, an apologetic smile painted on her face. "Lady Cosima, I apologize for this . . . inconvenience. Amara is unwell, and I thought it would be wise to begin training the girl."

"I do not want her touching my family's sustenance," Cosima stated. "I do not want to see her at all, in fact. Do you understand, Toula?"

Toula's hands fluttered. "Of course, Lady. I do apologize. It will never—"

"Come now, Cosima," Straton interrupted, his voice weary. "Evadne will be with us for five years. There is no need to be afraid of her."

Cosima set her eyes on her husband, defiant. "Is that what you thought of her sister, too, Straton? Before you chose her for our son? Before she slayed him?"

Evadne rose, eased away from their circle. Her ankle popped, but she somehow managed to walk smoothly to Toula, setting the wine jar into her hands. Toula did not stop her from striding through the camp, beyond the circle of torches, into the darkness.

She walked until she was swallowed by the wind, until she could almost fool herself that she was near the grove and none of this had happened. Evadne sat in the grass, closing her eyes. Her temples throbbed with anger, and she struggled to find her breath, to anchor her mind.

The moon had risen by the time she had steadied her emotions. She opened her eyes to see the stars were scattered across the night sky. And in the distance was Mount Euthymius, incandescent with celestial light.

Evadne was too tired to be afraid of its watchful presence. She had scarcely slept the night before, and she lay down, thinking she would rest only for a moment.

She jolted awake hours later.

Her right shoulder and hip were pressed into the earth, wild-flowers wilting over her like a blanket. And in the ground, she felt a tremble. The pound of something approaching.

Evadne sat forward, dazed. At first, she did not know where she was. The moon had set, and the stars were muted, veiled behind clouds. But then she saw the commander's camp in the distance, the torches struggling to remain alight as the wind blew, cold and ruthless, from the mountains. There was a song within the wind, a woman's voice, chanting.

Ivina.

The guardian of the mountain had taken note of them, sleeping in Euthymius's shadow. And she was about to send down an enchantment to confront them.

Evadne scrambled upward, fear making her limbs melt. She froze on her hands and knees when she heard the first howl. Something was approaching Straton's camp; the light gleamed upon its fur. And it was not just one, but many. Evadne counted six wolves, prowling closer and closer, waiting for the torches to extinguish.

No, she thought, straining her eyes in the darkness. They were not wolves. They were the same beast, multiplied. A dog she recognized.

Her blood went cold. It was the shepherd's dog from years ago, the one that had almost mauled her, that had left scars and pain in her ankle.

Halcyon had once come between them, had killed that dog to save her life.

This cannot be real. Evadne panted, fingers curling into the loam. But it was real. The dog had been resurrected by Ivina, over and over, according to Evadne's greatest fear. She told herself they were only apparitions; they could not bite. But then a torch went dark, and one of the dogs snarled, leaping into the camp through the river of shadows.

A scream pierced the wind.

Evadne flinched. She watched the servants rush with lit torches, frantically shouting as they beat the phantom dog back with fire. Toula dashed for the darkened torch, lighting it just before another phantom could slip into the camp. And then there was Straton, moving through the tents and wagons with calm precision, a spear in his hand.

He lit it on fire and hurled the weapon across the night. The spear caught one of the phantoms in its side. The dog howled and jerked before it evanesced into a swarm of sparks and smoke. The commander did it again, again, as effortless as breathing, and Evadne's fear eased.

The phantom dogs were splintering, dissipating, unable to withstand the fire.

Evadne pushed herself to her feet, shaky. She took a step forward but stopped when the nape of her neck prickled.

Slowly, she turned.

One more phantom dog stalked in the darkness, its luminous eyes fixated on her.

"Evadne!" Straton's voice cracked her indecision. It was a command to run—to run to him—and Evadne sprinted to the camp in her uneven gait.

The phantom dog gave chase. She could hear it snarl, snap its teeth in her wake. But she saw the commander striding to her, a fiery spear in his hand. She kept her eyes on him, even when she felt a tug on her chiton, when she heard the linen shred.

For one heady moment, Evadne thought about taking flight. She was one breath from it, but her heart was frantic. She could scarcely think, let alone command the wind to uplift her.

"Down, Evadne!" Straton ordered as he hurled the spear, and Evadne only had a ragged breath to decide if she wanted to heed him.

She hit the ground, and the fiery lance sank into the phantom directly above her. Smoke rose and sparks rained down on her arms, her tangled hair. She listened to them hiss in the wind, her face pressed into the earth. And then it went quiet, and Evadne found she was trembling so violently she could not make herself move.

"Can you stand?"

Gradually, she lifted her chin to see Straton standing at her side.

Evadne pushed herself up, wavering. The commander made no action to assist her, but he followed her as she limped back into camp. A few of the servants watched; they said nothing and offered nothing as Evadne leaned against one of the wagons, laboring for breath.

Damon appeared, as if he had risen from a shadow. His dark hair was tousled, his chiton smeared with ash as he approached her.

His gaze shifted to her legs, where the wind played with her torn garments. "Are you hurt?"

"No," Evadne said. She was trembling, and she could not quell it, no matter how much she tried. Nor could she resist the draw of Damon's eyes. Their gazes locked, reluctant yet hungry, and Evadne did not know what he saw in her. Longing, terror, pain. Resentment. She felt a hundred things, and then nothing at all. He was suddenly reaching for her arm, but the commander's voice stopped him from touching her.

"Toula? Bring Evadne something to drink, please. As well as some fresh clothes."

The servants drifted away, but the commander and his son remained with Evadne. No one spoke for a moment, and then Damon's sister called for his aid, and he departed, hurrying to one of the tents.

Evadne kept her mouth shut, waiting for the commander to break the quiet.

"Why did you stray from the camp?" Straton finally asked, his words clipped with anger.

She felt reckless, and almost laughed. *Why?* Because of his wife, with her fury and her sharpness. Because of the servants, who openly reviled her. Because Evadne had been so angry, she had craved to burn the entire camp to the ground.

"Were you attempting to run away, Evadne?"

"No, Lord. I felt like it was best for me to give your family . . . distance," she replied carefully. "I still do not know where my place is among your people, Commander."

He drew his hand over his face. His eyes were bloodshot when he looked at Evadne once more, and she remembered he had not slept the night before, either.

"I apologize for my wife," he said. "I hope you will understand and give us time."

She nodded, but her brow wrinkled, betraying her wariness. Why was he being so kind to her? *Do not trust him*, she told herself.

"Now, then. I would like for you to remain in the camp at night, where it is safe," the commander said. "You have a place among us, in the tents. Toula will show you."

Toula had just returned with a cup of wine and a tunic draped over her arm. She stopped short, hearing the commander's pointed words. The older woman almost appeared repentant when she saw how disheveled Evadne was. But that flicker of compassion was gone as soon as Straton stepped away.

"You fool of a girl!" she chided. "Straying from camp in the shadow of Mount Euthymius! What were you thinking?"

Evadne was silent, accepting the reprimand and wine Toula

handed to her. She took a fortifying sip and followed the older woman into one of the servants' tents. It was empty; everyone was still shaken by the phantoms, remaining on guard close to the fire.

Evadne stripped from her ruined clothes, keeping her back angled to Toula to conceal her relic. She donned the new tunic, spread the wrinkles from the linen. It was too large for her, swallowing her curves. She struggled to knot her belt, a tremor still racking her hands. Toula acted as if she did not notice, pointing to a bedroll in the corner that Evadne could claim.

"Was someone wounded?" Evadne asked, remembering how she had heard a scream.

"Yes. Amara."

Evadne felt ill, imagining it. "Where did the dog hurt her?"

"Dog?" Toula echoed. "Oh, you do not know. I suppose this is your first time passing Euthymius?" She beckoned for Evadne to keep drinking the wine. Evadne did, feeling the color return to her face. "If Ivina chooses to wreak havoc, which is common but not every time we pass the mountain, we each see something different. Our phantoms are shaped according to our fears."

Of course. Evadne had known that. But in the fray, she had assumed the rest of the camp had also seen the bane of her childhood.

"What did you see?" she dared to ask Toula.

The old woman snorted. "Now, *that* I would not even tell my closest friend, let alone you." And she must have realized how cruel she sounded, because she softened her tone. "Fears are intimate. Most of us never divulge what haunts us when we pass Euthymius."

"I understand."

Toula was quiet, but she stared long and hard at Evadne. Evadne did not know where to look and finished the wine before she crawled into her bedroll.

"You are very fortunate, Girl," Toula said, just before she slipped from the tent. "You are fortunate Lord Damon realized you were missing from the camp."

Lord Damon, indeed.

That thought kept Evadne awake, late into the night.

Travel was slow the following day. Amara's arm had been wounded, and she languished in one of the wagon beds, her face pinching in pain every time a rut jostled her. The commander's daughter, Lyra, chose to forgo her mare to sit beside Amara, keeping an eye on the girl's bandages and coaxing her to sip a pungent brew to keep fever at bay.

Evadne returned to being unseen, sitting in her designated uncomfortable spot, watching the land roll by as she worried about Halcyon. She did her best to particularly remain out of Cosima's sight, but it seemed the commander's wife was still rattled by the night attack, riding close to her husband at the front of the caravan.

When they made camp on the second night, Evadne had finally oriented herself with the chamber pots. Her initial task.

Straton had positioned them in a valley beside the River Zan, as far from the mountain's shadow as they could manage, and Evadne carried the brass pots to the bank. She was drawing water from the rapids, preparing to scrub the pots clean, when the commander startled her. She had not known that he had followed her to the river.

"Lord?"

"Put that down," he ordered.

Evadne stepped back onto the moss, lowering the water bucket. A note of dread reverberated through her as she waited for him to speak, wondering why he had sought her out. When he spoke at last, his words were a surprise, like a splinter catching in her palm.

"You are not to scrub the chamber pots, but to serve my family's wine."

She might have gaped at him. "But, Lord, I thought—"

"I know what you thought," he interjected with a sigh. "But I have spoken to my wife, and she has agreed that you will be the best replacement until Amara's arm has healed. Do you agree?"

Evadne swallowed her shock. "Yes, Lord. But . . ."

He arched his brow, waiting. "What is it, Evadne?"

"If I should die of poisoned wine . . . what becomes of my sister? Does she still have to settle the five years of servitude?"

"I am not going to let you die," he said, as if he truly were a god, holding the threads of life and death. "Now leave those pots for Toula and come prepare the wine." He turned and strode back to the camp.

Evadne hesitated for a breath before tracing his steps. She quickly braided the hair away from her eyes and brushed the wrinkles from her tunic, washed her hands with water and a drop of spikenard—fragrant oil harvested from a plant. She struggled to understand why the commander had made this arrangement for her as she arrived to taste the wine and tend to their cups.

Again, the family did not speak. They reclined on cushions of every color—indigo, saffron, olive, ochre. They rested beneath their hanging oil lamps, the firelight gilding the golden hues of their skin and their hair and their eyes. They gathered around a dinner they hardly touched, their hands holding empty cups, waiting for Evadne to fill.

It was only when Evadne poured Cosima's wine, when she felt her hard gaze, that Evadne finally understood. This had not been a test of wills, a spar between a husband and a wife to see who would prevail over the assignment of the new servant girl's task.

This was a tactic.

Because, Evadne was beginning to learn, when you had an enemy in your house, you did not make them scrub the excrement from your chamber pots.

You gave them a position of honor, of trust.

You kept them close.

You kept them just within your reach.

Evadne

Mithra exceeded Evadne's expectations, and her breath caught at the sight of the city's magnificent sprawl across the land.

The royal city was built around a small summit, where the queen's palace sat on the mountaintop. One main road led to the palace, branching into streets that flowed east to west and north to south, pooling about markets and temples, stretching as far as the eye could see. From a distance, Mithra gleamed like tarnished silver, trees and greenery blooming from private gardens. Divine pennants waved in the breeze with lazy flashes of color. The great River Zan cut through the eastern quadrant of the city like a blade, and on her wide banks rested docked vessels and barges. It smelled of smoke and moss and fish and incense.

Mount Euthymius was now out of sight, nothing more than a hazy nightmare to the south. But the common quarry, Evadne noticed, was visible; it lay to the west of Mithra, a wound in the Dacian foothills. There was a road winding from the western gate of the city, through fields of barley, all the way to the quarry out-post, a tall narrow building surrounded by an impenetrable wall.

Only a matter of miles would lie between her and her sister, Evadne thought, studying the place where Halcyon would soon arrive. It was as comforting as it was disheartening.

They entered the eastern gate of the city through the clamor-ous fish market, steadily wending their way on wide streets. But the noise and bustle became reverent and quiet as the people took note of the commander and his family, and the wagon that car-ried a coffin. The somber silence followed them all the way to the shadow of the summit, where Straton's villa sat like a sentry overlooking the eastern quadrant of the city.

Evadne's first impression of the commander's house was that it was grand, a smaller replica of the queen's palace. The villa was fashioned from white marble, its bronze roof upheld by a grand colonnade. A wall encircled the verdant grounds of the property, and within its embrace were trees and flowering shrubs and two small shrines to the goddesses Magda and Ari. There was a spar-ring circle and an armory and forge, and even a stable and pasture for the horses to graze beside a small pond. The entire villa boasted a striking view of the river.

And it was to be Evadne's home for the next five years.

She hardly had time to soak in the grandeur before Toula approached her with a scowl.

"You'll bunk on the lower floor, with Amara," she said, glancing at the injured servant girl, who was too preoccupied with pain to protest the arrangement. "You can draw water from the servants' well and find a bowl and the essence of spikenard in the cupboard, to wash with. A fresh tunic and sandals will also be there. The family is burying Xander at sundown, but they will return here for dinner, and you must be ready to serve the wine. Amara, show her the way."

Evadne's mind was spinning, and she felt like crawling into a hole to hide. But Amara walked into the villa, and Evadne had no choice but to follow her. The front doors were made of hammered bronze, so tall a giant could walk with ease through the passage. They ushered the girls into a receiving chamber; it was roofless, an open courtyard that welcomed a glimpse of the sky. The floors were set with hexagonal-cut jade and carnelian, and in the center of the courtyard was a reflection pool.

Evadne lingered as she walked by the pool, to gaze within it. A Pegasus mosaic gleamed just beneath the shallow waters, her wings outstretched, her body highlighted in gold.

"At night during the summer, the constellation Zephyra shines on the water, just between the Pegasus's wings," Amara said, surprising Evadne. Her arm was bandaged, and her movements were stilted, but a rosy hue had returned to her face. "It is my favorite thing about the villa."

"It is beautiful," Evadne confessed. She was quiet the remainder of the way to their chamber. She worked to memorize the corridors they took, and at last they arrived at a small room with two beds and a window, which was open to let fresh air flow.

"You have a few hours before night falls," Amara said, easing herself onto her bed. "I would rest, if I were you. Sometimes the family remains up late, and they expect you to be attentive at all times. Especially when Lady Selene is here."

"Who is Lady Selene?" Evadne asked, slowly sitting on the other bed.

"Lord Straton's sister. Do not let her cup go dry." And that was all she would say. Amara angled her face away from Evadne and soon fell asleep.

Evadne rested, as Amara advised, but she was too anxious to sleep, worried she would be late for dinner. When she rose, she did as Toula instructed, washing with water and a drop of spikenard. It smelled of sweet earth and musk, stirring Evadne's emotions. She longed for home.

She braided her hair, found a tunic that was better tailored to her body—high-necked, to conceal all traces of Kirkos's Winged Necklace—and followed the aromas of dinner up to the main floor. She located the kitchen, where servants were preparing the meal, and then farther along the corridor, Evadne found the dining room.

Small iron braziers provided light and warmth as the night crept closer, and long, transparent linens hung between columns, stirring with the slight breeze. A low-slung table made of polished oak anchored the center of the room. Silver plates and goblets were set, and a stream of flowers flowed down the spine of the table— knots of lilies and anemones and hyacinths and myrtle leaves.

A wine station sat between two of the pillars. Jars had already been brought up from the cellar, still cool from storage, their seals unbroken.

Night soon fell, and servants began to carry in platters of food, arranging them along the table.

The family arrived quietly. Evadne stood between the columns, listening to their footsteps on the marble, the whisper of their clothes as they entered the dining room. Straton and Cosima. Damon and Lyra, and then another woman Evadne assumed was Selene, the commander's sister. They gathered around the table, sitting on cushions, and Evadne took up her wine jar.

She approached Straton first. He watched as Evadne took the first sip of wine, and she waited to feel the heat of poison seep through her, counting her frantic heartbeats between breaths. But the wine was clean. Straton motioned for her to begin pouring.

Cosima was withdrawn and pale. She only put a few morsels of food on her plate, and she did not take note of Evadne's motions. No one did. Not Damon with his guarded face, or Lyra with her red-rimmed eyes. Evadne realized that the family would not notice her movements as long as she was quiet and did her task.

Not even Selene. She shared the commander's height and startling blue eyes, but that was where their similarities ended. Upon first glance, Evadne would never have surmised they were siblings. Selene was a contrast to him; her skin was pale and flawless, her face round and pleasing, her hair a light shade of brown, curly with threads of copper and gray within it. She was dressed in white, her chiton trimmed in purple. And as she reached for her cup, Evadne saw the flash of silver. A ring on the thumb of her right hand.

So, then. Selene was a mage. One with the deepest well of magic.

Evadne resumed her post at the wine station, the night breeze playing with her hair. She watched and listened as the family began to converse.

"I am concerned for you, Damon," Selene said. It sounded like she was resuming a previous conversation that had been abruptly ended.

"There is no need for it, Aunt. I will manage." Damon granted her a small smile, but he sounded exhausted. The gravel in his voice had roughened to a burr. He did not eat, even though food sat on his plate.

"Scribes are tricky," his aunt continued, swirling the wine in her cup. "Did you hear what happened to Orrin a few weeks ago? His scribe stole his enchantments and sold them to his rival. He is still recovering, but his reputation is ruined."

"As I heard," Damon said. He glanced to his father, but Straton was still detached. "I am sure Orrin will recover soon."

"Why do you even need a scribe?" Lyra asked, her voice wavering. "You have not needed one so far, Damon. It feels too risky, for you to trust someone else."

"Most mages hire scribes, Lyra," Damon explained. "It is to our benefit, even with the risk of betrayal."

"Is it because of your handwriting? Because it won't remain on papyrus? I could scribe for you, Damon," Lyra said. "If it is enchantments you need recorded, I could do it. I know I could."

"No, Lyra." The commander finally spoke, his eyes sharpening as he looked at his daughter.

Lyra appeared crestfallen by her father's curt tone. Cosima reached out to weave her fingers with her daughter's, trying to smile at her. It emerged more as a grimace on the lady's face.

"You know that I need you at the infirmary, my love. There is still so much illness in the northern quadrant."

Lyra nodded, but she refused to let the topic die. "But how can you trust them?" She looked at Damon again. Her voice dropped to a tremulous whisper. "I do not want anything to happen to you."

"Nothing is going to happen to your brother, Lyra," Selene said. "I am going to help him find the perfect scribe."

Damon cleared his throat, tracing the rim of his goblet. "I appreciate that, Aunt. But I am in no hurry."

"And why should you be? You only graduated from the Destry this past spring."

"Yes," Damon said. "It can wait."

Evadne was entranced by their conversation. She did not realize that Selene's cup had gone dry, not until it was too late.

Selene held her chalice up, lifting her gaze to where Evadne fumbled for the jar. And just like that, Evadne's aloofness vanished.

"Is this her?" Selene asked, staring at Evadne as she filled her cup.

For a moment, Evadne thought no one would answer, and she could not move from her place beside Selene. But finally, the commander's voice broke the stilted air.

"No. Her sister."

Selene continued to study Evadne, saying, "I thought I smelled the blood of Isaura. The unmistakable smell of spoiled ichor, the reek of a disgraced god."

Her words stung. Evadne felt her face warm, her hands quiver. She did not meet the mage's eyes, but oh, how she wanted to return Selene's cold stare, to reveal there was nothing less about her for descending from a broken god. Indeed, it only made Evadne all the more dangerous, for she had come from the one divine who was not afraid to break.

She wanted to give Selene a knowing smile, to touch the relic hiding beneath her clothes. To rise up on sightless wings and kick every single one of their chalices over, until the wine sprayed over their perfect clothes and ran like blood along their perfect floor.

But Evadne would have to be wise, as Halcyon had begged. She would have to be careful, as her parents admonished. She could not let these high-ranked people anger her. She must earn their trust. So she held her position and breathed, waiting with a placid expression.

"You must love your sister very much to take her place here," Selene stated.

"Yes, Lady."

At last, Selene looked away, and Evadne was released. She quietly stepped back to make her rounds to the other chalices, refilling them. Cosima began to speak of the illness she was treating in the infirmary, mentioning how wonderful it would be to possess Magda's Sunstone Ring of Healing at a time like this, and

Evadne felt the tension ease, the attention drifting away from her. Until she came to Damon's side. He stopped her without a word, laying his hand over the mouth of his cup, the silver on his finger glittering like a warning.

Evadne returned to the embrace of pillar shadows.

This time, she did not let herself become distracted by the family's conversations. She kept her gaze on them, watching their chalices. They soon forgot about her again, a girl in the shadows.

Save for one.

Damon did not eat; he did not drink. He hardly spoke again. But he looked at Evadne, meeting her gaze from across the room, and there his eyes remained. Directly on hers.

She looked away first, unable to hold that uncanny stare of his, brown and blue, like sky meeting earth.

And she knew that he had been aware of her the entire night, no matter what she had previously believed. He had kept track of her, as one does the height of wine in a chalice.

Or as one does a viper.

⟶ XIII ⟵

Halcyon

Miles from Straton's villa, down the winding streets of Mithra and beyond the western gates, through the moonlit barley fields, Halcyon finally arrived at the quarry outpost. She was chained in the back of an iron caged wagon, and she was alone, the only prisoner to be brought to the quarry that night. She could hear the howl of the wind in the foothills, and she stared at the distant fires of Mithra, a city that never slept. The queen's palace blazed on the summit, and Halcyon could hardly stand to look at it, to be reminded of how she had failed.

Evadne.

She breathed her sister's name, hoping the wind would carry it east, to where Evadne now dwelled in the commander's villa.

The guards unlocked Halcyon from the wagon and escorted her into the outpost. Torches were pegged along the walls, casting uneven light on the rough-hewn walls, and Halcyon walked mindfully, her back still tender. She was brought into a chamber. It looked to be some sort of workroom; there was a desk lit by a lamp, and a lonely chair positioned in the center of the floor. Shelves lined one of the walls, laden with scrolls and stacks of papyrus.

She was instructed to sit in the lonely chair. Halcyon obeyed, and the guards chained her to iron rings in the floor. As if she could run anywhere.

They left her in the workroom, and she sat in the quiet, listening. She must have sat there for hours, whoever she was to meet purposefully delaying to make her feel forgotten and inconsequential. She watched the moonlight drift across the floor at her feet; she watched the oil lamp almost extinguish. She counted the number of scrolls on the shelves. And then, at last, just when she was about to doze in the chair, the door opened.

She expected the quarry lord, imagining him to be a burly, weathered individual who would be overseeing her the next five years.

But a slender young man greeted her, dressed impeccably in the garments of a mage. A silver ring gleamed on his forefinger, his eyes probing as he stared at her. His hair was long, sleek and fair as corn silk.

He did not belong here any more than Halcyon did.

Mages were forbidden from overseeing or even visiting common prisons and convict quarries. For the mages who committed crimes . . . there was a special prison for them, on the eastern coast of Corisande.

But this mage was not a prisoner. And as he walked across the floor to settle behind the desk, dread pooled in Halcyon's stomach.

"Halcyon of Isaura," he greeted with an unsettling smile. "I must say, I never expected to meet you here." He unrolled a scroll with a flick of his fingers, dark words resting on the papyrus. It was a record of her trial, freshly inked. "You are convicted of accidentally slaying your lover and shield mate, and have been sentenced to only five years of work here, with five years of imprisonment to follow and . . . what is this? Your little sister took a portion of your punishment. Evadne of Isaura, correct?"

She hated the way he spoke Evadne's name, how it drawled in his voice. As if he had tasted it before.

"Come to think of it, I do believe I have met your sister," he continued. "On the road here. I shared a fire with her and your parents. She is a little shorter than you, but curvier. Long brown hair in dire need of a combing, big doe eyes, a dusting of freckles on her face. She might have been pretty, had she been raised in the upper class."

"You are fortunate I am chained," Halcyon said. Her voice was calm, but her blood was pounding. "Or else I would kill you."

The mage laughed. "You could try, Halcyon. In fact, I would welcome it. I am not at all intimidated by you, even though you were once considered Lord Straton's *most favored* of warriors. There was a rumor, even, that he was about to promote you to the rank of captain in his legion. Of course, this was *before* you killed his son."

Halcyon struggled to control her fury. But she could not stop imagining it: Evadne and her parents traveling to Abacus and coming across this mage, who oozed of deceit and wickedness. Had he harmed them? Had he said or done anything to Evadne?

"Do not worry, Halcyon. I would never dream of hurting your sister, or your rustic parents, for that matter. They might have been hungry and thirsty, but trials like that build character. As you should know."

"What are you doing here, mage?" she countered, to halt his words of her family before she lost her composure. "It is forbidden for your ilk to be here."

"You will address me as *lord*, for that is what I am to you. Do you understand, Convict 8651?"

Convict 8651. Halcyon was now the one to laugh. She laughed until she knew she had irritated him, until he pounded his fist on the table.

"Do you understand, 8651?"

She quieted. But she did not speak her agreement and was not planning to until she heard him utter a charm and she felt his magic gathering in the room. The flame from the oil lamp grew into a creature made of heat and rancor. It began to shift toward her, its fiery maw open and hungry, and she could feel the blistering temperature of it. The chimera was one moment from taking hold of her ankle, melting her skin in its white light, when she spoke, "Yes, I understand, Lord."

The mage relaxed. His fiery chimera faded, flickering back to the lamp wick, returning to a solitary flame.

Halcyon also appeared relaxed, but her panic was thrumming,

just beneath her skin. A mage had somehow wormed his way into this common quarry as lord. He was powerful and seemed to have no qualms with using his charms for violence.

This was going to bode very badly for her.

For the first time since her sentence had been announced, Halcyon realized she might not survive the quarry.

"What is it you want from me?" she whispered.

He tapped his fingers on the table. The guards returned to unchain her from the floor.

But the mage delayed in answering, waited until she was on the threshold, about to be dragged to her holding cell.

"I suppose we will soon find out, won't we, 8651?"

⇢XIV⇠

Evadne

"Here. You are scrubbing the floors today. And I do not want to see a smudge of dirt on them," Toula said, handing a bucket, lye, and bristle brush to Evadne the next morning.

Evadne accepted the task without a word, drawing water from the servants' well. She began on the southern side of the villa, slowly inching her way across the marble floor, one stroke at a time. She was not intimidated by this sort of work, as Toula no doubt had hoped. It gave her time to think of what she had overheard the night before, of Damon's need for a scribe. She also learned the layout of the villa, particularly where Straton's office was located, behind locked doors.

But soon the lye had turned her hands red, her skin itching and burning, and Evadne stopped to rest, sprawled in the center of the empty dining room. She groaned, drawing her right ankle closer to rub the stiffness away. That was when she noticed the dog, lying a few paces away in a patch of sunlight, watching her.

Evadne froze.

The dog blinked, raised his head as if he smelled her fear. His fur was long and copper brown, a few patches of white on his chest and paws. He did not have a malicious gleam in his eyes as the shepherd's dog had, but all the same, Evadne was terrified.

She crawled away backward, keeping her eyes on the dog, dragging her bucket with her.

"By the gods, girl, *what* are you doing?"

Evadne whirled to see Toula standing in the dining room, bearing a tray of silver plates.

"Th-there's a dog."

Toula frowned, glancing to where the dog still rested in the sun. "Arcalos is old and gentle. No need to be afraid of him."

Evadne still hesitated, and Toula hefted a sigh. "Go on, girl. Finish the floor."

Toula departed, and Evadne worked and silently cried, washing the floor with her tears. Arcalos did not move, but he reached his head out as if to nuzzle her.

She looked at the dog and saw nothing but gentleness in his eyes, his muzzle gray with age.

"You do not understand," she whispered to him.

Arcalos only blinked, drowsy from the sun.

Evadne finished the floor in the dining room and moved down the corridor. She heard the clicking of nails and turned to see, in horror, Arcalos was following her, leaving a trail of paw prints on her drying floor.

"No, stop," she pleaded.

Arcalos paused, smile-panting at her.

She would have to rescrub the floor again, to wash away his prints, and her back was aching and her skin felt like it would crack and peel away, and she knew she was one breath from sobbing. Evadne leaned against the wall. Arcalos approached her and lay down at her side, his fur warm against her legs. She had nowhere to go and was too exhausted to flee from him, and so she remained there in the shadows of the corridor, weeping quietly, with her worst nightmare curled up against her.

A whistle sounded down the hallway.

Arcalos's ears perked, but he remained next to Evadne. Evadne did not move, did not breathe, praying that whoever it was did not stray down the corridor to find her so unraveled.

"Arcalos? Arcalos, come," Damon called, and the dog instantly obeyed, struggling to rise as if he was just as stiff as Evadne.

Of course you would be Damon's dog! Evadne thought, hurrying to her knees. She plunged her brush into the bucket and began to clean the paw prints.

"Is he bothering you, Evadne?"

For the second time that day, she startled. She had not heard Damon approach, but now that she knew he stood behind her, she sensed his presence.

"No," she said, continuing to scrub. She kept her face angled away, her braid falling over her shoulder, to hide her tears.

He stood there a moment longer, watching her. And then he was gone, taking the old dog with him.

She worked until sundown, when it was time for her to serve the wine. And Evadne had discovered that every time she lifted the wine to her lips to taste it for poison, her desires sharpened. She felt cut by her own longings for life, for escape. To return home with Halcyon. Her desires bled as she waited to see if she would die for a man like Straton. But the wine was clean that night, as it had been all the nights before.

Evadne moved to Straton's side, doing her best to conceal her limp, which had flared with all the crawling and crouching she had done.

His chalice was half-full when he noticed it. "What has happened to your hands, Evadne?"

She paused, feeling Cosima, Lyra, and Damon look at her raw fingers.

"It is from the lye I cleaned with today, Lord," she replied, moving to the lady's cup.

"You need to wear gloves, then. Toula should be able to provide a pair for you," the commander said, and Evadne nodded, knowing she did not have the courage to ask Toula.

She arrived at Damon's side, but he covered his chalice, and she did not know if it was because he was abstaining from wine or he mistrusted her. But what did she care? That was one less cup for her to watch.

When Evadne returned to her chamber that night, she found Amara folding tunics one-handed on her bed, her wounded arm held steady by a sling.

"Toula delivered that for you," Amara said, indicating a small jar on Evadne's shelf.

Evadne opened its lid and found a fragrant healing salve inside.

She was stunned at first, wondering who had made it for her.

"You should also wear these on your hands," Amara said, tossing leather mitts onto Evadne's bed. "When I first began my time here, I had to scrub the floors, too. You will eventually progress to other tasks."

Evadne sat on the edge of her mattress, dipping her fingers into the salve. It burned at first, but then her skin went cold and numb, and she groaned as she spread it over her hands. She watched Amara fold by firelight for a moment, gradually building the courage to ask, "How long have you been here?"

"Since I was eight. My mother brought me to the healer's infirmary, to Lady Cosima, and begged her to take me on as one of their servants." Amara's voice held no emotion as she folded perfect thirds, smoothing wrinkles from servant tunics. "My father abandoned us when I was born, to hunt relics. I have not heard of him since. My mother worked the barley fields on the edge of Mithra. One year, the blight was so terrible we lost nearly everything. Every night when I lay down in my bed, I thought I would die of hunger in my sleep. But then one day, Queen Nerine came to our house and brought us two sacks of grain, jars of oil and wine, a pot of honey. She had heard about the blight and opened the royal storerooms, and she fed us when we had nothing. She saved us. I remember how warm and lovely she was, and she held me on her lap and told my mother and me that if we were ever hungry or needed aid that we should come to her at once. But the next year the blight was just as devastating, and when my mother went to the royal palace, to ask the queen for aid again . . . she was turned away by one of the court mages. That was the year my mother finally became too sick to work, to care for me. The year when I felt as if the Magical Court wanted to keep us common folk down and out of sight from our own queen. Since then, I have come to hate the mages, save for Damon."

Evadne was silent, aching as she listened.

"Lady Cosima tried to heal my mother, but she was too ill. She died, and Lady Cosima kept me on as a servant. When I come of age next year, my term will be over, and I will have the choice of whether to stay or to leave." Amara finished her folding. She stood and carried the laundry to the chest at the foot of her bed.

"Will you remain here?" Evadne asked, slipping off her sandals to crawl beneath her blankets.

Amara climbed into bed, careful of her arm. "Yes. What else is there for me? A barley field? Relic hunting? Hunger? I have no other family. Toula and the other servants are my family now. And here, as a servant, I am paid for my work and I never go hungry. Lady Cosima and Lord Straton are good to me. I am higher off than I was before."

She blew out the oil lamp; the darkness rushed in.

"Amara?"

"What?"

Evadne hesitated. "Has the wine ever been poisoned?"

"Yes. Once, years ago. I was still a girl scrubbing floors when it happened. Lord Straton discovered one of his former hoplites had poisoned his wine, in revenge for being dismissed from the legion." Amara fell quiet. When she spoke again, her voice had softened. "Are you afraid, Evadne?"

Evadne was tempted to lie. But the truth slipped out in a whisper. "Yes."

Amara shifted in her bed. Evadne could almost feel the girl's gaze on her, even in the pitch darkness. "Lady Cosima has antidotes if you were poisoned."

"You truly believe she would try to save me with an antidote?"

"To let you die would be foolish."

Soon, Amara's snores filled the chamber. But all Evadne could hear was Halcyon's voice, echoing in the deepest cracks of her soul.

Do not be afraid, Little Sister.

The days began to pass, one sunset bleeding into the next, Evadne repeating the cycle of her drudgery over and over. She scrubbed the floors, she tasted and poured the family's wine, and she thought about Halcyon until it was hard to breathe. But Evadne counted the sunrises, scratching a tiny mark for each one into the stone floor with Halcyon's kopis, just out of sight beneath her bed.

The twelfth day of her service began as all the others. The villa was quiet; Cosima and Lyra were at the infirmary, and Straton had gone to the palace to meet with the queen's advisors. Damon was the only family member to remain home, closed away in his chambers. The servants continued with their tasks: Toula washing and polishing silver, Amara folding laundry, Evadne scrubbing the floors.

She was cleaning the courtyard beside the reflection pool when a guest arrived at the villa. A young man with the air of a scholar, tall and well-groomed, his clothes practical yet perfectly laundered. Evadne watched as Toula greeted him.

"I have an appointment with Lord Damon," the visitor said, glancing around at the glamour of the commander's villa.

"Follow me," Toula instructed, leading him to the marble staircase.

Evadne slowed her scrubbing, keeping track of the time by the slant of sunlight on the floor. The scholar's appointment lasted only half an hour. Damon escorted him to the front doors and thanked the scholar for coming. It did not sound promising, and Damon returned to his chambers.

Evadne did not think much of it until another visitor arrived. A girl with hair the color of fire, her garments luxuriously tailored, her voice like that of a songbird.

"I am here to see Lord Damon," she said to Toula.

Toula guided the girl up to Damon's rooms, and Evadne slowed her scrubbing yet again, timing the appointment. Another half hour, and the girl was walked to the door with a gratitude for her time.

A third visitor soon rang the villa's bell. Toula muttered to herself as she hurried to answer it. A young man, broad and strongly built. An athlete, Evadne thought, watching him disappear up the stairs to meet with Damon.

He only lasted a quarter of an hour before Damon walked him to the door, the same *thank you* sounding on the mage's lips.

The doors closed behind the athlete. This time, Damon did not stride back to his chambers. He stood in the courtyard and looked at Evadne.

"That section of floor must be overwhelmingly filthy, Evadne."

She quickened her scrubbing, keeping her gaze on the tiles. "What makes you say such, Lord Damon?"

"You have not moved in over an hour."

"I might have found vast amusement in your appointments."

"Oh? How so?"

Evadne ceased her work, daring to lift her eyes to his. "All of them must lack something you seek. It is not brains, or you would have chosen the scholar. And it is not beauty, or you would have chosen the singer. And it is not strength, or you would have selected the athlete."

He looked amused. "Or perhaps I need a little bit of all three in one person."

"And good luck discovering such a person, Lord." She returned to her task, but her body was tense beneath Damon's steady gaze. "I fear you will only be able to find them in a myth."

"Then I am doomed. For what myth still lives and breathes?" He fell quiet, waiting for her to counter him. When she ignored him, he began to walk away, but he made it to the edge of the reflection pool before he returned to her. "Perhaps you would like to be interviewed, Evadne?"

His words sent a shock through her. She dropped her brush and gaped at him.

"Interviewed? For what?"

"I am looking for a scribe. You are right-handed. Perhaps you are the myth I seek."

Her eyes narrowed. Flattery. That was all he was doing. To soften her dislike for his family, for this place. To earn her trust.

All the same, she sat back on her heels, her ankle smarting with pain. She had no idea why it mattered which hand she favored. Confused, she said, "How do you know I am right-handed?"

"You pour with that hand."

"Are you watching me because you do not trust me?"

"No. I promised your sister I would look after you." He strode away, his answer astounding her.

Not once had Evadne imagined Halcyon asking it of Damon. But had he not visited Halcyon in her cell in the agora? *Why?* Evadne still wondered.

And here she was on bruised knees and burning hands, scrubbing floors when he had just offered her a chance to rise and come into his knowledge.

She stood and gathered her bucket, her brush. She was careful not to cross paths with Toula, rushing up the stairs, sloshing her lye and water all the way to Damon's door. It was cracked; a thread of sunlight escaped, flowing over her as she lifted her hand to knock. . . .

And she found she could not do it. Surely, he did not believe she could be his scribe. Evadne was backing away, her mitted hand still poised in the air, when the door unexpectedly swung open.

Damon, for once, seemed shocked to find her there. "Yes?"

"I came to scrub your floor," Evadne blurted, awkwardly

lowering her hand. "And then maybe, afterward, I could still have that interview. Although I understand if the offer has been revoked."

He was quiet. She thought he was about to deny her, and she continued to edge away, into the shadows.

"I do not need my floor scrubbed. Leave the bucket in the corridor and come inside."

Evadne set down her bucket, her brush. She struggled to pull off her leather mitts, but Damon waited patiently. She eased past him, stepping into his chambers for the first time.

"Forgive me. I reek of lye."

He snorted, shutting the door behind them. "I could think of many other worse things. Come, sit at the desk."

His receiving room was spacious. One wall was full of windows, welcoming rivers of sunlight. The other wall was built of shelves, each laden with scrolls, so many that Evadne's mind momentarily spun at the thought of all the stories that might be hiding within them. There was a desk with ivory legs, its oaken face covered by a stack of papyrus squares, a jar of quills, and several pots of ink.

She followed him across the floor and sat in the chair at his desk, her eyes continuing to flicker around the room, taking in the details. The lion-skin rug. The sword sheathed in one corner. The door in the far wall that must lead to his bedchamber. The fresco that spanned across the ceiling, begging to be admired. Arcalos sprawled in a patch of sunlight, tail wagging as he watched Evadne. She still felt a sliver of fear at the sight of the dog, but it was not as sharp as before, and she let out a breath, relaxing.

"Have you ever scribed before, Evadne?"

"No."

"I take it you are literate in Common Speech, but what of God Tongue?"

"Yes, I am fluent in both. I . . ." She stopped herself. She had almost told him of her hopes of becoming a mage, how she had tackled her literacy with fervency, believing any day her letters would magically slip off parchment. How fragile that memory was, and she swallowed the emotion it roused.

"Yes?" he prompted, waiting.

"Never mind, Lord."

"I am no lord to you, Evadne. I am simply Damon."

"Very well . . . Damon."

"Now, then. I am looking to hire a scribe, someone who can record my enchantments and even my daily correspondence. As you may know, I cannot write with my favored hand. The magic makes it impossible; my writing will not remain on papyrus. And as much as I would like to memorize all of my spells, some of them are long and complicated, and I would benefit from having them recorded. As such, my scribe will be privy to my secrets. I need someone I can trust, who I can rely on, who will not betray my spells to another mage who may want them." He paused, glancing down at the blank papyrus stacked on his desk. "If that is something you can agree to, Evadne, then I would like for you to take up a quill and write your favorite myth."

Evadne was perplexed, until she realized *this* was the interview. She thought for a moment before selecting a quill and opened a pot of ink, setting a square of papyrus before her.

She almost wrote the myth of Kirkos. How many times had she heard that legend, over and over, sitting on her father's knee?

But she did not want to draw attention to Kirkos, in case mysteries of his relic surfaced.

She traced through her collection of myths, and maybe it was because she was homesick, longing for the grove more than she thought possible, but she decided to write about the creation of Acantha's olive branch crown.

When she finished, Evadne set down her quill and walked the legend to Damon, going around the long way to avoid the proximity to slumbering Arcalos.

Damon's face was guarded at first, but then she noticed his brow grew heavy as he read her words. She couldn't explain why her heart began to beat fast and desperate. But it seemed that she had written the wrong thing, somehow, without even knowing it.

Damon lowered the papyrus and looked up at her. "Thank you, Evadne. You may go."

She should not be disappointed, or stunned, for that matter. For a wild moment, she had believed she could become his scribe, that he had not been flattering her for his cruel amusement. That he had not dangled hope before her only to snatch it away in spite.

Evadne left without a word. She found her bucket and brush just as she had left them and returned to the courtyard, an angry hitch in her step.

"Where have you been, Girl?" Toula caught her on the way down with a scowl.

"I was assisting Damon."

"*Lord* Damon," Toula corrected her. "And do not bother him again, do you hear? He is very busy."

Evadne did not respond. She returned to her scrubbing, letting the floor take the brunt of her ire, since she couldn't bestow it on Damon's face. But soon she grew tired, her frustration easing as her arms began to ache, and she leaned against one of the pillars, mortified.

Her interview had not been half an hour. Or even a quarter of one.

She had lasted all of ten minutes.

That night at dinner, Damon drank his wine.

It only fueled Evadne's annoyance with him, for now she had to watch his chalice, refilling it as needed. He did not speak of his appointments; it seemed that Straton and Cosima and Lyra had no idea Damon had been conducting interviews. The talk centered on taxes and illness and the legion, to which Straton would soon be returning.

When dinner was over, everyone left the table. Save for Damon. He remained, nursing his chalice of wine, reading a scroll he spread out before him by the light of the braziers. And Evadne could not leave, because his cup was still there, and he continued to sip it from time to time.

She leaned against one of the pillars, exhausted, watching

his chalice. A cool night breeze drifted into the room, stirring the white drapes. The villa was quiet, peaceful as a dreamscape; moonlight began to steal across the floor, and Evadne closed her eyes until Damon gently spoke her name.

"Evadne."

She straightened, reaching for the wine jug.

"Bring another cup to the table and join me," he invited.

She did as he beckoned, sitting on the cushion directly across the table from him. He took the jar and reached for the empty chalice, filling it with wine. And then he slid the cup over to her, and she could only blink at it, amazed he had served her.

"*This* is what you have kept me up late for, Lord Damon?" she drawled, letting her irritation ring. "So you could pour me a cup?"

"Yes and no. I wish to speak to you, alone."

"You spoke to me alone earlier."

He stared at her a moment. The blue flush in his left eye was bright, distracting. Evadne broke their gaze, looking down into her wine.

"Are you not going to drink, Evadne?"

"You hardly drink what I pour you, Lord Damon."

"It is Damon. Only Damon. And I drank it tonight."

"What do you want from me?" Evadne asked. She was so weary, so homesick that she lost her reservations.

"The myth you wrote today," he said, withdrawing a papyrus square from his scroll. Evadne recognized her script as Damon set the papyrus faceup on the table, between them. "Euthymius's creation of Acantha's All-Seeing Crown. Out of all the myths you could have chosen, why that one?"

Evadne rubbed her brow. "I do not know. It is just a myth, and I chose it on a whim."

He doubted her. His face was intense as he waited for her to explain.

"I know I displeased you today," she began, her anger rousing.

"You did not displease me."

"Although I hardly know why. Perhaps it was the slant of my handwriting—"

"No, your handwriting is more than fine."

"Or perhaps I did not write fast enough for you, or—"

"If I asked you to become my scribe, would you agree to it, Evadne?"

She froze. For a moment she could only breathe and stare at him, wondering if she had imagined his offer.

Damon continued to regard her, the firelight flickering across his face. "Before you give me your answer, I want you to know that it will be difficult. I need someone I can trust, yes, but I also need a partner who trusts *me*, who is not easily intimidated by challenges or opposition. Who would rise up to meet them alongside me."

Evadne did not think recording spells would be all that difficult, but she heard the earnestness in his voice. She could only wonder what these challenges could be.

"You teased me about the three appointments I met with today," he said when her silence continued to expand between them. "But I did not arrange for them. My aunt Selene did. She would like to keep me beneath her thumb. Any scribe selected by her would be a spy, reporting all my enchantments and movements to her." He paused, traced the rim of his chalice with his fingertip. "My aunt was one of my instructors at the Destry. She has been good to me, but she also expects me to follow her orders. She is powerful. And she will be very displeased that I have chosen you to scribe for me, because she has no hold on you."

Evadne was surprised he was revealing so much to her.

She drew in a deep breath. "All my life, I have wanted to be more than what I am. I wanted to be fast and strong, like my sister. I wanted magic, to have the ability to speak and sing charms to life. I wanted to be someone who made a mark on the world, even if it was a small one." She swallowed, hardly believing she had just said such things to him. But when she lifted her gaze to look at him, she saw Damon transfixed on her words, and a tentative current of friendship began to flow between them.

"You are making your mark, Evadne," he whispered.

And she thought about how he had broken laws for her and Halcyon, how he had cloaked her unseen and guided her into the agora's prison. How he had noticed she had been missing from camp and had told his father to look for her, to find her before the phantom dogs did. *Why?* she wondered.

"I do know God Tongue, but it has been a while since I used it," she said.

"I can refresh your memory."

"Lord Straton might not like this arrangement. I am supposed to be his cupbearer."

"He will have no trouble finding a new cupbearer."

"It does not bother you that my sister . . ." Evadne's words died. She could not even voice it, this pain that lived between her and Damon.

He was silent, encouraging her to finish her thought aloud.

"I imagine that when you look at me, you see Halcyon," she said. "That I am a constant reminder to you of what has happened."

"Is that what you feel when you look at me?" he countered. "Do you see my brother? What my father has done to your sister?"

Evadne held his stare, her pride too great to look away. She had to reckon with the truth: day by day, she saw Damon more for who he was, and him alone. "No. I see only a mage who irritates me from time to time."

He smiled, his eyes crinkling at the corners. "Good to know." But he would not say what he saw when he looked at her, and Evadne was too anxious to ask him.

She could not think of another excuse. She wanted to know the secrets of this family. Well, this was her chance. It would not come again, and Evadne wondered if the gods were blessing her, opening a door for her, just as her mother had believed they would.

"Yes," she said. "I will scribe for you."

"Thank you," he replied, and Evadne heard a warble of nervousness in his voice. Had he truly believed she would deny him?

He produced another sheet of papyrus and set it in front of Evadne, along with a quill and a pot of ink. She arched her brow, incredulous.

"You want to begin *now*?"

Damon looked like he might laugh. "No. But we need to draft a contract for our agreement. We must move quickly, before my aunt has a chance to interfere."

Evadne sighed but took up the quill. She dipped the nib into the ink and waited for Damon to tell her what to write.

He drummed his fingers against the table, lost in thought. She realized he was just as uncertain as her, remembering his conversation with Selene from a few nights ago. He had never had a scribe before.

"On this day," Damon began, "the fifth day of the Fire Moon, I hereby draw up a contract between Damon of Mithra, mage, and Evadne of Isaura, scribe . . ."

Evadne began to write, capturing his spoken words in ink.

"How long shall this contract's term last?" Damon interrupted himself to ask her.

She raised her eyes to meet his. "Five years."

He nodded and continued to dictate the contract. Everything sounded fine to Evadne until they reached the mind-sweeping clause:

Damon will have the power and authority to mind-sweep Evadne in only two cases: she chooses it or Damon has evidence that Evadne has betrayed him by sharing or selling his enchantments to another.

Evadne knew that all mages held the power to look into another's mind and memory, and because of such power, there were strict limitations to it. She had never had her mind swept, nor did she ever want to experience it.

She stopped writing in the middle of the phrase. Damon noticed.

"Is there a problem, Evadne?"

"The mind-sweeping . . . I do not like the thought of it."

"This is included in every contract between mages and scribes," Damon replied gently. "I will not do it, not unless you betray me."

Evadne was silent, staring at her writing. She would not sign her name to something like this.

She heard Damon slide another square of papyrus to her. "Let us begin anew, then."

Surprised, Evadne watched as he set the half-written contract in the brazier. As it burned, Damon spoke and Evadne began to scribe again, his words identical to what they had been before until he reached the mind-sweeping clause.

He omitted it, relinquishing his right to mind-sweep her.

When they reached the end, Evadne was ready to sign it. She inked her name at the footer before handing the quill and papyrus to Damon. He signed next with his right hand, the hand he could not cast magic with. His handwriting was weak and crooked, but his name remained on the paper beside hers, magicless.

"What happens now?" Evadne asked.

"We will go to the Destry to have the contract stamped and made public." Damon took the papyrus in his hand, the ink still glistening. "Meet me at daybreak in the courtyard. Good night, Evadne."

He departed the dining hall, and Evadne continued to sit at the table, staring at the flames burning on the brazier, overwhelmed by all that had just happened. And then she drank the wine in her cup and was just about to rise and drag herself to bed when a thought crossed her mind.

She stopped, reaching for the papyrus Damon had left on the table. The myth of Acantha's All-Seeing Crown. A missing relic.

Evadne sank back onto the cushion. She felt for Kirkos's Winged Necklace, traced the relic's hard shape beneath her tunic as she reread her myth.

Damon's demeanor had changed when he saw the myth she had chosen. He had grown suspicious of her, as if she knew something. Where to find the All-Seeing Crown, perhaps? But why would he think Evadne knew such a thing? Because the crown was made of woven olive branches and she hailed from a grove?

We all hold secrets like breath, Evadne thought, dwelling on her own, which hung around her neck, waiting for her to summon its magic into flight.

Halcyon was holding a secret. As was Straton.

What had they been protecting at the trial? What had Halcyon and Xander been doing, sparring privately all those times? Damon, Evadne was slowly coming to believe, knew the truth of it.

She thought of her Uncle Ozias, of Lysander, of Amara's father. All of them connected by the same desire—to find and claim a relic.

Evadne set her myth into the brazier fire and watched the

papyrus catch flame, curl, and turn into ash. As swift as breath. As irrevocable as stealing a life.

And she believed that she finally knew what her sister and Xander and Straton had been secretly trying to do.

❧ XV ❧

Halcyon

Work at the quarry began at dawn. Halcyon was the only woman among the convicts; most of them were relic hunters, and all of them were murderers. Her first day was just as terrible as her initial meeting with the mage. Her cell was small, and as soon as her iron door was unbolted at daybreak, three convicts meandered over to greet her. Their beards were long and knotted, their eyes hungry, their grins bent with suggestions that made Halcyon's heart beat cold.

"Welcome to the quarry," the biggest of them crooned at her. He was missing a front tooth, and his face was weathered from days squinting against the sun. "Although it is difficult to imagine you taking a life. Who did you kill, my sweet?"

Halcyon sat up from her cot slowly, her back still tender. She studied him, knowing he was strong. Most men who worked in the quarry were. Brute strength did not intimidate her; she had beaten plenty of men his size before. But she had also never felt such nagging pain in her body; everything felt arduous. Even something as simple as rising to her feet.

This was also her first time being approached by men such as him. In the hoplite camp, Straton had uprooted this festerous behavior in his legion. Rape and sexual misconduct were rare, because the commander considered them both intolerable, unforgiveable. His punishments for such crimes were harsh. Halcyon had always felt safe in the camp, among her fellow warriors.

"Did they cut out your tongue, then?" the missing-toothed man continued, taking a step into her cell.

Halcyon's fingers curled. Her fists were ready, her breaths lengthening. She was about to take out his other front tooth when there was a banging on her cell door.

"Out, all of you," a guard ordered. "To the mess hall."

The three convicts slunk away, their eyes still consumed with Halcyon. She waited until they were out of sight, the guard impatiently motioning for her to exit her cell.

"Move along," he said, prodding her back with his club.

She winced and followed the winding corridor. The cells were underground and hewn from stone. It was cold and dimly lit, the prison seeming to curl like a serpent. But the mess hall was up, toward the light, and Halcyon could smell the gruel and fresh air as she stepped into a wide chamber set with long tables and benches. There was a food line, and Halcyon hesitantly approached it. Every eye hooked to her; she felt crushed beneath the weight of those gazes.

Her hope of reuniting with Uncle Ozias vanished as she searched the faces around her. None of them she recognized. Although perhaps she might still cross paths with her uncle. There had to be hundreds of men here. She let that hope bloom; it kept her standing and moving and breathing.

The first three weeks, Halcyon told herself. *The first three weeks will be the hardest.*

And she was twelve years old again, standing in the camp of Abacus, shoulder to shoulder with other first-year trainees. The commander had paced before their perfect line and told them the first twenty-one days would be the hardest. They would be homesick; they would be exhausted; they would only be eating gruel and vegetables and water; they would vomit after training; their muscles would be relentlessly sore; they would want to quit; they would feel alone and bereft; they would hate him; they would respect him; they would wonder why they'd ever agreed to come in the first place; they could, likewise, leave at any time they felt like giving up.

But if they could make it to day twenty-two, he had said, then they would last in the Bronze Legion.

Day twenty-two, day twenty-two, she silently chanted, moving along the line.

A guard was doling out the gruel from a large iron pot. He paused to stare at Halcyon when it was her turn, his eyes raking down her body, and he purposefully gave her a smaller portion.

She accepted the gruel, but she was starting to realize how murder felt in one's pulse. The pounding chorus of it. Five men. Five men did she want to kill here, and it had only been a few hours since she had arrived.

"Let me help you with that," yet another man said as he suggestively bumped into her, snatching her bowl of gruel.

Six men, then. Halcyon stared at him, and he only smiled and laughed at her.

"That belongs to me," she said calmly. "Give it back."

"Oh, did you hear that, my friends?" he said, turning to glance across the room. "Mistress No-Hair is already giving orders, and she has not even proved her salt in the quarry yet." He chuckled and brought his face close to hers. Beneath the grime and dust and facial hair, he was not much older than her. But the hatred burned in him like a flame, and it stole her breath to see a stranger cast such enmity upon her.

"How about a trade?" he hissed. "I will give you your food, but you must give me something in return."

"Return her food, Cassian," a voice interrupted with a crackling depth. "Now."

Cassian straightened. But he spat in Halcyon's gruel before he returned it to her, sauntering away to a table where other young men were gathered, watching Halcyon with malicious interest.

Halcyon stood for a moment, staring down at Cassian's spit. She assumed the man who had spoken for her was one of the guards, but when she lifted her eyes, she was surprised to see he was a fellow convict, and while he was tall, he was not burly or seemingly strong. He was thin, his brow creased, his black hair shot through with silver, braided away from his eyes. He did not regard her with lust as the other men, but with a sadness that wrung out her homesickness.

He turned and walked back to his table, sitting on a bench to finish his gruel. Halcyon did not *want* to follow him, but she needed an ally, and this man was the only one who struck her as honorable.

She traced his steps, arriving at his side. "May I sit here?"

"Sit wherever you like."

She sank onto the bench beside him and did her best to fish out Cassian's spit. She lifted her bowl to her lips and began to swallow her gruel, forcing it down her throat.

"Thank you," she said after a few swallows.

"You have no need to thank me," the man said. "I only did what anyone should have done."

Halcyon paused, studying him from the corner of her eye. Something about him was different, but she could not name what it was. He obviously was not a relic hunter. He cast a different aura, one not lit by greed and ruthless ambition. And that aura must have granted him authority here, because despite his non-threatening size, the other prisoners respected him.

"Halcyon of Isaura," she whispered.

The man seemed surprised that she had introduced herself. He nearly dropped his bowl as he met her gaze, his eyes studying her with a shade of disbelief. "Thales of Zenia."

"You do not seem to belong here, Thales of Zenia."

Thales snorted. "No, and neither do you, Halcyon of Isaura. You should stay close to me for now. The first days here can be treacherous." He rose, his motions infused with grace, and carried his empty bowl to a washbasin.

Halcyon followed him. He was of the upper class, she suspected. That was why he felt out of place here. What had he been in his life before? A politician? An artist? A scholar?

Another line formed from the mess hall to an outside deck. Halcyon waited in Thales's shadow, watching as the convicts ahead of them checked in at a table. The guards were recording the prisoners' identification numbers and bestowing them with the tools they needed for the day: iron hammers, picks, chisels, saws, wooden wedges, jars of water.

"How can they trust murderers with such tools?" Halcyon said.

"It is a marvel, is it not?" Thales sounded amused. "You have a greater chance of falling to your death than being split open by a pick. Although there have been a few murders by hammers here. But there is great punishment for those who dare to do it."

Halcyon mulled over that a moment. Then she asked, "What sort of punishment?"

"A body part is removed. It's usually an eye; sometimes it's a tongue. But most important, if you murder another prisoner here, you are then granted a life sentence here. Most of us have only a matter of years or decades in this quarry before we move on to the next portion of our sentence. And after a few moons here . . . you will be more than ready to leave."

She was quiet, thinking about her next sentence: imprisonment in Mithra. She dreaded it, more than the quarry. Here, she would at least feel sunlight and breathe fresh air and work her body. In the prison, she would be chained to a wall in utter darkness.

She thought of Evadne, brave and beautiful Evadne, taking five years of her sentence for her. Halcyon's eyes burned; she struggled to diffuse the emotion, and it left scorch marks in her soul.

"Every morning," said Thales, breaking her thoughts, "your cell will open at dawn and you will come to the mess hall, to eat. Then you will walk to the captain, here on the deck, and tell him your number. He will rent the tools to you, and he keeps impeccable records. It is futile to try and smuggle one back into the mess hall or your cell."

"I was not thinking to," Halcyon said, although she felt her cheeks warm, remembering how she had wanted to kill six men, just minutes ago.

"Very good. Now, I am working on track twenty-seven. I could use your help and will ask the captain if you can work with me today."

Halcyon nodded, anxious as she and Thales approached the captain on the deck. He was a large man with a jagged scar on his face, his beefy hand swallowing the quill as he recorded the day's rentals. Thales reported his number; the captain wrote it in perfect penmanship, and a guard behind him handed Thales his supplies for the day: a bundle of fifty wooden wedges, a chisel, a hammer, a jar of water.

"I would benefit from having Hal—Convict . . ." Thales paused, expectant as he looked at her.

Halcyon had nearly forgotten her number. "8651."

"Convict 8651's assistance on track twenty-seven."

The captain slid his jaded gaze to Halcyon. He noticed every line and edge of her, just as the gruel guard had, and it took all her strength not to spew curses at him.

"Very well," the captain finally said, and Halcyon watched as he wrote her number—8651—onto his ledger. "I will rent you the same supplies as Convict 7909, and I will know if anything is missing come the end of the day."

Halcyon nodded and gathered up the tools, following Thales to where the wooden tracks along the quarry walls began to split and grow, like roots from a tree, down the steep face of marble. Several times, she worried she would slip and fall over the measly rope borders—the quarry was perilously deep—but the wooden tracks were built with footholds, and she eventually came to track twenty-seven and set down her supplies on a bench.

"My task is to make shallow cuts along the marble," Thales explained when Halcyon, back throbbing, moved to stand beside him, looking at the white marble face before them. "I then drive these wooden wedges into the cuts and soak them with water. The wedges will expand at an even rate, and it will fracture the marble into large sheets. The group behind me will come along and transport the sheet by pulleys. By then, I will be on the next track, repeating the cycle." He paused to look at her. "Do you think you can drive the wedges into the cuts?"

"Yes."

"Good. Let us begin."

Halcyon and Thales grasped their tools and started for the day. She did not notice it, not until he had taken the chisel in his grip.

Thales's right hand was crooked, his fingers bent at painful angles. It seemed that he could command a few motions with it, but he primarily worked with his left one. His right hand must have been brutally broken and healed without proper setting. And then Halcyon saw the scar on his right middle finger, like a ring had melted against his skin, leaving a mark.

She pounded her first wedge into the crack. "You are a mage."

"So I was," Thales said, turning it into a past statement. There was no emotion in his voice as he chiseled cracks into the marble.

Halcyon waited for him to explain, but he refrained. He moved farther away from her. Again, she wondered why he was in this common quarry. He still had his tongue to sing, and he still had his dominant hand to cast, even if it bore the evidence from past trauma. By law, he should be in the mages' prison, on the eastern coast.

"Can you still cast magic?"

"No."

"Is that why you are you here in a common quarry, Thales? Because you have lost your magic?"

"I am here because they claim I murdered someone, Halcyon."

"*They claim?* You do not know for sure if you did or did not?"

He refused to respond and Halcyon quieted, uncertain if he was humoring her or if he was serious with this notion that someone had framed him for murder. She resumed her work of hammering the wedges into the cracks he made. Soon, her back was on fire, and every pound into the marble was agony.

"You are injured?"

She turned to look at Thales, who was now the one to watch her closely.

"Yes. I was whipped, days ago."

Thales glanced up at the upper tracks. There was always a guard within sight, Halcyon realized. They carried clubs and swords, ready to beat prisoners if they slacked in their tasks.

"Here, let me hammer the wedges for a while," Thales said. "You can take the jar of water and pour it slowly. It will give you some time to recover."

Halcyon gave him the hammer and took up the water, doing just as he suggested. She was as suspicious as she was intrigued by him—his past was a mystery, as were his motivations in helping her, an utter stranger.

"Why are you being so kind to me?" she asked.

"Do I need a reason to be kind to someone who needs it?"

She was silent, displeased with how he perpetually evaded her questions.

He must have sensed her annoyance. Thales sighed and said, "A few years ago, I incurred a debt from a man I wronged. Since then, I have been waiting to settle my debt to him."

Halcyon frowned. "And being kind to the new convict is how you plan to settle your debt?"

Thales glanced at her. He had that shocked gleam in his eyes again. The same shock as when Halcyon introduced herself.

Her imagination began to roam, and she realized why the name of Isaura had startled him so greatly. Why he struggled to look her in the eye.

"You know my uncle," she breathed, and suddenly her heart was pounding in her throat. "Where is he? Is Ozias here?"

"Shh," Thales hushed her, his hand trembling. "Yes, I know him. And no, he is not here."

"Please, tell me where he is. My family has not heard of him in ten years, and I—"

Thales turned to her, his face grooved in fear, anger. "Do not ask me, Halcyon. I hardly know your uncle, and I am not here to give you answers but to keep you alive, to fulfill my debt to him."

She fell quiet, watching Thales hammer stakes into the marble. She could be patient; she had five years in this place. One day, she would get the truth out of him.

They worked in harmonious silence for hours. But as the heat heightened, Halcyon found herself desperate for a distraction.

"Last night, when I was first brought into the outpost," she said, "I was met by a mage."

Thales halted in his hammering for a beat. "Yes. That would be Macarius of Galenos. He arrived only a few days before you."

"And he is now lord of this common quarry?"

"So the rumors claim."

"But I do not understand *how*. It is illegal for mages to be on common prison grounds."

Thales hammered a few more wedges, moving farther down the wall. Halcyon followed with her pouring water, waiting.

"I have been here for two years now," he said. "But before I was sentenced . . . things were changing among the Magical Court. There was talk of laws being altered, amended. To set us in higher places of power among the people, to give us unprecedented liberties. To turn us into gods." He paused, despite the threat of a guard noticing his moment of rest. His shoulders stooped; his breathing was labored. He spread his left hand upon the marble, as if he could feel the pulse of the earth, of Corisande, hidden deep. "It is a dangerous belief, but the queen is not well. She has not been well for some time. She is not the queen I knew when I was young. And terrible laws are being passed through her, and it is going to change this land. Corisande will molt into something we will not recognize, and that grieves me deeply."

Halcyon was still. This was almost the exact speech Straton had once shared with her, when he had chosen Halcyon to help him.

You are my last hope, Kingfisher.

She thought of Xander. The final words he had spoken to her, just before they had sparred that fateful day, just before Halcyon had slipped the blindfold over her eyes.

We do this for Queen Nerine. And I am honored to be at your side.

A sound escaped her, the first breath of a sob. She wrestled it back, but it was like a cresting wave. It wanted to break; she wanted to break. All the things she hoped to do with her life, with her gift. All the people she had loved and hurt. There was a crack in her soul, a fracture. It was expanding. Soon, she would shatter, and what would be left of her?

"Step this way," Thales whispered to her. "Hurry."

She obeyed, just as the marble farther down the quarry cracked with a thunderous bellow, separating as a perfect sheet. She watched as a group of convicts worked to tether it, the marble gleaming like bone. It was incredible to watch such a heavy load be borne up into the sky on pulleys.

"Back to work."

Halcyon jumped. A guard was an arm's length away from her, prodding her with his club. She had not seen him approach, and she nodded and resumed her task, Thales already pressing onward ahead of her.

The back of her tunic felt wet. She prayed it wasn't blood.

Eventually, Thales slowed, so they could work side by side again.

And he whispered to her, between the blows of his hammer, "I do not know why you are here, Halcyon of Isaura. What your past holds. But do not trade your hope for despair. Yes, you and I are prisoners. But we are alive, aren't we?"

Yes, she was alive.

Although she daily wondered why.

Why Straton had refused to let her die.

→ XVI ←

Halcyon

There was a gift waiting for her in the cell that evening. A basket of fresh linen bandages, a jar of healing salve. Halcyon sat on her cot, locked within her cell, and marveled at it. Who would send this? Could her parents have managed it? Evadne, perhaps?

She waited until the sentry had passed by her door to remove her tunic, to redress her wounds. She struggled to spread the salve on her back, but the wounds she could reach became cool and numb beneath the tincture. Halcyon stifled a groan, rushing to wrap fresh linen bandages around her before slipping into her tunic. She collapsed on her cot, angled on her belly, drained.

She was woken some time later, the door of her cell clanging.

It was a guard, bearing a torch. "The lord of the quarry wishes to see you."

Halcyon wanted to melt into a shadow, to evaporate. But she made herself leave her cell, an escort of guards surrounding her. They guided her to the ground level of the outpost. She was brought to Macarius's workroom, seated in the lone chair, and chained to the floor by her wrists and her ankles.

This time, the mage was waiting for her. And with him was a politician, his saffron sash displayed proudly across his body. And a woman was also present. She was dressed gloriously, little diamond stars wound in her hair. She sat on the edge of Macarius's desk, staring at Halcyon as if she could see though her. Her hand was draped across her lap, stained with ink, and Halcyon knew exactly what she was: Macarius's scribe.

Macarius waited until the guards shut the door, and it was just the four of them: mage and scribe and politician and hoplite-turned-convict.

"Ah, one day in the quarry, and you still cling to your high spirits, 8651," Macarius said. "It is admirable, but I do wonder how long you will last here."

Halcyon did not respond.

"Beryl," Macarius said to his scribe, but his eyes remained on Halcyon. "Ready yourself."

Beryl slid off the edge of the desk, taking the seat he had vacated. Halcyon watched as she opened a scroll, her elegant fingers taking up a quill, opening her pot of ink.

The politician yawned and scratched his sandy-brown hair, completely disinterested. Why was he even here? When had lazy men like him been inducted into the senate? Halcyon wondered with disdain.

Macarius moved closer to Halcyon, standing directly before

her. His clothes were still clean and rich—not a speck of quarry dust marred him—and Halcyon could not resist speaking.

"I see that you hide yourself during the day, Macarius. Are you afraid to be seen here?"

"Careful, 8651," he said, his voice sharp. "This is the only warning I will grant you. I will resort to . . . other methods should your tongue forget its place."

Halcyon was quiet.

"Very good. Now, let us begin, shall we?" Macarius smiled. It was apparent that he expected this conversation to be effortless.

How little he knew her, Halcyon thought, preparing herself.

"I am going to ask you a question, 8651," he began. "It is not a hard one. You know the answer. And if you answer it truthfully, I will set you free from this quarry. Your sentence will be overturned. As will Evadne's. Both you and your sister can return home to Isaura and to your family and forget all of this ever happened to you." He paused only to watch the hope and yearning stir in her eyes. "Which relic did Lord Straton appoint you to find, *Kingfisher?*"

She was silent, her face like stone. Straton had trained her for a moment like this, anticipating it might come. But within . . . she was crumbling. The mage knew her code name. He knew who she was. This changed everything.

"There is no need for us to pretend here," Macarius said. "Lord Straton brought you and Xander into the queen's underground alliance, appointed you both to recover a relic, didn't he? And of course, there was an accident. You killed Xander before you could fulfill Lord Straton's command. And he has taken his vengeance on you by sending you here. It is not your fault, Halcyon. Nor do you belong in this den of murderers. So tell me. Which relic did the commander order you and Xander to find? Was it Irix's Sky Cloak? Kirkos's Winged Necklace? Magda's Sunstone Ring of Healing? Loris's Pearl Earrings? Or maybe it was Acantha's All-Seeing Crown?"

Halcyon felt sweat bead on her brow, on her palms. But she smiled, reveling in the way Macarius's eyes narrowed. "Yes, you and I do not need to pretend, mage. What would you give for the Sky Cloak, the All-Seeing Crown, the Necklace, the Pearl Earrings? The Sunstone Ring? You are so close to possessing them all for your mistress." Her voice dropped to a husky whisper. "What reward has Selene promised you, then? How did she attach such strings to you, so she could yank you around as her puppet, *Hemlock*?"

Macarius struck her. The silver glinted on his forefinger, as if his magic was eager to spark now that Halcyon had uttered his code name.

Her cheek throbbed, but she leveled her gaze at the mage, unbowed. She had taken a wild presumption that he was Hemlock, the enigma that liked to taunt the commander, the person she and Xander had taken great pains to outwit. And by Macarius's response . . . she was not wrong.

"I had hoped it would not come to this," Macarius said. His voice was calm, but his eyes were livid.

How strange, she thought, her ears beginning to ring. How strange that she wanted the very thing this mage desired to possess. They were so different, Kingfisher and Hemlock. They were nothing alike, belonging to different sides, and yet they were on the same path.

"I will ask you *one* more time, and as Cyrus is my witness"—Macarius turned and gestured to the politician, who nodded blearily—"I have been exceedingly patient with you. I have given you ample opportunities to comply. Which relic did Lord Straton appoint you to find, and where is its location?"

Halcyon was silent.

"You disappoint me, 8651," Macarius said. "Beryl, prepare to write everything I say."

Beryl dipped her quill into a pot of ink, smirking.

Macarius approached Halcyon. His confidence was edged with cruelty, and her heart began to pound. She felt her mouth go dry, her body quiver as the mage loomed over her.

She knew what he was about to do, and still she could not forget her oath to Straton. To the queen.

"You break the law, Hemlock," she said. "I have not given you permission to mind-sweep me."

"Speak that name again, and I will cut out your tongue," Macarius threatened. He waved his hand at the politician. "What is the law, Cyrus? The one that just passed by the queen 8651 so valiantly serves?"

"Mind-sweeping can be enforced on convicts without their consent," Cyrus said, yawning. "Particularly when the convict is harboring information that is vital to the safety of the kingdom."

"Did you hear that, 8651?" the mage said, returning his gaze to Halcyon. "You are a murderer, and you have no rights. And if I want to delve into each of your memories, I can and I will."

Halcyon gripped the arms of the chair, the chains heavy, biting into her. "You will not get away with this."

"Who is going to stop me?"

And Halcyon had no answer. For there was no one to stop Macarius.

She had only a moment to prepare herself, to hammer a shield mentally into place. Macarius set his fingertips upon her brow, and she felt his magic sifting through her memories. He saw her and Evadne at the oil press, leading the donkey and watching the millstone crush the olives. He saw her racing the boys of Dree, leaving them far behind to choke on the dust she kicked up. He saw her envious of her little sister, of all the evenings when Evadne had sat on their father's lap, adored, while Halcyon sat on the floor, watching. He saw her tied to the stave, a flash of gold— Euthymius's Golden Belt—girded around Bacchus's waist as the priest approached her. . . .

He was getting closer, closer to the truth. And Halcyon felt vulnerable, helpless. She was in his hold, and he was searching through her, as if she were nothing but dirty rags on the floor.

She shifted in the chair. She pressed her back against the wood. A flare of pain. Of agony. She jerked harder, inflicting it upon herself, her wounds weeping. He could not search her mind if she was unconscious.

Macarius's hold faltered. He made a sound, as if he was disoriented. And then a curse, hot and angry.

Halcyon pressed her wounds against the chair one last time and finally met the safety of darkness, her mind slipping entirely from the mage's grip, like wind passing through his fingers.

XVII

Evadne

At daybreak, Evadne found Damon waiting for her in the villa's courtyard. They departed through the front doors unnoticed by the guards, all due to one of Damon's charms, and Evadne followed him along the path that led to the gates. They did not speak—it seemed too early for words, and Evadne did not mind sharing quiet company with Damon. The sunrise set the clouds on fire above them and the wind blew strong from the east, carrying the scents of the River Zan.

This was Evadne's first time leaving Straton's villa since she had arrived over a week ago. It seemed as if she had been here for ages, and walking the streets felt like freedom. She kept pace with Damon as they wove from street to street, and she watched Mithra awaken: scholars rushed to the university toting scrolls and wax tablets; servants carried baskets to the market; potters and weavers and bakers all started their trades; politicians and tax collectors meandered with their money purses and the latest decree tucked into their belts.

Damon and Evadne soon joined the current of young mages, who were hustling just as the scholars had, only the scholars hurried to the west and the mages hurried to the south, where the Destry stood proud and magnificent.

The school of magic reminded Evadne of the agora in Abacus, but where the agora enforced strength and vigor, the Destry radiated with beauty and grandeur. The colonnade was massive, its pillars embellished with curling architecture. Its body was built with the gleaming white marble harvested from the common quarry, and the lower halves of its outer walls were covered with ivy and flowering vines. Its windows were arched and guarded by bronze screens pierced with stars, and its oaken doors were carved with the nine symbols of the divines. For once, Kirkos's emblem of a wing was included.

Evadne's heart raced as she and Damon approached those magical doors. She stepped into the Destry's shadow and smelled the sweet nectar of the flowering vines, and for a moment, she let the wonder overcome her as she ascended the steps.

But then she felt her ankle, jarring with pain, and her hands, cracked from lye, and reality returned, like a cold tide rushing about her.

The doors groaned opened for them, and she followed Damon into the cavernous lobby, the floors made of black and white checkers. Nine pillars upheld the ceiling, each of them carved to represent a divine. Evadne could have stood there for hours, admiring the beauty of the gods and goddesses. She looked for Kirkos and found him instantly, hewn from marble, tall and strong, dressed in a knee-length chiton, a laurel crowning his head. His hair blew in loose waves to his shoulders, and his wings were tucked behind him, but they were great and carved as feathers. A marble falcon accompanied him, the bird perched on his forearm, and above him the ceiling flushed with sunrise, as if it were the real sky beyond the roof.

"The ceiling is an enchanted reflection of the sky," Damon said, noting Evadne's awe. "It is easy to lose sense of time when creating and casting spells. Come, we must hurry now."

Evadne lowered her eyes and noticed a wide stairwell. Tardy students continued to dart up the stairs, but soon the Destry fell quiet. Beside the flight of steps was a desk, where an older mage and her scribe stood, receiving visitors.

"Damon," the mage greeted as they approached. Her voice was polished, her eyes the color of the ocean as she looked at Damon, then Evadne. "What brings you back to the Destry?"

"Good morning, Professor Cinta. I have a contract I need sealed." Damon handed her the papyrus he and Evadne had written on the night before.

"You must be Evadne of Isaura," Cinta said, drawing Evadne's attention. A crease formed on the mage's brow when she noticed Evadne's simple tunic and amulet. "Do you come into this contract of your own volition?"

"Yes."

Cinta's scrutiny returned to the contract. "There is no mind-sweeping clause, Damon."

"I know, Professor. It was a deliberate choice."

Cinta did not look pleased, but she held her opinion as she warmed a golden square of wax over a flame. "You both understand that when I seal this contract, it will be magically binding for the time frame agreed upon, unless there is a severing?"

Evadne glanced at Damon. He was watching her, ensuring there was no hesitation in her eyes. She nodded her consent.

"We understand, Professor."

Cinta poured a circle of wax on the papyrus. She briskly took up a seal and pressed it into the wax, and the contract became active.

Evadne felt no different. She'd half expected to experience something . . . an invisible shackle, a slight weight heaped on her shoulders, a constricting of breath. But there was nothing to mark her new status, nothing but the words on papyrus, which Cinta explained would be made public, posted in the Destry courtyard.

Evadne turned to follow Damon through the lobby, her pace slow so she could admire as much as possible before they departed.

"I think we should purchase you some new clothes, and then find something to eat," Damon said, squinting against the sunlight as they left the shade of the colonnade. "What do you think, Evadne?"

"I think my clothes still reek of lye."

"Is that a yes, then?"

Evadne nodded, a smile playing on her lips. She could not

remember the last time she had smiled, and it almost felt traitorous to do it now, knowing that Halcyon was still west of the city, down in the quarry.

She walked with Damon back to the eastern quadrant of Mithra, into a small clothier's shop, worries of Halcyon catching in her thoughts like burrs.

"Lord Damon!" an elder woman greeted him fondly. She stood behind a table, arranging bolts of linen and wool, every shade of earth and sky. "What brings you here today?"

"Good morning, Rhode. My scribe, Evadne, needs some new garments."

"Oh! How wonderful!" Rhode came forward, eyes bright as she looked to Evadne. "Come closer, Daughter, so I may measure you."

Damon remained at the front of the shop, his back angled to them as Evadne followed Rhode behind a privacy curtain. It was only when the clothier began to measure her body that Evadne remembered with a frantic pang that she was wearing Kirkos's relic.

"And how long have you been scribing for Lord Damon?" Rhode asked, her hands flickering with a measuring rope over Evadne's chest.

Evadne did not breathe for a moment, thinking the woman had surely felt the chain hiding beneath her tunic. But when Rhode arched her brows, expectant, Evadne found her voice. "Today is my first day."

"How marvelous! My daughter became a scribe years ago. She

works in the Destry." Rhode turned to begin sorting through a rack of chitons, and Evadne took that slender moment to draw forth her relic, hiding it in a clenched fist. "Here, this one will fit you perfectly. Let us get you out of this tunic, shall we?"

With Rhode's assistance, Evadne stepped into the new raiment. The chiton was soft and sleek, shimmering with the hint of gold when the light touched it. Evadne thought it was far too fine for her, but when she tried to say such to Rhode, the clothier waved away her excuses.

"Scribes are just as important as the mages they write for. What do you think of this belt?" She brought a gold band of woven threads about Evadne's waist.

The relic was still hidden in Evadne's palm, growing slick with perspiration. She waited until Rhode was preoccupied with sandals before Evadne began to search her new chiton for pockets. To her dismay, there were none. And the chiton's neckline was far lower than her tunic's.

"Here we are. These sandals will be perfect." Rhode knelt so Evadne could slip her feet into them, crosshatching them up Evadne's legs to knot them just below her knees. "Now for your brooches. Follow me to the table."

She pinned back the curtain, and Evadne realized she would have to wait to slip on her necklace. Hopefully Damon would not notice its addition later, but Evadne's heart did a strange lurch when she watched him turn toward her. His eyes traced her. They touched her hair with its wild tangles, the lines of her collarbones, her long, bare arms, the belt at her waist, all the way down the golden rush of her new chiton, to where her toes peeked from beneath the gilded hem. And she knew right then that he would take note of the silver chain later, should she dare to wear it.

She would have to keep it hidden in her fist, then, as impossible as that seemed.

"Do you hail from divine blood, Evadne?" Rhode asked, opening a wooden box brimming with brooches. Gold and silver, bronze and brass. Some burned with jewels, some intricately etched.

"Yes. Kirkos."

Rhode's smile waned. "Oh. Oh dear. I do not have a brooch of Kirkos. Forgive me, but . . . I have never had a request for it." And she anxiously began to sift through her baubles, as if she could magically find wings at the bottom of the hoard.

"That is all right," Evadne was swift to reassure her. "These will be perfect for me." She touched a pair of olive wreath brooches, crafted from bronze.

"Let me see if I have a golden pair," Rhode said, continuing to search her treasure box. "The bronze will not look as nice with your chiton."

Evadne wanted to say that the bronze was more than enough for her, but Rhode was beaming as she found two golden olive wreath brooches, and Evadne could not find the heart to refuse them.

Rhode gathered the chiton on her shoulders, slipping a long golden pin into each olive wreath. The linen became narrower, exposing even more of Evadne's shoulders and chest.

Her heart continued to beat anxiously, but she managed to smile and thank Rhode.

"Is this to your liking, Evadne?" Damon asked, his voice close behind her. "I will have Rhode send a few more sets up to the villa, if you approve."

Evadne glanced down at the shimmer of her clothes, her right hand continuing to clench the relic as inconspicuously as possible.

"Perhaps I could have a second chiton made with pockets?" she asked.

Rhode was speechless for a moment, her brow wrinkled. And then she laughed. "Of course! I can make you a chiton with pockets."

While Damon was placing the order, Evadne wandered a few paces away, bending to tuck the relic beneath the toes of her right foot. She would have to keep her toes curled as they walked back to the villa, but Evadne already bore a limp.

She straightened just as Damon turned toward her, ready to depart.

The market was busy and loud; it was midmorning, and Damon bought them each a skewer of roasted meat and fruit, and a flask of honeyed wine to share. They stood beneath a canopy, too hungry to speak, and Evadne thought she had never tasted anything so delicious. She was licking her fingers when Damon finally glanced at her.

"We will make one more stop at the Gilded Owl," he said. "That is the shop you should go to if you need ink, papyrus, or quills. And then we will return to the villa and begin for the day."

Evadne did not have a chance to respond. A crowd was suddenly gathering on the edges of the street, jostling her and Damon, who frowned, glancing across the market well.

"What is happening?" Evadne asked as a man bumped her.

"The queen is about to ride by," Damon replied, eyes focused on the distant curve of street. And then he looked at Evadne and smiled. "Have you ever seen Queen Nerine before?"

"Only her profile on an Akkia coin."

"Then come with me. You need to see her." He held out his hand, waiting for Evadne to take it.

She hesitated, and Damon sensed it. His smile faded, his hand began to fall away when Evadne darted hers forward to meet it, and their fingers wound together as if they had done it countless times before.

He led her forward, forging a path for them in the crowd.

Evadne struggled to keep Kirkos's relic bunched beneath her toes. She was limping more pronounced because of it, and Damon stopped to look at her, a question forming on his lips, when Evadne, terse and impatient, said, "I'm fine."

He did not seem surprised by her tone, but he moved slower through the crowd, and she was secretly grateful for it.

They emerged at the front of the crowd, and Evadne waited for the queen to arrive, anticipation like sparks along her skin. She felt Damon standing in her shadow, and then the press of the crowd moved him closer, until the space between them melted, and his chest was aligned with her back.

The solid warmth of him was a shock to her. Evadne was

suddenly aware of everything: the difference of their heights, the way their bodies curved to fit each other. How Damon's breaths quickened, stirring her hair.

She should move; she was obviously making him uncomfortable. And yet she did not want to, and she realized her breaths were flowing just as swiftly as his. Like their hearts were beating the same chorus.

Queen Nerine appeared at last—a blessed distraction—leading her procession on a great horse.

She wore a purple chiton, its hem resting just above her knees, and golden sandal strings glittered up her calves. Ari's enchanted relic, the Shawl of Stars, was draped across her, guarding her front and her back, a shield made of hundreds of small, exquisite diamonds. Any arrow or spear that dared to hit that shawl would be rebounded, hurtling back to lodge within the would-be assassin. Many foolish relic hunters had tried to assassinate the kings and queens of Corisande for that shawl, which had been found a hundred years ago by a princess who had kept it in the royal line's possession.

A laurel crowned Nerine's brow, and her dark hair streamed out behind her like a pennant, her coarse waves shot through with silver. Her arms were adorned with chased gold and lapis lazuli. And yet while she smiled at her people, there was a tangible sense of weariness about her, as if she was only half-awake.

Evadne soaked her in, trying to remember every detail, but her fascination broke when the person standing beside her in the crowd shouted angrily at the queen, "Your taxes will starve us!" And then another man, across the street, raised his fist and screamed about the relic decree, about hunger and inequality and the divide between courts. Murmurs and shouts began to kindle in the crowd, spreading like fire.

Evadne was jostled; someone stepped on her foot, and she flinched in pain. Damon stretched his arm out to ward people away from her. And the glory of the moment was eclipsed by the resentment of the crowd. Queen Nerine did not stop; she did not falter. She continued on her way, that distant smile on her face. It would almost seem as if she did not hear her people at all.

Evadne's focus shifted to the woman riding in the queen's wake.

It was Selene.

At first, Evadne blinked, unable to believe it. Damon's aunt was riding *with* the queen, in her procession. Closer than any guard. And she was singing in God Tongue, her voice a current of sweetened words.

Evadne leaned back into Damon, longing to disappear just as Selene drew close, about to pass them. The mage's eyes flickered, and she looked directly at Evadne and Damon. Her lips never stopped moving; her chorus never faltered. But her eyes cut through Evadne, and a sharp smile curved the corners of Selene's bloodred mouth.

And then she passed them, the wind stirring her hair and her purple cloak as she followed the queen, shouts of anger continuing to spawn along the street.

The queen's guards followed at a respectful distance, armored and bearing spears. They heard the dissenters, but they made no action against them. Soon, the street was empty, and the crowd began to dissipate.

Evadne continued to stand, softened by shock. Eventually, she turned to look at Damon.

"Your aunt . . ."

"Is Queen Nerine's hand. Her closest advisor."

"She was singing in the queen's wake."

"Yes. A spell of protection."

That was why the guards had held back, why no angry dissenter had charged forward. Selene had formed a sightless barrier around her and the queen, created by enchanted song.

Evadne glanced away, to where the market had resumed its bustle, as if nothing had interrupted it. "Your aunt is very powerful, then."

"Yes." He began to walk back to his father's villa, forgoing the stop at the ink shop. Evadne fell in stride beside him. "When Xander and I were boys, our father would caution us every night about power and pride. 'If you find yourself to be strong, use that strength not just for yourself but for those around you. And if you find yourself to be smart, use that knowledge to uplift others.'"

Evadne could not imagine a man like Straton saying such things. "Your father sounds wise."

"He was worried about us," Damon said. "My brother had begun to show great skill as a warrior, and magic had just revealed itself in my literacy. My sister, likewise, was very young, but she was already adept in healing. It would seem the three of us were destined for greatness, to rise up as near divines in the eyes of society. It would not be worth it, my father often said to us, to rise so high by standing on the backs of others. We must earn it in an honest way, and should we find our lives to be exalted one day, it would only be because we had served, respected our peers.

"Xander and I both grew tired of our father cautioning us so much. I did not understand it then, but now I do, after seeing my aunt's ascension. She and my father both worked diligently and came into their own power, but my father was adamant about forming boundaries, while my aunt was not. She became a professor at the Destry when another instructor fell mysteriously ill. She then was made a member of the queen's inner circle soon thereafter, and when the queen's hand suddenly died, Selene was chosen to replace her, even though the vote was rushed and took place when my father was gone."

Damon paused, glancing at Evadne. "Sorry. I should not bother you with such things."

"No, it is all right." She wanted to hear more, but Damon fell silent.

They were quiet the remainder of the walk, and Evadne could not shake the sensation that she was being watched, followed. But every time she glanced over her shoulder, the streets were quiet and ordinary. She wondered if Selene had cast a charm on her, but even that seemed unlikely, and Evadne continued to reimagine her and the queen—one possessing the distant smile, one sporting the angry smile. As if the queen were a puppet. And suddenly, Damon's desire to choose his own scribe felt palpable, and as Evadne entered the villa at his side . . . she worried that she was not strong enough to weather whatever storm was brewing between Damon and his aunt.

"Lord Damon," Toula greeted with flourish in the courtyard, bowing. And then she looked at Evadne and startled, as if she had not recognized her. *Evadne?*

"Evadne has agreed to become my scribe, Toula," Damon said. "Will you please let the others know so they may begin to address her accordingly?" He continued to walk, and Evadne trailed him, trying to ignore Toula's horror.

She was relieved to finally be in the safety of Damon's chambers. It felt as if they had walked through a battle and had miraculously emerged with only dust on their clothes.

But there was Arcalos. The dog seemed to sleep most of his life, curled up in a patch of sunlight on the floor. He lifted his head to blink adoringly at Damon, and then Evadne.

Well, the dog suddenly did not feel so threatening anymore.

"This desk is now yours," Damon said, standing beside it. "You may arrange it however you like. Fresh scrolls can be found on that shelf. Papyrus and wax for correspondence on that one. I would like for you to record my spells in dark ink—nothing fancy, like some mages I know—and keep them organized by scroll. So, for instance, today we will begin transcribing what I call my *sorah* spells. These are spoken spells, very simple and effortless to cast. Eventually, we will progress to the more difficult spells—my *charena* spells—which are sung enchantments. Have I . . . have I overwhelmed you, Evadne?"

He had—her eyes were glazed. "No, I am just . . . taking it all in." She moved across the chamber to her desk, mind whirling. She could not wait to remove Kirkos's relic, which had become as obnoxious as a thorn in her foot. But she procured a new scroll from the shelf Damon had indicated, and she sat at the desk and oriented herself with the pots of ink.

"Why does it matter that I am right-handed?" she asked, remembering how he had noticed this fact about her, as if it was vital. "Is it to represent balance, because you are left-handed?"

"What? Oh. It does not matter. It is simply convenient as all the quills I have are for right hands."

She looked at his jar of quills. People who wrote with their left hands needed feathers harvested from a bird's right wing. The opposite was true for right-handers. They needed the feather from a left wing.

Damon could not write with his left hand because of his magic. But the fact that he only possessed right-handed quills made Evadne wonder if he often tried to write with his weaker hand.

"Very well," she said, opening the scroll. The parchment was smooth as silk beneath her fingers, blank with possibility. It stirred the awe in her again, and she traced its perfect face before taking a swan quill in her fingers. "This shall be your *sorah* scroll."

Sorah. Which was translated as *spoken* in the God Tongue.

She wrote it in the scroll, a word built from elegant curves and dots.

And then she thought of the other word he had mentioned: *charena*, which translated as *sung*.

She became aware of the silence and glanced up to find Damon standing on the other side of the desk, staring down at her handwriting. That one ancient word had him utterly bewitched, the ink still glistening.

"What I would give to be able to write, to see my words shaped perfectly by my own hand, to know they will remain long after I am gone," he whispered, and then seemed to remember Evadne's presence, and he flushed, embarrassed.

Evadne decided to also share a confession. "And what I would give to be able to cast magic, to see my words transform into spoken and sung power."

Damon smiled mournfully. "I suppose this is our fate, then? That the mage will envy the scribe's power, and the scribe will envy the mage's?"

She had never thought of it that way. And she began to see the gift she held, this ability to write in beautiful strokes, to write as much as she wanted. There was power within it, a small seed. But how it could grow, should she allow it to.

And she remembered that she *did* possess a small trace of magic, thanks to Kirkos's relic. And Damon *could* write with his right hand, should he truly want to.

"*Sorah*," Damon breathed, as if recalling why they were here, and began to pace.

Evadne waited, quill ready.

Soon, he began to voice his spells from memory.

A spell to move a shadow. A spell to extinguish a flame. A spell to mend a garment. A spell to distract another person. A spell to draw light. A spell to call an animal. A spell to make an object move. A spell to unlock a door.

All spoken charms.

Evadne recorded them, word for word. Most of the *sorah*s were only several words long, easily spoken in one breath. A few progressed to multiple lines, and although they were deemed "simple" by Damon, they were exquisitely worded. Evadne found herself desiring to go back and reread them, to speak them aloud, just to hear how they would sound in her voice.

She realized something, as if she had been struck. And she sat back, hand aching, and laughed.

Damon seemed to jolt at the sound. He frowned.

"What is it, Evadne?"

Her laughter eased, but its buoyancy lingered, lightening her heart. "I now see that I could never have been a mage. I am no poet."

Damon snorted, the tension leaving his face. "Yes, you could have. Every mage has their own taste in words and rhythm. You would have found your own."

Suddenly, the door blew open with a bang.

Evadne startled, her quill streaking ink across the scroll. Even Arcalos jumped, raising his head at the intruder, and Evadne was shocked to see it was evening. The daylight had faded, and she and Damon had been completely lost in another world. The oil lamps were the only source of light throughout the room.

Straton stood on the threshold, glaring at both of them.

"Father," Damon spoke calmly.

"I want to speak with my son, alone," the commander said to

Evadne. His face was guarded, but his eyes were livid, burning a path to Damon.

She stood and swiftly departed, shutting the door behind her.

The corridor was quiet, cloaked in shadows. Fresh night air drifted in from the open window at the end of the hall. And Evadne breathed in that air, wondering if she should descend to the main floor and prepare the family's wine, even though Damon had told her she was no longer cupbearer. But she chose to remain by the door, pressing her ear to the wood . . .

"You have defied me, Damon," Straton hissed. "I told you this needed to be approved by me."

"If I remember correctly, Father . . . you have now passed the mission *back* to me to fulfill. And that is what I am doing."

"You cannot take this girl with you!"

"And why not? It seems only fitting that Evadne finishes what Halcyon began."

"And what happens if she does not survive? Have you thought about that? Would you make me tell her family that she perished by an unknown cause?"

"Do not act as if you suddenly care for Evadne's family, Father. You have all but torn them into pieces."

Another moment of rigid silence. Evadne continued to breathe against the door. The hair rose on her arms.

"Is this how you perceive me, Damon? Do you think I take delight in shattering people's lives? That I enjoy what has happened to Halcyon?"

"Of course I do not want to believe my father is heartless. But if you want my honesty . . . I feel as if you and I have begun to esteem very different things in life."

"You and I want the same things, Damon."

"If that is so, then why are you opposing me on my choice?"

"Evadne can hardly walk without limping, Son," Straton continued, trying to calm his tone. "The chances of her being a successful partner for this mission are very slim. It is wrong of you to put it upon her."

"Have you not been paying attention this last week, Father?" Damon sounded incredulous. "Evadne has scrubbed your villa's floors five times over, on her hands and knees, with lye burning her skin. Before that, she stood up in an assembly and asked to take half of her sister's sentence! No one I know would do that. And I cannot look the other way, telling myself that she is not worthy of this mission. My magic is drawn to her."

"Scrubbing a villa floor is nothing compared to what you are about to ask of her."

"You act as if physical strength is all there is to life!"

"That is not true."

"It *is* true, and that is why you favored Xander over me. That is why you gave the mission to him and Halcyon, and not to me, even though I was the one who forged it. I was the one who helped you discover where the crown was! And now my brother is *dead*."

"*Enough!*"

The silence was painful. Evadne blinked back tears, told herself she should move away. But she remained at the door, transfixed.

"You should have come to me first, Damon," the commander

said. "You should have asked for my input before you ran to the Destry this morning."

"And what would that input be, Father? *Evadne is a foolish choice*, even though I sense she is a good balance for me? Even though when I asked her to write a myth, she chose the creation of Acantha's All-Seeing Crown?"

The commander made a noise in response.

"Yes. She chose that myth," Damon reiterated.

"I thought she did not know anything. I thought you told me Halcyon did not betray her oath."

Damon was quiet. And then he said, low but not at all repentant, "I did not mind-sweep Halcyon."

"*What* did you say?"

"I did not mind-sweep her. Nor do I ever want to. And you should be ashamed, Father, that you asked it of me."

"You lied to me."

"Yes, I lied."

"Evadne knows, then?"

"I do not know what she knows. But she is not a fool. We need to either bring her into the mission, or we need to come up with a new set of plans."

Evadne could hear the commander pacing. And then he growled, "You ask why I chose Xander for this? Because I do not trust you. When I give you an order, I expect you to follow it."

"Yes, well, I am not one of your hoplites, Commander. In case you forgot, I am your *son*."

Evadne rushed away from the threshold, melting into the

corner's shadow just before Straton departed, slamming Damon's door.

She stood in the corridor, trying to make sense of it all. And then she realized why Damon had gone to see Halcyon in her cell the night after the trial: to follow his father's orders to mind-sweep her. The fact that Damon had not done it, instead risking himself to sneak Evadne into the agora, made her ache. She waited until she had blinked away her tears before she cautiously returned to Damon's room.

He sat on the floor, his back against the wall, Arcalos curled against his side. Damon's eyes were closed until he heard Evadne's soft tread. His face was pale, haunted when he looked at her.

"I have been waiting for you to return. Come inside so we can talk."

Evadne joined him on the floor, hesitant to be so close to Arcalos until Damon stroked the dog's copper-and-white coat. Arcalos was half-asleep, his head resting on Damon's thigh.

"Your dog seems gentle," she murmured.

"He was Xander's dog." Damon's caress slowed on Arcalos's back, as if the memory was taking hold of him. "For years, he begged our parents for a dog. A few seasons before he left for the Bronze Legion, Arcalos was given to him. And we both knew Xander would be gone for a long while, and he was worried about the dog and asked me to look after him. So I did, although sometimes Arcalos still watches the door, waiting for Xander to return home."

"Were you close with your brother?"

"I was before he left for Abacus. I saw Xander again a few

weeks ago, and while I was in awe of who he had become . . . I felt as if he were a stranger."

Evadne wondered if Damon had also seen Halcyon in that moment, discussing this mission Straton was trying to spearhead. She could not help but think of what she had overhead earlier—Damon choosing Evadne for some difficult challenge that Halcyon was supposed to triumph.

She reached out to pet Arcalos. Her fingers trembled until they disappeared in his soft fur, and she could have wept, to be touching something that had once terrified her.

"There is something I need to tell you, Evadne," Damon said, drawing her eyes to his. "It is something that cannot be shared beyond this chamber."

Evadne waited patiently, and when Damon finally spoke, she gathered his words like they were gold.

"Two years ago, I was a student in the Destry. I was in my aunt's class, and she was teaching one particular enchantment that surprised me: the spell of thought. You could go so far as to call it manipulation. By its power, a mage can plant thoughts or steal them from someone's mind. It is a shade of magic that we rarely perform, and we are taught to be wise and careful in such casting. But my aunt showed me that day that she was alarmingly good at casting it.

"I began to watch her more closely. I noticed she was missing from the Destry every morning. That she would arrive late. And then the news broke that she had been selected as Queen Nerine's hand, so Selene was beginning every day in the palace, and then coming to the Destry. And decrees soon began to pass, laws that seemed counterintuitive to Nerine's reign, and I started to worry that my aunt was using the spell of thought on the queen, planting ideas in Nerine's mind, manipulating her slowly. I did not know what else to do, so I went to my father. He was in Mithra for a brief visit, but he listened and believed me, and we began to forge a plan.

"He asked if I could break Selene's enchantment. There is only one way I could, and that would be for me to steal her written spell and to create my own in opposition to it—a great crime among mages. And then I would have to sing it in the queen's presence. Selene's scribe is loyal; he guards all her spells with his life. But even if I could have stolen her enchantment, my aunt possesses a very deep well of magic. She is far more powerful than I am. It would be foolish for me to think I could unravel what she had cast. So I began to think of another way. I turned my mind to enchanted objects, which brought me to the study of divine relics, something I had scarcely given a stray thought to before. There are only two of them that can break enchantments: Nikomides's Devouring Sword, which is carried by the lord of the mage's prison, to keep convict mages from enchanting a breakout, and Acantha's All-Seeing Crown.

"Not long after this, a spymaster for the queen approached my father and claimed that there was a group of people—mainly mages—who were striving to find and collect all of the relics. They desire to hoard them, so no one but mages have magic. And this group is currently working in opposition to Queen Nerine.

"Because I had already done so much study on the relics, my father brought me into this knowledge, inviting me to become a member of Nerine's underground alliance. There is a race to find and reclaim all of the relics—our group desires to protect and save the queen by doing such, while our opposition plans to use them to spur the queen's decline.

"Nerine's spymaster asked me to study Acantha's legends, which I did in the beginning, until I found no trace of where her crown might rest. But then I reread the myth of its creation with Euthymius, and it soon became clear to me that he was vital in all of this. So I dared to approach the only priest of his within the kingdom: Bacchus of Dree."

"Bacchus?" Evadne breathed, leaning closer. "Bacchus knows about this?"

"Yes," Damon replied. "Bacchus is loyal to Nerine and has secretly supported the queen's underground alliance for years. He spoke to Euthymius in prayer, and Euthymius granted the priest knowledge of where the crown rests, as well as a map, so we could recover it.

"Prior to all of this, my father, who began to believe my magic was not strong enough to fulfill this mission, decided to pair Xander with his most favored of hoplites. Your sister, Halcyon. They, too, were brought into our confidence. They began to train with one another, and my father covertly sent them to Dree, to speak with Bacchus and procure the map. It was dangerous for me to leave Mithra at this point, because my aunt began to suspect me, and I also did not have a scribe yet. And I knew that it would be impossible for me to recover the crown without a scribe. So it would fall to the warriors: my brother and your sister. They would memorize the map and recover the crown, and we would present it to the queen and break the hold my aunt has on her."

He paused and closed his eyes. His dark hair was draped across his brow, a hint of blue gleaming within it, and there was a sheen of perspiration on his face.

"And then you know what happened next," he whispered, looking at Evadne. "Everything has come apart, and I wish that I had never agreed to let my brother take this mission from me."

"This is not your fault, Damon," Evadne said, her mind reeling from all he had shared with her. "Nor is it my sister's fault." She hesitated for a moment. "You said you need a scribe to recover the crown. You have me, and I will go with you."

Damon met her gaze. His eyes were full of sorrow. "You have yet to ask me where the crown rests, Evadne."

"Where does it lie, then?"

He was silent, and she sensed his dread. His fear. "Acantha's crown hangs on the door to the Underworld. In the heart of Mount Euthymius."

ᐳXVIIIᐸ

Halcyon

Thales . . . I think I am being poisoned."

Halcyon kept her voice low as they sat in the mess hall,
eating their morning gruel. Ten days had come and gone since she
had first arrived at the common quarry. Ten days, and Macarius
had not summoned her again. It filled Halcyon with unspeakable
dread; had he found what he wanted in her memory, then? Before
she had defiantly slipped from his grip?

She must have inadvertently given something vital away during
the mind-sweep.

"What makes you think such, Halcyon?" Thales asked, just as
quietly as he continued to sip gruel from his bowl.

"I have been weakening more and more each day. I can hardly
sleep. I feel . . . unwell."

Thales met her gaze, soft with understanding. "The first few
weeks in the quarry can cause that."

"No, Thales. The quarry work does not intimidate me. This is something else." She stared down at her untouched gruel. "I think Macarius has ordered poison to be stirred into my food. I have noticed the past few days that when I reach the gruel pot, the guard does not serve my portion from it. He has a bowl waiting on the shelf beneath, already filled."

Her stomach growled and throbbed with hunger. She wanted so badly to eat. But her mouth was dry; her head felt foggy. Her arms were slow to respond. Something was wrong, and it would only grow worse if she ate what the guards were giving her.

There was a flash of movement, and Halcyon glanced up to see Cassian approaching their table. The relic hunter who had spit in her food the first day.

"Is Mistress No-Hair too good for her gruel, now?" Cassian said with a sneer, leaning across the table from Halcyon. "Or perhaps you need me to flavor it for you again?"

"Why should you care if I like my gruel or not?" Halcyon said. "I will eat it when I want. Go back to your table."

Cassian grinned. He did just as she wanted; he snatched her bowl and carried it over to his table, where his companions were smirking and chuckling.

Halcyon and Thales both watched as Cassian did not share with his friends but drank the entire gruel himself.

"Well," Thales said, brows arched. "I suppose that is one way to see if your food has been tampered with."

Halcyon almost smiled. The feeling felt stiff on her lips. "Yes. Exactly as I hoped."

"Here." Thales edged his bowl to her. "Eat part of mine."

And she wanted to refuse, to insist that he needed his entire portion. But she was so hungry, so desperate to ease her pangs, to give her body fuel. She took only a few sips and tried to hand it back to him. But Thales was already rising, heading to the deck line.

They worked on track thirty-two that day. The sky was bright above them, the sun hot on their hair as they chiseled and hammered and poured water and listened to the marble crack. Halcyon moved slow and heavy; she was in a fog, and her head continued to ache. She was hammering the wooden wedges into the cracks, but every time she blinked, the wedges multiplied before her, and she could not tell which was the real peg and which was the mirage. She wavered, close to the edge of the track. Thales dropped his chisel to grab her arm, a moment before she would have lost her balance and slipped over the rope, plunging leagues to her death.

She blinked at him, saw two Thaleses before her, gripping her arm. His faces were pale; his eyes were wide.

"Halcyon?" His voice sounded distant.

"I told you," she said. "I am being poisoned."

He guided her away from the ropes, making her lean on the marble. "Here. Drink." He opened a jar of their water and gave it to her, glancing around to ensure none of the guards were watching.

The water washed through her, easing her symptoms. When she looked at Thales again, there was only one of him, and he hovered close, concerned.

"I am fine. I just . . . needed a moment."

A guard began to approach them, his sandals thrumming on the tracks. Thales quickly picked up his chisel and resumed work. And Halcyon began to pour the water over the wedges, although it pained her to waste it when she wanted to drain it herself.

"Why would Macarius want to poison you, Halcyon?" Thales asked when the guard had passed them.

Halcyon fell quiet. She could not tell Thales the truth, and so she eventually answered, "Because he dislikes me."

Thales made no response. It irritated her, and Halcyon pressed, "You do not believe me, do you, Thales?"

"I *do* believe you," he was quick to respond. "But Macarius would not risk something so foolish. Not unless there was a reason for it."

Thales studied her. She kept her blurry gaze on the marble, schooling her face to be calm.

"If he is poisoning you," Thales said, low and urgent, "then he is doing so to weaken you. And if he is trying to weaken you . . . he must want something. Something you know, perhaps?"

She felt the draw of Thales's insistence. Her eyes shifted, meeting his concern.

"What could he possibly want to know from me?" she said, but Thales was not convinced. No, his eyes were dark and shrewd, as if he were seeing into her. It made her shudder, even though Thales no longer wielded power to mind-sweep.

She moved away from him, but he followed.

"Has he harmed you, Halcyon?"

"I can handle it."

"Look at me."

Halcyon bristled but turned to glare at him. It was only then that she realized it, reading it in the lines of his brow. "You knew Macarius before you were sentenced here. And you are not surprised that he has wormed his way into this quarry, that he has targeted me."

Thales was silent, but his distress was evident. "I was one of his professors at the Destry."

"Was he a menace as a student?"

"He was once a good student. One of my brightest. But he was easily influenced, easily swayed. He eventually joined a group of friends who led him down a sinister road."

Halcyon thought about Queen Nerine's secretive opposers, seeking her destruction. She knew Macarius was one of them. He was Hemlock, Selene's puppet.

And the longer Halcyon stared at Thales, the more she sensed there was more to him, too.

No one was quite as they seemed.

She wanted to continue asking about Macarius, but there was a sudden thump above them, on one of the higher tracks, and then a groan.

Thales and Halcyon glanced up, just in time to see Cassian on his knees, leaning over the track, vomiting into the quarry void.

"I think you have proven your theory, Halcyon," Thales said, mournful, as if he did not want to believe it.

"And what am I to do about it?" She felt her own stomach

clench at the sound of Cassian's heaving. She turned away and snuck another sip of water from the jar.

"I am not sure yet," Thales whispered to her, returning to his work. "But we will think of something."

Thales's plan was for Halcyon to continue taking her poisoned bowl of gruel from the guard, let as much of it as possible slosh over the side as she walked to the table, so it would appear that she had eaten some of it. And then she was to set her bowl down and wait for one of the relic hunters to come and steal it. Which they would, every time. Even when they noticed how Thales drank half his porridge and gave the other half to Halcyon. Even when the ones who drank her gruel wound up vomiting a few hours later.

This plan lasted all of two days before a guard finally noticed.

On the twelfth morning in the quarry, Halcyon rose and waited for her cell to unlock. She could hear the other cells around her clanging open. She could see the other prisoners walk by, up to the mess hall. But her cell door remained bolted.

Eventually, a guard approached her, slid a bowl of gruel beneath her door.

She merely stared at it. The past two days, she had felt her strength return, a slow but steady trickle, now that she wasn't ingesting the poison. But it seemed she had arrived at an impasse. To eat poison or to go hungry.

"I am going to stand here and watch you swallow every drop of that gruel," the guard said.

Halcyon did not respond. She sat on her cot and removed her sandals.

The guard waited all day, leering at her. Halcyon had nothing to eat, nothing to drink. She lay on her belly and closed her eyes, trying to go deep into her mind, to draw out her determination. When the prisoners returned to their cells for the night, the guard left his post. But he returned with four others, and they entered Halcyon's cell like a storm.

It took three of them to hold her down. One of them pried her mouth open, and they forced the gruel into her.

She spluttered, choked.

"Do not kill her, you fool," one of them growled.

She spit most of it out, all over the guards. But some of the gruel went down, and she could feel the poison begin to warm her throat, simmer in her stomach. She made herself vomit it up after the guards left her.

Two more days passed, so similarly that Halcyon could hardly discern the difference between them. She felt herself weakening: her thoughts were cloudy, her body was sore, her lungs felt heavy, as if water was trickling into them. Soon, her hand came away bloody when she coughed, and she felt as if she would die soon.

She lay on her cot and stared at the wall. There was a faint drawing etched into the stone. The prisoner before her must have created it, and the longer Halcyon studied it, the more it comforted her. It was a great serpent, and it stirred the dregs of her memory. No, it was not just a serpent, but a basilisk, and her breath caught, entranced.

The Basilisk.

She had met the queen's spymaster once, when Straton had welcomed her and Xander into Nerine's underground alliance. It had been a brief meeting, in the dark. She had not seen the Basilisk's face, but she had heard his voice, a rough baritone that hardly rose above a whisper.

"You are willing to do this, Kingfisher?" he had asked her. He meant the plight for the crown, hidden in the heart of the most dangerous mountain in the realm.

"Yes," she had said, standing beside Xander. "We need a few moons to train, but we are confident we can succeed."

The Basilisk was silent, but she had felt him stare at her in the moonlight. She had been so worried that he saw a flaw in her, that he thought her a poor choice.

"Let it be done," he had said to Straton. "Let the hoplites venture into the mountain."

Halcyon's memory faded, but she continued to stare at the etched basilisk in the wall, wondering if it was truly there or if she was hallucinating. She wondered what the Basilisk thought of her now: a failure, a disgrace. And her strength, her glory began to slip away from her breath by breath, until there came a whisper in the dusky light.

"Halcyon."

She turned her head. Thales stood at her cell door, gripping the iron bars.

She struggled to sit up. She was too weak to walk so she crawled to him. "Thales . . . they will catch you," she rasped, knowing his cell was farther up the serpentine corridor, that he had risked himself to walk this far after dinner.

"Shh, here." He knelt so his eyes would be level with hers. He slipped a full bowl of his gruel to her, beneath the slender space of her door. "Drink it quickly."

Her hands were shaking uncontrollably. She took a sip of the gruel; it dripped down her chin, onto her tunic in her desperation. And all the while, Thales knelt and waited, his eyes rimmed with tears as he watched her.

"Why has he done this to you?" he whispered, mournful, angry.

Halcyon choked down the rest of his gruel—her stomach knotted, and she could hardly swallow. She edged his bowl back to him, and he hid it in his tunic.

"Thales, I am going to die here."

"You are not going to die, Halcyon. I will find a way to free you. Just . . . hold on. Please. Please do not give up."

"I am going to die here," Halcyon repeated, feeling it in her bones. "Whenever you are liberated from this place, I want you to write to my parents and my sister in Isaura, and tell them—"

"Away with you!" A guard ordered, approaching Halcyon's cell door. He kicked Thales aside, threatening him with the club until the former mage had moved back up the corridor.

Halcyon crawled to her cot, breathing heavily. She coughed until she thought her lungs had been shredded, until she vomited up all the good gruel Thales had risked himself to sneak to her.

She lay down on her cot and stared at the basilisk again, and the world grew hazy. Her breaths were becoming more and more shallow when the cadre of guards entered her cell to force more poison into her. Only this time they didn't. They held her upright, slapped her face. One of them sounded frantic.

"You put too much into her gruel!"

"Quick, give me some fresh water."

They fumbled around her, opened her bloody mouth, and nearly drowned her with water. Halcyon could not help but swallow it, even though she wanted to defy them.

She did not remember them leaving. She fell asleep and drifted on the boundary of life and death, until she felt her arms being gripped, her feet dragging over cold stone. She was brought into the workroom of the outpost again, sat down in the lonely chair. And there was Macarius, standing in wait for her arrival.

Just the sight of him stirred her dying embers back to life, and she felt her will sharpen in fury, holding her spirit in place.

Macarius looked aghast at the sight of her. Indeed, Halcyon hardly recognized her own body. It was gaunt and pale, as if she had become a wraith.

"Should we chain her to the chair, my lord?" one of the guards asked, uncertain.

"I told you to *weaken* her while I was away," the mage snapped. "Not kill her, you fools!"

"Apologies, my lord. We . . . we were uncertain of the dosage . . ."

"Chain her to the chair," Macarius ordered. "And then leave us. I will deal with the four of you later."

Halcyon stared unflinchingly at the mage, and he returned it as her thin arms and ankles were bolted. She realized how much Macarius feared her. That he would still have her bound when she was so weak.

"Beryl?" Macarius said, and his scribe shifted behind the desk. "Prepare to write."

Halcyon felt Beryl's stare. She met the scribe's gaze and saw a gleam of horror in Beryl's eyes, as if she could not believe Halcyon's state of health.

"Are you certain we should proceed, Macarius?" Beryl hesitated. "She does not look well."

"Are you questioning me?" Macarius hissed, glancing over his shoulder to pin her with a glare.

Beryl sat, chastened, and unrolled the scroll. She took up her quill, but she looked at Halcyon again, and there was doubt in the scribe's face.

Macarius moved to stand directly before Halcyon, and she prepared her mind, hammering her mental shields into place just as his fingers touched her brow and his magic began to sort through her memories. He searched and searched, but every time he grew near to the truth—anything that touched Xander and Straton and the location of Acantha's crown—he was deflected. And he knew it. He cursed at her, and he marveled at her, too, unable to hide it. That he had weakened her with poison, repeatedly, and yet he could not break her mind.

"What is this, Macarius?" a cold voice spoke into the room.

Macarius broke his magical hold on Halcyon, stumbling back. His brow was beaded with sweat, and he was trembling, exhausted, as he looked to the visitor.

"Lady Selene. I . . . I am very close to finding what you seek," the mage stammered, bowing to her. "I just need a little more time."

Halcyon did not turn her head. But she felt the commander's sister step deeper into the room, her presence withering the air like a trace of winter as she approached Halcyon. And then Selene moved into her blurry sight, and Halcyon had no choice but to meet her gaze.

Selene studied her. This was the first time the two of them had met, but they had certainly heard of each other. In private conversations, in pieces of gossip, in breath that was destined to sing them into legends. Selene, one of the strongest mages the kingdom had seen in centuries, and Halcyon, the humble warrior who had risen up and gained the elusive respect of the Bronze Legion's commander.

"I see you have almost killed her, Macarius," Selene said, and her voice was sharp with displeasure. "I thought I told you to take care with this one. My brother loves her as if she is his own daughter. And should he see her like this . . . well, it would spoil everything."

"Yes, Lady. I apologize once again. I was away, and left behind orders to poison her—"

"And why would you need to poison her?" Selene cut him off, as effortless as wind extinguishing a small flame. "Is her strength too great for you, even now?"

Macarius swallowed. Halcyon could see his throat bob. She relished his mortification. She almost smiled at him as his gaze darted from her to Selene.

"Lady . . . she is very resilient. I cannot break through her shielded memories. I did, however, procure the belt from the priest, as you wanted. The priest would not talk or reveal the location, either, so I have returned to Convict 8651 for the information."

Selene was quiet for a beat, and then she murmured, "Is the priest dead, then?"

Halcyon's pulse spiked. The room began to warp around her, and she struggled to control her breaths. *Bacchus.* They were speaking of Bacchus and his relic, Euthymius's Golden Belt. She realized now why Macarius had been absent; he had been at Dree, torturing Bacchus.

"He is dead. I took care to hire one of the local hands to do it, and he is here at the quarry now, for the time being. He and his followers will support us."

"Very good. Leave us," Selene said.

Macarius and Beryl retreated, quietly shutting the door behind them.

Selene drew up a chair and sat across from Halcyon. Her eyes were a vivid blue and just as keen as the commander's. Halcyon held the stare and waited, her breaths raspy.

"I remember the first time I heard my brother speak of you," Selene began, her voice pleasant. "It was two years ago, and I was sitting in one of Queen Nerine's advisory meetings. We were waiting for the queen to arrive, each of us conversing to pass the time. Straton was speaking to the land advisor, and he mentioned a hoplite who was unsurpassed in her speed and her prowess with spear and sword. A young woman who had come from the lowest of the low, and was destined to become a legend, who he would soon rank as captain when her eight years of training came to an end. 'Who is this hoplite, Straton?' the old land advisor asked. And my brother spoke your name, reverently, as if you held more magic than all of the mages at the Destry combined. 'Halcyon of Isaura.' And I never forgot your name, the way it rang in the air, like a blade leaving its scabbard. I knew it would return to me one day, and that you would either be a sword in my hand or a thorn in my side."

Halcyon was silent. But her chest was aching so vibrantly she worried that Selene's words would eventually crack her in two.

"I surmise you know which one you have become to me, Halcyon of Isaura," Selene whispered. "But it does not have to be like this. I acknowledge that you are a woman to be reckoned with, a woman who was created to challenge and champion. A woman who has been deceived by my brother. It angers me, to see what he has done to you."

"And what has he done to me?" Halcyon countered. "Lord Straton has granted me grace. He has given me life when I deserved death."

"This is grace to you, Daughter?"

"This work in the quarry does not intimidate me. I *do* deserve to be here, Lady Selene. With every crack I give to the quarry wall, I think of Xander and I strive to work off my sentence. But what I do not deserve is to be poisoned and mind-swept without my consent, to be treated less than because I am a woman among a horde of men."

Selene was quiet, but her eyes betrayed her frustration. "It is difficult for me to understand you, Halcyon, when it was my brother who sentenced you here. Are you so faithful to him, then? Is there nothing I can say to you to usher you into the light, to bring you under my care and my protection?"

"That would be an insult, Lady Selene, to the memory of your own nephew Xander. Nor would I ever join the side of one who tortures and murders innocent priests."

"Yes, all because my brother asked something terrible of you," Selene was swift to add, brushing over Halcyon's accusation. "I know Straton asked you and Xander to search for a relic. And since my brother is so lawful, I know he would never go after Nikomides's Devouring Sword. He would chase after something missing, something that could break an enchantment, would he not?" She leaned forward, her chiton rustling with her fluid movement. The silver on her right thumb caught the light, gleaming in the shadows of her lap. "He is going to lose this battle, Halcyon. And I would hate to see you destroyed by it. Come join me and my forces. You and I would be unbeatable with Acantha's All-Seeing Crown. Whatever relic you desire, I would find it and grant it to you. I would name you commander of the Bronze Legion, and you would be the sword in my hand. Together, we can raise Corisande higher than it has ever been before. We can return to the era of the gods, when the divines walked among us."

Halcyon did not even have to contemplate the offer. "Anything I obtain is to be earned. Not stolen or undeserved. And lest you forget, Selene . . . I am common. My family has suffered beneath your heavy taxes and the hateful rhetoric you have spread among the Magical Court. I will never join forces with you."

"One day," Selene began calmly, "you will look back on this moment and regret your decision. One day, you will find yourself beholden to another with an amulet on your arm, and you will work the fields and clean the gutters of the streets. You will hate your former self when you realize you could have been one of us, ruling the kingdom. But instead you will labor the rest of your poor, insignificant life. Although perhaps you will not mind it so much, since you were born as a land steward. The lowest, the dirtiest of your Common Court."

She stood and called for Macarius.

The young mage was swift to return. "Lady Selene?"

Her gaze remained on Halcyon, even as she spoke to him. "You will need to get creative in obtaining what I seek from this one. It is of the utmost importance that we obtain the crown before they do. Continue to poison her if you want, but do not kill her. Keep her imprisoned in her cell, out of sight. I want her alive when I take the throne. Use the memories you have gained from her to your advantage. If you succeed, I will name you my hand when our time comes."

Selene smiled down at Halcyon. And finally, the dread poured into Halcyon's heart, stunning her more that the poison ever had.

"Yes, of course, Lady Selene," Macarius said. "Any suggestions?"

Selene walked to the door, but she lingered on the threshold. "Perhaps you should resume your work at a different angle. My nephew Damon has just recently taken a scribe. I think you should target her. She will be easy to draw information from. Procure it however you want."

"And who is this scribe, Lady?"

"Evadne," Selene said before she vanished, leaving behind a trail of her perfume, and Halcyon was screaming as the realization tore through her. Her voice was fraying, and she coughed blood as she strained against her binds, as she bruised herself on the chains.

This time, when Macarius began to sweep through her mind, Halcyon could not guard everything. She could not shield the details of the mission and all of her memories of Evadne, and when Macarius's tentacles found one particular moment, bright and beloved and sweet, Halcyon knew he would take it and use it against her and her sister.

And Halcyon wept, her spirit breaking at last.

❖XIX❖

Evadne

"Charena," Damon said, handing a new scroll to Evadne. "This is how we shall make our way through the heart of Euthymius. With one of my sung enchantments."

Evadne accepted the scroll, unrolled it on her desk.

"What do you know of Mount Euthymius?" he asked, standing in his usual place on the opposite side of her desk, staring down at the blank papyrus she was about to mark. It was still night, and they were both weary and yet strangely invigorated, holding the secret of the mission between them like a second heartbeat.

"Well, I know Euthymius and Loris carved into the mountain by power of earth and water," Evadne said.

"Which means that no flame of Pyrrhus can burn in the mountain's passages. The fire would be extinguished as soon as it was lit within Euthymius." He set a small scroll down before Evadne, his fingers quickly unfurling it. It was a map of the mountain's inner passage, a descending drop that led to the door of the Underworld.

"Is this the map Bacchus drew for Halcyon and Xander?" Evadne asked, tracing its boundaries with her fingertips.

"Yes. Euthymius gave the knowledge to the priest, to then bestow to Xander and Halcyon," Damon said. "This is why our siblings were training to fight in the dark, because they would not have the ability to carry fire into the mountain."

Evadne remembered her sister's terrible confession: *Xander had yielded, but I did not . . . see it. I was already in motion, and my sword caught him in the throat.*

She pushed the memory aside, focusing on the map. "This looks like a cistern . . ."

"It is," Damon said. "And there are three levels. The water begins ankle deep. It flows to the west, where a staircase is carved in the midst of a waterfall, to lead down to the next level. It is a steep drop. Finding the stairs will be difficult, but I believe we can avoid the draw of the falls." He pointed at the first waterfall and the stone staircase that divided it. Evadne's eagerness dwindled as she tried to imagine them navigating it without slipping or drowning or falling to their deaths.

"The next level will be more arduous," Damon continued, moving his finger to mark the path. "The water rises to the knee, and again, its currents will pull to the west, to yet another staircase and waterfall. These stairs will lead to the lowest level of the mountain. The water will be deep, and it will hold no current. We will have to swim to where the door to the Underworld resides, and there will be stairs that rise up from the water, leading to its threshold. The crown is hanging on the door. Above all, Bacchus warned, we must not open the door and release Pyrrhus, no matter how much the god might pound or beseech us."

"And what of the immortal mage, Ivina?" Evadne asked.

Damon was silent for a moment. "She presents a threat. I have no doubt she will try to impede us. Xander and Halcyon were preparing for a battle with phantoms in the dark."

"I am not sword trained, Damon."

"And neither am I," he said. "We will still carry swords, to ease my father's mind, but our greatest defense will be my enchantment. Ivina's phantoms cannot withstand fire. Keeping them at bay will be paramount to our success."

Evadne took up her quill, twirled it in her fingers as she pondered on what he had just spoken. "You will cast enchanted fire, then?"

"Yes."

"That sounds simple enough."

His eyes flashed. "It would be simple for a mage of great power. To cast fire, or light at all, is a very demanding spell. Compare it to common fire: it needs kindling and breath and constant nourishment or it will burn out."

Humbled, Evadne fell quiet. She realized that she truly knew nothing of magic.

"I am not powerful," said Damon. "But nor am I weak. I am an average mage."

His words resonated within her. Because that was how she thought of herself. Not powerful, not weak. Somewhere in between the two.

"Much to my father's dismay," Damon said with a sad smile,

"I am not as strong as someone like my aunt. I can only cast an enchantment for so long, and there are many factors that influence the depth and length of my enchantments. How tired I am, for example. If I am sick. If I am hungry or thirsty. Casting fire will be difficult for me. That is why . . . I must ask you to sing the enchantment with me, Evadne."

Surprise flickered across her face. It was the last thing she'd expected him to say, and she tried to imagine what it would be like to sing a spell with him. She could not envision it, but nor could she imagine moving through the water and terror that was the heart of Mount Euthymius to claim a divine relic.

"It will be an enchantment composed of six verses," Damon said. "I can deepen my magical well by letting my voice carry the brunt of the magic. So we must sing the stanzas in order, and then repeat them, over and over until we are safely out of the mountain."

"Is this common?" Evadne asked. "Is it expected for a scribe to sing with their mage?"

Damon nodded. His eyes were bloodshot, his hair tangled. He seemed exhausted until he looked at her, and something stirred in him. "It is. Scribes record our enchantments, but they also learn them, so they can sing with us when we cast the more arduous spells. It will be like singing into the wind, like swimming upstream. I will grow weary and forgetful, and I will need you to guide me when my memory begins to slip." He paused, the gravel in his voice softening when he continued to speak. "If I had been a more powerful mage, I could have gone on my own. Casting fire would be easier if I had a deeper well. But I do not."

Evadne was pensive, surprised by how eager she was to sing his magic. He mistook her silence for unwillingness.

"Have you changed your mind, Evadne? You do not have to go into Euthymius with me if you do not want to."

She stared at the map, its challenges and falls and water. She thought of Halcyon and Xander. She remembered how Straton did not think Evadne was capable of such a daunting mission.

"I have not changed my mind."

Damon tried to hide his relief, but it still shone in his eyes as he turned away, pacing the chamber. "I think we can perfect the spell in two days. And then we should prepare to go to the mountain. But for now . . . you and I both need sleep. It will do us no good to weary ourselves before Euthymius. Return to me in the morning, when you feel rested."

The night was deep beyond the windows, although Evadne had no inkling as to what hour it was. The curtains drifted with the breeze, and the villa was silent, slumbering.

She rose, her neck and back sore from sitting. She reached the door and was one breath from leaving Damon for the night when she paused and glanced back at him, watching as he continued to restlessly pace.

"You never asked if I am an acceptable singer," she said.

Damon stopped to look at her. "It would not matter."

"Really? You would be fine if I sound like an off-tune kithara while singing your enchantments?"

"*Do* you sound like an off-tune kithara?"

Evadne smiled and stepped into the corridor shadows. "I suppose you will find out soon enough. Good night, Damon."

Toula intercepted her the next morning. Evadne was on the stairs, heading to Damon's chambers, when the older woman motioned for her to halt.

"Here," Toula said gruffly. "This is for you."

Evadne's brows arched when she saw it was a letter, folded and sealed. Her first thought was that it was from her parents. But then she noticed the seal and the handwriting. Both were unfamiliar.

She accepted the papyrus from Toula and ascended the stairs, waiting until she was out of sight from the servant's keen eyes before she opened the letter.

The message was sparse:

Evadne—Meet me at the Gilded Owl this afternoon. Come whenever it is most convenient for you.

There was no signature. Only the stamp of a winding basilisk in the bottom right corner.

Evadne had seen this mark before. She remembered the strange message she had found in the commander's satchel her first night as a servant.

Who was this person, and what did they want with her? How did they know her name? Why did they desire to meet with her?

A tremble went through her as she tucked the letter into her belt. She did not have time to dwell on it, to wonder if she should meet this enigma, and she found Damon sitting at the desk, writing painstakingly in a scroll with his right hand. He startled at the sight of her, as if she had caught him doing something criminal.

"Have I come too early?" she asked.

"No, no," Damon said, but he sounded flustered. He uttered a charm to dry his ink, which sat crooked and miserable on the papyrus, hardly legible. And then he rolled the scroll up before Evadne could make out a single word he had scrawled. The scroll handles were gilded, and they caught the sunlight, as if they had just swallowed a secret.

"Here, sit, Evadne." Damon rushed to stand. He smeared ink on his face as he gathered the gilded scroll in his arms, bearing it into his bedchamber.

Evadne tried to douse her curiosity as she sat, the chair still holding his warmth. It was apparent he had been working for a long while, she thought as she rearranged her desk the way she was coming to prefer it, opening the *charena* scroll.

Damon returned to her. He was still wearing yesterday's clothes, and he looked tired as he arrived to stand on the other side of the desk.

"Did you sleep at all?" she asked, concerned.

"Hmm? Yes. A few hours," he said, preoccupied. He drew his hand through his hair and sighed. "Shall we begin?"

Evadne opened a pot of ink and prepared to write. Damon began to pace, seemingly aimless, but she knew he was sorting words and thoughts, preparing to speak his enchantment into existence.

He finally came to a stop before his window. She watched from beneath her lashes as he raised his hand to a ray of sun, as he studied the way the light illuminated his fingers.

"A Song of Firelight," he said, and Evadne wrote everything that spilled from his mouth, capturing the random words and pressing them into the papyrus. He was trying to describe the essence of fire, as if he had never encountered it before.

He began to pace, still seeking the right words, the right bones to build his enchantment, and eventually he came to a stop before Evadne.

He ceased speaking; she looked up at him. Damon was watching the way the sunlight touched her hair, the golden pins at her shoulders. At last, his eyes dropped down to the parchment, where her handwriting was drying.

"Scratch all of that," he said, with a growl of dissatisfaction, and he began to pace again.

Evadne wanted to argue, but she did as he wanted, drawing a line through them.

She soon realized that Damon was not easily satisfied. Word after word, phrase after phrase, he spoke and then told her to scratch, as if nothing was good enough, and she began to worry that they would not have the enchantment ready in two days, as he hoped.

By the time the light aged into afternoon, Damon had perfected the first half of the song, with three more stanzas remaining to create. Evadne's last quill finally snapped, and she thought it must be providence, because she was hungry and weary.

"That was my last quill," she announced, groaning as she stood. "I suppose I should go to the Gilded Owl to purchase another bundle? And we should probably eat something."

Damon collapsed in his chair and leaned his head back. Arcalos was not in his room today; Evadne wondered where the dog was, shocked by how much she missed his sleeping presence.

"Yes," Damon murmured, closing his eyes. "Let me accompany you, though. I do not want you to go alone."

"No, you should stay here and rest," she insisted, thinking of her mysterious appointment. "I remember where the Gilded Owl is. I will return soon."

"You can put the quills on my tab," Damon said, his words smudging together in exhaustion. "And go ahead and purchase another pot or two of ink."

She departed quietly and was almost to the stairs when she heard Straton and Cosima speaking as she passed their cracked door.

"I want you to be very careful, Cosima," Straton said, low and urgent. "Do not drink the wine until the cupbearer has tasted it. Keep your antidotes with you at all times. Make sure Lyra is also aware of this, that she does not drink anything outside this villa."

"You do not think . . ."

"I do. It is happening again. The land advisor has fallen ill. It will not be long before Selene has ravaged the entire inner circle."

"Must you go so soon, Straton?" Cosima pleaded. "What is in Abacus that is more important than your family?"

"I have responsibilities," the commander said. "I must return to the legion. I told you such a week ago that I would need to leave today. My warriors are waiting for me."

"Your legion can wait. Please, Straton. Please stay another week with us."

Evadne hurried down the stairs, her heart beating in her throat. She did not know why it bothered her, why she felt an echo of Cosima's pain. But it reminded Evadne of the day Halcyon had left for the legion.

She was anxious as she passed through the villa's gates, storm clouds beginning to blow in from the west. The streets soon cooled in the shade, and Evadne walked the way Damon had taken her the day before. Was she a fool to answer the letter's summoning? Part of her believed she was. But she could not stem her curiosity, her hope that maybe this person would be willing to help Halcyon.

Evadne was almost to the eastern market when she felt a prickling sensation on the back of her neck, as if someone was following her.

She slowed her pace and studied the street—the Basilisk could be anyone, she thought—but no one took note of her. Evadne continued on her way until the warning shivered through her again. And she remembered how once she and Damon had gone unseen.

A mage was trailing her, invisible. She was almost certain of it.

The rain arrived and Evadne took shelter beneath the same canopy she and Damon had shared a meal. She watched as the merchants and vendors hastened to close up their market stalls; she watched the way the rain hit the paved stones, hissing with steam, and she noticed there was a small circle of street that was shielded.

The mage was standing there, a stone's throw away, watching her.

She acted as if she had not noticed, darting across the market to where the Gilded Owl sat on a street corner, the door nearly covered up in ivy.

Inside, the shop was quiet. Evadne was overcome with the sight of all the papyri and scrolls, and pot after pot of quills. Crow quills, goose quills, swan quills. And the different-colored inks sitting within glass jars! They ranged from madder red to lapis lazuli blue. One ink was even a shimmering gold; she wondered if it was the captured ichor of a divine. By its enormous price, she imagined it could certainly be.

"May I help you?"

Evadne turned to see the shopkeeper standing behind a table, white frizzled hair sitting on his head like a cloud, his eyes gentle as he regarded her.

"Yes, I am Damon of Mithra's scribe, and I am here to purchase a bundle of quills," she said, stepping closer to his table.

"Damon is one of my finest customers. I take it you are right-handed, by the ink on your fingers?"

Evadne nodded.

"Come and choose which quill will suit you the best. I have all kinds of right-handed ones," the shopkeeper said, setting out his quills for Evadne to evaluate.

She was brushing her fingertips over the swan quills, the

shopkeeper telling her all about where these feathers had come from and how he had cut their nibs, when she heard the door open and close. She did not breathe as she listened to soggy footsteps draw close to her, knowing they were the ones that had stalked her in the streets, and she kept her gaze on the shopkeeper, watching as he lifted his eyes expectantly, as they dimmed when he beheld his second guest.

"Ah, Macarius," the shopkeeper greeted in a flat tone. "It has been a while since I have seen you here."

Macarius.

Evadne recognized his sinister presence. The mage who had stolen from her and her parents with one of his sung enchantments. And he had the audacity to stand at her side, far closer than she wanted, his sleeve brushing her arm.

He was the mysterious stamped basilisk? Her heart fell with anger, disappointment.

"Hello, Sophus," Macarius said in that polished voice that made Evadne grit her teeth. He looked at her and feigned surprise. "Evadne? I almost did not recognize you in those fine clothes!"

Evadne frowned, as if she had never seen him before, and said, "I do not think we have met. Who are you?"

Macarius's confidence wavered. "Of course. It was a dark night when your father was kind enough to share his fire with me."

"Oh. Yes, I remember you now. And my parents were gracious enough to feed you for days, weren't they?" Evadne said sharply and then looked to Sophus, who was regarding her and Macarius with wariness, as if their stilted exchange made him nervous. "I think I will take this bundle of quills, Sophus. And I would love to have a pot of black ink."

Sophus nodded, shuffling to the far shelf.

Macarius waited to speak until the shopkeeper was out of earshot. "I trust Damon has been treating you well?"

Evadne refused to meet his gaze, focusing her attention on the quills. "I never told you I was Damon's scribe."

"It is public knowledge now," he drawled. "I thought you knew such. The contract is posted in the Destry."

She elected to ignore him. But Macarius, strangely, seemed intent on capturing her attention. "Evadne, Evadne. You are angry at me. Why?"

"Are you such a conceited fool that you must ask?" she hissed at him, her cheeks flushing in fury.

"I must say you are beautiful when you are angry."

"You have no right to speak to me in such a way. As a matter of fact, I do not want to speak to you at all." She took her quills and met Sophus on the other side of the store, thanking him for his assistance. He gave her an oiled leather pouch to carry her purchases in, and Evadne dashed out of the shop into the storm.

She was halfway across the abandoned market when Macarius's voice chased after her, nearly desperate.

"Wait, Evadne! Contrary to what you may believe, you will want to hear the news I bear."

"No, I do not think so," Evadne shouted back at him, walking as quickly as her ankle would allow.

"But I have news of your sister. Of Halcyon."

That brought Evadne upright. She halted, torn. Wasn't this the very thing she was secretly hoping for? That the stamped basilisk would be able to help with Halcyon's current situation? "How do you have news?"

"Come, let us get out of the rain and share a meal at this corner tavern, and I will tell you everything you wish to know." Macarius now stood before her, his flaxen hair dripping rain, his hand outstretched, waiting for her to agree.

It was the last thing she desired. To sit in a tavern with him and share a meal.

But Evadne followed him into the corner building. It felt like a prelude to betrayal, and she hoped word of this would not trickle back to Damon.

The other patrons were reclining, sipping wine and listening to a musician play a seductive melody on her flute. They were dressed in fine garments, their hair perfumed, chased gold on their wrists. Evadne had never felt more out of place in her life as she reluctantly sat across from Macarius in a shadowy nook.

She watched him pull the curtain closed, granting them privacy. Again, that sense of unease swarmed her, and Evadne glared at him.

"What is this news? How have you come by it?"

"Patience, love," Macarius murmured with a smile. "Have a drink first, to soften that edge in your voice." The alcove curtain parted, and a servant girl brought a pitcher of white wine and two golden cups. Macarius waited until she had retreated, and then he poured a cup for him and one for Evadne.

"I do not want anything to drink," she said, terse.

"Suit yourself." Macarius reclined on his cushion, his eyes on Evadne. She was still drenched and disheveled, and his gaze lingered a beat too long on her wet raiment, where the linen clung to her skin. "How do you like it? Being a scribe, that is."

"I am not here to converse about scribing, Macarius. If you do not speak news of my sister in the next few moments, I am going to leave."

He sipped his wine, unhurried. But she could tell her bluntness was irritating him.

"I do not understand the rush, Evadne. Is Damon strict on your errand time?"

She made to leave, and Macarius sat forward.

"Very well. Sit down and I will tell you everything I know."

Evadne stared at him, her dislike for him evident in the crinkling of her nose. But she sat back down on her cushion and waited.

"I spoke with Halcyon," Macarius said, swirling the wine in his cup.

"When? Where?" Evadne sounded desperate. She struggled to rein in her emotion, knowing Macarius would only use it against her.

"At the common quarry."

"How? You are a mage. You are not allowed there."

"I was granted entrance the other night by the quarry lord," Macarius said. "There is a former mage among the convicts, and he was causing some trouble, planning to escape. I was invited into the quarry to speak sense back into him. Turns out he has convinced your sister to escape the quarry with him."

Former mage? Did that mean a mage could lose their magic? Evadne had never heard of this, but her curiosity was overshadowed by her dread. "Escape?"

"Yes. And while in any other case, I would be against it . . . I am not this time."

"Why?"

"Because your sister is very sick. I do not think she will survive another moon in that quarry."

Evadne was trembling. She laced her fingers together, trying to hide it. "What is she sick with?"

"She has quarry lung. Some of the convicts procure it from breathing in so much dust. It is almost always fatal."

"What did she say to you, then?"

"She asked me to help her and her friend escape the quarry. I have agreed to do it, but I will need your assistance, Evadne."

Anything, Evadne nearly said. But she caught the word on the tip of her tongue. Her thoughts unspooled. Why would Macarius, who had brought her only harm, want to help her now?

"I do not believe you," she said.

Macarius blinked. "You do not believe me? Although I should not find this surprising—Halcyon did say you would doubt me. So here. This is my proof, since you are slow to trust." He reached into his chiton and procured a fold of papyrus. Evadne watched, impassive, as he set it down on the table between them. When she made no movement to retrieve it, Macarius whispered, "Go on,

Evadne. You will want to know what it says."

She took the papyrus in her hands and let it unfold.

She recognized the inked symbols as if she were looking at a reflection of herself. Her heart leapt, her blood sang, and she nearly cried as she read the Haleva message:

Evadne, my prayers follow you, little sister. I hope you are well. I have fallen ill at the quarry—I do not think I will survive much longer here, but Macarius has agreed to help me escape. Please, Sister. Help me escape this place.

Evadne read it twice, her eyes blurring with tears. She felt speared, imagining Halcyon's distress. She folded the papyrus and tucked it into her leather pouch.

"What is your plan?" she whispered, and Macarius drained his wine, as if revitalized by her interest.

"I cannot speak of it yet. There are still parts I need to coordinate. But meet me here again at midnight. I will be ready for you then, as will Halcyon. Do not be late, Evadne."

He departed, so hastily that Evadne was momentarily stunned. She continued to sit, staring at the wine pitcher, her world seeming to crack beneath her.

Until her mind cleared and she realized something. Slowly, she retrieved Halcyon's Haleva message. She read it again carefully, scrutinizing the symbols. Ones that she and Halcyon had carefully chosen and memorized.

Evadne knew her older sister's handwriting well, almost as intimately as her own. She had traced Halcyon's letters, over and over, when she had been learning to read and write.

This was not Halcyon's handwriting.

One of the Haleva symbols was crooked. The sparrow wing. It was drawn in the wrong direction.

Halcyon had not written this message.

But someone had. Someone who would have had to sift through her memories to know it.

Evadne lurched up from the table, stuffing the parchment into her leather pouch. The rain had passed, the sun had broken through the storm, and the streets were steaming like a bath. Evadne rushed back to the commander's villa.

She saw Straton's horse, tacked and ready, waiting for him before the colonnade. He was about to leave Mithra, she recalled, to return to Abacus, and for some reason that filled her with alarm.

It galled her that the one man she had vowed to despise was now the one she needed to beseech for help. She did not want to trust him, but she had a greater enemy now.

She nearly collided with the commander on the great threshold, decked in his armor, his helm in the crook of his arm. He looked down at her, a frown creasing his brow, and he was about to speak, but Evadne's voice overshadowed his.

"My lord, I must speak with you. Now, before you depart."

Straton sighed. "I do not have time, Evadne. I am late as it is." And he moved to step around her.

"Lord Straton," she implored. *"Please."*

He continued on his way, descending the stairs, splashing through the puddles.

"Commander, this is about my sister," Evadne said, and she noticed how he slowed. "I believe she is in peril."

Straton halted halfway down the stairs and turned to look up at her.

"What do you mean?"

"I cannot say it to you here, Lord."

He hesitated, glancing to where his horse waited. But then he looked at Evadne and ascended the stairs, motioning for her to follow him up to the privacy of his office.

"Sit, Evadne," he said, pouring her a cup of barley water. "You do not look well."

She sat in a chair before his desk, feeling her pulse in her ears. She accepted the water and drained it as Straton leaned on the edge of his desk, watching her.

"Now, then," he said. "What is this peril you speak of?"

She was shaking when she procured the cipher. It took her a moment to spread the wrinkles from the papyrus, to find her voice, but she told Straton the history of Haleva, of how Macarius had stalked her and invited her into a tavern booth. Of the message and the handwriting and the crooked wing.

"You claim Halcyon did not write this?" the commander said, taking the papyrus when she offered it.

"No, she did not. I know it."

Straton met Evadne's gaze. "Then who did?"

"The mage. Macarius."

"But he is forbidden from the common quarry, Evadne."

"He has been there, Lord. And he has mind-swept my sister."

Straton's face was calm. But his eyes blazed. She saw the fear and the fury within him.

"I know of the mission, Lord," she whispered, and flinched when he looked at her. "Damon told me. And I swear that I will go with him and recover Acantha's crown for you. I will finish what Halcyon began, if you will only go to the quarry and ensure my sister is well, that she is not dying as I fear she might be."

Straton was silent. But he handed the Haleva message back to her and stood, his eyes continuing to smolder.

"Do not worry about your sister," he finally said. "I will go to the quarry now and ensure she is hale."

He did not fully believe her, she thought. But it did not matter. Because he was a man of his word, and if he said he would go and check on Halcyon, she knew he would.

Evadne rose and bowed to him, clutching the papyrus to her heart.

The commander left her in his office. She listened to his footsteps until they faded away, and Evadne moved to the windows, parting the linen curtains.

She watched him ride away to the west, where the quarry lay. And only then did Evadne finally let herself melt to her knees, to silently weep into the crook of her arm.

⇢XX⇠

Evadne and Halcyon

Half an hour later, Evadne sat at her desk in Damon's chambers, rain-damp hair wound back in a braid, tears washed from her face, her body draped in a clean chiton and shawl. The *charena* scroll was open before her, a new quill in her fingers, and she watched Damon pace the floor, in and out of the waning light. She thought of Halcyon, trying not to worry. The commander would be with her now, and for once, that reassured Evadne. Macarius would not dare harm her sister with Straton present.

She had not told Damon about the meeting with Macarius, about the Haleva message. And yet he sensed something was wrong.

"Are you sure you feel well enough to scribe, Evadne?" he asked. "We can always return to the task tomorrow."

"I am fine." She dipped her quill into the ink to express her resolve. "We do not have much time left."

"I know how I want the rest of the song to sound," Damon said. "It is not to be an enchantment of *fire* as I originally thought, but a chorus of *stars*. The last three stanzas should come swiftly now."

Evadne remained poised over the scroll, ready, eager.

Damon began to speak again, words and fragments and phrases. It seemed like he called them down from the sky, and Evadne hurried to keep up with him. He spoke quickly, and then just as quickly did he scratch his previous ramblings, but not as much as before. Evadne could see his words building as a storm, as a mountain, something for their voices to climb.

The final stanza came together effortlessly, as if all the dangling threads of before, which had seemed to hold no purpose, found their place, weaving together. Evadne felt nearly drunk by the beauty of it, her hand aching as she inked his last words.

She set down her quill, leaned back in her chair. The song for Mount Euthymius was complete, sitting before her on papyrus, drying in the light.

Damon stood across from her, staring down at her writing, just as mesmerized.

"What now?" she asked.

He met her gaze, a mischievous gleam in his eyes. "Now, we sing."

"Has she eaten anything?"

"No, Lord."

"Has she woken or said anything today?"

"No, Lord."

A pause. Halcyon kept her eyes closed as she lay on her cot, shivering and feverish, but she could feel Macarius's gaze on her as he stood at the door of her prison cell, regarding her.

"Halcyon?" he called to her, impatient. "Halcyon, look at me."

She refused. Her breaths were coming slower, slower, and her pain was unbearable now. Body, mind, spirit. All broken.

She wanted to die.

"Halcyon, you are going to have a visitor tonight," the mage continued. "Get up and eat your gruel. It is not poisoned anymore."

Still, she did not move, did not open her eyes. All she could do was breathe and burn and listen to her heart beat in her ears, a sad chorus that was about to reach its end.

"If she does not eat within the next hour," Macarius said to the guard, "I want you to force-feed her. And make sure she drinks a cup of water."

"Yes, my lord."

It grew quiet. Halcyon seemed to float in a landscape of red earth, red sea, until the guard entered her cell to force cold gruel into her mouth. There was only one of them now; four guards were no longer needed to hold her down.

When he left her, she retched the food up.

She lay on her belly again, cheek pressed against the hard slope of her cot, and waited for death.

"Halcyon."

The voice was poignant, familiar. She did not think death

would sound like that, but then he spoke again, urgently.

"Halcyon."

She opened her eyes; the world was dim, blurry, until she saw Straton standing on the other side of her prison door, illumined by a torch he held.

I am dreaming, she thought and closed her eyes again.

"Unlock this door," the commander ordered.

"My lord, I cannot do that," the guard replied.

"Unlock this door. Now."

A frantic jangle of keys. The iron door squeaked open.

Halcyon could see the torchlight through her eyelids. She felt a stirring of air, and then a large hand—wondrously cold against her skin—cupped her shaven head.

"Halcyon, what has happened? Who has done this to you?"

She struggled to open her eyes, to look at the commander. He was kneeling beside her cot; tears were in his eyes.

"I have never seen you cry," she said, her voice nothing more than a wisp.

"Sit up, Kingfisher."

She made no effort to move.

"Sit up," he ordered gently. "There is strength within you. Find it, Halcyon."

"I cannot, Commander."

He paused. She closed her eyes again, unable to keep them open, to look at his tears.

"You have never said such to me before," he said. "Why have you given up?"

"I am dying."

"No. I will not allow it."

She almost smiled. "Why, Lord, do you care if I live?"

He was quiet. His voice trembled when he finally spoke. "Because I love you as if you are my daughter. The world would darken without you. Sit up, Halcyon. Do not go out like this."

She did not move.

But he did. He stood and gathered her into his arms, holding her as he sat on the edge of her cot, and a sound escaped him when he finally felt how frail she was.

Once, long ago, when she was a girl who had not joined the legion yet, she had yearned to be held by her father as he had held Evadne. Gregor had cradled Evadne on his lap every evening after dinner, as if she were part of his heart. And how Halcyon had wanted that, too. She would have given anything to be her youngest sister—the adored daughter.

And now she was finally being held by the father of her soul, the man who had loved her in his own quiet, steel-sharpened way. Who had taught her everything he knew, who understood her, who had trusted her. A small part of her wanted to be mortified that she was being held at her very worst: bloodstained and filthy and reeking of vomit. But she was too exhausted to care anymore.

Her head lolled until he supported it on his breast, the scales of his armor biting into her cheek. His voice echoed when he ordered the guard to bring him fresh water.

"Do not drink it," she whispered, spending the last of her strength on her voice. "It is poisoned."

She began to drift into the red landscape, and the commander felt it.

"You are burning," he said, touching her brow. "Stay with me, Halcyon. Open your eyes."

But for once, she did not have the will to follow his command.

Evadne stood beside Damon, and they each held one end of the scroll as they read and sang in unison. At first, it was just their voices, cautiously melding, seeking balance with each other. Evadne could hardly remember the last time she had sung; it had been in Isaura, with her father, weeks ago. In another life entirely.

Her voice was a whisper, uncertain. But with every word she sang, the stronger and bolder she became, until she was filling her lungs with night air, setting her voice free.

And that was when it finally happened.

The first enchanted fire bloomed to life. A star hung, suspended between her and Damon, aligned with their shoulders, radiant.

She knew it was not her voice that had inspired it. But for a moment, she imagined that she alone had cast an enchantment.

They were singing the second stanza now. And another star bloomed, and then another. The constellations gathered about them, bright and glorious, and Evadne felt as if she were walking in the night sky.

She did not sing for Damon, or for the mountain, or for Acantha's crown.

She sang for Halcyon.

Halcyon would have remained beneath the surface of her ocean. She planned to wait for the end to come. She would go quietly, which struck her as a surprise. Never did she imagine this was how she would slip from the world, her lungs filling with water, breath by breath.

Which divine would come and greet her on death's threshold?

She heard a voice she did not recognize. She felt cold hands on her face, slender and gentle, like her mother's.

Mother, Halcyon wanted to cry out, to reach for her. But her arms were heavy as iron. She could not find them, or her voice. *Lost*, she thought. *I am lost. I do not know the way back.*

"Hold her steady, Straton," the motherly voice said. "She must drink all of this."

Halcyon felt those cold fingers open her teeth, and she wanted to fight them. No more; she wanted no more. And yet the liquid was soothing and sweet, and it coated her mouth like oil, the oil from home, and Halcyon helplessly swallowed it all.

She saw stars gathering above the water. They beckoned to her, and she did not know where they had come from or how they had found her, but when Halcyon finally opened her eyes, she had broken the surface, and she was breathing. She knew who had guided her back into the world.

Evadne.

Evadne felt Damon glance at her, his voice slowing, as if he was beginning to forget the words of his own song. Perspiration gleamed on his brow; she noticed how his hands were trembling, betraying his exhaustion.

It will be like singing into the wind, like swimming upstream.

That is how he had described it. To sing a difficult spell.

He fell quiet, his tongue snared. But Evadne continued to sing his enchantment, the stars slowly dimming without the magic in Damon's voice. She sang and Damon eventually rejoined her, drawing strength and guidance from her. The fire flared again, and more constellations winked into existence.

A drop of blood fell upon the scroll.

It took a breath for Evadne to realize it was Damon's blood, dripping from his nose.

She stopped singing just before Damon went silent, easing himself to the floor, his half of the scroll tumbling from his hand. She caught it, sank to her knees before him. He looked dazed until Evadne tentatively reached out to him, pressing the edge of her shawl to his nose to stem the blood.

She did not want to feel anything for him. And yet she did. She was concerned, anxious for him the longer his blood soaked her shawl. She blamed it on the circumstances surrounding them both—secrets and loss and uncertainty. But Evadne knew that despite it all, she was changing. She noticed every time Damon looked at her; she noticed the grace in his hands. She liked the sound of his voice. She found pleasure in singing with him.

She was grappling with how she saw him: a mage, a partner, a friend. The son of the man she despised.

They remained on the floor a while, until all but one of the magical stars had extinguished, and Damon's nose had ceased its bleeding.

"Sorry," Damon whispered to her as she lowered her shawl.

"What for?"

"That I am so weak. I . . . did not expect the spell to make me bleed so soon."

Evadne was quiet as she regarded him. It had surprised her, too, and also made her apprehensive. What if he bled the entire time in the mountain's heart? What if he could not make it all the way to the door and back? But she watched the final star fade away, and she yearned for it to return. To sing with him again.

"You are not weak. There is steel within you," she whispered, remembering how Halcyon had once spoken those very words to her. How they had sustained her.

"That sounds like something my father would say," he said.

"Yes, well, my sister did say it to me."

"Then he probably once said it to her."

"Probably."

Evadne stood and held her hand out to him.

He stared at her a moment, and then he smiled, a warm smile that reached his eyes, and she thought he looked much younger, much softer.

"Off-tune kithara, indeed," he mused in a wry tone, slipping his hand into hers.

She drew him up. And by the way his fingers were reluctant to release hers, Evadne knew that her voice had been far more than he had ever imagined it to be.

→XXI←

Halcyon and Evadne

A woman sat in Halcyon's cell. It was not her mother or Evadne, and Halcyon slowly recognized her, surprised. She had seen her only one other time, at her trial. It was Cosima. The commander's wife.

Xander's mother.

The moment Cosima saw Halcyon awaken, she stood and drew closer, to kneel beside her cot. Cosima said nothing at first, hesitantly touching Halcyon's brow.

"Your fever has broken," she said, still avoiding eye contact. "I have another brew for you, one that will help flush the remaining poison from your body."

Halcyon watched as Cosima searched through a leather satchel on the floor. She sorted through small jars of herbs, a few pots of salves, rolls of linen bandages, and a flask of clean water, swiftly working to mix the brew together in a clay bowl. She poured it into a small wooden cup, the herbal remedy refreshing the stale air of the cell.

"Can you sit?" she asked, and when Halcyon struggled to push herself up, Cosima helped her.

The world spun for a moment, but Halcyon's eyes began to focus, and while she still felt hollow and weak, she sensed a trickle of her strength returning. Cosima held the cup to her lips, and Halcyon drank.

The healer seemed reluctant to look at her. It reminded Halcyon of her transgressions, and she suddenly could not swallow anymore. She sputtered and turned her head away, but Cosima waited, determined and patient.

"You need to drink all of this, Halcyon."

Halcyon was silent, listening to the ragged edge of her breaths. And then she whispered, "Why are you helping me?"

Cosima shifted, pulling her stool closer, and she sat with the cup in her lap, directly before Halcyon.

"Because Xander loved you," she said. "I imagine he is dwelling in the villa of the clouds, watching and fervently hoping you will choose to live. Drink the rest of this, for him."

The sound of his name released the tension between them, and Halcyon met Cosima's gaze. She did not find anger or resentment within the healer's eyes, as she expected. There was a gleam of sadness, of hope.

Straton must have told her the truth of Halcyon and Xander's doomed mission, of Halcyon's blindfolded error for which she would never be able to forgive herself.

She consented to drink the rest of the brew, and Cosima helped her lie down again, so she could redress the wounds on Halcyon's back.

"Do you know who has been poisoning you?"

"Yes," Halcyon replied. "The mage Macarius of Galenos."

"Did he do anything else to you, Halcyon?"

Halcyon hesitated. She hated how shame crept upon her, how her throat narrowed. "He mind-swept me. Two different times. I . . . I did my best to shield certain memories, but I might have betrayed a few important pieces of information. The priest Bacchus . . . Macarius saw Bacchus in my mind and has since killed him and taken the Golden Belt."

"It is not your fault, Halcyon. Macarius has committed a grave crime against you." Cosima spread a cooling salve on Halcyon's back. "We can find no trace of him anywhere, but do not despair; we will catch him."

Halcyon was not surprised Macarius had fled. Of course, could she fault him, when she herself had fled in fear? Her hopelessness unfurled as Cosima had her sit up again, to wrap fresh linen bandages about her. Halcyon tried to remember the day before—or had it been two days?—and her memory felt foggy. "Was . . . was Lord Straton here? Or did I imagine it?"

"He was here. When he saw how ill you were, he sent for me." Again, there was a flicker of sorrow within the healer.

"How did he know to come?"

"Your sister asked him to. She sensed you were in trouble."

Halcyon marveled. She wanted to see Evadne, so fiercely she

could feel her pulse in her ears.

"My husband has returned to Abacus," Cosima said. "But he is meeting with the archon to submit a request for you to be brought to the infirmary for a few weeks, so you can fully heal beneath my care. Evadne can visit you then."

Halcyon was stunned. Tears burned her eyes; she struggled to hide them as Cosima helped her change into a fresh tunic.

"Straton did not want me to leave you here unattended." She stood and began to clean up her herbs and the soiled linens. "But I must take a moment of reprieve. My daughter, Lyra, will be coming to replace me for a while. She is going to bring you some broth, and I would like for you to drink all of it. I would also like for you to keep drinking this water throughout the day." She set a flask beside Halcyon's cot and slipped her satchel over her arm, preparing to leave. But she paused and dropped her voice so low Halcyon almost did not hear her. "Straton also left a gift for you beneath your blanket. He said you would know what to do should you see your poisoner again."

Halcyon's mind whirled, but she nodded. "Thank you, Lady. I am in your debt."

"There are no debts here, Halcyon of Isaura. I will return soon."

Halcyon watched her leave, her cell door closing and locking in her wake. But the guard no longer leered at Halcyon. He seemed fearful, and Halcyon could only surmise it was a lingering result of Straton's presence.

She looked to the blanket Cosima had referenced, soft and clean from the infirmary, folded at the foot of her cot. With a trembling hand, she reached beneath it and found the gift.

She unsheathed the small scythe, her heart swelling as she recognized it. A blade she had often seen but had never held. No one had ever held it but him.

Straton's kopis.

Evadne woke with a start. Her cheek was numb, and she was drooling on the *charena* scroll. She eased herself up, rubbing the crick in her neck. She had fallen asleep at her desk, in Damon's chambers. And there he was, slumbering in his chair, morning light spangled across his face.

Slowly, she remembered.

They had sung most of the night, over and over, until the Song of Stars had settled into both of their memories, until they had grown bone weary. Eventually, they had both needed a moment to rest—Evadne had sat at her desk and Damon his chair—and they must have drifted into sleep.

The door creaked.

Evadne glanced to the threshold to find Damon's mother entering the chamber. Cosima did not seem surprised to find Evadne there. In fact, it seemed the lady was looking for Evadne, not Damon, and Evadne struggled to rise.

"You do not need to stand," Cosima said gently.

Damon stirred at the sound of her voice. "Mother? What is it?"

Cosima glanced to her son, noting the bloodstains on his chiton and the corresponding bloodstains on Evadne's shawl. "I bring news of Halcyon."

"How is she, Lady?" Evadne whispered, suddenly terrified to hear the answer.

"Your sister is very ill. She has been repeatedly poisoned and mind-swept, but I was able to get her the antidote in time. Halcyon is weak, but I believe, with time and proper care, she will make a full recovery."

Evadne trembled as she sat in her chair.

"Who has been poisoning her?" Damon demanded.

"Macarius," Evadne said, and the truth spilled out of her: the cipher, her encounter with him, his lie and his ploy to use her against Halcyon. Damon and Cosima both listened intently.

"He fled the quarry as soon as Straton arrived," Cosima said. "But I will bring your sister to the infirmary as soon as Straton can speak to the archon about the arrangement. We will eventually catch the mage, Evadne. He has broken many laws, and the queen will see that he pays for them accordingly."

The queen.

Evadne met Damon's eyes from across the room.

How could the queen grant justice if Selene was enchanting her?

"You will be journeying to the mountain soon, I take it," Cosima said, surprising them both.

"Father . . . told you?" Damon asked carefully.

"Yes. And he should never have withheld it from me." She reached within her leather satchel, procuring a vial of herbs. "I know you have a long journey ahead of you. These herbs will ward off exhaustion." She set the vial in her son's hand. "When do you depart, Damon? Your father said he did not know."

Damon looked to Evadne. Evadne with her disheveled hair and

ink-smeared hand and dark eyes.

They shared the same thought.

Macarius had mind-swept Halcyon. The confirmation made Evadne shake in fury. She knew he had seen the Haleva cipher, but what more had he pilfered? Had he gleaned the truth about where the crown rested?

Damon could take no chances, and Evadne nodded to him.

"Today," he said, his eyes remaining on her. "We leave as soon as possible."

It was difficult to leave the villa for a mysterious journey without the servants taking note. Toula packed their provisions, and Amara found Damon and Evadne the proper clothes to wear: modest but comfortable woolen tunics that would keep them warm, shawls to cover their heads, and durable sandals to protect their feet. Damon procured two swords from the armory and requested two of the swiftest horses to be tacked in preparation. And then it was time to leave, even though Evadne felt as if she was lacking something.

She did not feel ready.

Cosima waited to say goodbye to them in the shade of the inner courtyard.

"When should I expect you back?" she asked as she embraced Damon.

"It should hopefully only take us three days to reach the mountain," he replied. "And maybe half a day to recover what we need. I did not have time to send word to Father in Abacus. I hoped you could let him know."

"So I can expect you to return no later than a week, if all goes well?" Cosima sounded calm, but Evadne heard a warble of apprehension in her voice. A week of uncertainty would be like a year to her.

"Yes. Do not worry, Mother."

"That is like telling me not to breathe, Damon. Regardless, I will let your father know you have departed." She would worry, for he was the only son she had left. And her eyes traced him, memorizing him. Just as Phaedra had done the last morning she'd had with Evadne.

Cosima glanced to her. "Thank you, Evadne. For accompanying him."

Evadne thought she saw a spark of shame in the lady's eyes, as if she was dwelling on the first night of Evadne's service, when she had insulted her.

"I will bring him back safely to you," Evadne said.

Cosima nodded and turned away, unable to watch them leave the villa.

Just before they stepped through the doors, Damon sang a charm over them. A *charena* enchantment, one that did not render them unseen but slightly changed their appearance, hiding their true selves. Those they passed on the streets and then later on the road would see not a mage and his scribe but a farmer and his wife, traveling to their barley fields in southern Corisande.

The magic settled over Evadne; she saw that her hair had become lighter, curlier, and her nose felt longer, her jawline softer.

She watched Damon's transformation, his sable hair lightening to the color of olive wood, his face becoming broader, the blue flush of his left eye fading.

She would not have recognized him, just as his magic wanted, and it sent an unfamiliar pang through her.

"Are you ready?" he whispered, gathering their provision packs and handing one of the swords to Evadne.

"Yes." She accepted the blade, buckled it across her chest. She wondered if Xander had spoken the same words to Halcyon, weeks ago. How could one truly be ready for something they had never encountered?

Evadne followed Damon through the doors, into the afternoon sunlight, to where their horses waited.

She carried only three things with her as they departed Mithra:

The sword sheathed at her back.

Kirkos's relic around her neck, hidden beneath her tunic.

And Halcyon's kopis at her belt.

Lyra rode along the path to the quarry outpost, two guards trailing her. Of course, her mother would not allow her to come to the common quarry without an escort, and Lyra tried not to let it irk her. But deep in her heart, she knew her father believed her fragile, and her mother never let her stray anywhere unwatched. It would only worsen now, with Xander gone. Damon was the only one in the family she felt like she could speak freely to, but he had been heavily preoccupied for weeks. And even then, he could never understand. Their parents treated them differently.

Lyra thought of Xander, and her chest ached.

She had been a child when he had left for the Bronze Legion. But hardly a morning passed when she didn't wish that she had known him more.

She cast thoughts of her oldest brother aside, or else she might approach Halcyon in hatred, and her mother had been adamant about Lyra being pleasant to the murderer. To treat her as she would any of her other patients.

She passed no one on the road but a farmer and his wife, cantering to the south in a rush, and Lyra sighed as she finally arrived at the quarry gates.

She had never been here. And she could not stifle the shiver that moved through her as she entered the outpost with her bag of supplies, her mother's appointed escorts trailing her. She followed one of the quarry guards as he led her down the serpentine prison corridor, and she listened to the echoes that haunted the air: the chisels and the cracks and the shouts.

It reeked in the prison. Stale air, refuse, vomit, unwashed male.

She began to breathe through her mouth, preparing herself. Her mother had warned her that Halcyon was in terrible shape and that Lyra should guard her emotions, her face. To give the murderer only hope, not disgust or despair.

The guard unexpectedly stopped. Lyra almost plowed into him.

"What is it?" she asked, annoyed.

But he was silent, staring at a cell. Lyra moved around him to see the iron door was wide open. She drew closer, her heart beginning to pound . . .

"Lyra," one of her escorts reached out, trying to grasp her arm, to hold her back. "It is not safe. Wait."

She slipped through his fingers and entered what she knew to be Halcyon's prison cell.

A blanket was torn on the floor. The bucket of refuse spilled. A stool overturned.

And Halcyon . . . was not there. Lyra knelt and reached for the one thing she recognized, her hand shaking.

Her father's kopis lay abandoned on the floor.

And the blade was stained with blood.

⇢XXII⇠

Evadne

W e should make good time," Damon said, kneeling in the moonlight to set out their meal. "The wind is blowing in our favor."

Evadne nodded, wrapping her shawl closer around her. They had ridden hard that day, their horses kicking up clouds of golden dust, the southern road bending like a sickle toward the mountains. It was now midnight, and Damon's *charena* charm had worn off, and the horses needed water and rest.

They had taken pains to find a flat ridge among the Dacian foothills, hidden from sight of the road. But Damon did not want to take any chances. They would burn no fires on their journey, and the night was cold.

Evadne shivered; she felt battered from the hours of hard riding, and she was too weary to speak. She ate her bread and smoked fish by starlight and then lay down, struggling to keep warm. She listened to the wind, to the horses as they munched on the mountain grass, to Damon as he moved around nearby, trying to settle.

She knew she would not be able to sleep with her bones rattling from the cold.

"Damon? Are you cold?"

He was quiet for a moment. And then he drawled, "I am freezing, Evadne."

"Should we share a blanket? I could keep you warm."

Within an instant, he was crawling to her, dragging his shawl and blanket. "I will set my back to yours," he suggested. "If you think that will keep me warm the best."

Evadne smiled. "Yes, I think so." She turned on her side and he lay down next to her. Their backs aligned, and they shared their blankets.

Damon's warmth began to seep into her, and Evadne looked at the stars with heavy eyes. They burned silver against the night, and she thought of Ari's Shawl of Stars. She thought of the way Damon's voice had sparked constellations.

She drifted into dreams, anxious and puzzled by the mystery of him, of the magic she had always wanted and yet struggled to fully understand.

When dawn arrived, Evadne woke. The back-to-back arrangement had become null sometime in the night. She found that her legs were entwined with Damon's, and his chest was flush with her back, his arm draped over her. She could feel his breath warm her hair as he dreamt, and Evadne did not move for a while, waiting for him to wake.

He finally did, and they carefully untangled themselves from each other and their blankets, as if nothing had happened. They ate a quick meal, drank from their water flasks, and while Damon prepared their horses, Evadne bundled their bedrolls, drawing stray grass from her hair.

He sang his *charena* spell over them once more, and then they were off, galloping to the south.

Their second night of camping was the same as before, only Mount Euthymius had crept into view. Evadne felt uneasy at the sight of it, a peak that rose higher than all others. Damon still insisted that they should burn no fire yet, but when he lay down next to Evadne, he set two ember stones near them. To be breathed upon and sparked in an instant, should they need fire.

"Do you think Ivina will send our fears to oppose us in the mountain?" Evadne wondered as Damon set his back to her, drawing their blankets over them. The wind blew harsher that night, bitterly from the mountains. And there were no stars; the clouds veiled them. Evadne missed their presence.

Damon was silent for a moment, pensive. "Yes. I expect she will."

She wondered what he feared, what sort of phantom haunted him, a ghost that Ivina could raise with a mere swipe of her fingers. But Evadne did not ask, remembering Toula's reprimand from weeks ago. To reveal a fear was to be vulnerable.

And she dwelled on her own fear, pulling her right ankle farther beneath the blankets.

If Ivina resurrected the phantom dog again, Evadne would

think of Arcalos. Sweet, gentle Arcalos.

"Have you ever seen Ivina?" Evadne asked.

"No. But I have heard her laughter on the wind," Damon answered. "She takes delight in tormenting others."

"I wonder if she was always like that, even when she was a mortal mage."

"I suppose it is possible that she was different before Euthymius granted her immortality," Damon said around a yawn. "Being alone in a mountain and guarding a trapped god for hundreds of years surely takes a toll."

"Do you think she can be killed?"

"Maybe. But one would have to get close enough to her to even attempt it. And as far as I know . . . that has never happened."

Evadne slept uneasily that night, waking frequently. Damon's back remained to her, and this time Evadne turned to him, her face and hands freezing until she pressed against him and stole his warmth.

They were up again at dawn, riding the final approach to Euthymius. When darkness fell, Damon led them on a deer trail among the foothills, and they battled rocks and tangles of shrubs, but he claimed it would be the safest way to approach the mountain door.

This had been the path that Xander and Halcyon had once planned to take.

Damon eventually brought them to a cleverly hidden grotto. They fed and watered their mounts, leaving the horses hobbled in the safety of the shadows. Damon mixed Cosima's herbs into both of their water flasks, to ward off exhaustion as they approached.

They took the mountain path beneath their feet, quietly carrying their swords on their backs and the Song of Stars in their minds. The horses would have drawn Ivina's attention, he claimed as the way soon grew steep and treacherous. Several times, Damon crouched behind a rock, pulling Evadne with him, as if he could feel the immortal mage's eyes sweeping the mountainside. But nothing came for them.

Dawn arrived with a sigh. Evadne watched the light increase breath by breath, turning the rocks and shale around her to rosy hues. Mount Euthymius seemed to be a pillar of fire against the brightening stars, catching the light of both sun and moon. Despite the beauty of the summit, Evadne did not let her gaze linger upon the slope, for fear of drawing Ivina's attention.

She was drenched in sweat, cold and hot all at once, soft with exhaustion in the rare moments when the fear did not sharpen her, her ankle singing in pain. And then Damon came to an abrupt halt; she narrowly avoided stepping into him, peering over his shoulder to see what had brought him upright.

The threshold of the mountain was paved as a courtyard. One great door was hewn in the rock, arched and carved with the nine symbols of the divines.

"How do we gain entrance?" Evadne whispered, and even with her voice lower than a hum, it seemed far too loud.

"Entrance is simple," Damon whispered in return.

He reached for the coil of rope he had fastened to his belt. Evadne watched as he bound the rope about his waist, knowing the other end was for her. They would tether themselves together, to keep from being separated. She stepped closer to him, and Damon carefully brought the cord about her waist, knotting it with trembling fingers. It was the only evidence of his fear.

"Come, let us go now."

She felt his every step. The rope between them yanked, but it kept her close to him. She could smell the earth and salt on his skin, the wind in his hair as they approached the door. No matter the position of the sun, the door of Euthymius was always draped in shadow. Only the carvings caught the light.

Damon stared at them a moment, as if he was lost in thought. Evadne waited, feeling the sun rise with each haggard breath.

"Damon . . ."

"If my voice should falter," he said, continuing to stare at the divine symbols, "if I should forget the words, above all else, do not cease your singing. Your voice will be my guide, Evadne."

He turned and looked at her. She could see herself reflected within his eyes: the sunlight sat upon her hair like a crown; the hilt of the sword smoldered like a star on her shoulder.

She must have appeared ready, because Damon withdrew a kopis from his belt. He sliced his palm in one fluid motion, laying his bloodied hand upon Ari's carven symbol. His ancestor.

The door shuddered. It was too loud, Evadne thought with a wince, preparing to see the wild-eyed Ivina emerge at any moment.

But no one came to greet them.

The door fully opened, and Evadne smelled the cold heart of the mountain. Slick white stone. Creeping moss. Endless water.

The rot of something dying.

If not for the tether, she would have lurched back.

She wanted to run. But Damon stepped forward.

Evadne followed him into the mountain, the light from the open door waning the deeper they ventured. They were walking in a tunnel, the floor beneath them gradually declining. The walls on either side of them were damp; water dripped from the ceiling, beading in their hair, on their shoulders. Evadne imagined Euthymius and Loris carving their way into this mountain, long ago. One by earth, the other by water. Both divine, both smoldering with the intention to trap their brother.

Soon, there was no light. The darkness was supreme, permeating. Evadne could not see her hand when she held it before her face, and the air boasted a brutal chill. It was a dank cold, a cold to sink deep into bones. Evadne began to shiver, and they had not even reached the first tier of the cistern.

"Evadne," Damon whispered, slowing his pace.

She wondered if he wanted to turn back. She wondered what she would say if he asked her to.

She wanted to turn back, too. But she needed to fulfill this mission. For Halcyon.

"I am here," she said, touching his back in reassurance.

He continued to lead her, and soon she felt the ceiling heighten, the tunnel widen. They were almost at the cistern. She could hear the trickle of water; she envisioned the map in her mind. There would be a stone arch that marked the stairwell. That is how they would be able to find the safe way down the first waterfall.

She heard Damon step into the water.

He stood for a moment, the water lapping at his ankles, and then he began to sing his enchantment, to light their way and ward off phantoms. Evadne merely listened at first, transfixed by the haunting beauty of his voice. It echoed along the water of the cistern, taking her back to a tender moment when life was sweet, gentle. It stirred a nameless thing within her, a flame that burned in her lungs. She watched as he summoned the fire. A star bloomed, inspired by his voice and his magic, and it floated in the air between them. She could see the planes of his face, limned in silver, and his voice grew stronger, braver.

She stepped into the water with him, and joined his song. Her voice soft where his was rough. She was his balance, his accompaniment. And the stars began to multiply; they gathered around them and lit their path, their reflections just as luminous on the trembling surface of the water.

Ivina would know they were here. She would hear their song, and yet they did not sing meekly. They sang to defy her, to announce their presence. They sang without fear, walking through the cistern. With each stanza Damon sang, more and more stars gathered until Evadne could see the mountain ceiling, white and glittering. She could see the pillars Euthymius had shaped, narrow and sleek, blooming from the floor like trees to uphold the dome, and she and Damon wove among them.

The resistance did not come until they had sung through the entire song, their voices circling back to repeat it.

Evadne felt Damon tug on their tether as he stumbled, losing his breath. He hunched over, and Evadne worried he was bleeding. His song was slowing, and she knew his magic was thinning. And yet the stars continued to unfold around them, incandescent. And Evadne continued to sing, her voice a guide for him.

Damon straightened and rejoined her in song, and they struggled to walk and sing through the frigid water, following the draw of the currents. Sweat began to bead her brow; surely, they were close to the first waterfall. In between breaths, she listened for it—the distinctive roar of rushing water.

"Eva! Eva, where are you going?"

Evadne stopped, shocked to hear a beloved voice echo across the water to her, cutting through Damon's enchantment. She nudged past him to see Halcyon standing a few paces before them. Her older sister was decked in armor—it was brilliant, as if she was dressed in every color of earth and sky. She smiled, and her eyes were mirthful, as alluring as molten gold. Halcyon radiated strength and health and beauty; her hair was long and iridescently dark in the firelight, brushing her collar.

"Halcyon?" Evadne cried, astonished. "Is it truly you?"

"Yes, Little Sister," Halcyon said.

"But I thought . . ." Evadne suddenly struggled to remember. Where was she? What was the annoying tug at her back? "But I thought you were somewhere else."

"Where else would I be?" she countered with a laugh. The sound only heightened Evadne's desperation to reach her, to throw her arms about her sister. "I have been with you all this time. Not once have I left you. Now follow me and let us go home. Let us return to Isaura."

"Yes, I have longed for it, more than anything!" Evadne almost wept, the desire threatening to burst in her chest.

"Come, then! Follow me." Halcyon invited, but she turned before the words had fully left her lips, striding away into the darkness.

"Hal, wait!" Evadne was terrified of losing her. She rushed forward to chase after her sister, only to discover something was resisting her. It almost felt like hands on her waist, hands rushing along her arms, hands cupping her face . . . She struggled against them, but there was such gentle persistence within that haunting touch. "Hal! *Halcyon!*" Evadne shouted, dragging the mysterious weight behind her. Everything felt muddled in her mind, in her heart. It was dark, and yet there was light. She could not remember where she was. All she knew was her sister was about to abandon her. Halcyon at last paused, casting prisms on the stone pillars. "You are stronger than that, Little Sister."

"Something is holding me back!"

"It is yourself, Eva. You have a sword at your back, remember? Unsheathe it and cut away the part of yourself that is hindering you."

Her order bewildered Evadne. Why would her sister tell her to wound herself?

But Halcyon was not waiting for her to decide. Unusually impatient, Halcyon pressed on again. She was about to disappear in the darkness, and Evadne would not lose her.

She rallied her strength and dragged that encumbering weight behind her like it was a mere grain sack. She thought she heard her name, as if shouted from a long distance. But she was too focused on her sister to stop and heed it.

She felt the water rushing faster at her ankles. It was guiding her to her sister; it was aiding her. And then she realized Halcyon had brought her to the first waterfall.

Halcyon stood at the very edge, the water roaring down the long drop behind her. She seemed utterly unaffected by it. She stood upon the foaming surface and held her hand out to Evadne, smiling.

"The only way out is down," she said. "Follow me, Eva." And she stepped over the edge.

Evadne rushed to follow her, but the weight she had been battling finally overcame her. It pushed her to her knees in the shallow water, and her head caught the edge of a nearby pillar; the jarring pain sent a spasm through her, as did the freezing water, which swelled about her, drenching through her tunic, soaking her hair.

She gasped, suddenly aware that she was on her back, her head just above the surface as she divided the current, and a man was all but lying on her, his body speckled in fading starlight.

"Evadne," he breathed. "Return to me. She is not real . . . *She is not real.*"

She recognized him slowly, her eyes adjusting as if she had just stepped from sunlight into a shadowed room.

"Damon?"

"*Yes!* Yes, I am here, and I am the only one with you." His relief was so sincere it brought tears to her eyes.

She realized what had just happened. Halcyon had been a phantom, one of Ivina's enchantments. And Evadne had almost dragged her and Damon over the edge of the waterfall, chasing after it.

She trembled as she tried to calm her pulse. The fire of the song was fading, withering without Damon's voice. But the stars were slow to burn out; the silver light continued to illuminate them, and Evadne watched as Damon reached for her, threading his fingers through her hair to find the wound on the back of her head. It was not deep, but his fingers came away bloodied.

"I am fine," she said. "Help me stand."

Damon found her hands and drew her up. They leaned on the pillar that had almost knocked Evadne unconscious—which, she now realized, had saved their lives by bringing her senses back—and they sought to reconcile what had just happened.

"You saw your sister," Damon stated.

Evadne nodded. A lump suddenly formed in her throat, and she blinked away her tears. "Yes. And it was as if I completely forgot myself as soon as she called out to me. I couldn't hear or see you." She looked at him and his dying stars, a few constellations fading in his damp hair. "It was not a fear, though. As we were expecting."

"No, but it was something just as sharp and visceral," Damon said. "You saw what you wanted."

And it had been more painful than the phantom dog encounter. Because Evadne ardently longed for it to be true. To return home to Isaura with her sister. To see Halcyon whole and well and laughing and joyful.

And then a thought crossed her mind, rendering her numb.

"You do not think that something has happened to Halcyon. That she is . . . dead, and Ivina has resurrected her as a phantom, and . . ."

He drew her close, and his touch was confident, reassuring. "No, Evadne. My mother said your sister should make a full recovery, that she will be caring for Halcyon. Your sister is well."

Evadne inhaled a deep breath. She nodded, and Damon waited to move until she was ready to find the stairwell.

He began to sing his enchantment, and the stars flared to life again. Together, they carefully skirted along the waterfall until they saw the stone arch that marked the beginning of the stairs. At first, Evadne was relieved to be standing on something solid. Until she saw how long the stairwell was—it seemed to plunge endlessly—and the stairs were carved from stone, treacherously slick from the mist of the falls.

Every step was painful to her. Her right ankle throbbed, and she did not know how much longer she could endure it. Her voice thinned, and it was fortunate that Damon seemed to be slaying the enchantment's discomfort on his own, because Evadne would not have been much help to him.

She heard Straton's voice behind her, speaking into her ear. *Evadne can hardly walk without limping . . . The chances of her being a successful partner for this mission are very slim.* She almost believed he was a ghost, too, stalking her steps to pour hopelessness within her. But when she glanced over her shoulder, there was no ethereal commander. Only the stairs she had conquered.

They finally reached the second tier of the cistern.

Evadne's legs trembled as she followed Damon into the knee-deep water. The cold was like a balm to her aches and pains; her ankles and feet soon went numb as she labored to cut through the currents.

Damon stopped abruptly, in movement and song. Evadne worried he was feeling another bout of pain until the tether between them went taut.

"Xander?" he cried, his voice rising in joy, in disbelief.

Evadne's heart constricted. "No, Damon!"

"Xander, wait! Where are you going? Where have you been?" And just like that, Damon began to drag Evadne through the water.

"Damon!" she screamed, desperate for him to hear her, for him to slow. "Damon, he is not real! *Stop!*"

"Arcalos and I have been watching the door, waiting for you to return," he said, charging onward as if the water were nothing, as if Evadne were weightless. "Yes, Arcalos is still alive! I have taken good care of him, as I vowed. Wait, slow down!"

The stars began to burn out, one by one. And the water began to deepen and pull harder. Soon, it was lapping at their waists, and Evadne's pulse throbbed as she reached out to wrap her arms around Damon, frantic to stop him before he dragged them over the second waterfall.

"Damon, please," she panted, her fingers curling into his chest, her heels trying to find purchase on the slick floor. She could feel his heart beating, a drum of doom.

He broke from her grip and Evadne momentarily went

underwater, the tether yanking her in his wake. She broke the surface, gasping. The current was unyielding. Evadne could not have swum against it had she been alone.

They were almost to the falls. She could see the edge of it, the way Damon's constellations glittered upon the water.

They were going to die here.

The panic stunned her, stole her breath.

And there was a moment when everything stilled, when it seemed as if the water eased and the stars gathered around her. She reached out to hold on to Damon, and she felt a shiver move through him as he realized Xander was a phantom, his senses finally returning to him.

A woman laughed in the distance, her amusement echoing off the rocks and water.

It was too late.

Damon's fingers wove with Evadne's as the water bore them over the edge, into a cold, endless plummet.

⟶XXIII⟵

Evadne

They fell together, entwined, stars dying in their hair. Evadne's heart was pounding so fiercely she couldn't think. Of all things, her mind clung to one image: the grove, home. She saw mighty Kirkos fall and break his wings, his body hanging limp in the branches of the olive tree.

Fly.

Evadne commanded her heart, and the screaming rush of air quieted, answering to her. Damon's weight, though, was heavy, his face pressed against her neck, his hands clinging to her as she clung to him.

Fly, she breathed again, and while she could not hold them both suspended in the air, she brought them down gently, slowly, the cascading water roaring beside them.

They reached the bottom. It was slick bedrock, the water shallowly spilling over it to tumble into a deep pool. Evadne set

Damon down on the rock first. Exhausted, she settled on his lap, gracelessly straddling him, the mist in her face and the water rushing about her knees. There were just enough stars remaining for her to behold Damon's awestruck face as he gazed at her, his dark hair a shade of blue in the bewitching light.

He said nothing, but he reached around her, to lay his palms upon her back. Where her wings should be.

And a delicious shiver moved through her; she didn't know if it was from his touch, his wonder, or the way her blood still hummed from the fall and the flight.

She pulled Kirkos's relic out from beneath her drenched tunic, and the lapis lazuli wing rested against her chest, gleaming like a spoken secret. Damon's gaze riveted to it, and he began to shake beneath her. She realized he was laughing—in relief, in amazement. It seemed ridiculous to laugh at such a dire moment, but she joined him, and it eased the knot of horror that had been winding tight within her.

"You never told me you possessed a relic, Evadne," he said when his laughter quelled.

"You never asked," she replied, hiding the lapis wing back beneath her tunic.

"No, although I should have. You are full of mysteries." And yet his eyes revealed far more, seeming to say, *You are a mystery I want to know, to slowly unravel.*

And she knew her gaze reflected the same longing.

"Come," she said, to hide the lambent desire she felt. "We are almost to the door." She moved away from him, ignoring his slight groan. His hands slid from her back, and she helped him stand. That was when she saw the gleam of bones, scattered and fused to the rock around them. Testaments of shattered bodies.

If Damon noticed them, he said nothing. But he eased into the pool first, turning to help her in.

She could not feel the bottom. There was no telling how many leagues deep this water went, and Evadne shuddered as she thought about what creatures might swim its depths.

"Try not to think about it," Damon whispered, and she knew he had been dwelling on the same thing. But what could be worse than treading mysterious water? Only one of his stars remained, and he began to sing his enchantment again, rousing the fire. He started to swim, searching for the stairs that would rise from the water and lead to the door, Evadne at his side.

But swimming and singing was exhausting. They both grew tired, and Damon was becoming more and more forgetful. Evadne sang for him, to help him remember, but when she glanced at him, she saw blood trickling from his nose.

He stopped, treading in place. Evadne stiffened in dread, thinking he was seeing another phantom.

He broke his singing to breathe, "There it is," and Evadne looked ahead of them, where his constellations framed their path, lighting the stairs. They were carved of white rock, rising out of the water, spotted with moss. They led to the door of the Underworld.

The sight reinvigorated them, and they swam to the stairs, their garments drenched and heavy as they stumbled out of the water. It was almost over, Evadne thought as she sang, her voice turning hoarse. She followed close behind Damon, the path to the door suddenly narrowing.

The door was not huge as she thought it would be, but it was exquisitely carved. Evadne admired the grapevines and ocean waves and mountains that were etched upon the stone. And over its center hung an olive wreath, its leaves lustrous in the light, eternally green and silver.

Acantha's All-Seeing Crown.

Evadne reached forward, to brush it with her fingers, to claim it with her hands. And a hiss met her, flowing from the cracks of the threshold.

"Evadne, Evadne of Isaura," said Pyrrhus, the trapped god of fire, his voice hungry like the flickering of a flame. "Open the door and set me free, esteemed daughter of Kirkos."

Her hands froze just before she could take the crown.

She knew Damon heard it, too, because he stopped singing.

"Evadne, *Evadne*, girl of wind, release me," the god of fire begged, and she heard him scratching at the door.

"Take the crown," Damon said, his eyes fixed upon the door as it shuddered. "Quickly, Evadne."

She lifted the crown from the door, and she felt Pyrrhus's anger in the floor, warming the rock beneath her. The door shuddered violently, as if Pyrrhus was throwing all of his weight against it.

"*Evadne*," he screamed; it sounded like a screech of claws on instrument strings, and the hair rose on her arms. "Evadne, do not leave me here!"

She would have remained rooted to the floor had Damon not

taken her hand and led her away. The crown rustled against her; she slipped it farther up her arm, to hold it in the crook of her elbow.

They reached the stairs and stepped back into the water. Damon was moving swiftly; he no longer sang, his stars gradually winking out one by one. He guided her back across the pool toward the roar of the falls and the stone staircase that was almost hidden in mist, and she knew he was trying to save his voice. She could still hear Pyrrhus's screams, and it chilled her blood, more than the cold of the mountain.

Damon crawled onto the bedrock, mindful not to slip, and drew Evadne up behind him, his grip like iron. They found the foot of the seemingly endless stairs, but Damon paused, unsheathing the kopis from his belt. With unfaltering confidence, he cut the rope that bound them.

"What are you doing?" Evadne demanded.

"I want you to fly, Evadne," Damon said calmly, slipping his kopis back into its scabbard. "I will meet you at the top."

She opened her mouth to protest, but she felt a shudder in the rock beneath her, then another. She glanced over her shoulder, watching the ripples form on the surface of the water. But it was not in response to Pyrrhus's tantrum. Something was rising from the depths.

"Now, Evadne!" Damon began to run up the stairs, taking two at a time, and Evadne leapt into the air, flying just above him. She watched, anxious as he began to slow and tire. But she could hear him singing in between pants, snatches of his enchantment so the stars would remain to light his path.

Pyrrhus fell quiet, but over the roar of the falls, Evadne heard a splash of something stirring the pool. She strained to see in the darkness and saw a horde of golden eyes, gleaming as they emerged from the water. The phantom dogs were charging up the stairs in pursuit of Damon.

Evadne flew to him. "Take hold of me. I will carry you."

Damon shook his head. "Go, Evadne. Leave me," he struggled to say, his chest heaving.

The phantoms were gaining on him. He did not look behind to see what fear was chasing him, but he knew it would catch him. He was reaching to unsheathe his sword and Evadne wound her arms about him, lifting him into the air.

She barely got him high enough, his arm coming about her to hold on, just before the phantoms snarled and jumped to snap at their heels. She toiled to draw her and Damon higher, her mind pounding, *If only I were stronger, faster.*

And she heard Halcyon's voice respond, *There is steel within you.*

Evadne grit her teeth and honed her will, flying higher, faster, the constellations remaining about them. Damon was laboring to breathe; she could feel his exhalations warm the front of her tunic, and his grip on her began to ease.

"Damon, hold on!" She adjusted her hands, terrified that he would slip away. Water was rushing beneath them now. They had reached the second tier of the cistern. They were halfway back.

The phantoms continued to pursue them, running along the surface of the water, growling and snapping whenever Evadne dipped too low. Her back was aching, her muscles burning and cramping. But she could see the final waterfall, the final staircase. She flew to it, every fiber of her blazing, alive. She sensed the ceiling closing in, and she adjusted herself, remembering the first tier was shallower, and then it went dark.

"Damon, I need light!"

His hands tightened on her as he began to sing, his voice so shredded she almost didn't recognize it. But the stars returned, just in time for Evadne to see she was hurtling toward one of the pillars. And she did not have time to redirect herself.

She slammed into it, her shoulder taking the brunt of the impact. She and Damon were separated, and down she went, into the shallow water. It was not a long fall, but she sprawled on her back, gasping for breath, the crown amazingly unharmed as she embraced it to her chest.

She heard something rushing to her, splashing through the water. She cringed, waiting for a phantom dog to maul her. "Evadne!" Damon cried, taking hold of her and dragging her up. "Draw your sword, now!"

She found her footing and clawed for the hilt of her sword, withdrawing it with a groan of pain. The phantoms finally caught up to them, circling her and Damon. There were eight of them, and while they prowled and snapped, they could not touch the enchanted fire. Damon's stars continued to burn all around them, and he sang again, enflaming the constellations even brighter.

Evadne walked at his side, raising her voice one final time to join his. They stepped carefully through the water, as stately as if they were a mage and a scribe at court. They did not rush, not even when they saw the mouth of the tunnel that would lead them up, back into the world. They did not run or swing their swords.

And their phantoms relinquished them at last.

Evadne led the way into the passage, Damon close behind her. The floor began to tilt upward. In the distance was a tiny door of light.

When she could feel the sun on her face, she ceased singing and sheathed her sword. She ran to the promise of blue sky, hands outstretched as if she could catch the light in her hands. Acantha's crown rustled on her arm, soaking in the sun.

They staggered into the open air blinking and stumbling, kneeling on the smooth flagstones when their legs gave out. Evadne held herself up and wept. And Damon knelt before her, cupping her face in his hands. He wiped her tears away, and the same thought passed through them.

Halcyon and Xander would not have survived this mission.

It did not matter that they had been the strongest in their legion. They both would have perished in the heart of Euthymius without fire.

"Your shoulder, Evadne," Damon whispered, his hand drifting to it. His thumb traced her collarbone beneath her tunic, searching for a break.

"I hardly feel it," she confessed, the pain eclipsed by her relief to be alive. "It is bruised, not broken." But when she made to roll her shoulder, it throbbed in response, and she winced.

"Let me see."

Evadne nodded, and Damon's hands carefully rolled up her sleeve. The crown rustled between them, and their gazes met, full of wonder.

"I think we make a good team," she whispered to him, smiling.

Damon's lips parted to speak, but a different voice sounded from a distance, smooth as river stone, polished with mockery. A voice Evadne never wanted to hear again.

"Well, this is fortunate."

Damon stiffened. His hands drifted from Evadne as they both looked toward the voice.

There stood Macarius, only a few paces away, a nasty cut marring one of his cheeks. He was not alone. A feeble woman stood before him, and he held a kopis blade to her throat. A sound escaped Evadne when she realized the woman was *Halcyon.*

"Hello, Evadne," Macarius greeted with a cold smile, but his eyes were on the crown she held. "How about we strike a trade? Your sister in exchange for Acantha's All-Seeing Crown."

➻•XXIV•➻

Halcyon

No," Halcyon rasped. "Do not give him the crown, Eva."

Evadne continued to kneel and stare at her, soaked and flushed from the frigid water of the mountain. She was stricken, horrified. Halcyon knew she had not recognized her at first, and pain bloomed in her chest, to realize she looked so terrible that her own sister had not known who she was at first glance.

But she could not dwell on such agonizing things.

Because her little sister had the All-Seeing Crown in her possession. Her little sister had just done the impossible, and Halcyon felt humbled and awed and proud of her.

She wanted to weep, to collapse and crawl to Evadne until she felt the warning of Macarius's kopis on her neck.

"How much is her life worth to you, Evadne?" Macarius taunted. "Surely, Halcyon means more than a mere crown."

It was not a mere crown, Halcyon thought, clenching her teeth.

It was their last hope for the queen.

Evadne finally took her eyes from Halcyon and looked at Damon, who was still on his knees, close beside her. Halcyon watched the two of them stare at each other, as if they were holding a private conversation in their minds. Macarius, ever impatient, stomped his foot.

"Evadne! This offer will not last for much longer. Answer me now, or I slit your sister's throat."

Halcyon expected Evadne to plunge into panic. But her little sister continued to surprise her.

Evadne met Macarius's gaze, her expression calm, her eyes heavy-lidded with contempt for him. Slowly, she rose, her tunic dripping water onto the courtyard.

"My sister means everything to me," she said. "I will give you the crown, but you must first set her free, Macarius."

Macarius laughed, the crackling sound of wood burning. "You think me a fool, Evadne? Hand the crown to my scribe, and I will let Halcyon go."

Beryl appeared then, from behind an outcrop of rocks. She stopped halfway between the two groups, waiting for Evadne to close the distance with the crown.

Evadne stared at Beryl. They were both scribes, and yet how different they were. Halcyon watched as Evadne began to walk the crown to Beryl, the limp prominent in her gait.

No, she wanted to shout at her sister. *No, Evadne. Do not give up that crown for me.*

But then Halcyon saw the wicked gleam in her little sister's eyes, the way her hand was clenched. She thought of all the times Evadne had been underestimated and overlooked.

And yet it was Evadne who had just stolen the most revered relic in all of Corisande, surviving Ivina's phantoms and Mount Euthymius's precarious water.

Halcyon waited, heart suspended.

Her little sister stopped directly before Beryl. Evadne studied Acantha's crown, glittering in the sunlight. She offered it up to Beryl with her left hand.

Beryl, greedy for the relic, set her gaze upon it and took the crown, the leaves rustling in protest. She did not see Evadne's swift motion until it was too late, and Evadne flung a handful of shale into her eyes.

Beryl squawked and tripped backward, dropping the crown, and Damon surged to his feet. With his hand outstretched, he uttered a charm that rang like a blade—*dessanos vor*—and Macarius was magically disarmed before he could slice Halcyon's neck.

His kopis arced through the air. Evadne dashed beneath the steel's flashing descent, recovering the crown as she made for Halcyon. Halcyon lunged to meet her, slipping from Macarius's grasping hands, her body quivering from strain. Her feet were numb; she stumbled into Evadne, and her sister took hold of her thin arm, holding her steady, before she frantically dragged her toward the outcrop of rocks.

From the corner of her eye, Halcyon could see Beryl, seething on her knees as she wiped the grit from her eyes, and Damon and Macarius engaging in a duel, hissing charms in God Tongue, words that flew and sparked like hot iron on an anvil, scorching through their clothes, leaving the tang of lightning in the air. Macarius's shadow rose and stretched into a creature, long talons and sharp teeth, slithering across the courtyard. And just before she ducked out of view with Evadne, Halcyon saw Damon summon his shadow in response, but it was not a monster. It was the shadow of a hoplite, armed with spear and shield, and she knew it was inspired by Xander.

A lump welled in her throat, and she slipped, losing her footing. Evadne lost her footing, too, and the sisters slid down a gentle incline of shale. Evadne had to stop their tumble by catching them on a rock with her feet, and Halcyon heard her grunt in pain.

"Hurry, Hal," Evadne whispered, ragged. She rose and helped Halcyon stand, her dark eyes glancing up the hill to the marks they had made in the shale. Flickers of searing light and shadows continued to play on the mountain threshold. The clouds darkened overhead, and the wind began to howl. She was worried about Damon, Halcyon sensed. But they also needed to hide, because Beryl would come for them.

Halcyon strained to follow her around a knot of rocks, hidden from view. But her lungs were weeping, and her body was trembling. Cosima's care had given her back a tiny portion of her strength, but it was not enough to sustain running and fighting. How easily Macarius had overpowered her at the quarry, Halcyon remembered. He had waited, unseen, for Cosima to depart, and then he had struck, dragging Halcyon from her cell. She had given the mage a cut to his face, hoping it would catch his eye. But she had been too weak to put up a proper fight, to sink the blade into his throat.

This was all her fault. Macarius had mind-swept her again, and in her exhaustion, she had not been able to shield the mission. He had gleaned it with glee, taking her and Beryl to the mountain only to discover the door was already open. Macarius, coward that he was, decided to wait and see who emerged.

Halcyon crouched beside Evadne in the shadow of the rocks, struggling to breathe, tucking her hands into her chest to hide how they shook.

She felt like a stranger in her own body.

But then there was a flash of something familiar before her. Evadne held Halcyon's kopis in her palm, waiting for her sister to claim it.

"Eva, I—"

"Take it, Hal," Evadne ordered, and Halcyon obeyed.

Her scythe seemed to sigh in pleasure the moment she wrapped her fingers about its hilt. The blade remembered her, and she did not dwell on how Macarius had wrenched the commander's kopis from her hand. She would not let him disarm her again.

Evadne unsheathed the sword at her back. Halcyon wanted to smile, to see her little sister wielding a sword. An image she would never have imagined she would encounter.

They waited in the shadow of the rock, breaths far too loud, blades shivering light in their hands.

And then they heard footsteps. Graceful, poised on the shale. It had to be Beryl.

Evadne and Halcyon did not move, waiting for her to come

around the rocks and find them. But it never happened. The footsteps retreated, and Evadne sagged in relief. But Halcyon knew better.

"She is playing with us, Eva," she whispered. "We need to move."

Evadne met Halcyon's gaze. She looked exhausted; how long had she and Damon been in the mountain's heart? But Evadne nodded and shifted to a crouch, moving away from the shadows to study the plunge of landscape before them.

Halcyon heard the spell first. A sharp enchantment that whirred in the air like an arrow.

It struck Evadne, and Halcyon shouted, all of her combat training forgotten as she watched her little sister fall facedown on the shale, limp, sword clattering uselessly beside her.

No, no, no, no, no.

She lumbered to her feet, only to trip and fall like her bones were melting. And here came Macarius, strolling down the incline as if he were taking a pleasure walk. His cheek was scabbed from her cut—it would scar, no matter what healing salves he slathered on it—and his clothes were shredded from his magical duel with Damon. But his eyes were gleaming in victory, and he gave Halcyon a cruel smile.

Beryl followed close behind, staring at Evadne's prone, unmoving body.

"It truly has been a pleasure, Halcyon," Macarius said. He snapped his fingers, and Beryl walked to Evadne, stealing Acantha's crown from her lifeless arms.

Halcyon's chest heaved; spit swarmed through her teeth as she moaned, angry that she could not fight, agonized that her sister was lying on the ground. Had he killed her?

"Beryl, please," Halcyon whispered, and Beryl hesitated for a beat. "You do not have to go with him. You can join us. There is nothing for you in the future he plans. Has he told you what has been promised to him if he hands that crown over to Selene?"

The scribe hesitated, betraying her confliction.

"Common people like you and me will be forced into labor, to work for the mages," Halcyon said. "They will take away our rights, our voices, and Macarius will have no need of you when he finds himself living in the luxury of the palace as the queen's hand, with all of the relics in his possession. He will have you killed, Beryl, for knowing too much—"

"Enough!" Macarius cried, furious. "She lies, Beryl. Remember the reward I have promised you?"

Beryl resumed her walk to him. She came to a stand behind him, and when he held his palm up, she hung Acantha's crown on his fingers.

It was all over.

Halcyon wanted to kill him. She vowed she would, soon, and she began to crawl to Evadne.

She heard his spell, the same one he had shot at her little sister. It struck her like a fist in her ribs, and Halcyon went down. On her belly, she could hardly breathe, she could hardly move. Her blood thickened, pumping slower and slower, but she willed herself to reach Evadne.

She touched her sister's cold fingers just before her body froze.

But her mind was still present. She still saw from her eyes. The storm broke, an aftershock of the magical duel. Rain began to fall, beading on her face, spilling into her lashes.

And she watched Macarius and Beryl leave them helpless and exposed on Mount Euthymius, taking the resplendent crown with them.

THE THIRD SCROLL

A Ring
Made of Fire

⟐XXV⟐

Evadne

Evadne listened to the storm and felt Halcyon's fingers on hers and watched the darkness arrive like ink spilling across papyrus. How long would she be frozen here? Would Ivina send her phantoms again, once night fell?

She thought of Damon, of Halcyon, of Macarius, of the crown. Her mind lived in a loop, reenacting the disaster over and over.

She heard footsteps crunching, sliding on the shale toward her. It was Damon, and her heart warmed in relief, to know he was still alive. He knelt beside her, his clothes torn, small lacerations bright on his face. He caressed her cheek, her hair. His hand smelled of earth, and his voice was rough as he spoke the reversal to Macarius's charm.

"Evadne," he whispered. The frost melted, and Evadne moved her arms, pushing herself up to look at Halcyon.

Halcyon was frail, like the wind could snap her in two. Her

dark hair was slowly growing back, but her eyes were glazed in pain, her lips cracked with scabs.

It took everything within Evadne not to weep as she stroked her sister's hollow cheek, as she watched Damon liberate her from Macarius's snare.

Halcyon flinched, blinked. Her gaze found Evadne, as if it was all she wanted to see, and Evadne eased her up to sit on the wet shale.

"We cannot stay here," said Damon. His gaze remained on Halcyon, mournful, disbelieving. And angry. Coals stirred in his spirit; Evadne could see it in his eyes when he returned his gaze to her. He was furious to see Halcyon so broken and feeble. He was furious Macarius had defeated them, stolen from them, dragged Halcyon around with a kopis to her throat.

That fury was electrifying.

Evadne let it catch and spark within her, and when she looked at her sister, she saw the fire smolder in Halcyon, too.

The three of them knelt in the rain, unified.

Evadne recovered her sword and her sister's kopis while Damon stood and helped Halcyon rise. He looped her left arm over his shoulder, Evadne did the same with her right, and they bore Halcyon's slim weight between them, helping her walk.

"The grotto, Damon?" Halcyon whispered.

"Yes, we left the horses there," Damon replied, finding the path he and Evadne had originally taken.

They did not speak again after that, saving their strength to pick through the brush and scale the slopes. The rain fell and the darkness was thick by the time they found the grotto. The horses whickered in greeting, and Evadne had never seen a more inviting sight.

She and Damon eased Halcyon down to a dry segment of the stone floor. He was quick to rummage through their packs, drawing forth clean tunics and their bedrolls, their provisions. He brought it all to Evadne, silently setting it into her hands before he returned to the rain, granting them privacy.

Evadne could scarcely see in the darkness. She found an ember stone and breathed upon it. A small flame danced on the rock, its light just enough to allow her to behold her sister.

Gently, Evadne began to undress her.

She saw how thin Halcyon had become, the bandages for her back still wrapped about her chest. She saw the bruises made from chains and hard hands. She saw the dirt and the nicks on her hands, the blue branching of veins beneath her lackluster skin.

She saw the ravaging evidence of the poison that had all but eaten Halcyon from the inside out, and Evadne wanted to shake them both awake, as if this were all some nightmare.

But the waking never came.

Halcyon was dying, and Evadne could not heal her, could not stop it, could not save her.

She brought Damon's spare tunic over Halcyon's head, easing her arms through the sleeves. Evadne was sorting through the food, hiding her tears as she sought something soft for Halcyon to eat, when her sister finally spoke.

"You did not recognize me, did you, Eva?"

Evadne's throat closed. She wanted to say, *I recognized you. I would know you anywhere, even if your soul was in another body.*

But she could not lie to Halcyon. She reached for the water flask and whispered, "No, not at first." She brought the flask to Halcyon's lips, and her sister swallowed only a mouthful of water before spluttering.

"I hardly recognize myself, either," Halcyon said with a cough and a smile, as if she wanted to ease Evadne's dismay. "It will be all right. I just need some time to heal."

"Yes," Evadne agreed, her heart lifting at the thought even as her tears fell.

She helped Halcyon drink a few more sips before she disrobed from her own sodden tunic. The flame was almost extinguished on the ember stone, but Evadne could see a mottled bruise beginning to form on her shoulder. A painful reminder that she knew nothing about flying. Gingerly, she drew the clean garments over her body. She and Halcyon were eating fruit by the time Damon returned. There was not a fresh tunic for him to change into, but he did not seem to care. He tended to their horses and then built a fire from the wood they had packed.

Evadne was too weary to ask if the fire was a foolish choice, if it would draw Ivina to them. She shifted to the warmth with a groan, holding her hands to the flames before she made Halcyon a bed beside it.

Her sister crawled into the bedroll with a sigh of gratitude, the light illuminating her haggardness. Evadne tucked the blanket and shawl about her, watching her sister fall asleep. She counted her breaths, took note of how shallow and raspy they were. She feared the moment when they might cease altogether, and Evadne wrestled with her thoughts, trying to remain hopeful.

She felt Damon watching her from across the fire, and she lifted her gaze to meet his.

"Where do you think Macarius will scurry away to?" she asked.

"He will go to Mithra, to give my aunt the crown," Damon replied heavily. "Without it, we have no way to break the enchantment on the queen. Selene has the upper hand now."

Again, that sense of despair crept over her.

Evadne was exhausted. All she wanted was to curl up beside Halcyon beneath the blanket, like they had done when they were girls, and sleep for days.

"I am sorry, Evadne."

"What for?"

He stared at the fire, as if he could not bear to look at her. "I am sorry that I could not defeat Macarius. If we had not just come through the mountain . . . if I had not been so tired, I would have killed him. What he has done to your sister . . ."

"It is not your fault, Damon." She thought of how Macarius possessed deeper magic than him. The fact that Damon had been able to fight at all after singing the entire time in the mountain was extraordinary to her.

"It is," Damon insisted. "He should not have gotten away."

Evadne traced the edge of Halcyon's blanket with her fingertips, imagining justice for her sister.

"What do you want to do, Evadne?" he asked.

She was quiet, sorting through her heart, her worries. But then a path forged itself in her mind. And she knew it was the right choice.

"I want to take my sister home. To Isaura."

"How many days will that take from here?"

"I think I can make it in three."

"You can take both of the horses," he said, accepting the water flask when Evadne handed it to him. "One for you and one for your sister."

"But what of you?"

"I will be fine."

"But where will you go? Back to Mithra?"

Damon drank. A beard was beginning to shadow his face, and his eyes caught the firelight when he looked at her again. "No. To Abacus. To my father."

They fell silent, the fire dancing between them.

"You should get some sleep," he said. "I will keep watch."

And she wanted to say that he needed rest, too. More than her.

But Evadne sank to the ground. She curled up beside her sister, listened to her breaths, and fell into a dreamless slumber.

Dawn arrived, foggy and warm, the wind having borne the rain to the east. Evadne woke before Halcyon and quietly worked to prepare the horses and pack the provisions with Damon.

"When you camp tonight," Damon spoke in a low voice, rushing his hand over one of the horses' manes, "I want you to burn a fire. Keep your sword near, as well as a long branch that you can wield as a torch."

Evadne felt her fears stir. "Do you think Ivina will come after me?"

"I do not know. But it would ease my mind to know that you are prepared if she does."

Evadne nodded, words caught in her throat. She was afraid, although she did not want to be. She closed her eyes until she felt Damon's caress in her hair, gentle as a spring breeze.

"You will make it home safely," he whispered.

She breathed in that promise, felt its wings unfold and beat within her chest. As if a part of her had awakened, come to life.

She leaned into him for a moment, until she felt overwhelmed by the feelings he roused in her. Evadne stepped back, watching his hand ease away, the silver flashing on his finger.

She turned and knelt beside Halcyon, waking her sister. Evadne had hoped that Halcyon would look better come morning, but her face was still bloodless, her eyes still glazed, her movements still arduous. Yes, they needed to get home. As swiftly as they could.

The three of them ate a small repast, and then Damon helped Halcyon mount her horse.

Evadne climbed into her saddle, waiting to speak to Damon before they departed. He walked to her side and whispered a phrase to her in God Tongue, low and sweet, the words radiant. And then he let her go, the distance growing between them. Evadne had heard him clearly, but she did not translate his words, did not swallow them until she and Halcyon had ridden to the southwest and Damon had departed on foot to the southeast.

I will come for you soon.

→XXVI←

Halcyon

Halcyon did her best to keep up with Evadne's harried pace. She did not know why they had separated from Damon; she did not care, as long as she was with her sister. But her head was throbbing, and every breath she took felt like she was drawing a saw over wet wood. Splintered and damp and painful. And then she realized where they were going, that the mountains remained to their right.

Evadne was taking her home.

She longed for Isaura, to see her parents. She longed to sleep in her childhood bed and savor Aunt Lydia's stew and braid Maia's hair and listen to Lysander's whines and soak in Uncle Nico's stories.

But . . . she could not imagine them wanting the same of her. She was a stranger, a criminal. She had humiliated them.

Mount Euthymius was still visible when Evadne stopped to

make camp for the night. She helped Halcyon down from the saddle, and Halcyon shakily set out a meal while her little sister tended to the horses and made a fire and gathered two long branches from a dead tree. They were camping on a high ridge, a promontory that jutted into a deep ravine. Halcyon knew exactly why Evadne had chosen this place. It was strategic. It afforded them clear vantage points, and there was only one way to access it. If Ivina decided to send their fears to them, the phantoms would have to approach from the mouth of their promontory, a narrow strip of land.

"Do you think we are too exposed here?" Halcyon carefully asked. "And I am fine without a fire tonight, Eva. We can keep each other warm."

Evadne hesitated a beat but continued to set kindling in the fire. "The fire is our only defense against Ivina. Her phantoms cannot withstand it."

Halcyon nodded, submitting to Evadne's decision. But she took note of how steep the walls of the ridge were. It would be a deadly drop to the ravine below should one of them misstep.

Evadne did not seem to mind the height, finally settling beside Halcyon. They sat with their backs to the ravine, their faces to Euthymius, the fire blazing at their feet.

Despite her desire to regain her strength, Halcyon struggled to eat the flatbread and fruit Evadne set before her. She knew her sister was watching everything, even when she seemed not to. Evadne took note of her breaths, her motions, what she ate, how much she drank. And Halcyon wanted to tell her not to worry, but what a lie that would be. Her hands still trembled, and she knew she needed more of the antidote. She sensed the poison lingering in her stomach and her lungs, haunting her blood.

To distract herself from the inevitable, Halcyon thought of all the things she wanted to ask her little sister: How had she come to be Damon's scribe? What was it like? Had Straton taken good care of her? When had Evadne been brought into the mission? Had Macarius tried to use Haleva against her? How had she known it was false? What had it been like in the heart of Euthymius?

"Eva . . ." Halcyon began, but her voice died. She did not have the strength to ask all of her wonders.

"Sleep, Hal," Evadne whispered. "I will guard our camp."

"I can keep watch," Halcyon insisted. But eventually, she began to ease down to the blankets, her feet facing the mountain. "Will you wake me if they come, Eva?"

"Yes. Do not worry."

Halcyon woke hours later to Evadne's touch on her shoulder. A gentle yet urgent squeeze.

"They are coming, Hal."

Halcyon struggled to sit. She held up her hand to block the fire from her sight so her eyes would remain keen in the darkness. Evadne helped her rise, and they stood side by side, staring toward the mountain. The moon was a fingernail above them, the grass whispered in the wind beneath them, and the phantoms raced across the foothills to challenge them. Halcyon counted only three, starlit and gleaming and impossibly swift. When she saw what Ivina had spun for her, her heart began to pound.

No.

But it was. She would recognize them and the flash of their bronze armor anywhere. By moon or by sun.

Iason. Symeon. Narcissa.

Her erstwhile friends had been turned into phantoms to torment her. The three hoplites in her squad who had testified against her at her trial. One who had been her captain, who Halcyon still highly esteemed. Who had whipped her, shredded her back before countless witnesses.

No.

Halcyon swayed when she realized that she would have to take up fire and slay them into sparks. She could not let Evadne conquer them all.

It does not matter. I am a murderer. Halcyon's soul wept. *I am already doomed.*

She reached for her branch, set it into the fire so its end would catch the flames. Evadne mirrored her, unsheathing her sword.

"What do you see, Eva?" Halcyon asked, her voice wavering.

"I see three dogs," Evadne replied, and her voice trembled, too. "The dog you once saved me from."

Halcyon met Evadne's wide-eyed gaze. Her little sister's hair was bound in a braid, but threads of it had worked their way free, and the wind tangled them over her face. She did not look so young anymore, Halcyon thought. It had always been her instinct to protect Evadne, ever since the day she had proudly held her in her arms, a wailing bundle of life. But Halcyon suddenly realized her sister did not need it. Evadne could defend herself.

And Halcyon let her mind descend, deep into her dust-streaked memories. There had been a moment in hoplite training when she had been afraid, when she had wanted to bolt. But the commander had stood at her back and spoken words to her that she had branded into her mind.

"This is your moment, Eva," Halcyon said, and her voice was strong, clear. The strongest it had sounded since she had arrived at the quarry. "Stand and meet it. For it belongs to you."

Evadne was silent. But her eyes remained on Halcyon as if Halcyon were a divine. And then she took her torch and her sword and turned to meet the phantoms.

Halcyon grasped her long branch, the end writhing with fire, and prepared herself.

She stood and watched the phantoms close the distance, so perfectly re-created they appeared to be flesh and blood. Iason, Symeon, Narcissa.

It was Iason—sweet, loveable Iason—who charged for her first, sword thrusting, and Halcyon hesitated before her reflexes overtook her. She swung her branch, piercing him in the heart. He turned into a swarm of sparks and smoke, his face contorting as it melted into the darkness. She felt sick at the sight.

I am a murderer. I am guilty. I am unforgiven.

Beyond the sparks, Evadne swung at Symeon with her torch, catching him in the arm. He howled and jumped back, but Evadne pressed him, refusing to give up ground, falling into a dangerous dance with him. She was seeing a dog, but Halcyon was seeing an old friend, and she grappled with the sight of her sister battling Symeon.

He is not real. It is just a ghost of Symeon. He is not real . . .

Narcissa took advantage of that distracted moment to slither through the shadows, spear raised, teeth clenched. She looked nothing like a phantom. Even the red-and-white horsehair of her helm blew in the breeze. Again, Halcyon wanted to kneel and toss down her torch. But she swallowed and swung, severing Narcissa's right arm with her fire.

Her former captain hissed as her arm dissipated. She regrouped and charged, this time taking the kopis from her belt, swinging and hacking.

Halcyon stepped back, felt the blade catch the front of her tunic, ripping it.

She parried Narcissa's second thrust, shoving her into the fire. She watched, trembling, as the captain surrendered into smoke, drifting up to the stars.

Halcyon dropped her stick. She retched into the grass as cold sweat dripped down her back. The night had gone quiet. It felt like hours passed, but it was only a moment when she lifted her face to see Evadne standing on the other side of the fire, watching her with large, mournful eyes.

The third phantom was gone. Evadne had killed it, and Halcyon was grateful.

"Hal?"

Halcyon retched again, unable to stop it. Her eyes were blurry, her mouth burned, and she felt her spirit cling to her bones, still broken and wounded, uncertain how to heal itself.

"Here, Hal." Evadne was on her knees, frantically looking through the provisions for the water flask. Her head was down, intent on her task, so she did not see the fourth phantom's approach.

But Halcyon did.

She straightened, wiped the back of her mouth and watched the phantom come, swift and silent and brilliant, just as she remembered him being. He did not glance at Evadne. His eyes, furious, were for Halcyon alone. And it was justified, she told herself.

She had been waiting for this. Halcyon's fear melted away as she held out her arms to him.

"*Xander*," she breathed.

In the distance—so far away that she could have been a star in the sky—knelt Evadne. Halcyon could see her from the corner of her eye. She saw Evadne's hair stir as the phantom rushed past her. She saw Evadne startle, scramble to relight her torch, to take up her sword. She heard Evadne scream her name, trying to rouse her.

"Halcyon, Halcyon, your torch! *Take up your torch!"*

But Halcyon let the torch be, burning out on the grass. Because she would not—could not—slay him again. Her shield brother. The one who should be living.

Xander came for her. Their bodies collided, and he felt solid, tangible, alarmingly real. The bronze of his armor caught the front of her tunic. He knocked the breath out of her, and her arms came around him, and she was weeping into his long, flaxen hair.

I am sorry, I am sorry. Forgive me. The words escaped her; she sounded like a wounded creature. She released a wail she did not know she could make.

But no matter how perfectly Ivina had re-created him . . . this was not Xander. And he lifted Halcyon up in his arms, but it was not to embrace her or forgive her. He took her to the brink of the promontory.

And together, phantom and girl, they fell over the edge, into the howling darkness.

⤙ XXVII ⤚

Evadne

Evadne twisted her ankle trying to launch herself into flight, the pain keeping her earthbound, as if the grass had turned into manacles. She was too late, too slow. Even as the magic thrummed in the air, she could not fully summon her wings. The moment had passed; Halcyon could not be caught and saved. Her sister was *gone*. As if she had never been.

Evadne crumpled to her knees. She tore her tunic, she screamed at the stars, at the sliver of the moon, at the mountain.

She had been so close to bringing Halcyon home. Two days away from the safety of Isaura. And Halcyon had just fallen to her death.

"How could you leave me?" Evadne screamed at Halcyon's memory, at the place where she had plummeted, where the edge of the earth met the moan of the wind. *"How could you leave me like this?"*

But Evadne knew why, even in the haze of her fury and the

creeping numbness of her shock. She had heard Halcyon breathe his name—*Xander*—and had known it was over. Halcyon would not slay his ghost.

Ivina had gotten her revenge.

Time passed, even when it felt like everything should stop.

The fire burned down to embers. The wind tore at her braid. The horses were gone, spooked by the phantoms.

Evadne was alone.

She crawled to Halcyon's bedroll and lay facedown on it, uncertain what she should do.

Before long, she heard a voice. "Is this truly Evadne of Isaura, the crafty girl who snuck her way into my mountain and stole a divine crown from the door I guard?"

The voice was lovely, amused. There was also a flicker of steel within it, a cadence honed to cut.

Evadne sensed the immortal mage's presence.

She swallowed. Her throat ached; her voice felt torn away in her grief. But Evadne lifted her head and beheld Ivina.

She was old, as the legends claimed. She was also beautiful.

Evadne wanted to look away from her, and yet she could not find the strength to do it.

"I expected to find a warrior here," said Ivina, her words like thorns Evadne would have to extract later. "I expected to find a courageous woman. For not many mortals dare to journey into Euthymius's heart, let alone live to tell about it."

Evadne was silent. But she could feel the indignation, the fury brewing in her.

"You conquered your other fears so beautifully, Evadne," the mage continued. As if she had found great delight in watching Evadne's turmoil. "The dog that terrified your childhood. Damon dragging you over the falls. I find it hard to believe you are a mere mortal, a girl who was destined to remain in her father's grove, picking olives until her fingers turned green." She paused. "Even now, you are not afraid of me. Why, Evadne? What has wrought this change in you?"

"Why have you come to me?" Evadne raised herself up, to stand on her feet. "Say what you must and be gone, mage."

Her defiance brought a smile to Ivina's face.

"Ah yes. That is better."

Evadne fell silent. More than anything, she wanted Ivina to leave. She wanted to lie down and mourn her sister in private.

"But you have always harbored this fear, haven't you?" Ivina said, stretching a long white finger to where Halcyon had fallen. "Nursed it since you were nine, the day Halcyon left you for the Bronze Legion. Halcyon, who was strong and revered and destined to become great. The daughter who would gild your family's name in honor. And what would you be, in comparison? Well, nothing. Because your sister outshined you, always, and you secretly resented her for it. You were often overlooked. And yet you loved her, and you feared she would leave you far behind, that she would go to a place you could not follow. That she would forget you. That you would lose her."

"Leave me," Evadne warned through her teeth. "I have nothing to say to you."

"That may be, but someone must say this to you, Evadne of Isaura, girl of flight. It is time for you to remake yourself."

"You know *nothing* of me, of what I need!"

Ivina snickered. She turned to leave, her white raiment whispering as she moved. But she stopped and looked back at Evadne one final time, her hair like gossamer on her shoulders.

"I do know, Evadne. Once, long ago, I was the same as you. I was a mortal girl, a young mage who did not know who she was or what she wanted. And look at me now. I see a shade of myself in you. You, Evadne, who have lived your entire life in comparison to Halcyon's. You measure yourself according to her. And the past moon, you have not lived for yourself, but for her. You gave up your freedom and took an amulet on your arm, all for her. You risked yourself in Euthymius, to finish what she started. Do you even know who you are? Can you be your own person without her? Or are you destined to be the moon, always reflecting the sun? Who is Evadne of Isaura?"

Evadne cursed her until the mage vanished into smoke that the wind carried back to the summit.

She was alone again, and the silence of the night crushed her. Evadne fell on her knees, stunned.

The things Ivina had said . . . some of her words had been terrible, intended to wound Evadne at her weakest moment. But some of her words had been truth.

And that truth broke the last of her.

Who *was* Evadne without her sister?

She did not know.

~

The sun rose.

Evadne packed her provisions. She banked the fire. She bundled the bedroll, strapping it to her shoulders. She sheathed the sword and began to walk.

She could find only one horse, grazing in the meadow. The other gelding was gone, and Evadne led her horse down into the ravine to begin the terrible search for her sister's body.

The ground was pebbled, rocky, choked with weeds. Evadne walked on foot, the gelding following delicately behind her. She was afraid to look ahead, to see Halcyon's remains. She expected to find her broken, her blood pooled about her.

She stopped suddenly, closing her eyes, hiding her face in the gelding's neck. She would never get home like this, though. And Isaura waited, just over the foothills.

Evadne continued to walk along the ravine's floor. But there was no sign of Halcyon.

She was beginning to wonder if the enchanted Xander had taken her into another world—perhaps they had slipped away through a secret door in the air—when Evadne finally saw a flash of movement, high on a ledge, halfway up the perilous slope.

A girl, holding to a wiry shrub. Bleeding, breathing. *Alive.*

"Halcyon!" She dropped the reins and took flight, her voice echoing off the rock, but Halcyon heard and tilted her head. Her eyes widened as she watched Evadne glide, hover in the air beside her.

And then Halcyon did the most remarkable thing.

She laughed, just as Damon had done in the mountain. She laughed until she was weeping, and Evadne embraced her, waiting for Halcyon to trust her enough to carry her, to let go of the shrub that had saved her life.

"Am I dreaming, Eva?" Halcyon whispered, still clinging to the plant. Her face was scratched from the fall, as were her hands, her arms. Dried blood and tears cut paths down her dusty cheeks. "Or are you truly flying?"

"This is real," Evadne said, smiling. "And you are about to fly with me. Trust me, Sister. Let go."

It took her another breath. But then Halcyon did.

She trusted Evadne's arms, her unseen wings. And she let go.

There is a meadow in Isaura. In summer, it is a field of gold, and in winter, one can see it from Gregor's villa. It is like catching a glimpse of another realm, a place that only the divines know. This was sacred childhood ground, a piece of earth that Halcyon and Evadne had often explored as girls. This was the ground where Evadne had sat with her wax tablet, practicing her letters, waiting for magic to arrive. Where Halcyon had raced the mountain boys. Evadne remembered how her sister had once run through the grass—dauntless, victorious.

This was the path they took home.

Halcyon rode the gelding, and Evadne walked ahead with the reins, leading her sister through the tall grass, a world of gold and wildflowers. Dragonflies and beetles flew in lazy circles, their iridescent wings gliding on the breeze. A pair of doves startled, their melodies like a welcome banner above the sisters. And as Evadne walked deeper into home, she no longer felt exhausted and discouraged and bruised. She did not feel the pain in her shoulder or her ankle, or the blisters on her feet. Even Halcyon lifted her face to the sun, breathing in the fragrance of the meadow, breathing in the memories of her childhood.

She smiled at Evadne. For a moment, they were girls again.

The breeze rushed to meet them. Evadne could smell the grove within it. She could see the olive trees, their branches dressed gloriously in leaves. She could see the roof of her father's home, waiting to shelter them.

She shielded her eyes as she saw someone emerge from the shadows of the trees, from the back courtyard of the villa. He ran into the meadow, cutting through the gold and the sunlight. He ran to meet them, and Evadne dropped the reins, trembling.

"Evadne!" Gregor called, like he was afraid she was a mirage, and would fade before he could reach her.

Evadne ran to him. He swept her into his arms, he lifted her off the ground, his face pressed into her hair. She held him as he wept, and she was worried he might break. But then Gregor set her down and took her face in his hands.

"Eva, Eva," he said, over and over like her name was a chorus. He smiled through his tears. "I cannot believe it is you. How can this be?"

She took his hand, her voice suddenly lost in her chest. She led him to the horse, where Halcyon still waited, gilded in sun.

He had not recognized her.

"Halcyon?" Gregor startled, drawing in a jagged breath, his fingers slipping from Evadne's as he moved to his oldest daughter. He saw her thinness, her bruises, her wounds, her weakness. Gently, he reached up to touch her hand, to press a kiss to her knuckles.

Evadne turned away, to grant them a moment.

And she saw her mother now running to them, shawl falling away from her head, her black hair tangling behind her. And her cousin Maia was waving and shouting, her smile so broad Evadne could see the gleam of it. And Uncle Nico, who was slow, and Aunt Lydia, who never ran, were both sprinting, and Lysander was passing them all with his great, hungry strides.

One final person hurried into the meadow. One more person who Evadne almost did not recognize.

He looked just like he had ten years ago.

Uncle Ozias.

Her long-lost uncle had returned.

They were all home now, Evadne thought, and suddenly it was difficult to breathe.

She watched her family rush to greet her and Halcyon.

And that was when Evadne finally dropped to her knees, smiling, weeping, laughing. Overcome.

⤙XXVIII⤚

Evadne

Home was just as Evadne remembered. The frescoes were still woefully cracked on the walls, and the corridors still smelled like warm bread, and the common room was still too small to hold all of her family. But that is where they gathered, Gregor carrying Halcyon. He carefully set her down on cushions.

Halcyon groaned in pain.

Phaedra knelt beside her, stroking her daughter's shaven head. Evadne sat on the other side of her sister, anxious, as she watched her mother's hand trace the scabs on Halcyon's brow and jaw, the bruises. Her voice trembled when she said, "Gregor? One of you should ride to Dree, to summon the healer."

Gregor seemed struck motionless, staring down at Halcyon. The joy of reunion was dimming into fear, disbelief as the family realized how ill Halcyon was. As they listened to her labor to breathe.

"Nico, you go," Aunt Lydia said to her husband. "Now!" Tears gleamed in her eyes.

The men departed the chamber, closing the door behind them. And the women began to undress Halcyon.

"Mother . . ." Halcyon whispered.

"I am here, love," Phaedra said, caressing Halcyon's hollow cheeks. "I am going to take care of you. Close your eyes and rest."

Halcyon obeyed, resting her head on one of the pillows, closing her eyes.

Evadne cut away Halcyon's tunic, Phaedra unwrapped her wounds, and Aunt Lydia and Maia prepared a bowl of water.

Despite everything Evadne had just gone through, it was one of the worst moments she had experienced: to witness her mother behold Halcyon's poor state of health.

"Lydia?" Phaedra said, serene although her hands were shaking. "Will you go fetch my pot of salve and one of my old chitons? We can shred it into new bandages."

Lydia moved at once, slipping from the room. And Evadne noticed that Maia was trying her best not to weep as she stared at Halcyon, her face crumpling. Evadne took her cousin's arm. "Can you bring down a fresh set of clothes for Halcyon?"

Maia nodded and was gone, and it was only Phaedra, Evadne, and Halcyon.

Quietly, they bathed her, minding Halcyon's raw forearms. Evadne could see the countless questions in her mother's gaze, but she held them captive.

Halcyon's eyes fluttered open. Her chest rose and fell as she breathed, shallow and wet.

"I know, I look terrible . . ." she rasped.

"You are beautiful, Halcyon. So beautiful." Phaedra stroked Halcyon's face again.

Evadne sensed that she should leave. They needed a moment alone.

She departed the chamber, closing the twin doors behind her only to discover her father in the corridor. He stood against the wall, arms crossed, waiting.

"Father?"

"I need to know everything, Pupa," Gregor murmured. "Did you sneak Halcyon from the quarry? Are you fugitives? How did your sister come to be so ill? Was it Lord Straton? I will *kill* that man if he ever steps foot on my lands again."

Evadne hesitated. What could she possibly say to her father? She could not tell him everything. Not yet. She would have to tell him bits and pieces.

She reached out to touch Gregor's arm. "Father . . . I . . ."

She noticed Uncle Ozias from the corner of her eye, tentatively approaching.

"Uncle Ozias," she breathed, and when he held out his arms, she went to him.

He embraced her, holding her tight for a moment. He was just as she remembered him being, save for the long scar on the right side of his face. His chiton smelled of sun and smoke, and she wondered where he had been for the past ten years. Why he had stayed away so long. She felt Kirkos's relic beneath her tunic, and she stiffened, hoping he could not feel it.

"How you have grown, Evadne! The last time I saw you, you did not even reach my elbow," Ozias said, pulling back so he could study her. "Gregor said you favored him, and yet I could not imagine it. But now I see . . . he was right."

Gregor was still overwhelmed, trying not to cry. Evadne glanced to her father, watched him run his hand through his messy hair.

"Yes," Evadne said, looking back to her uncle. "I am happy you have returned home."

There was an awkward beat of silence. Ozias cleared his throat and said, "I know, I have been away for too long. But when I heard the news of Halcyon and how you had left Isaura to take a portion of her sentence . . . I wanted to come home. To see my brothers."

Evadne's heart warmed, and she was opening her mouth to say more when Lydia and Maia returned to the corridor, bearing fresh clothes and bandages and warm tea for Halcyon.

"I will tell you everything soon, Father," Evadne promised Gregor. She began to follow her aunt and cousin into the common room when Ozias took a gentle hold of her arm.

"Wait, Evadne."

She paused, expectant as she looked at her uncle.

Ozias glanced down the corridor, where Uncle Nico and Lysander stood, curious. "I told Nico not to ride for the healer."

"Why?" A flash of anger coursed through Evadne.

Ozias's eyes shifted nervously. From Gregor's scowl to Evadne's anger to Nico's and Lysander's confusion. "When you have finished dressing Halcyon, will you invite us back into the chamber? There is something I need to say to her, and I would like the entire family to be present."

Evadne did not like his request, and she found that she did not wholly trust Ozias. But she only nodded and slipped into the common room, leaving the men in the shadows of the corridor.

Aunt Lydia and Phaedra were making swift work of cleaning and rebandaging Halcyon's wounds and cuts. Soon, they had Halcyon dressed in a clean chiton, and Maia was helping Halcyon sip the tea.

"Where is the healer, I wonder?" Phaedra asked, rising and gathering the soiled linens.

"Uncle Ozias has something to say to Halcyon," Evadne said. "Before the healer arrives."

Her mother and aunt looked bewildered and irritated, but Evadne opened the door, and the men returned to the room.

They gathered around Halcyon, who seemed to shrink into her cushions as if she was afraid. Afraid of her family?

Evadne knelt at her side and wove her fingers with her sister's. She felt Halcyon's grip tighten on hers, apprehensive.

Ozias gazed down at Halcyon, a crease in his brow. And then he said, "Quickly, quickly. Move her and the cushions there, into the sunlight."

Gregor gaped at him. "Cease this, Ozias. My daughter is ill!"

"Do as I say, Gregor," Ozias said calmly, his gaze remaining on Halcyon.

Gregor gently scooped Halcyon into his arms, and Evadne

grasped the pillows, moving them into a large patch of warm sunlight. She helped her father ease Halcyon back down onto the cushions, and Halcyon stifled another groan.

And all Evadne could think was her Uncle Ozias was mad.

But then he knelt on Halcyon's other side, the sunlight brightening his tawny hair. He reached for Halcyon's hand and held it a moment, and he smiled at her.

"I knew the night you were born, when I first held you, that you were destined for something more, that you heard a calling beyond this grove as I once did," he said. "I remember how fast and strong you were as a girl. You could run so swiftly, as if you had wings. A kingfisher bird."

Halcyon's eyes flooded with tears. *He is needlessly upsetting her*, Evadne thought, wringing her hands. But then she saw a change overcome her sister. Halcyon's emotion eased into a reverent peace, as if she saw something in Ozias no one else could.

He reached beneath the collar of his chiton. Evadne stared at him, heart thundering, and her family pressed closer, anxious, mistrusting. But it was only a silver chain that he removed from his neck. A silver chain that carried a ring.

Ozias freed the ring from the chain and held it to the light. It was a golden band, intricately etched with vines and flowers, and a great sunstone glittered in its setting. Red and amber and incandescent with fire, with life.

Lysander's jaw dropped in disbelief.

And Evadne finally understood. She knew what this ring was, and tears swarmed her eyes.

"I give you this ring, Halcyon of Isaura," Ozias said with a gentle smile. "Wear it and be healed."

And he slipped Magda's enchanted relic—the Sunstone Ring of Healing—onto Halcyon's finger.

Evadne found Uncle Ozias that night after dinner. He sat alone on the edge of the courtyard, staring into the starlit grove. He heard her approach and droned, "No, Lysander. For the hundredth time, I will *not* tell you where I found the ring."

"Thank the divines I am not Lysander, then," said Evadne.

Ozias turned and saw her. "Ah, Evadne. Forgive me. I thought you were your cousin. Come, sit beside me."

She did, and they were quiet for a moment, watching the night breeze play with the branches.

"I wanted to thank you, Uncle," Evadne said. "For giving your relic to Halcyon."

She could only imagine how difficult it was for him to surrender the ring. She knew how much her uncle had once craved possessing a relic, almost more than anything. His former greed had tragically driven a wedge between him and his brothers.

Ozias was quiet, and then he glanced at her with a smile. "I am honored to give it to her."

"Thank you."

"Your sister should keep it on her finger and bask in sun as much as she can," he said. "It will take her a while to fully heal, but she should. The enchantment is fueled by the sun, but moonlight will work as well. The ring is not as effective at night, but that should be a given. For Magda is the goddess of the sun, is she not?"

Evadne agreed. She was thinking of all the windows in the villa they could open to let as much sun in as possible. And then maybe they could bring Halcyon outside, to the meadow, where the light was full and golden.

Ozias cast his gaze back to the grove. "It is humbling to return here after I swore I would stay away."

Evadne sensed this was an invitation and roused her courage to ask the question no one dared speak to Ozias. "Where have you been all these years, Uncle?" By the scar on his face, she surmised he had once been held prisoner in the common quarry. But even that presumption felt odd, because Ozias wore fine clothes and had the Sunstone Ring of Healing in his possession, a relic that had been lost for years.

"I have been many places, Evadne," Ozias replied. "I have walked the queen's palace and supped in thieves' taverns. I have been in court and in prison and everywhere between."

"Is that where you received your scar?"

"You are the first of the family to ask about it," he said, glancing at her. "For that, I will answer you truthfully. A mage once tried to kill me. He was unsuccessful but left me with a scarred face."

His words troubled Evadne. "Why would a mage attempt to kill you, Uncle?"

"We wanted the same thing."

"A relic?"

Ozias smiled. "Ah, it is always about the relics, isn't it?"

Evadne waited for him to further explain, but he fell quiet, his hand retrieving a small square of papyrus from his chiton. He held it in the space between them, and Evadne's breath caught when she saw what was inked on the papyrus: the stamp of the mysterious basilisk.

"I saw you the day the queen rode through Mithra," said Ozias. "I stood in the crowd and watched you and Damon, and I knew then . . . I knew that he was about to drag you into this quandary, and I did not want that for you. Not after what had befallen Halcyon. I sent you the letter to meet me at the Gilded Owl, hoping you would recognize this symbol, that you would connect it to me."

Evadne took the papyrus, studying the basilisk. She finally saw it, now that she knew it was him. The basilisk was like the old fresco on her bedroom wall. The chamber that had once been Ozias's.

"I thought it was Macarius," she confessed. She was overwhelmed, realizing that her uncle was also woven into Straton's secrets. "I thought Macarius had written to me, not you."

"So I suspected the moment he followed you into the shop," Ozias said. "I could see you from the storeroom, but you left before I could redirect you."

She handed the papyrus square back to her uncle, distressed. "So you have been working with Lord Straton and Damon?"

"I work for and serve the queen," he said. "When I first set out from Isaura all those years ago, I sought relics for my own gain. I was the lowest of the low. But my life changed when Queen

Nerine granted me mercy for a petty crime. She gave me a renewed purpose, and I vowed to serve her in her secret alliance, to be her eyes and her ears in places she could not tread."

"You are a spy," Evadne blurted, amazed.

"Your words, not mine," Ozias said, amused. "But yes. I began to work closely with Straton when we both suspected that Selene was manipulating the queen. That led me to uncover her plan for the relics. Selene's group of mages are trying to gather all of them together and use them against the queen by making it seem that Nerine has turned her back on the common people. Selene has already passed a few laws through her that have sparked dissention and inequality. We have been trying to find the relics before they do, to keep them out of their hands."

Evadne remembered how the common people around her had shouted and booed at the queen that day in the street. She thought of the relics, how the divines had left them behind for common people to wield, to keep the mages in check. Her stomach ached when she dwelled on Acantha's crown, now lost to them.

"We lost the crown, Uncle. I am so sorry, but Macarius was waiting for Damon and me at the mountain threshold. He overpowered us. And I know that the crown was the most important relic of all. That it was the last hope for Nerine, to break whatever enchantment Selene has cast upon her."

Ozias gently touched her shoulder. "You do not need to apologize to me, Eva. I am still in awe of you, that you were able to survive the dangers of Euthymius."

And yet it was not enough. Evadne covered her face for a

moment, breathing in the scent on her palms. "Damon has gone to Abacus, to see his father." Her hands fell away, and she looked at Ozias. "Why have you come home, Uncle?"

Ozias glanced to the grove. And she knew why he had returned to Isaura. It was not to see his estranged family, to comfort his brother, to mend the past.

"You have returned here to search for Kirkos's relic," Evadne whispered.

"Yes. It makes me sound callous, does it not, Eva?"

She remembered how he had once wanted to dig up Kirkos's grave, thinking the relic was buried with the god. And how all this time, her own father had been keeping it. Her family, it seemed, was built upon secrets.

"Father does not know that you are Nerine's spy," she stated.

"No. And he should not, Eva."

"And what of the other relics?"

"Three are still unaccounted for. Irix's Sky Cloak. Loris's Pearl Earrings. And Kirkos's Winged Necklace."

"The Sunstone Ring of Healing . . ." She hesitated, worried.

"It can remain with Halcyon for now," Ozias reassured her. "She is a member of our alliance, a servant of the queen. She knows to guard it well."

It was the response she'd been waiting to hear.

Evadne lifted the silver chain from her neck, the lapis wing centered in her palm, and held it out to her uncle.

Ozias merely stared at it for a breath. Stunned. And then he brushed it with his fingertip.

"By the gods," he whispered. He met Evadne's gaze. "Where did you . . . ?"

She shook her head. "No. I will not tell you where I found it. Just as you will not tell Lysander where you found the ring."

"Fair enough, Eva."

"But I would like to give it to you, Uncle Ozias. For Queen Nerine." Evadne set it into his palm, the chain whispering as it left her.

She wanted it back as soon as she let it go. She wanted to keep it around her neck until she died, to revel in that one piece of magic. But she knew that relics were not to be hoarded. There was more at stake now. More than she had ever thought possible.

"Thank you." Ozias enclosed the relic within his fingers. "When this is all over and we have prevailed, Queen Nerine will be honored to know what you have done for her, Eva."

Evadne nodded and smiled. But within? Her heart was churning. Because it seemed that victory was as distant as the stars.

❧XXIX❧

Evadne

He's gone!" Lysander cried, bursting into the common room the following morning.

Evadne sat beside Halcyon in the sun, feeding her soaked oats and honey. She stopped to stare at her cousin, his anger disturbing the tranquil air like a storm.

"Who, Lysander?" Maia asked around a yawn. She sat on Halcyon's other side, holding a cup of steaming tea for her cousin to sip.

"Who do you think?" Lysander growled. "Uncle Ozias!"

Evadne's eyes drifted to where her father sat on his bench, finishing his breakfast. Gregor frowned and said, "No, that cannot be. Ozias said he was going to be with us until next summer."

"His chamber is empty. His possessions are gone, and so is his horse. He's gone, just like that. No goodbye. No farewells. Just . . . *gone*. Like some thief in the night!" And Lysander collapsed onto the floor, fuming.

Evadne knew why Ozias had left without word: he had Kirkos's relic, and he needed to return to the queen in Mithra. But her throat narrowed when she saw a gleam of pain in her father's eyes. Her mother touched Gregor's shoulder, a wordless comfort. Aunt Lydia began to mutter—*good riddance to him; why did we even welcome him home in the first place?*—and even Uncle Nico appeared crestfallen that his brother had slipped away from the villa without a word.

"I am sure he will return soon," said Phaedra. "Perhaps he had an errand in Dree."

"Unlikely," Lysander said, pouting into the oats his mother set down before him. "Ever since Bacchus was murdered, Dree has been different. All the men have left. It is like the eve of war in that village. Why would Ozias go there?"

"Bacchus has been murdered?" Evadne cried, nearly overturning Halcyon's bowl of oats.

Her family looked at her, surprised by her passionate outburst. She felt Halcyon's hand, stronger than it was the day before, take hers and gently squeeze.

Halcyon knew, then.

Macarius, Evadne thought. Macarius must have had something to do with this, and Evadne felt like killing him. Again.

"Yes," Lysander said. "Bacchus was murdered by that brute Laneus. And Laneus stole the Golden Belt, and who knows where he took the relic? He has all but vanished, like some worthless uncle I know."

Laneus.

Evadne met Halcyon's sorrowful gaze.

"The vile boy of Dree?" Evadne whispered to her. And Halcyon nodded.

It took everything within Evadne to calm herself, to draw in a deep breath. To continue feeding Halcyon her oats. Because that was what mattered most in this moment: restoring Halcyon's health.

The days began to pass. Evadne often sat at Halcyon's side in the light, watching her sister's health gradually return. Halcyon slept more than anything else, but she was never alone. There was always someone near her. Phaedra mended garments; Gregor sang, low and sweet. Maia wove crowns, and Aunt Lydia shelled beans. Uncle Nico balanced ledgers, and even Lysander took a turn sitting beside Halcyon, reading an old scroll of legends, trying his best not to gawk at the ring on her finger.

It revived Evadne to see her sister safe at home—sleeping, dreaming, mending.

But with every day that passed, Evadne's worries heightened. They were isolated here in southern Corisande. News did not come to them; they had to go to Dree to glean it, and ever since Bacchus's slaying, her family had avoided going to the mountain village. And so Evadne wondered what was occurring outside the boundary of the grove. Did Selene have the All-Seeing Crown yet? What was Macarius's next move? Why had all the men left Dree? Where had Laneus taken the Golden Belt?

She tried not to watch Isaura's gates, which her father kept locked in case the commander arrived to demand Halcyon back. Which he would not, Evadne knew. Straton had more pressing matters to attend to now. But Gregor still kept the gates locked, and Evadne continued to glance to them, expectant.

Damon, where are you?

Whenever she thought of him, a small ache drummed in her chest. It was only because she was waiting for news. Because she was anxious. Not because she missed him. Or so she tried to convince herself.

Perhaps he would not come, then. Perhaps he had changed his mind and he did not need her anymore. Perhaps he had forgotten her.

The thought was strange, and she could not understand why it made her feel vulnerable.

Almost a week had passed before he finally arrived. Evadne, of course, was dusted in flour, kneading bread with her mother in the kitchen. She did not hear the gate bell ring, so lost was she in her thoughts, but Lysander came stomping into the villa, and she heard his announcement drift down the hall: "Uncle Gregor, there is a mage at the gate. Should I let him in?"

Evadne deserted her dough and was down the corridor, out the front doors before her father could so much as rise from his bench in the common room. She was barefoot; she felt the flagstones and the grass beneath her as she walked, the courtyard warm from the midday sun. There was not a cloud in the sky, and the air was bright, painful at first. But then her gaze found the tall gates of Isaura, and waiting behind the iron vines was Damon.

When she could see his face, when his gaze met hers, she could not breathe.

She stopped at the gates, and they stared at each other as if they had been apart for years.

"Evadne," he whispered. His voice rushed about her like the tide, revealing his relief to find her here, safe. "I—" He was about to say more, but Gregor arrived.

"Who are you? What business do you have here?"

Damon looked at Gregor. Evadne flushed, to hear how rude her father spoke to Damon.

"I am Damon of Mithra. Evadne is my—"

"Evadne is *my* daughter, and you have no right to come here," Gregor countered. "Be gone, back to wherever you came from!"

Damon took a step back.

"Father." Evadne gently took her father's arm. "You remember what I told you? I am Damon's scribe, and I have been waiting for him to come."

Gregor's jaw clenched. But he met his daughter's gaze, and she watched as he struggled to reconcile what he felt with what his daughter was asking of him.

"Are you certain about this, Pupa?" Gregor whispered to her.

Evadne nodded, smiling up at him. It was a rare thing for him to deny that smile.

With a sigh, Gregor relented and unlocked the gates.

"*Pupa?*" Damon asked her half an hour later, when they were finally alone, walking through the grove.

The sun trickled over their shoulders, and Evadne had to press a smile to her lips, her cheeks warm with embarrassment.

"I was hoping you did not hear that," she said.

"I thought I misheard at first."

"No. My father affectionately nicknamed me after *larvae*. For as long as I can remember, he has called me such."

Damon was quiet. Evadne snuck a glance at him to see he was trying his best not to laugh.

"It suits you, Evadne."

She swatted at him, and his laughter unfolded, startling a sparrow from the boughs. For a moment, the world was not a treacherous place. They were not a mage and a scribe with an impossible challenge awaiting them. They were just a young man and a young woman, walking together in a grove, their arms brushing, their hearts content and luminous.

But when the moment passed, Evadne and Damon both fell quiet again. She saw the god tree in the distance, the tormented olive tree inviting them into its shadows. They came to a stop beneath the ancient branches, and Evadne sat in the grass, her ankle plaguing her, while Damon rushed his hand along the gnarled trunk.

"This grove is a hard place to find," he said, admiring the tree. "I rode all morning trying to locate the road that would lead to your gate."

"It is intended to be that way," Evadne replied, leaning back on her elbows, tilting her head up to the sky. "Kirkos's last enchantment, before he fell."

"Your home is beautiful, Evadne."

She felt his eyes trace her, and she met his gaze. He stood close by, his shadow cascading over her, and her heart ached. That small ache she had felt for days, waiting for him.

"I have news," she said, ignoring the spark she felt.

Damon sat down beside her, a few hand lengths away.

"I met with the Basilisk last week," she announced, watching the shock move across Damon's face.

"*What?* How did he know where to find you?"

"He is my uncle." She was not surprised Ozias had kept his connection to her and Halcyon a secret. But Damon was.

"Your *uncle?*" He laughed, incredulous. "My gods! He should have told us. That could have risked the entire mission."

"But it didn't, did it?" Evadne said, despite knowing that Ozias would have opposed her going into the mountain.

"Does Halcyon know it is him?"

"I do not know. I gave him Kirkos's relic, and he left, returning to Mithra." She picked a blade of grass, wrapping it around her finger. "He did not tell me much at all. I have been waiting for you to bring me news."

Damon let out a long sigh. "My father believes Selene is going to press on with her coup. The heralds have proclaimed that Queen Nerine has ordered all the gates of Mithra to be locked, that no one may leave or enter. It is an act of war and my aunt's way of summoning my father to come and challenge her, one final time. Because my mother and my sister are now trapped within the city, beneath my aunt's power. And my father cannot abide that. He has rallied his legion, and he plans to march with his hoplites today. They will march to Mithra and breach the city to save the queen."

Evadne was quiet, soaking in this terrible thought. And then she whispered, "Will Selene send the queen's army to fight your father?"

"My father does not believe so. The queen's army respects him. He has trained many of them. Selene would be a fool if she thought she could turn the queen's hoplites against my father."

"Then who will the legion have to fight?"

"That we do not know."

Evadne was uncertain on what to say, because it suddenly felt as if she was not needed. She and Damon were not hoplites. What could they do in the face of a siege and a battle?

"Despite all of this," Damon said, and his hand drifted closer to hers, "my father has asked for my support. He wants me to march with his legion to Mithra."

She resisted the temptation to look at him. "Do you want me to join you?"

He was silent for a moment. "Yes, Evadne. I want you to come with me. But before you answer . . . I need you to know that this will be dangerous, perhaps even more than our journey into the heart of Euthymius. And I will understand should you choose to remain here with your family. In fact, I want to beg you to stay, and yet I want to beg you to come, and I can hardly understand how you have inspired this in me, that I should desire two different things in the same breath."

He stopped speaking abruptly. As if he could not believe he had just said it aloud to her.

But his eyes . . . they continued to speak.

What have you done to me?

She glanced away. To hide her own longings. But she felt his warmth and heard his breath falling swiftly, as if it was both pleasurable and painful to be so close and yet so far from her.

At last, she was finally beginning to understand why Kirkos had chosen to stay on Earth. Why he had chosen to give up his wings and his divinity.

Not yet, her mind said. *Do not lose your reason just yet.*

She tilted her head back until her hair brushed the grass. Sun and shadows on her face, she closed her eyes, knowing Damon was still watching her.

"Will there be endless stairs or waterfalls or angry immortal mages involved?" she drawled.

He snorted, amused. "Divines, no."

She relented to open her eyes, to look at him.

What have you done to me? She wanted to return to him, like the whisper just before lips touched. Because she wanted to stay and she wanted to go. She wanted the same things as him.

But she did not speak them. *Not yet, not yet.*

She smiled and said, "Then yes. I will go with you."

Halcyon still slumbered in the sun, deeply trenched in healing dreams. Evadne knelt beside her, dressed and packed, the hair braided back from her eyes, moments away from departing with Damon.

Their mother worked nearby, mending a new chiton for Halcyon. The villa was quiet, and the walls almost felt sad, to know that Evadne was about to leave them again.

"Should I wake her?" Evadne whispered.

Her mother glanced to Halcyon. Her dark brows lowered. "I do not know, Eva. If she wakes . . ." And her voice trailed.

But Evadne knew what her mother was thinking. *If Halcyon wakes, she will want to go.*

Evadne dropped a kiss on her sister's brow, marveling at how much color had returned to her skin, how her wounds and bruises had all but faded. It felt wrong to leave Halcyon without a goodbye, but Evadne had never been fond of farewells, and she managed to rise and turn, striding from the common room before her resolve broke.

Phaedra followed her out into the courtyard, where Damon waited with two horses, Gregor speaking to him in a stern voice.

"Father," Evadne said, and Gregor stopped midsentence to look at her.

His eyes lost their sharpness. He walked to her and gathered her close. "Why must you leave, Pupa?" he whispered into her hair. "You only just returned."

Evadne leaned back to meet his gaze. "Remember how we like to sing, Father? We sing all of the stanzas, or else the song hangs unfinished in the air. And so I must go now, to finish something I began. I must honor my word, as you have taught me to do."

Gregor cupped her face, and she worried he would cry again. But he only smiled—a sad, painful smile—and kissed her brow. He released her, and she embraced her mother next.

"You will return soon, Eva?" Phaedra asked, smoothing a few unruly threads of hair in Evadne's braids. "And Lord Straton's legion will protect you?"

"Yes, Mother." Evadne resisted the urge to look at Damon, knowing he had mentioned the legion to ease her parents' minds. He had not, however, mentioned the siege and the imminent clash at Mithra's gates.

Uncle Nico and Aunt Lydia waited next, to hug her goodbye. And Maia, with tears streaming down her cheeks, and Lysander with envy in his eyes.

She turned to Damon. He waited for her, mounted on one of the horses, and Evadne walked to him, drawing herself up into the saddle.

She followed him through the gates. And Evadne looked back, just once, to catch a fleeting glimpse of her family. All save for Halcyon and Uncle Ozias.

But she memorized the image of them, pressed it into her memory like a wax seal.

And she rode without fear to the east. She rode with Damon to meet Straton's legion.

To finish what Halcyon had begun.

Halcyon and Evadne

When Halcyon woke, it was evening. The air was calm, tranquil.

And yet something did not feel right.

She sat up, surprised to discover she was in her bedroom. An oil lamp burned on her wash table. By its gentle light, Halcyon studied Evadne's side of the chamber. Her little sister's bed was perfectly made. Her tablet sat on her oaken chest, the Haleva symbols still pressed within the wax.

Halcyon rose and walked to the tablet, holding it in her hands. She studied the symbols, traced them with her fingertips, Magda's sunstone glittering with the movement. And that was when Halcyon realized what the nagging feeling was. Every time she had woken, Evadne had been present.

She set the tablet aside and left the room, following threads of voices down the stairs into the common room. Her family was eating supper by firelight, and they startled at the sight of her standing on the threshold.

"Sprout," her father said. "Come and eat with us."

Halcyon's gaze flickered from face to face, all beloved but none the one she sought. "Where is Eva?"

Her family seemed to freeze.

"Eva?" Maia echoed with a nervous twitch, like she had never heard of her before.

"She is away for a little while, Halcyon," Phaedra said in a smooth voice. She filled a bowl of stew, extending it for her to take. "Come, my love. Join us."

"Where is Evadne?" Halcyon asked again, her voice sharpening.

Uncle Nico looked away first, and Halcyon's suspicions multiplied.

"Father," she said. "Father, where is my sister?"

Gregor rushed his hands over his face. He sighed and stared across the room at her, and even though he parted his lips, he seemed unable to speak.

Lysander said, "Evadne left with Damon to join up with the legion."

"The legion?" Halcyon looked at him. Her face was guarded, but her stomach was aching. "*My* legion?"

She did not need them to answer. She knew it then, studying their faces.

Evadne had left her. Without a word.

Halcyon backed away, out of the firelight, out of the room, her thoughts a tangled blur, her breaths coming fast and hard. It felt like someone had just punched her.

Phaedra stood, spilling the stew in her haste. "Halcyon, please. You must remain here!"

Halcyon was already halfway up the stairs by then. She blew into her bedchamber and began to dress and pack her things, a tremor racking her hands.

She had fastened her belt and draped a shawl about her shoulders when she felt her father's presence in the room.

Gregor stood and watched her, and Halcyon hesitated when she looked at him, at his sorrow.

"Father, I must go. You know that."

"I know, Halcyon."

He was silent, regarding her. Halcyon shifted her weight, clenched and unclenched her hands.

"But your mother is worried, Sprout."

Sprout. She could not believe her father still called her by that old nickname. That it still held such a gleam in his voice.

"About what? My health is fully restored." That was a lie. Halcyon knew she was not whole yet. Her strength was still striving to regain what had been stolen from it. But she would not confess that.

"About Lord Straton. Your sentence still stands, Daughter. What if he decides to shackle you? Or send you back to the quarry?"

Halcyon exhaled a long breath as she thought of her commander. She remembered how he had held her, wept over her. He had striven to keep her alive, even after all the pain she had given him.

The world would darken without you.

He had wounded her, but she had wounded him, too. And the final portion of her healing could not begin without him.

Her redemption was not here, in Isaura. It lay to the east, where the commander walked among his hoplites in the moonlight, preparing for the unknown.

"Lord Straton needs me, Father. I am one of his warriors, and I must answer the call he has sounded. Sentence or no."

Gregor nodded, weary. And yet there was something else within him. A spark of pride. "Then let us prepare you the best we can, Sprout."

She followed him into the kitchen. To her surprise, her mother and aunt and Maia had already packed her provisions. A sack heavy with food and two water canteens. And then Lysander came rushing into the room with a set of leather gloves.

"Hal, you need to cover your ring."

Halcyon had become so accustomed to the relic that she nearly forgot its presence on her finger. But Lysander was right; Magda's sunstone needed to remain hidden.

Halcyon slipped her hands into the gloves, grateful. And then she looked at her family, gathered close about her, watching her with dewy eyes.

"Thank you," she murmured. "I will return soon. Or I will send word with Eva." And she began to walk away from them when her father cried, "*Halcyon!*"

She stopped and turned, stunned by the emotion in his voice.

She thought he had changed his mind, that he would not let her leave. But it was his arms, open wide. For her.

She stepped into his embrace, wrapping her arms around him, holding to him tightly. She embraced her mother, her aunt, her cousins, her uncle. And it surprised her how the affection rekindled her. All this time she had been telling herself to *let go, let go.* But there was beauty and strength in the *holding on.*

Without another word, she turned and strode from the courtyard of Isaura, past the gates, to the road. She waited until she felt the wind push at her back with invitation.

And she set her eyes on the eastern sky and ran.

It took her two full days to find the legion.

Halcyon spotted them midafternoon, marching harmoniously in the distance, the bronze of their armor reflecting sun like a river. She trailed at a safe distance, anxious and exhausted and coated in dust. Whenever she thought she was prepared to approach, she decided to delay.

She watched as tents were erected in the early evening—Straton's sat at the heart of the camp—and as small fires bloomed among the sea of warriors. They would be resting, breaking bread together. Sharing ale from their flasks. Preparing to bed for the night. She also knew there would be a guard patrolling the camp. And she found them swiftly, figures who walked the perimeter. Mount Euthymius was in view, so torches burned at the edges of camp.

There were no shadows that Halcyon could use to slip her way into camp undetected. Too many guards, too many eyes, too much light.

She was looking for a glimpse of her sister when Halcyon recognized one of the hoplites on guard. A scorpion etched on her helm and shield. Her former captain, Narcissa. And Halcyon knew she had delayed long enough.

She began to walk down the hill, the grass long and thick with wildflowers, brushing her knees. She set her eyes on Narcissa, waiting for the captain to see her. Narcissa did, before Halcyon was truly ready.

"Halt!" Narcissa ordered, spear poised in her hand. "State your name and purpose."

Halcyon stopped, held up her hands. Narcissa still did not know it was her. Halcyon was not sure if that relieved her or pained her. Gently, she said, "It is me, Captain. Halcyon of Isaura. And I have come to speak with Lord Straton."

Narcissa did not move. She continued to aim her spear at Halcyon's heart, but her eyes widened. She took a step closer. Another. Her armor clinked with her graceful movements. And then she saw Halcyon's face, and she lowered her spear.

"Halcyon? How can this be?"

Halcyon swallowed. She was trembling as she lowered her hands. "It is a long story."

Narcissa stared at her a moment. Stricken. "You are not one of Ivina's phantoms, are you?"

Oh, the irony. Halcyon almost laughed. "No. But if you doubt me, then hand me a torch."

The captain continued to study her. At last, she smiled. "I almost did not recognize you, Hal."

"Yes, I have changed." And she read the trail of Narcissa's thoughts. It had been a full moon since they had last seen each other. A handful of weeks, and Halcyon's appearance was drastically altered. Not even the relic on her hand could resurrect the Halcyon of old. She was no longer that girl. In body or in spirit.

"How is your back?" Narcissa whispered.

"Fully healed."

The captain nodded, but there was a sheen in her eyes, as if she doubted Halcyon. "Lord Straton informed us all that he was not to be disturbed after sundown. But I sense he will make an exception for you."

Halcyon waited for Narcissa to shackle her wrists, to parade her into camp as a criminal. But her former captain did none of that. She motioned for Halcyon to wrap her shawl tighter about her face, to conceal it.

Halcyon was grateful that Narcissa brought her into the camp quietly. She breathed in the dust of her shawl and followed the captain into the camp, winding around fire rings and tents, keeping her eyes on the ground as she passed other hoplites.

All too soon, they arrived at Straton's tent.

"Wait here," Narcissa murmured.

Halcyon nodded, lingering outside, heart beating in her throat. But she watched as Narcissa ducked within the tent flaps. Halcyon could hear her say, "Lord Commander, I am sorry to interrupt you."

"Yes, what is it, Narcissa?"

"A visitor you will want to see."

"Can they not wait until morning?"

"No."

A weary sigh. "Very well. Send them in."

Halcyon took a step back. Gods, what was she doing? Why had she come here? But then Narcissa returned, standing in the mouth of the tent, beckoning her to come forward into the commander's light.

This is your moment, Halcyon told herself.

She stepped past Narcissa, into the tent. The commander sat at a table, staring at a map unrolled before him. He seemed bowed down, heavily preoccupied by his thoughts. And then he heard her footsteps, he felt her presence, and he looked up.

He frowned, seeking to know who she was.

Slowly, Halcyon let go of her shawl and revealed her face.

For a moment, Straton merely stared at her, as if that was all he could do. And then he rose, so abruptly he shook everything on his table.

And Halcyon knew she needed to be the one to speak first.

She held out her gloved hand and said, "Lord Commander, I have not followed your legion expecting to be welcomed back into the fold, or to be forgiven. I know I still bear a sentence I must fulfill. All I ask is that you allow me to fight at your side with my former squad, with your legion, for the battle that lies ahead of you. That you permit me to fight in memory and honor of your son Xander of Mithra, whom I loved as my own brother. And when this battle is over, I shall willingly return to the common quarry, to continue my penance."

Halcyon met his gaze, attempted to read the lines in his brow.

"I thought you were dead, Halcyon," he said.

She saw a flicker of pain and remorse in his face. But it was as fleeting as a star falling in the cosmos. Quietly, she said, "I live, Commander. Because of your mercy."

He glanced away, overcome. "Was it mercy, Kingfisher, that I gave you?"

Halcyon was silent. But her heart was thrumming in her chest. Did he regret it now? His choice to sustain her life?

"You must forgive me, Halcyon." Straton returned his gaze to her. His eyes were bright and keen, the blazing shade of the summer sky. "In anger, I wounded you. In anger, I struck your spirit when you were broken. I have wronged you. I do not deserve to have you in my legion. And I must ask you to forgive me."

She held his stare. And she knew his wounds—she saw them as if he had lowered his shield, at last. She beheld them just as he beheld hers. Wounds they had inflicted upon the other—in fear, in anger, in vengeance, in pride. As if they carried these marks on their bodies, visible to the eye. This moment was raw and painful and glorious. A fiery lance to close the final wound.

She could not give him complete forgiveness. But nor could she lie.

"Every morning, I wake and I inevitably dwell on what I have come through, what I have endured," she whispered to him. "It is still so fresh in my mind. How I long to forget, to have the power to be joyful again, to rise as the old Halcyon." She paused, a tremor in her voice. The commander hated tears and quivering, she reminded herself. And yet there were tears in his eyes as he listened to her. "But you have trained me to be stronger than that, Lord Straton. I am no longer that old Halcyon, nor will I ever be her again. I am something new, and it will take me time to fully heal. It will take me time to fully come to forgive you."

He was quiet, but her words had been meekly accepted by him. And she realized that he was not the old commander, either.

He nodded, seemingly at a loss, which she had never witnessed. Straton always knew what to say, which order to give.

"Then I will wait, Halcyon," he finally said.

And how those words refreshed and comforted her. To know that he did not expect it of her yet. That he would not drill her or hover over her. He would step back and patiently wait for her forgiveness, and she could suddenly breathe.

She nodded, glanced down to the ground as she blinked back her tears.

"Your sister said you were recovering," Straton said after a moment, "but I never imagined to see you this restored so soon."

"I am capable and eager to fight, Commander," she replied. She would not reveal that she wore Magda's ring, even though it was evident the commander sensed the enchantment about her. "If my captain and my squad will have me."

"Let us speak to Narcissa, then," Straton said, moving to the front of the tent, where Narcissa waited outside.

The captain stepped back into the tent, trailing the commander. She glanced from Halcyon to Straton.

"Halcyon of Isaura would like to rejoin your squad," the

commander said. "Does she have a place among you?"

Narcissa studied Halcyon. Studied her thinness, the lingering hollowness of her face, which no amount of food would fill. The golden, hungry gleam in Halcyon's eye.

"What of her sentence, Commander?" the captain asked.

"Her sentence has been absolved," he answered, and Halcyon had to swallow the shock that rose in her. "She has paid for her mistakes and has full restitution from me. She is a free woman, and so is her sister."

Narcissa walked around Halcyon, still intently studying her former warrior. "She is fully healed, then, Commander?"

"She says that she is."

Narcissa came to a stop again, directly before Halcyon. "She will have to earn back her place among us."

Halcyon held the captain's gaze. She expected no less from Narcissa; this was how it was done in the legion. Honor was always earned.

"Set a challenge upon me, Captain," Halcyon said. "I will prove that I am worthy."

"Very well, then." A smile curved the corner of Narcissa's mouth. "If you can disarm me in a spar, I will welcome you back into my squad."

"I agree to it," Halcyon answered, confident. She had disarmed Narcissa plenty of times before. But as she followed the captain out of the tent to be dressed in armor and weapon, her breath caught.

It had only been a little over a moon, but how much she had changed since then.

Because the last time Halcyon had wielded a sword and sparred had been with Xander. The day she had killed him.

"Damon . . . I swear, if you make me cross out another word . . . I will kill you."

Damon leaned on the makeshift desk Evadne was scribing at. They were in one of the camp tents. Oil lamps hung above them, filling the tent with light, and a rug was spread on the grass beneath them. Evadne sat on a pile of grain sacks, a new *charena* scroll spread before her, line after line marked through. She and Damon planned to work late into the night, but they would not get very far like this. Three words spoken, two words revoked.

A wily grin spread across his face. "Scratch that, Evadne."

"But . . . *why*? These words are . . ."

"Are what?"

Evadne set down her quill. She met his gaze and breathed, "They are beautiful."

"That they may be. But they are not perfect. And this spell must not lack anything."

"You have yet to tell me what, exactly, this spell is," she said.

"That is because it has no name yet." He continued to stare at her, almost as if he was memorizing her face and her hair. Even the way she was glaring up at him, ink smeared on her chin.

"Why are you looking at me like that?" she asked. "As if you are worried you might forget what I look like."

To her surprise, he stepped away. He did not answer her but posed a question in return. "What does this spell evoke in your mind, Evadne?"

She glanced down at the remaining words that had survived the cut. "The words evoke an imagery of earth: ancient olive trees, the scent of the wind just after a storm, the color of the sky at sunset." She paused, then said, "It sounds like beauty, like harmony."

Damon turned to regard her. "Beauty and harmony?"

Evadne kept her gaze on the scroll. Indeed, his spell made her think of home. Of Isaura. "Yes. Am I wrong?"

He started to pace around the tent. It was close quarters. Several times he narrowly missed hitting his head on one of the dangling oil lamps.

She had grown accustomed to his patterns. He liked to pace while he thought, and then he liked to look out a window when he spoke his magic for her to record. Only there were no windows, and Damon eventually came to stand before her again, staring at her handwriting.

He was just about to say something when they heard a commotion beyond the tent. The sound of shouts and the ring of swords.

"What is that?" Evadne asked, standing. She closed the *charena* scroll and carried it in her arms like a child, for it never left her or Damon's sight, and she followed him into the night. They wove through a crowd of warriors and campfires, growing closer to the sound of conflict. At first Evadne believed one of Ivina's phantoms had wormed its way into the camp, wreaking havoc. But as Evadne and Damon came to the front of the crowd, she saw it was no ghost that had inspired an audience.

It was Halcyon.

Evadne watched, unable to breathe, as her sister sparred with the captain.

Halcyon wore a cuirass and leg greaves, a helm with a plume of black horsehair. She bore a round shield on her left arm and wielded a sword in her right hand. She jerked and moved in a stiff manner, as if her muscles were cold, fatigued.

The captain easily deflected Halcyon's cuts, seeming to wait for Halcyon to remember herself, to come to life.

Evadne was not surprised her sister had pursued the legion. She had anticipated Halcyon would upon discovering Evadne had left. But despite that prediction, Evadne felt a pang of alarm. She had never seen Halcyon spar before. It was as beautiful as it was daunting. It took everything within Evadne to remain where she was, to not utter a sound. She held the scroll to her chest and felt Damon's warmth at her side as he, too, watched the spar unfold.

Halcyon spun, arced her sword in a powerful swing. The captain met it with her shield, deflecting Halcyon with little effort. Halcyon tried again, grunting and swinging. Still too slowly, as if her arms were struggling to keep up with the lightning-swift orders of her mind.

Narcissa took a cut at her. Halcyon blocked with her shield, but the impact made her stagger.

To everyone watching, it seemed apparent that Halcyon was not ready to return to the legion.

Evadne closed her eyes and listened to the sound of her sister's grunts, of the hiss of clashing blades, the thunk of swords meeting shields, the pounding of sandaled feet.

The spar continued like that for what felt like moons, dancing at the captain's unrelenting command.

But then Evadne felt the shift, and heard Halcyon's feet become agile, her grunts no longer defensive but offensive.

She opened her eyes and watched as her sister warmed to the spar, remembering herself. The stiffness was gone. Halcyon moved with smooth heat, her teeth bared, her sword catching the starlight.

She completed a sequence that had Evadne's heart in her throat, both awed and terrified. And then it happened, swift and unexpected.

Halcyon disarmed the captain.

The captain yielded on her knee, a slender smile on her lips.

And the hoplites cheered for Halcyon as she continued to stand with her sword in her hand, victorious.

Evadne watched it unfold like a bittersweet myth. And she knew that Halcyon had finally found her way home.

❧ XXXI ❧

Evadne and Halcyon

The moon continued her arc across the sky and the stars continued to burn as Halcyon was welcomed back into the legion. There was no talk of the past, and Evadne sat beside one of the fires, eating a stale piece of bread, watching it all with contentment.

Damon had retired to his tent, claiming they were done working for the night, and Evadne was inwardly relieved, for her mind was awhirl, and all she wanted was to remain near her sister. She abandoned her own tent and brought her bedroll out to the fire, laying it beside Halcyon's, to sleep beneath the stars as most of the hoplites did. And while she was weary, she waited patiently for Halcyon to finish with her reunions.

The amulet was gone from Evadne's arm. It had been the first thing Straton had done when Evadne and Damon had arrived days ago. The legion blacksmith had cut away the silver, and she had looked at the slight tan line left behind. Halcyon's sentence had been overturned, and with it, Evadne's. And while she could hardly describe the emotions this inspired in her, she also wondered what had brought this change in the commander.

Eventually, Evadne rose, walking through the camp to warm herself. She began to pass Damon's tent but stopped when the light within caught her eye, and she saw a glimpse of him sitting at the makeshift desk.

She silently drew the tent door open a sliver so she could fully see him.

He was writing in a scroll. One she had never seen before.

He wrote laboriously with his right hand, and it trembled from exhaustion when he lifted the quill to dip it in the ink pot.

She should go to him, offer to scribe. And yet she sensed he did not want her assistance. He was not working on enchantments; no, this was something else.

He felt the draft and started to turn toward the door, and Evadne backed hastily out of sight, hurrying along her path.

But her heart was pounding a doubtful chorus.

What is he hiding from me?

Deep in the night, Halcyon lay beside Evadne, listening to her sister sleep. Her stomach and heart were brimming, the fullest they had been in weeks. Even so, Halcyon was worried. There was too much to think about, too much uncertainty to come.

She felt Evadne stir, yanking on the blankets they shared.

"Evadne?" she said quietly.

A pause. And then a groggy "Yes, Hal?"

"Do not do that to me again."

"Do what?"

Halcyon swallowed, staring up at the stars. "Leave me without saying goodbye."

She felt Evadne turn to face her, yanking more of the blankets away.

"I am sorry for leaving you behind all those years ago," Halcyon whispered. "And I do not know what the future holds for me or for you, what lies ahead of us. But I promise that I will come and see you often, wherever you are. I know that the legion is my home. But it is also with you."

Evadne was silent. But Halcyon felt her shift, Evadne's hand moving to find hers in the dark.

"You know I hate goodbyes, Hal."

Halcyon snorted. "Yes, I know. But promise me you will not do it again."

Evadne threaded their fingers together. It was the hand Halcyon had killed with, the hand Evadne had written spells with. Two very different hands and two very different women, and yet they had sharpened the other, upheld the other. Defended and protected and healed one another.

Evadne tightened her hold on Halcyon.

"I promise."

It was strange to put armor on again.

Halcyon admired the pieces Narcissa had given her. A red tunic trimmed in white squares, a cuirass of bronze scales and linen pleats, leather sandals to crosshatch their way up to her knees. A sword, a spear, and a round shield painted with the scorpion. She kept her gloves on to hide the relic on her finger, and she strapped her kopis and belted her sword to her side. Last, she slid the helm upon her head, the bronze cold against her scalp.

She stood as the camp stirred to life, breathing in the morning light.

Evadne began to bundle their bedrolls, and Halcyon found food in their packs. They broke their fast with a quick meal. And then it was time to march.

Evadne mounted a horse, to ride at Damon's side while Halcyon walked through the throng of warriors, finding her squad assembled at the forefront.

The legion marched to the north. Halcyon kept stride and soaked in as much sun as she could, battling the nagging desire to sleep. She felt her health like it was the edge of a blade; it was sharp, but not perfect yet. And then the clouds merged and swallowed the sunlight, spitting thunder and rain, but she continued to march until evening arrived and the commander came to a stop in a field, to make camp.

She kindled a fire and watched as Evadne entered Damon's tent. Halcyon knew her sister would be with him most of the night, working on some enchantment. She did not want to sleep yet—she wanted to break bread with her squad—but the moment she lay down on her bedroll, Halcyon lost her battle with slumber.

She woke in the middle of the night to the sound of shouts in the camp.

Halcyon lurched to her feet, dizzy as she followed the clamor.

She passed a few hoplites, stopped long enough to ask them what had happened.

"An outsider tried to sneak into the camp," a warrior replied. "He is with the commander now."

Halcyon strode to Straton's tent. Narcissa and the commander stood side by side, gilded in lamplight, staring down at a ragged man. The stranger was on his knees, his hands bound behind his back. He was barefoot, dressed in a tattered, bloodstained tunic.

"*Thales?*" Halcyon cried.

The stranger stiffened at the sound of her voice, turning toward her. His disbelief and joy were tangible as he gaped at her. "Halcyon?"

She stepped closer, astounded, when Straton came between them.

"Do you know who this man is?" he asked in a cold tone.

Halcyon paused, glancing from Straton to Thales. "He was my only friend in the quarry. I would be dead without him."

"Did he tell you why he was in the quarry, Halcyon?"

"He told me he was framed for murder," she said, but when she looked at Thales, her own doubts began to surface. There was guilt in his eyes. Shame.

"You should tell her the truth," the commander said to Thales. "Before I behead you."

Halcyon stared at her friend, waiting. Her stomach knotted when he was unable to meet her gaze.

"You are one of Selene's followers," she said, hollow.

"I *was*," Thales corrected, at last lifting his eyes to her. "Years ago, before I realized what she was planning. We were good friends at the Destry. But things began to shift. Before I knew it, I was surrounded by a group of mages with ideas I did not want to be a part of."

There was more, Halcyon knew. She waited, feeling as if she had been struck.

"Selene sensed my reluctance," Thales continued. "She decided to test my loyalty by asking me to kill someone she believed was a threat."

"She wanted you to kill one of us in the queen's alliance," Halcyon surmised, remembering all those nights the commander thought his wine had been poisoned by Hemlock. How cautious she and Xander had to be when they were training for the mountain, so no one would know they were involved in the alliance's plans to thwart Selene.

"I was ordered to identify and kill the spymaster who was giving Selene the most trouble," Thales said. "A spy who had vast knowledge of missing relics. The Basilisk."

The Basilisk, an enigma Halcyon had briefly met seasons ago. She had only just realized it was Ozias when her uncle had knelt at her side in Isaura to slip the Sunstone Ring of Healing onto her hand. When he had called her by her code name. All this time, he had withheld his identity from her, even as they both sought to bring justice for Nerine.

Halcyon never had a chance to speak of it with him; Ozias had vanished from the grove like a shadow. But the scar on her uncle's face? She now knew whose hand had inspired it. And Thales's debt to keep her hale and alive in the quarry? A small atonement for the crime he had inflicted on Ozias.

She stared down at Thales, overcome with emotion.

"But you know as well as I do, Halcyon," Thales continued, ragged, "I could not go through with the killing. And so Selene framed me, punished me for it. She broke ties with me, sentenced me to the quarry. If you doubt me . . . I can prove it all. I have detailed written accounts that span the years of my reluctant involvement and my falling-out with her."

"Selene would allow you to record such dealings?" Straton asked, suspicious.

"Of course not," Thales said, his patience waning. "But I kept an account regardless. Mages must be very careful, meticulous with . . . certain things."

Halcyon frowned. "And where are these recordings of yours?"

"In Mithra. Hidden in a place Selene does not know."

"Well, that is not helping us now, is it?" the commander said through his teeth.

"Why have you come to us, Thales?" Halcyon asked.

"Because I bring news of Selene's plans."

Halcyon looked at Straton. It was evident he wanted to kill Thales, not listen to him.

"A moment, Lord Commander?" Halcyon tilted her head, inviting Straton to step outside the tent with her.

Straton nodded to Narcissa, who remained behind as a guard. He followed Halcyon into the night, and they stood beside a torch, both lost in thought.

"You want to grant him mercy," Straton eventually stated in a low tone. "You think we should heed his message."

Halcyon drew in a deep breath. "Yes, Lord."

"Why should we trust a man who was an enemy?"

"I met Thales the first day at the quarry," Halcyon whispered. "When I introduced myself to him . . . he startled, as if he knew who I was. Now I realize he knew who I was *related* to, and Thales did everything in his power to aid me, protect me. Because he owed a debt to a man he once tried to murder."

"What are you saying to me, Halcyon?"

"I am saying my uncle gave mercy to the man in question. And if he can forgive the hand that once attempted to steal his life, then we should as well."

The commander's eyes flashed like cold silver. He was shocked by Halcyon's admission—the Basilisk was her uncle, and Straton had been given no knowledge of their connection. She could see his indignation rising.

"You have questions, Commander," she said, "and I will answer them soon. But our time is short, and we have been given an unexpected asset."

"I am not certain about this, Halcyon. What if—"

"He misleads us?" she finished, reading his thoughts. "But what if he joins us, gives us the advantage we need to win this battle?"

"I do not trust him."

"Then trust *me*, Commander."

Straton met her gaze, shadows playing over his face. Could he trust her? The girl who had killed his son and run as a coward?

He motioned for Halcyon to lead the way back into the tent. "Very well, Kingfisher. Let us hear what news he brings us."

Evadne was scribing for Damon when the commander interrupted them. It was past midnight, and she and Damon were finally making good progress. Stanza after stanza they had brought together. Words that made Evadne ache when she dwelled on them, when she imagined singing them, tasting them.

Damon was moving faster in his creation. He was keeping more words than he revoked, and Evadne knew he had found the magical vein he had been seeking.

It would not be long, she thought. The spell would be finished soon, and she would finally understand what this enchantment meant.

That was when the commander arrived.

"Damon, Evadne. I need you both in my tent, now," he said tersely, ducking back out into the night.

Evadne looked at Damon. He appeared just as surprised but he nodded to her, and she rolled up the *charena* scroll and carried it with them into Straton's tent.

Halcyon was there, sitting beside a strange man. He was finishing a bowl of stew, his skin streaked with dried mud, his matted hair bound at the nape of his neck. He looked up at her and Damon when they entered the tent. A strange moment passed among the three of them, as if this stranger could see through her, see through Damon. He noticed the scroll she carried, and Evadne felt Damon stiffen at her side.

"Eva, this is Thales," Halcyon said, breaking the moment. "He was at the quarry with me. He is a friend of mine, and he has brought us news of Mithra."

Damon and Evadne drew closer to the table, where a map was spread out. Narcissa and the legion's five other captains were also present, and they listened as Thales began to speak.

"Macarius returned to the quarry a week ago," he said. "But while he was gone, I began to notice more and more convicts arriving to the quarry. It did not take me long to realize they were not true convicts but recruits who had gathered under the guise of being imprisoned, waiting for Macarius to return. I stayed out of their way, but word soon began to spread. The leader of the new group is named Laneus, from the mountain village of Dree. He killed Bacchus under Macarius's orders, and Macarius promised Laneus the Golden Belt as a reward for the evil deed.

"Four nights ago," Thales continued, his voice hoarse, "Selene visited the quarry. And she brought Macarius the Devouring Sword of Nikomides and a seemingly endless group of convict mages, who she has liberated from the prison to the east. Mages and common convicts now wait in the quarry, preparing for war, to defend the city. They will meet you in the field just before the gates, to fight for Macarius and the queen's promise of freedom, should they successfully hold the city against you, Lord Straton."

Straton was motionless, his face like carven stone. But Evadne could see a gleam of surprise in his eyes. He had not been expecting a battle with convicts.

"Is Selene still in the quarry?" he asked.

"No, Lord," Thales replied. "She holds Mithra while Macarius holds the quarry. I escaped the night after the mages arrived; it was chaos, a few of the common convicts getting into fights with the mages. But then Macarius belted the Devouring Sword to his back, and the mages ceased their threats of enchantments, and the convicts calmed with their weapons. Just the mere threat of the sword seems to instill obedience in them."

"Macarius with the Devouring Sword is almost unfathomable," Evadne said. "The power he now wields . . ."

Unsheathed, the sword could cut down enchantments, but it also turned enemy weapons into dust. If Macarius drew that sword in opposition to them . . . how could Straton's legion triumph?

"They have the Golden Belt," Damon said, his gaze on the map. "They have the All-Seeing Crown. And they have the Devouring Sword."

Three powerful relics.

It seemed hopeless. Evadne knew Halcyon carried the Sunstone Ring of Healing and Ozias—wherever he was—had the Winged Necklace, but that was all they had.

But then Halcyon said, "They have three relics, but they do not have honor. They do not have training and experience on their side. Only greed and lust. And their unity is shallow; it will not hold. Because convict mages and the common men of the quarry are going to want different things. The mages may want their sentences lifted, but the common men want relics." She paused and then rose to her feet, eager. "We can defeat them, Commander. Even if Macarius vanishes our weapons . . . we can defeat them."

Straton was silent for a moment. "So Macarius bears the sword.

Laneus bears the belt. And Selene bears the crown."

"The sword and the belt are at the quarry," Halcyon added, studying the map. "Macarius and Laneus will be eager to meet us in the field with such power. But what of the crown?"

"Selene will have it in Mithra," the commander surmised. "She will watch the battle from the safety of the city, near the queen. But we must come up with a way to distract her from it, a way to keep her preoccupied, to ascertain that she will *not* join the battle should we begin to overtake Macarius."

Straton set his eyes on Damon, on Evadne.

And suddenly Evadne knew what Damon had been preparing for. Because Damon had already sensed it, long before his father had asked. She understood now what he had spoken of in the grove: the challenge that awaited them was to take back the crown that had been stolen. To confront Selene by magic.

"Evadne and I will sneak into Mithra," Damon said, and his voice was calm, deep. "We will preoccupy Selene long enough for you to defeat Macarius and his followers."

"I do not want my sister involved in this," said Halcyon.

"And I concur," Thales added. "You speak of a magical duel, Damon. It is very dangerous, very risky. For both of you."

Evadne was shocked. Her sister and this strange, bedraggled man were speaking for her. She felt her face warm, her anger stir as she stared at Halcyon.

"It will be dangerous and risky for *all* of us," Damon said. "But you cannot make decisions for us. This is my choice, Evadne's choice."

A beat of awkward silence encompassed the tent.

Straton was the one to break it. "Do you have a plan, Damon?"

"I am currently working on it."

"Will you be ready in two days?"

"Yes." Damon sounded confident, but his eyes shifted to Evadne. "Although we should return to our work."

Evadne followed Damon back to his tent, the rain softly falling again.

She placed the *charena* scroll on the table and looked at him.

"Damon, what is this plan? What is this enchantment supposed to do?"

He reached for the jug of wine on the table, poured a cup for him and Evadne. He held it out to her, and their fingers brushed as she accepted the cup.

"This enchantment is inspired by things that have sharpened me, strengthened me," he said. "It is the deepest and most intricate spell I have ever drafted, and it will catch my aunt by surprise. She believes me average, middling toward the weaker end. Let her think such. Because I have grown stronger in the past moon."

Evadne remembered how Damon and Macarius had dueled on the mountain threshold. Her dread quickened. "You will challenge her to a duel?"

"Yes. And more than anything . . . I do not want to involve you, Evadne. But I can only defeat her by a *charena* spell, by drawing from the deepest portion of my magic. By singing it."

Evadne dwelled on that thought, on the spell Damon was currently constructing. An enchantment that made her think of beauty and harmony. Of all the good things in the world.

"My intention is not to kill my aunt," Damon said, "but to distract her until my father's legion triumphs."

And Evadne wanted to believe Damon was strong enough, but Selene had an endless well of magic. Damon's was not as deep. She vividly recalled how he had bled, how exhausted he had been just trying to rouse a spell of stars.

How would he be able to last against Selene?

"Damon . . ."

He seemed to read her thoughts. He smiled at her, and there was no fear in him. It was as if he had known this moment would come.

"I know it sounds impossible. But so was Mount Euthymius, was it not? With its endless stairs and waterfalls and angry immortal mages. I will render us unseen, and we will sneak into Mithra," he said. "I will send a missive to my aunt, to challenge her to meet us at the Destry. She will not refuse me. And that is where I will distract her. While she and I duel, my father and your sister will meet Macarius's challenge beyond the gates. It will all be over before we know it."

Evadne smiled and nodded, looking down into her wine. She could hear the rain tapping on the tent, and it seemed strange to imagine the violence that awaited them when the world felt so quiet and peaceful.

"Now," he whispered. "There is only one thing left for me to ask you."

She lifted her eyes to his.

He studied her for a moment. "Will you sing the enchantment at my side, Evadne?"

"Yes." She raised her cup to his. They clinked together, the agreement like a musical note between them.

The rest of the enchantment came quickly after that, as if Damon had been holding back, waiting for Evadne's reassurance. They worked all through the night, polishing a song made of eight stanzas, each one more beautiful than the one before it.

It was not until the sun rose and the camp began to disassemble that Evadne finally realized it—why he had been so attentive when he looked at her. Parts of Damon's lyrics were mysteries, concealed within the image of nature. But then there were other parts, words that resonated within her when she read them, as if she were seeing a reflection of herself, a gleam of her soul. And she knew one of the things that had made him stronger, something that had inspired an entire stanza of magic . . .

It was inspired by her.

❧ XXXII ❧

Evadne

Evadne found Halcyon among her squad just after dawn in a sea of bronze and painted shields.

"Eva?" Halcyon called, stepping forward to meet her.

"I came to tell you that I am leaving," Evadne said, clearing her throat. "Damon and I are going to ride ahead so we can position ourselves within the city before you arrive."

Halcyon said nothing, and it was hard for Evadne to read her expressions with the helm guarding her face.

"This is not a goodbye," Evadne added, even though it was in some sense. She did not know if Halcyon would survive the battle with Macarius, and Evadne tried not to dwell on that painful thought.

"Do you know where Damon will be challenging Selene?" Halcyon finally spoke.

"Yes. The Destry. Do not worry about me, Hal. If anything, I have the right to worry more about you."

She sensed Halcyon would not want to be embraced before her squad. Evadne began to turn away when Halcyon surprised her by taking hold of her arm, gently pulling her back around.

She opened Evadne's hand and set her kopis in it, curling her ink-stained fingers over the sheathed blade. How many times had this blade been passed between them?

"I want you to wear this into the duel, Eva," Halcyon said. "Do not be afraid to use it. Stab in one of these three places if you are in danger." She pointed to the armpit, the throat, the eye. "Promise me?"

Evadne nodded. "I promise, Hal."

Halcyon kissed her brow and watched as Evadne walked to Damon. He sang a *charena* charm over them, altering their appearance as he had before. And then they mounted their horses, ready to ride ahead of the legion.

The commander intercepted them, just before they departed. He squinted against the light, his eyes lingering on his son. Evadne saw a storm of emotions in the commander's face now that she had come to read it better: worry, regret. *Hope.*

"I will await your signal, Damon," Straton said.

Damon nodded. He did not see the apology hiding behind his father's pride like Evadne did. He did not hear the words that Straton silently said to him between breaths—*be safe, I love you, I am proud of you*—and Damon gathered his reins and looked at Evadne. Evadne with her wind-tangled hair and mud-stained chiton, his enchantment resting upon her like starlight.

They took the road together, side by side in a furious gallop. And they left the legion, Straton, and Halcyon far behind them.

"You will not like this, Evadne," Damon whispered to her the next day, his fingers laced with hers. His unseen enchantment covered them both as they stood on the outskirts of Mithra, their horses left behind in a nearby grotto. "But the water is going to be our way in."

Evadne was exhausted as she stared at the eastern quadrant of the city, where the River Zan cut through it like a silver blade. It was an hour before dawn, and Mithra was strangely quiet. The gates were closed, the firelight flickering over the iron and wooden doors, locked against the world.

"All right," she whispered in return, even though she hated the thought of it. Ever since the mountain passage, the thought of submerging herself in water was horrifying. She felt Damon's hand tighten on hers for a moment—wordless reassurance.

He led her on foot around the eastern portion of Mithra. They walked as close to the wall as they dared, even though Damon's enchantment held steady and tangible as their own skin. Evadne glanced up to see the queen's guards patrolling the wall, and she wondered where Queen Nerine was now. If she was in the palace, safe and well, or if Selene was with her, poisoning her mind as Macarius had poisoned Halcyon's body.

They reached the riverbank and stood in the reeds. The Zan was wide, shallow at the edges, deep in the center. But the current was slow; they could easily swim across it to the Mithran port.

"What about the scrolls?" Evadne asked. The scrolls were tucked into a leather satchel Straton had given her, the strap tight across her chest.

"They will be safe," he replied. "I enchanted them days ago. Nothing can destroy them."

She had no other excuses. And the sun was beginning to rise behind them, the stars beginning to melt. Straton's legion would be arriving that afternoon, and it was paramount that Damon and Evadne find a way into the city.

"Do you trust me, Evadne?"

She did. And he waited until she breathed the word *yes* before stepping into the river. Deeper, deeper. And Evadne followed him, tentatively at first, the water cold, seeping into her clothes.

"I will not let go of you," Damon whispered.

And she believed him. Just as she had not let go of him in Mount Euthymius.

The floor of the river was slick and soft; it fell away suddenly, but Damon held fast to her, and they made their way across the river, the current bearing them slowly and steadily downstream, to the port.

Vessels bobbed in their berths. The queen's guards walked along the docks, armed. Damon and Evadne emerged from the water alongside the quay. They waited until the guard had turned, his back angled to them before they drew themselves out of the river with a small splash.

There was still a gate bolted between the port and the city. But there was also a door nestled in the wall beside it, nearly hidden among ivy, and Damon worked his magic to quietly open it. He and Evadne slipped over its threshold into the open courtyard of an armory. They passed a group of guards sitting at a table, playing knucklebones. The guards would notice the door was ajar, but by then Damon and Evadne would be halfway through the deserted eastern market.

"Where are you taking me?" Evadne whispered.

"Home."

The commander's villa sat somber and silent in the predawn hues. It almost felt abandoned as Evadne and Damon worked their way through the gates and down the path through the garden, to enter through a shadowed servants' door.

At last, they were safe within the villa's walls. And yet Damon did not let go of her hand or his enchantment. He guided her to the main floor, and then up to his chambers. They only passed Toula, who was beginning to light the braziers, who would indeed notice the strange duo of dirty footprints that mysteriously marred her freshly scrubbed floors.

Damon relinquished Evadne's hand once they were in his room, and she watched her body return to sight. Her clothes and hair were still wet, and she dripped river water onto the floor as Damon broke his enchantment, appearing just as disheveled as her.

They looked at each other for a moment. Breathless. Uncertain.

Evadne turned first, walking to her desk. She removed the leather satchel from her shoulder and set it in her chair, noticing there was a stack of beautiful chitons folded on her desk. Upon the clothes sat a small carven box.

"Your clothes order," Damon said, trailing her.

Evadne traced the soft linen; it glimmered gold beneath her

touch, as if sunlight had been woven into the fabric. Damon took the small box in his hand, sliding it into his pocket without a word. "I am going to go speak to my mother and sister. Ensure they are well and see if there is any other news I can glean. You should change into dry clothes, and I will bring us back something to eat."

Evadne nodded, listening to him leave. And then she was alone in his chambers, and she slowly unwound from her clothes, wringing the water from her hair. She drew one of the new chitons onto her body; it whispered and shone, and she found her old brooches in the sodden heap of her discarded clothes. The golden olive wreaths that Rhode had chosen for her weeks ago.

How distant that day felt now, Evadne thought, pinning the wreaths into place on her shoulders.

How distant, as if that memory belonged to another person.

She sat at her desk, opening her satchel. She intended to study Damon's latest enchantment, which still had no name. She found the *charena* scroll perfectly dry and intact. And then she saw the second scroll. The one Damon had been writing in the other night.

She hesitated. Her fingers hovered above its wooden handles, and she wanted to take it into her hands, unroll it on her desk, read it.

But she could not bring herself to do it. Whatever he had been writing, he did not want her to see.

She took up the *charena* scroll and began to study it, pressing his words into her memory. The light was streaming into the room when Damon returned, carrying a tray of food.

"How are your mother and sister?" Evadne asked.

"They are well. Been under house arrest for days now, as have all the other citizens of Mithra. Selene's orders to 'keep them safe,' of course." Damon noticed she was reading the *charena* scroll. And as he set the tray down, she saw how his eyes glanced to the open satchel, where the other mysterious scroll still waited. He had forgotten about it. The tension creased his face as he bent down to gather the satchel, carrying the strange scroll into his bedchamber.

He closed the door behind him. Evadne could hear muffled movements through the wood as he changed, and she sighed and began to eat.

Damon returned dressed in clean garments, the tangles combed from his damp hair. He sat across from her and joined her in the meal, and they were quiet. Uncertain again.

When their hunger had abated, Damon moved the tray aside.

"Will you write the missive to my aunt?"

"Yes, of course." Evadne found a square of papyrus from the shelf, and Damon had her trim it to be a small rectangle.

She opened her ink pot, dipped her quill, and waited for him to speak.

To Selene—
I challenge you for Acantha's All-Seeing Crown.
Today. In the lobby of the Destry. Three hours past midday.

Evadne watched as he charmed the ink dry, as he rolled it up and bound the papyrus with twine. He set it on the desk and then stared at the *charena* scroll, which lay open and vulnerable. Evadne's handwriting dark and elegant on its papyrus.

They still had a few hours.

Damon spent them sleeping in his chair by the window; Evadne spent them memorizing his enchantment.

But soon her worries began to multiply. She closed the *charena* scroll and stood, her body teeming with anxious energy. She did not want to wake Damon, so she paced his room quietly, the marble floor cold on her bare feet.

She was missing something.

She touched her waist, where her chiton now had pockets. Halcyon's kopis, she recalled. It sat in her dirty clothes, and Evadne bent to retrieve it, buckling the little scythe to her golden belt.

She remembered her sister's stabbing instructions, felt her stomach clench. Why would Halcyon say that to her? Surely Evadne would not need to stab anyone . . .

"Evadne." Damon's voice was deep, roughened by sleep.

She looked at him, still sitting in his chair. Dust motes hung in the light between them. And a sweet note of longing, waiting to be sung.

"I have not changed my mind," she said, sensing he was about to pose the question to her. To give her a way out. "I am simply . . . anxious." And she resumed pacing, and he merely watched her at first.

It was almost time, she thought. Why couldn't she catch her

breath? Why did he appear so calm?

She heard Damon rise, but she elected to ignore him until he said, "I have a gift for you."

She ceased her restless pacing and watched as he withdrew the wooden box from his pocket.

Her fingers were cold as she took the box from him, opening the lid.

Two bronze wings sat within, waiting for the light to touch them. The wings of Kirkos, fashioned as pins for her to proudly display on her raiment, proclaiming who she had descended from. Stunned, she traced their beauty, and she knew Damon had ordered them custom-made for her. Because they were not cast in gold or silver, as most people would desire. They were crafted from bronze. Bronze as Halcyon, as Xander, as the legion.

"They are beautiful," she whispered.

"May I?" Damon asked, and Evadne nodded, tears in her eyes.

Slowly, he unpinned the golden olive wreaths from her clothes. He selected one of the wings and gathered the loose linen at her shoulder. She felt his knuckles brush her bare collar as he pinned the first wing, then the second, in place.

Damon's hands lowered, but his eyes continued to admire her, the bronze wings flaring in the light.

"I think we are ready now," he whispered with a smile.

And yet he did not move. And neither did she.

Not yet, her mind, her reason, was begging again. *Not yet, not yet . . .*

But her heart swallowed the warning whole, and Evadne lifted up on her toes. Her ankle throbbed, but she hardly felt it as she framed Damon's face in her hands, as she raised herself closer to him. He did not move. For once, she had cast her own enchantment, and he was at her mercy.

She kissed him softly at first, a brush of butterfly wings against his lips. She breathed in the scent of his skin, emboldened, and kissed him again, deeper.

Still, he seemed unable to move, to respond. But then he drank her breath, he caught her fire. The air became amber, electric between them. His arms came around her and he pressed his palms to her back, bringing her against him, the last of the distance melting.

Her fingers lost themselves in his hair as she learned the secrets of his mouth, as he learned hers. Tentatively and then eagerly.

Time did not exist for them anymore. Nor did conniving aunts and stolen relics and an impending battle. They were entangled with each other, edging across the floor breath by breath, and his hands were in her hair and his mouth was on her neck and Evadne was warm and vibrant from the splendor they had sparked. And then she stepped into the desk, and Damon all but toppled onto her, his hand reaching out to catch himself. He overturned the jar of quills, the missive for his aunt falling to the floor.

His breath was heavy as he leaned his brow against Evadne's. The bronze wings were skewed, a moment from slipping away from her shoulders, when Damon stepped back, distance blooming between them again.

She rolled her swollen lips together as she straightened her garments, as Damon bent to retrieve the missive.

Without a word, he walked to the window and summoned a nightingale. Damon whispered a spell, and the bird took the missive and flew, carrying it to wherever Selene presided in the city.

And then he turned to Evadne, hand outstretched.

It was time.

The Destry sat like a jewel in the afternoon sunlight. Damon and Evadne entered the solemn, dim lobby, their footsteps echoing.

At first, Evadne believed she and Damon were alone, standing among the divine columns. But then she caught a glimpse of light, and she turned to see Selene standing between the pillars of Magda and Ari. Her scribe was beside her, a tall man with arms cut with muscle, his head shaven, his eyes green as jade.

The All-Seeing Crown was in Selene's hands.

"Hello, Damon," she said, ignoring Evadne's presence. "Do not be shy. You called this challenge. Come forward."

Damon still held Evadne's hand. Selene took note of this as they approached, coming to a gradual stop. A good portion of distance still remained between the two groups.

"I thought I taught you better, Damon," Selene said, her voice cold.

"You have taught me many things, Aunt," he replied. "Once you were a great mage. One I trusted and respected."

"But no more, I take it?" Selene arched her brows. "All because you have chosen to side with your father's illogical choices. He and Nerine will run the kingdom into the ground, Damon. It is time for people like us to rise and reclaim our status in this society."

"I am sure the queen will have something to say about that, Selene. When she is finally free from your cloying enchantment."

Selene smiled. The light gleamed on her teeth. "I suppose that depends if you can win back this crown. Because that was your plan from the beginning: to crown Nerine with Acantha's relic, to break through my spell. I confess, your tenacity surprised me. But unfortunately for you . . . the crown is now mine."

She lifted the crown, as if she was about to set it upon her head.

Evadne felt Damon's grip tighten on her hand, and she heard his breath suspend. She knew they were doomed if Selene crowned herself. She would have the power to look into their past, their present. Their future, should she desire, to see the outcome of this challenge.

Selene stopped just before the crown touched her hair. That scathing smile of hers returned, and laughter trickled out of her.

"You think I have not already worn the crown, Damon? That I have not already seen what comes of this?" She lowered it again. "Cast off your pride and heed me. You do not prevail here. But there is still time to change your course." She paused, her eyes softening as she regarded him. Evadne could see that once, long ago, Selene had loved Damon.

Damon was silent. Evadne could feel him trembling. And she feared he was about to consent, to give up the plans.

She is lying to you, Evadne wanted to say to him. *She cannot look into our futures without us being present.*

Damon set his gaze on Evadne, as if he had heard her thoughts.

He stared at her, and his eyes were haunted by sorrow, by desire. By fear.

She shook her head. *Do not surrender to her.*

"Come," said Selene. "Let us put aside this challenge and the threat it poses. Let us mend our relationship."

Damon, resolved, looked at his aunt again. "I will not side with you, Selene. Deliver the crown to me and Evadne or answer the challenge I have given you."

Selene's face hardened.

"Then know that what befalls you is your own doing, Damon of Mithra." She held up her hand, her silver ring winking in warning as her magic gathered.

She breathed in every possibility, every particle of shadow and light. And she began to sing.

⇢XXXIII⇠

Halcyon

Halcyon crouched behind an outcrop of rocks, her eyes set on the distant city of Mithra. Iason and Narcissa were both with her, watching for Damon's signal. The sun baked the field between them and the city gates. Heat rose up in waves. The grass wilted and locusts whirred in crooked lines. Perspiration dripped down Halcyon's body, drenched the tunic beneath her cuirass. But she hardly noticed. Her eyes were for the city, for that barely visible rooftop of the Destry.

Any moment now, she thought, Evadne and Damon would be arriving at the Destry.

She thought of Thales's words, spoken to her in confidence, just before Evadne and Damon had departed yesterday.

Ensure your sister is armed before she leaves with the commander's son.

Halcyon had asked why, but Thales had not answered.

And so all she could do was wonder and worry about her sister.

"There," Iason said, eager. "There is Damon's signal."

Halcyon squinted and saw the nightingale. It was a speck in the haze, but it became clearer as it flew closer to them. It would glide to the commander before circling back to the city, reassuring him that Damon had set Selene's distraction in motion.

"Let us go," Narcissa said.

The three of them jogged out of Mithra's sight, down the hill to where the legion waited. The horses had been left behind miles ago, due to the fact that Laneus had the Golden Belt, which he would no doubt wear into battle. Because he could command animals, Straton and the captains would approach on foot among the hoplites. But that was not to say that other animals might not be summoned to fight them.

The thought made Halcyon's stomach clench. She felt the tension, the excitement in the air, thick enough to divide with a blade as the hoplites prepared themselves for battle. Narcissa's squad was ready. Halcyon and Iason merged back with their brothers and sisters, and Narcissa waited among them, watching for Straton to give the motion to progress.

The commander stood before his legion, gazing at them— a moment that seemed to stretch long and endless. And then he slid his helm upon his head, the black-and-white horsehair catching the breeze, and a shout rose from his warriors that made the earth tremble and the sun hide behind a wisp of clouds.

Straton led them over the hill into the field that stretched to Mithra.

The hoplites walked in unison, arranged in tight formation eight warriors deep, their long spears held upright, their shields hooked on their left arm. Halcyon was at the front of the phalanx, with the strongest warriors. The younger, weaker warriors were in the middle, and this was where Thales had been positioned after he had insisted he fight alongside them.

The front line also experienced the heaviest casualties. But Halcyon knew why she had been appointed here.

Narcissa's squad had been given one important order: to pressure Macarius to draw the Devouring Sword from its scabbard.

It had first seemed daft to the other hoplites in Narcissa's phalanx. For Macarius to wield the relic meant all of his enemy's weapons—the legion's—would vanish in their hands. They would be magically disarmed, but the common convicts would still boast their iron. The hoplites would have to fight with their strength, their weight.

But if Macarius drew the sword, then all the convict mages beneath his command would also lose their power. Whatever enchantments they wrought in battle would be broken.

It was a dangerous, brilliant move.

"I want you on the front line," Straton had told her that morning. "You are to take the Devouring Sword from Macarius."

And Halcyon had bowed to the command, honored. Once the relic was in her possession, her opposition—the quarry convicts—would also lose their weapons.

But most of all, Straton was wordlessly giving Halcyon the chance to kill Macarius.

And her breaths skipped like stones tossed over water. Her blood was pounding, fast and thin and bright as gold heated over fire, and her heart was expanding, filling her chest. She marched and felt as if she could rise from the earth at any moment on sightless wings.

Macarius heard their approach.

Soon, Halcyon could see the convicts pouring out of the quarry gates, forming their own shallow line before Mithra. Straton raised his arm, and the legion came to a halt. A mile stretched between them and the convicts. But Halcyon could see Macarius at the center of them, outfitted in leather armor, the Devouring Sword sheathed at his back, the ruby in its pommel glittering in the sun. And there was Laneus with the Golden Belt at his waist and a sword in his hand. And Cassian, the prisoner who had spat in her food, with his cronies gathered about him, wielding iron picks.

The mages were interspersed among the quarry men. They carried no weapons, but Halcyon knew their unbridled magic had the potential to be devastating.

Straton began to walk the distance alone, to meet Macarius in the middle. The two talked, the commander's final attempt for peace. Halcyon knew it was futile. Macarius would not settle for anything, and the commander strode back to the hoplites while Macarius hurried to the protection of his line.

The hoplites formed their shield wall and began to close the distance at Straton's command. Halcyon lowered her spear, preparing for impact. She felt the shield of her hoplite brother at her back, pressed tight against her so there would be no space between them. Narcissa shouted, sensing her phalanx was drifting. It was hard to resist pulling **to** the right, Halcyon thought as she struggled to march straight. Apprehension and fear made them all want to seek shelter in the shield of the hoplite to their right.

The convicts did not know how to fight in a formation. They were foolish and zealous, the first line of them charging the phalanx, axes and picks and swords raised. Halcyon watched them come, felt the earth tremble, felt her mind calm as it always did before she sparred.

How many days of her life had she practiced, trained for this?

How many hours, by sun and by night?

And yet nothing could prepare her for the first moment of impact.

There was a clash, a blow of resistance as the two sides finally met. She plunged her spear into the neck of a common convict just before he could swing his pick into her. She watched the blood gurgle from his mouth, his eyes bulge. He fell, and Halcyon withdrew her spear and continued to move forward in a perfect line, the hoplites at her back pressing her forward.

Hold formation, hold formation, she chanted to herself as the screams and shouts and groans began to spiral in the air around her. As long as the phalanx held, they would be unbeatable. They were like a wall of bronze, surging forward.

She could see Macarius, nearly dead ahead of her. He stood at the very back of his convicts, observing with a frown. Soon the phalanx would reach him.

She watched as he lifted his hand and started to sing, and her courage began to unravel.

Hold formation, hold—

There was a crackle in the wind. Sparks unfolding, rending the air like thunder.

And his magic exploded, striking the phalanx several warriors down from Halcyon. It broke their line. Halcyon was hurled to the side, narrowly missed being impaled on Iason's spear. She hit the ground, her ears ringing.

The dust billowed—she struggled to rise, to see through the clouds of gold—and then chaos spawned. Hoplites were combating convicts hand to hand, and it was a tumbling mess of shields and screams and blood-splattered iron. And woven among it all were fiery tendrils of magic that sparked explosions and bone-splintering pain, and shadows that rose up with teeth and malice, shredding through armor and muscle.

The world became nothing more than fire and shadow and dust and iron.

"Halcyon!" Narcissa was screaming at her.

Through her daze, Halcyon saw her captain standing a few yards away, as strong and immovable as a pillar, summoning Halcyon to her mission

Macarius.

Halcyon found her footing and surged to join Narcissa. The dust was thinning, but there were shadows writhing within it. And they were not magical shadows. They were the shadows of countless birds, swarming in a circle, preparing to attack.

Halcyon had only a breath to raise her shield before the birds began to plummet and strike her. She hated the sound of their feathered bodies thudding on her shield, on her armor. Some of their talons caught her arms, leaving bright lacerations on her skin. But she pressed onward, slow but steady in Narcissa's wake. These were songbirds. Sparrows and doves and nightingales. Gentle creatures.

Laneus was a fool. He had summoned little songbirds into battle, forcing them against their will.

And Halcyon would kill him.

She moved out of the bird windstorm and lowered her shield. And there he was. The vile boy of Dree. Who was cruel and rotten within. He stood only a few paces away, sword held in his hand. He was too preoccupied with trying to direct his birds to see her coming. And then he saw her, a moment too late.

She watched his eyes go wide, his mouth slackened in fear.

She speared him in the stomach. Again and again, just above the Golden Belt.

Laneus screamed and crumpled to the ground. She stood above him and watched him begin to bleed out. The birds were soon released from the summoning and flew back to their roosts, and Thales appeared, as if he had been in Halcyon's shadow.

"Take the belt, Thales," Halcyon ordered him.

"Yes." Thales dropped to his knees, hurrying to unbuckle it.

Halcyon strode onward, over dead bodies and scorched earth and trampled grass. She saw the red-and-white plume of Narcissa's helm as she continued to cut, stab, down convict after convict.

But Macarius was lost from Halcyon's view. And she sought him, hungry for his blood.

A flash of light, bone white with heat, shot past Halcyon's shoulder. Her armor warmed uncomfortably in response, and she heard a hoplite scream in pain behind her. A convict mage was about to shoot another bolt of that lightning, his fair hair matted to his brow, his teeth rotten to the gums as he smiled.

Halcyon hurled her spear and caught him in the heart. He went down and she recovered her lance, his fingertips steaming from the magic she had interrupted. She progressed with her search for Macarius, her eyes peeling through the chaos. The shine of iron and bronze and the tang of blood and the song of magical choruses mixed like a sickening tonic, churning her stomach.

She saw the commander fighting in the fray, his helm and his red cloak drawing her attention. He did not see Macarius suddenly emerge nearby, casting off his invisibility. But Halcyon did.

Coward, she raged as she sprinted, spear raised. She hurled her lance; it arced and gleamed, and Macarius spun to see it hurtling toward him. His eyes widened, like all the men who Halcyon had killed. But then the mage reached behind him, unsheathing the Devouring Sword.

Halcyon's spear turned into dust just before it would have pierced his heart.

And the mages' enchantments broke instantaneously, rising from the field like smoke.

Her lost weapon did not stop her. Her hands were empty, but they were angry, and she began to close the distance to Macarius.

He did not know it was her at first. He was smiling, triumphant about how he had vanished her weapon. How he had vanished all of the legion's weapons. But Halcyon continued to stalk to him as if the victory were already hers, and Macarius's smile melted.

He recognized her. Even in her helm and armor, he knew it was her.

And he began to stumble away. Frantic, even though he held an enchanted sword and she held nothing but her vengeance.

But then again, he had always been afraid of her.

Halcyon smiled at him. Her teeth cut the dust and the light, and Macarius tripped over one of his dead men and fell. He sprawled on his back, and Halcyon leapt on him.

She struck his face, once, twice. She felt his nose crush beneath her fist. He finally roused himself, remembered he held the sword in his hand. Macarius began to lift it, but Halcyon took hold of his arm before he even knew what had gripped him. She pressed her thumb into the tendons of his wrist, and he whimpered, releasing the sword.

It clattered to the ground, a full arm's length away.

Halcyon reached to take it, to end this, when Macarius uttered a spell. He stole a flash of light from her armor and roused his fiery chimera.

The monster unfolded in an array of sparks. Halcyon felt them fall on her, burn her skin, hiss on her armor. The chimera did not attack; it was devoted to guarding the Devouring Sword. She could not believe it at first. The relic should have stopped all enchantments. But then she realized that its hilt had to be held for its power to be active.

She turned to Macarius and struck him, again and again, his blood streaming back into his hair. She heard his chimera let out a keen wail, and she sensed it was about to maul her when someone came between them.

Straton. He had no weapon to cut the monster down, but he took the brunt of the chimera's charge. Halcyon heard his cloak rip, the scratch of fiery talons on bronze, the commander's grunt of pain. She lunged for the sword and took it into her grip.

The hilt burned through her glove, hot from the chimera's presence. But the chimera morphed into smoke instantly, joining the wind with a hiss.

Halcyon held the Devouring Sword, her reflection bright upon its steel. She looked down at Macarius, who was whimpering.

"Please . . . please don't kill me." He held up his quivering hands.

Halcyon waited, watched his groveling.

"Have mercy, Halcyon. *Mercy.*"

Once, long ago, Halcyon would have granted mercy. But she was no longer that girl.

And she plunged the Devouring Sword into his throat.

Once the dust settled and the last of the convicts were defeated, Halcyon sheathed the Devouring Sword. She wanted to give it to the commander, and she found him sitting in the shade of the Mithran wall.

She knew something was wrong immediately. His cloak was

draped over him, his complexion sallow, his eyes glazed when he looked at her.

Halcyon knelt beside him, drew back his cloak, and saw the wound.

It was a trio of deep gashes in his thigh. Macarius's chimera had cut through the hard pleats of the commander's cuirass, down to the bone of his leg. And this was not a wound of iron or steel. It was weeping a steady trickle of blood, and the edges of it were a mass of melted flesh, mottled purple and red.

A poisoned wound.

Halcyon could not breathe at first, remembering all the poison she had been forced to endure. But then she felt the commander's gaze on her face, and she looked at him. She knew he was dying.

She could not imagine a world with him gone.

"Commander," she said, and he weakly tried to draw his cloak back over his leg.

"Leave me, Kingfisher."

Leave him? She gaped at him a moment. Angry, she said, "You want to die alone, then?"

Straton closed his eyes. He chuckled, which made his blood pool faster. "I only want to rest a moment. Ask if they will open the gates for us. I would like to see my wife and daughter."

Halcyon ignored him. She pulled off her leather glove, which prompted him to crack open his eyes. When he saw what glittered on her hand, he raised his brows.

"Ah. It is as I thought."

Halcyon did not reply. She slipped the ring onto his forefinger and stared at him, unable to conceal her worry.

It would take time, she knew. He needed to be in the sun.

She helped him shift away from the wall's shadow, and he lay down in the light, which was beginning to thin as the sun set behind the mountains. By now, Narcissa had noticed them. She ran to see why Straton was on the ground, grinning into the sun as if he was drunk. And then she saw his wound, how the blood and mottled colors were slowly easing, and the sunstone on his hand, and she only slid her eyes to Halcyon, grateful.

"We need to get inside Mithra," the captain said. "And then find a wagon for the commander. Will you see—"

"I do not need a wagon."

"If they will open the gates?" Narcissa finished.

Straton was still half smiling, half wincing into the sunlight. Halcyon glanced to his leg, relieved to see the ring was already working its magic, closing his wound.

"Yes, I will go," Halcyon said and began to stride over the bloodstained ground, aiming for the southern gate.

Thales approached like he had been waiting for her. He no longer wore the Golden Belt, and Halcyon was too exhausted to wonder who he had given it to. He fell into stride beside her, anxious.

"What is it, Thales?"

"Your sister. I am worried about her, Halcyon."

Halcyon lost her temper. "Why? Why do you keep tormenting me about it?"

Thales rushed his hand over his face. He was trembling.

Halcyon did not know if it was the aftershock of battle or if he was truly that concerned about Evadne.

"I was unable to murder the Basilisk, as you know," he said. "But I still deserved to be in the common quarry."

"Yes, why?"

"Because I did kill someone. After the failed assassination, I tried to sing an enchantment to end Selene. But she was too powerful, her magic much deeper than mine. My magic ran dry and sundered."

"Sundered?" she echoed, glancing to his right hand, the scar where his mage's ring had once gleamed.

"Yes," he stammered, his brow furrowed as if the memory still caused him pain. "Selene drained my magic dry to the bone. It broke my hand, and my magic departed. And in that moment, in my turmoil . . . I ended up killing someone very dear to me."

"Thales . . ." Halcyon began to understand his worry. She felt her pulse in her throat. "Who did you kill?"

He looked down at his right hand. Scarred and out of alignment. A constant reminder of who he had once been, of what he had lost.

He brought his eyes back to hers, and there was nothing but sorrow, deep and terrible sorrow, within him when he answered.

"I killed my scribe."

⟶ XXXIV ⟵

Evadne

Evadne was not afraid of Selene's magic. Not even as it gathered overhead, drawing her eyes upward to the glorious ceiling of the Destry. She watched as it ate the sun, the clouds, the blue illusion of the sky. A hungry fog that swirled and obscured and began to billow downward, shrouding the divine pillars. It reached for Damon and Evadne, ready to swallow them whole.

Evadne's heart quickened as Damon began to sing his unnamed enchantment.

He sang the first stanza only, repeating it over and over.

This was not the slow-burning magic of stars, or the fire he had made in Mount Euthymius. This light was brilliant and piercing; it was the gleam of sun on a sister's sword, the reflection of light on a brother's helm. It warmed the air like midday, and ripples of heat flowed outward.

Halcyon, Xander, Evadne thought. This golden light and warmth were inspired by them. And she raised her voice to join Damon's. Her heart was filled by the lyrics. Because as she sang with Damon, she sensed her sister and his brother with them. There were four of them in that moment, and no fog could withstand such fire.

Damon's magic cut through Selene's, and the fog dissipated, the light flashing over her and her scribe's astonished faces.

Selene's shock morphed into anger, and she lifted her hands and brought a different song, her scribe singing in beat with her.

Kirkos's pillar began to shift and move. The falcon perched on his arm woke from the marble, rustling its wings. He took flight from his master and transformed in the air. Evadne kept her eyes on the enchantment, watching as the marble falcon mutated into a griffin. And then he multiplied, until there was a horde of them, flying toward Evadne and Damon.

But Damon's song had been waiting for this, for creatures of wings and flight, and he began to sing the second stanza. Evadne sang with him, their voices rough and soft—perfectly matched. And this enchantment was no longer mere words on a scroll, words she had scribed. This was a fragment of her, and it rose from her mouth like an offering, something so pure that it could not be overcome.

The griffins circled about her and Damon; they reached for her hair with their talons, but Evadne's voice and Damon's magic stirred their feathers. The creatures hovered and then yielded to Evadne of Isaura. The descendant of Kirkos.

The girl who knew the taste of flight.

One by one, the griffins landed. They bowed to Evadne and to Damon as if they were the queen and king of myths and wings.

Furious, Selene shattered the creatures into dust.

She raised her hands and brought a different song. Her voice was still strong, resounding with power. And since the pillars had not heeded her, she called to the ground. The black-and-white checkered floor began to crack around Damon and Evadne, opening to swallow them.

But this was not the first time Damon and Evadne had stood at an edge.

They had both fallen before, and Damon was not intimidated. He began to sing his third stanza, Evadne's voice accompanying his. Water began to rise in the cracks, filling the broken places that Selene had made. The water shimmered and solidified into marble, and every crack she created, Damon's song was there to fill and mend, to bring everything back together.

That was when Damon's voice began to falter. He was singing slower, as if the words were fighting him.

The resistance had finally come.

Evadne looked at him. A trickle of blood flowed from his nose, over his lips, as he struggled to sing. His shoulders drew inward, as if the pain was unbearable inside of him and he was rallying the last of his strength to keep himself standing.

While his voice began to fade, Evadne's only grew brighter, stronger. A beacon for him to find and follow.

He turned his face to look at her, to listen to her sing his magic.

And all around them the floor was sundering, and yet Evadne continued to stand and sing, waiting for him.

He straightened. He still bled, but her voice brought him back to the lyrics, and his magic returned, flooding the shattered floor again, healing Selene's destruction.

She was growing weary, too.

Evadne could hear Selene's voice in spurts, as if she could not draw a full breath, and her scribe was singing a steady flow of words to her.

How much longer would they need to outlast her? Evadne wondered.

Selene rallied, just as Damon had.

She summoned the columns again. Euthymius's pillar began to crumble, threatening to topple.

Damon sang the fourth stanza. He was pale and trembling now, blood dripping from his chin, but he sang and he raised his hand to the pillar. He summoned a wind, fragrant and strong, a breeze that he had felt in Isaura's grove. It caught the pillar's tumble and gently set it back in place, rooted to the floor and the ceiling.

And then there was a crack in the air, like wood splintering on stone.

Damon gasped. He fell to his knees, all his magic flooding back into him, into his open mouth. Light, wind, water, myths. His eyes shut, his face agonized.

Evadne stopped singing. She forgot the words, forgot where they were, what they were supposed to be doing. She was frozen, watching Damon writhe and groan and hold his left hand.

She could see the skewing of his fingers—his hand, *his hand was broken*—and the sight robbed her breath.

Damon rocked on his knees and cradled his broken hand. His moans turned into coughs, and he coughed up blood, spitting it onto the floor he had just mended. But there was something else within it, glittering shards that looked like gold. He coughed up more of it, and Evadne realized it was ichor. Pieces of divine in his blood, in his breath, in his voice. He was coughing up his magic, and it was no longer sinuous and beautiful. It was sharp and bitter and hard, cutting him up from the inside, leaving his body ravaged in its wake.

He ceased coughing, and the silver ring on his finger boiled and hissed into steam. He cried out in pain, his hand knotting into a fist. And the last of his magic abandoned him, evaporating in a plume of smoke, leaving behind a burned scar on his finger.

Evadne melted to her knees, unable to fathom this, unable to listen and watch him suffer and break and come undone.

"Damon," she whispered, ragged. *"Damon."* She crawled across the floor to him.

He bowed over his brokenness, his blood and the splinters of magic. But he stiffened when he heard her voice, when he caught a glimpse of her approach.

Damon lifted his head, his eyes wild and glazed. He looked at Evadne and whispered to her, "Who are you?"

⇾XXXV⇽

Halcyon and Evadne

Halcyon pounded on the southern gate of Mithra. She called up to the queen's soldiers, who patrolled the wall, staring down at her. And when that did not work, she screamed orders at them.

But they would not open the gates for her or the commander and his legion.

"We cannot defy the queen's command," one of the soldiers shouted down at her. "We must wait for Queen Nerine to lift her order."

And Halcyon knew it was futile. Of course they would not open the gates without the queen's approval. Which was Selene's order to begin with.

Halcyon felt like weeping as she stepped back from the gate, her knuckles torn and bloodied. Thales was still with her, worry marking his brow. And the sun was setting. The first stars were arriving, and there was no word from Damon and Evadne. No sight of Selene. What did this silence mean?

In Halcyon's frustration, she did not see the man standing among the queen's soldiers on the wall. The man who, if she had looked closer, was not decked in armor and who looked uncannily like a younger image of her father with a scar on his face. A man who had watched the entire battle unfold, knowing she was somewhere amid the flash of bronze and iron.

She did not see him step off the wall and hover in the air. She did not see him glide down to her on invisible wings.

"Halcyon."

She startled, finally noticing the man who was approaching her. Uncle Ozias. The Basilisk.

"Uncle, how did you . . . ?"

"You need to enter Mithra?" her uncle surmised. "Come, I will carry you over the wall."

She was speechless. But then she noticed the relic hanging around his neck. Kirkos's relic, which Evadne had once worn.

The air stirred at her elbow, and Halcyon remembered Thales was beside her. The man who had once attempted to kill her uncle. She glanced between the two men, suddenly uneasy.

Thales had the right to appear wary. He took a step back, head bowed in submission, but Ozias was not paying him any attention. He looked only at Halcyon, knowing time was wearing thin.

She stepped into her uncle's arms, and he flew her, slow and careful, over the wall of Mithra. The queen's soldiers gaped, but they did not interfere, still awaiting orders from Nerine.

Ozias brought Halcyon down in the southern market, which was empty and forlorn. Halcyon, breathless from the flight, stepped out of his embrace and looked at him with gratitude.

"Will you swear to me that you'll refrain from killing Thales, Uncle Ozias?"

Ozias granted her a sharp smile. "I have not killed him yet. I suppose I can wait another day."

She could not tell if her uncle was jesting or serious, and she was too exhausted to spend more time on the matter. "I need him. Can you carry him over the wall as well? And Lord Straton? He is wounded."

"I will carry them both," Ozias said, watching as Halcyon began to hurry away from him. "But Halcyon! Where are you going?"

"The Destry," she called over her shoulder.

She did not watch her uncle take to the sky again. Her eyes were set on one thing only.

It was two streets away. Its burnished roof basked in the fire of sunset, beckoning her to hurry.

And Halcyon ran to the Destry.

"Who are you?" Damon rasped at Evadne again. Frantic, bewildered. He edged away from her, like her presence was overwhelming him.

Evadne halted, felt his golden shards cut into her knees. She watched Damon's anguish as he continued to move as far from her as he could, like she would harm him.

He does not know who I am.

And her heart broke into pieces; her chest felt like it was caving under the pain. She could not breathe. She could not think. All she could do was kneel in his blood and watch him tremble.

"Leave him be, Evadne," a cold, pitying voice said.

Evadne, numb, looked up to see Selene, standing beside her. She regarded her nephew's distress with a sigh.

"What . . . what has happened to him?" Evadne whispered, hoarse.

"He reached the bottom of his magical well and ran it dry. His magic has broken. And it has taken a portion of his memories with it." She looked down at Evadne. "I am sorry to tell you this, but he will not remember who you are, Evadne."

Selene's revelation dripped off Evadne like rain. She could not grasp it. She could not imagine a world where Damon did not know her.

Evadne looked at him again, trying to suppress her devastation. She watched as he glanced up at his aunt, and the lines of pain eased in his face.

"Aunt Selene," he said. "Aunt . . . help me."

"I will help you, Damon. Give me just a moment." Selene offered Evadne her hand. "Come, Daughter. There is nothing else you can do for him. It is best that you leave."

Evadne stared at the mage's elegant hand. The silver ring on her thumb. Selene had known Damon would sing his magic dry to the bone, and that was why she had cautioned him before the duel.

And yet his aunt had still partaken in the challenge, knowing her strength would outlast him. Selene had broken him, and she did not seem to care.

Reluctantly, Evadne accepted Selene's hand. The mage drew her to her feet. A strained moment passed between them as Evadne saw pity within Selene's eyes—pity Evadne did not want. And then that pity disappeared like it had only been an act, and Selene's eyes narrowed with ire and hatred. She moved swiftly, gracefully. There was a gleam of steel in her hand.

Evadne stepped back, but she was not fast enough. Selene plunged a dagger into her belly, deep and jagged.

A sound of shock escaped Evadne. And then a wave of pain cascaded through her, shook her bones. Pain that made her want to drop to the floor. She felt the dagger withdraw, and Selene prepared to stab her again.

Evadne did not move, not until Selene had stabbed her a second time, the blade fully embedded in Evadne's side, just beneath her ribs. Only then did she find her sister's kopis, like a promise waiting to be fulfilled. She took the hilt, and with her teeth bared, she drove Halcyon's scythe into Selene's soft neck.

Selene jerked, surprised. But it was over—she had been defeated—and she knew it as she gazed at Evadne. Her blood began to pour down her neck, fast and bright. She stepped back and gurgled, clawing at the hilt.

Evadne's mind went blank as she watched Selene succumb to the floor. Her blood spread out beneath her like a red cloak, and then the malevolent light dimmed in her eyes.

Evadne had just killed someone.

The truth echoed through her like she was hollow, and she felt changed. Culled. She felt as if she had just crossed a threshold that could never be found and recrossed again.

"You killed her."

Evadne lifted her gaze to where Damon still sat on the floor. "Damon . . ." Her heart welled at the sight of him. She was overcome with the desire to go to him, to touch him, kiss his face. To hold him in his brokenness. And yet his eyes betrayed his anger at her. He pointed at her with his right hand.

"Stay away from me."

She did not know what to do. He crawled and groaned, unable to walk. She could not leave him, and yet he did not know her. He did not want her.

A beat of footsteps. Dazed, Evadne glanced up to see Selene's scribe was staring at her, backing away. She had forgotten about him. He fled from the Destry, and it was only her and Damon now.

She and Damon and a glimmer of something enchanted in the shadows.

Evadne realized the All-Seeing Crown was on the floor. Selene must have set it aside during the duel. The olive wreath waited in the shadows, silver and green and full of secrets.

Evadne started to move to it and discovered that walking was suddenly very arduous and painful. Selene's dagger was still buried in her side, and Evadne looked at its hilt, wondering if she should remove it or if that would make her bleed out faster.

She set her teeth against the pain it provoked, and she walked with the blade still trapped in her side. It took her a moment to kneel and take the crown within her hands. And then it took her another stilted moment to rise to her feet and turn to where Damon sat, staring at her with suspicious eyes.

She walked to him. "Damon," she whispered, and her love for him turned his name into a melody, a chorus.

He drew himself up to his feet with the help of Euthymius's column. "I do not know you . . . Stay away from me."

Evadne gently progressed, watching as he turned to face her, his back pressed against the pillar. He was angry and terrified and confused. And she could only hope that this crown would be enough.

"Damon, let me help you," she whispered.

He stared at her, his breath ragged. But he did not move, and he did not protest.

"Please." Evadne closed the distance between them. With a dagger in her side and blood soaking her chiton, she crowned Damon.

She waited, trembling and wondering.

The crown enabled its bearer to see either the past, present, or future of the one they looked upon. And as Damon studied her . . . Evadne could only hope that he would see her past. That he would see how they had come together as friends, as a mage and a scribe. That he would see all the trials they had walked through, all the pain and the worry and the magic and the desire.

Once, she had been reluctant for him to look into her mind. She had vowed she would never welcome him into her thoughts.

But now . . . she *longed* for him to see her, to remember her.

She watched the change come over him, the tension fade from his body. His eyes—brown and blue—softened like earth after a long rain. He reached for her with his right hand; he traced the edge of her jaw and whispered her name, and she felt her heart stir and fight to continue beating even when it was slowing . . . slowing . . .

"Evadne."

She smiled at him. He was blurring before her; she realized she was crying. Damon kissed the tears from her face, and she clung to him. Her body was turning cold. It felt like a shadow was creeping over her.

She groaned in agony when he brushed the hilt in her side.

He eased her back and saw the dagger. The joy in his eyes morphed into terror. Her chiton was red; she had smeared her blood on his clothes. She struggled to breathe and took hold of the hilt and withdrew it, let it clatter to the floor.

"Damon," she whispered, and he held her, slowly eased them both down to the floor.

"Evadne, *Evadne.* Stay with me . . ."

She felt his warmth, his breath as he held her close. She could hear his heart beating, frantic. The contrast to hers.

She tilted her head back. The last thing she remembered was the ceiling of the Destry, how it was a mirror of the sky.

She watched it blush mauve as evening deepened. The first stars were awakening when she slipped away, into the darkness.

～

Halcyon entered the Destry, the doors slamming in her wake as she stepped into the lobby. She noticed the blood first. So much blood glazed the floor.

"Evadne?" she called, walking deeper into the cavernous chamber. She saw Damon sitting, holding, and weeping over her sister.

Her sister, drenched in blood.

No.

Halcyon hurried to them, slipping on Evadne's blood. She hit the floor and crawled, distraught.

"No, no, no."

Damon had killed her sister.

Damon had killed her sister.

She could not comprehend it, even as she saw the evidence of it. And then it hit her like a blow, and Halcyon felt her heart shatter. Trembling, she reached out to touch Evadne's face.

She finally understood the pain she had given Damon, for now he gave it back to her.

"Help her," Damon whispered to Halcyon. *"Help her."*

Evadne was alive.

Halcyon uttered a desperate sound. Damon's left hand was curled in a fist, but he opened his arms, and Halcyon gently eased Evadne from his lap onto hers.

"Eva? *Eva.*" Halcyon prayed, feeling her pulse.

Her sister still breathed, slowly bleeding out on the floor.

And Halcyon could save her. Halcyon had Magda's Sunstone Ring of Healing. She could save Evadne, and she shifted her arms so she could withdraw her hand from Evadne's back . . .

Her hand was bare. Reminding her that she had given the relic to the commander.

"Halcyon," Damon struggled to speak, and she finally looked closer at him. He was bent over, as if he could not breathe. "Save her."

Halcyon wanted to blister him with her words. To flay him like a fish. And then she saw the other body, lying in a pool of blood. Selene. With Halcyon's kopis in her throat.

Halcyon strove to make sense of it.

Evadne had killed Selene. Selene must have stabbed her. Damon . . . Damon was innocent, but he was broken, just like Thales.

And Halcyon could not save her sister.

"Oh, Eva." She held Evadne, brushed the hair back from her sister's face.

Time contorted. She did not know how long she sat there, cradling Evadne to her breast, Evadne's blood streaking her armor. But she suddenly realized they were not alone. Ozias, Thales, and Straton arrived at the Destry. The three men approached her, walking the bloodstained floor.

"Halcyon."

She met Straton's gaze as he knelt beside her. Beyond him stood Thales and Uncle Ozias, their faces grieved as they watched her hold Evadne.

The commander removed Magda's ring from his finger. He held the relic out to Halcyon, his eyes gentle.

"Take the ring, Halcyon."

But he needed it, too. She looked at his wounded thigh, which the sunstone's power had begun to mend. His skin was still mottled from the poison. It would take days, possibly weeks of the ring's power to flush it from his body. Halcyon knew this all too well.

If she took the ring from him, she knew he would die.

"Commander—"

"Put the ring on Evadne's hand," he said. "It is all right, Halcyon. This is how it is meant to be."

She stared at him, tears burning her eyes. He only smiled at her tenderly.

She took the ring and slipped it onto Evadne's finger.

Instantly, Evadne's breathing shifted, deepened. A small flush returned to her cheeks, the moon and constellations from the enchanted ceiling dusting her in silver light.

Relieved, Halcyon cradled her close, feeling Ozias move to stand behind her, his hand on her shoulder. They watched as Straton crawled to where his son was writhing on the floor.

The commander touched Damon's hair gently, drawing him up into an embrace.

"I have you, Son. I have you," Straton whispered, holding Damon to his heart.

Damon clung to his father, weeping into his neck. The sounds that emerged from him were painful, haunting to hear.

Halcyon knew she would never be able to forget them.

Thales lowered himself to his knees, covering his face. He was the only one who could truly understand the agony Damon was experiencing. And he cried for him, for the young mage who had broken and lost his magic.

And as Evadne's wounds began to close, Straton's wounds began to reopen.

Their blood mingled on the black-and-white floor of the Destry. Mingled among glittering shards of gold.

Hold on, Commander, Halcyon wanted to order him. *Your son needs you. Your family needs you. Do not go out like this.*

And Straton lifted his eyes to hers.

He was in pain, for himself and for his son. But he would hold on. Just long enough, Halcyon knew.

He would hold on.

⤐ XXXVI ⤏

Halcyon and Evadne

Halcyon followed her uncle through the winding streets of Mithra, Evadne cradled in his arms. She was only vaguely aware of Thales behind her, because her hands and armor were still stained with her sister's blood. They turned down one street, then another, the Destry soon far behind them. Eventually, Ozias used Kirkos's relic to glide up a set of stairs to a third-story flat, Halcyon taking two steps at a time to keep up with him.

"Quickly, Halcyon," Ozias said when they reached his door. He handed her a key, and Halcyon fumbled to open it.

She entered her uncle's apartment. It was dark and smelled of sandalwood, and she tripped over a chair in her haste to reach the veranda doors, swinging them open to the night. She arranged some cushions on the porch floor, and her uncle eased Evadne down onto them.

Evadne was still unconscious, lost deep in healing sleep.

Despite it all, Halcyon wanted to wake her, to see her sister's eyes and hear her voice.

She brushed a tangle of hair away from Evadne's face. The moonlight was not as bright as Halcyon wanted, and she yearned for dawn, for a flood of unhindered, bright sunlight to limn her sister. To quicken her healing.

This would be a long night.

"Let me see if my neighbor has some clothes I can borrow for Evadne," Ozias said, panting. He turned and nearly barreled into Thales, and a string of low murmurs were exchanged between the men.

Halcyon was too preoccupied to listen to them and she sank next to Evadne. Ozias departed, but Thales remained on the veranda, his presence a quiet comfort.

Halcyon listened to the nightingales, to the distant echo of a child crying. She remembered the sounds Damon had released, and her heart beat with sorrow.

"Has he lost his magic for good, Thales?"

Thales was silent, gazing at the sprawl of the city. "Yes, Halcyon. He will never cast magic again."

She exhaled a long, deep breath. Her eyes were still on Evadne, and she felt ill at the anticipation of having to reveal this to her little sister. Because Halcyon had seen it—the way the air shimmered between Evadne and Damon. The way they looked at each other.

"How long will it take him to heal?" she asked.

"It depends." Thales did not elaborate, and Halcyon sensed it was a sensitive topic.

Ozias returned with a white tunic draped over his arm. He also brought a sponge and a bowl of water, for Halcyon to wash the blood from Evadne's body.

The men left her on the veranda, and Halcyon began to undress her sister. She unpinned the bronze wings at her shoulders; she unfastened the golden belt at her waist. She removed the bloodstained chiton and saw the wounds that marred Evadne's skin. Two stab marks on her abdomen. They were still in the process of closing. The moonlight was not strong enough, Halcyon lamented, praying for a short night. Gently, she cleansed the blood from Evadne's body and dressed her in the new tunic. It was too big; it swallowed Evadne, and Halcyon felt like weeping.

She lay down beside her sister. And she did not intend to sleep, but slumber soon snared her, and Halcyon drifted into a sequence of bitter dreams.

She woke to her uncle's hand on her shoulder, gently rousing her.

"Halcyon? Someone is here to see you."

She sat forward, a crick in her neck. It was still night, and Evadne still slept, incandescent with silver light.

"I will sit with Evadne," Ozias reassured her, and Halcyon rose stiffly and walked through her uncle's flat to the open front door.

A girl waited on the threshold. Halcyon had never seen her before, but an amulet was fastened on her arm. One of Straton's servants.

"Halcyon of Isaura?" she asked.

Halcyon nodded.

"Lord Straton has summoned you to his villa," the girl said, a quiver in her voice. "He asks that you come as quickly as you can."

Halcyon hesitated. She wanted to go to the commander. But she wanted to stay. To remain beside her sister.

Torn, she turned to where Thales stood nearby, watching and listening.

"Tell my uncle I will return soon," she said hoarsely. And she slipped out of the flat before she could change her mind.

The girl ran with Halcyon, struggling to keep up with Halcyon's long strides. The commander's villa was not far. Halcyon ran to it with her heart in her throat, with her stomach aching. The gates were open; she ascended the stairs, and the guards wordlessly opened the great bronze doors for her.

She had never been here before, but Xander had often told her about it. In some ways, she felt like she had walked these floors before, in her dreams.

Lyra was waiting for her at the edge of a reflection pool. Wordlessly, she led Halcyon up a flight of marble stairs, down a corridor bend, into Straton and Cosima's private bedchamber.

At once, Halcyon wanted to flee.

Incense burned. Halcyon recognized the sweet, woody aroma of frankincense, the oil that was burned on the altars of Nikomides. All of the shutters were open to welcome in fresh night air, the white curtains billowing in the gentle breeze. Halcyon came to a reluctant stop beside the wash table, which was covered in jars and pots—herbs and tinctures and salves—and a roll of linen. A basin full of bloody water.

She felt like she was intruding on a private moment. She wanted to retreat until she saw the commander.

Straton was sitting upright in his bed, supported by cushions. Waiting for Halcyon.

His wife stood beside him, her face exhausted, her fair hair lank across her brow. Damon sat on a stool on the other side of the bed, still wearing Acantha's crown on his brow. His left hand was bandaged; all of his fingers had been reset—Halcyon did not want to imagine the pain of that, having experienced a broken thumb years ago. He held a cup of tonic in his right hand; Halcyon could smell the pungency of it, and she surmised his mother had made him a brew to dull his pain.

"Kingfisher," Straton said, but his voice sounded wrong. It was weak, frail. "Come closer."

As soon as Halcyon moved to his bedside, Cosima, Damon, and Lyra all departed the chamber.

Numb, Halcyon took the stool Damon had vacated. She felt the commander looking at her, waiting for her to rouse her courage, to meet his gaze.

Slowly, she did.

She saw the sheen of death in his eyes. The color of life was leaving him, breath by breath. And Halcyon wanted to rage and weep; she did not want him to leave her. She had never been one to pray much, but how tempted she was now to beseech the divines. To heal Straton, to let him live.

"Soon, I will be gone," Straton said. "And I wanted to see you. To ask something of you."

Halcyon waited, her throat thick with emotion.

"I want you to be there," he continued. "To help Narcissa and my other captains. To help them lead the legion."

"I am not worthy of this," she whispered.

"You are more than worthy. One day, you will take my place." He reached for her hand. It was large, scarred, feverish. She could see the veins in his wrist, stained by poison. "Look at me, Kingfisher."

It took everything within her to hold back her tears, to meet his gaze again.

"I have named you my successor. Narcissa will lead the legion in the meantime, until you have served your time as captain. And then . . . it will be you. It is my desire to see you command the Bronze."

Her mind was a whirlwind. Her thoughts tangled and chimed, and she could not breathe, to imagine taking his place one day.

"Will you do this, Halcyon of Isaura?"

She swallowed the lump in her throat. She tightened her hold on him. "Yes, Commander. It would be an honor."

"Good." He leaned back into his cushions. His strength was almost spent.

"Let me get you something to drink." Halcyon tried to rise, but he held on to her fingers, keeping her in place.

"There is one more thing I must ask of you, Kingfisher."

Straton drew in a raspy breath and set his bloodshot gaze on her again. "Damon is wearing Acantha's crown. But it is time for us to complete the mission. I want you to carry the All-Seeing

Crown to the palace and set it upon Queen Nerine's brow. To break the enchantment."

It was the final leg of the mission, one that she and Damon and Xander and Straton had forged together. This was the end, what they had dreamt of: to crown the queen with the relic.

"Do it as soon as you can," the commander said. "For the legion still waits in the field for the gates to open."

"I swear it will be done, Lord."

He was languid; he was fading. And Halcyon had still not fully forgiven him for all the wrongs that had been committed against her.

She had believed it would take her moons, maybe even years. But how death changed things. How death sharpened and sobered a soul. She could not imagine a world without Straton. And she knew that she had forgiven him, and the forgiveness had come softly. It had been the moment when she saw him sitting against the wall, when she saw his wound. A wound he had taken for her.

She lifted his hand, held his knuckles against her cheek. She whispered, "The world will darken without you."

Straton smiled. "And yet I am at peace, to know you will be its light."

He knew she had forgiven him. She saw it in his eyes, and she let him go.

She stood, battling the urge to run. Cosima entered the room, smoothing the wrinkles from the commander's blankets, and Halcyon slipped from the chamber. Lyra was waiting for her again in the corridor.

"My brother is in his chambers," she said, leading Halcyon farther down the hall.

They found Damon sitting in a chair, staring at an empty desk. Arcalos was curled up at his feet, and Acantha's crown gleamed against his dark hair. His face was strained when he looked at Halcyon. He knew she was coming to take the crown from him. The crown that was preserving his memory.

Lyra fixed another tonic for him, set the cup in his hand. Damon stared at it a moment, reluctant, before draining the liquid. At once, the tension in his body began to fade. It was a brew to usher him into sleep.

"The past five moons," he said, staring at the desk again. "When I wake from this tonic, I will not remember what has happened the past five moons. From the moment I graduated the Destry until now . . . all of it will be wiped from my mind. When I wake, I will think that it is the day after my graduation." He met Halcyon's gaze, and she heard the words he did not say.

He would not remember Xander's death. He would have to relive the pain of it.

He would not remember all the magic he had created and cast the past five moons.

He would not remember his venture into Mount Euthymius, how the mission he'd planned had come to fruition.

He would not remember his challenge with Selene, a challenge that had rendered his breaking.

He would not remember his father had been mortally wounded.

He would not remember Evadne.

Halcyon did not know what to say. But she saw Damon's heartbreak, to know that he was about to lose so much from his life.

"Halcyon," he said, his words beginning to slur, "tell Evadne . . . that I will find my way back to her, as soon as I am able."

He leaned his head back and drifted unconscious.

Halcyon delayed a moment, staring at his face, at his bandaged hand. She was trembling when she finally took the All-Seeing Crown from his brow.

She ran with the crown, up the winding road to the summit where the queen's palace rested. None of the guards hindered her; they merely watched Halcyon stride in her bloodstained armor through the palace gardens and up the stairs into the grand hall.

Incense burned from silver bowls. Torches flickered from ornate columns, the light illuminating carven vines and falcons and moons. The floor was so polished it was like the face of water; Halcyon's reflection shone vividly upon it. At the end of the hall was the golden throne, smoldering like a fallen star. And Queen Nerine sat upon it, frozen in time, her eyes closed.

Enchanted into sleep.

Halcyon paused, gazing upon her queen. When she began to close the distance, a guard finally intercepted her.

"What are you doing?" he barked at her.

"I am . . ." Halcyon halted, but she had no words within her. She was exhausted, broken, bloodied, devastated, hopeful.

"Let her pass," another guard said, seeing the crown Halcyon carried.

The guards backed away, and Halcyon continued her walk to the throne. She walked for Xander, for the commander, for Ozias. She walked for Damon and Evadne. She walked for herself, for all that she had done, all she had sacrificed to reach this moment.

She stepped upon the dais. Throughout the haze of the past few hours, she had forgotten that she still carried Nikomides's Devouring Sword, sheathed on her back. She could take the hilt, draw forth the blade, and the enchantment would break. But Halcyon did not choose the sword this time. She held up Acantha's crown. The green-and-silver olive leaves shivered in the firelight. They whispered of another era, another time. They whispered of hope and healing.

She set the crown upon Queen Nerine's brow.

And then quickly, quietly, Halcyon stepped down off the dais and knelt before the queen, her palms turned upward, her heart and mind ready. For the queen needed to know what had occurred, and she would need to look within Halcyon's past and present to come into that knowledge.

Queen Nerine's eyes fluttered open. Selene's enchantment melted away from her, like rime in sun. She was liberated, and she drew in a deep breath, confused until she met Halcyon's gaze. The two women were silent and still, their gazes united, their thoughts and hearts woven together. One gave; the other received.

And Halcyon did not know how much time passed, but at last, Queen Nerine rose. She wore Ari's Shawl of Stars, and the diamonds glittered with ancient light when she moved. She stepped off the dais and came to the hoplite.

The queen smiled and cupped Halcyon's face in her hands.

"Halcyon of Isaura, woman of bronze and courage . . . you have done me a great honor. Your sacrifice will be never be forgotten. Nor will Xander's and Damon's, Ozias's and Lord Straton's and your sister Evadne's. Your names will be carved in the palace walls, a testament to all you have done, to all that you are, to all you are destined to become."

The tears and emotions Halcyon had been suppressing surged forward. It was finished; it was done. And she turned her face into the queen's hands and finally wept.

When Evadne stirred, there was only one star left in the sky, hanging like a promise as the sun rose. She watched it fade, and she began to remember what had happened. She tried to sit forward, but her wounds ached in protest, and she groaned, lying back on the cushions.

She was on a veranda. Where? Where was she?

"Eva."

She heard Halcyon's voice and turned to see her sister was lying beside her. And Uncle Ozias was sleeping in a chair nearby, his mouth open as he snored, and another man—Thales—was also asleep, sitting against the wall.

"Where are we?" Evadne whispered.

Halcyon quietly sat forward and helped Evadne drink a few sips of water.

Gradually, her sister told her what had happened. Damon's breaking, Lord Straton's passing, Queen Nerine's liberation.

"It is over, Eva," Halcyon whispered and lovingly caressed

Evadne's tangled hair. "You have been so brave and strong, Little Sister. We have done everything that we could, and we have triumphed."

Then why did Evadne feel like she had lost? Why did tears crowd both of their eyes?

She thought of Damon. As soon as she did, she felt all the pieces of her heart, still scattered and agonized, struggle to beat within her chest.

Halcyon read her thoughts. "Just before I took the crown from him . . . Damon wanted me to tell you that he will find his way back to you, as soon as he is able."

Evadne said nothing, but her tears began to fall. *How?* She wanted to scream. How would he find his way back when his memories were culled?

He had only said it to ease her pain. And yet the pain was bright and sharp; she labored to breathe.

"Halcyon?" Evadne whispered.

"Yes, Eva?"

Evadne closed her eyes, and her tears continued to fall, streaking down her face into her hair. "Will you take me home to Isaura?"

Halcyon wiped away her tears. "Yes, Sister. I will take you home."

And Evadne finally understood the pain of breaking, the pain of trying to mend after loss. She felt an echo of Kirkos's anguish, and she wept as she finally understood the cost of his fall.

~XXXVII~

Evadne

Four Moons Later

"Pupa? Pupa, do not wear yourself out, now. We still have to sing tonight."

Evadne continued to move her small hand rake through the olive branches, smiling at Gregor's concern. "Do not worry, Father."

Despite her full recovery, her father had fussed over her, far worse than her mother. He stood beside the wagon, its bed brimming with olives, and he watched her harvest a few more moments, olives tumbling down around her onto the linen tarp, until he was certain the flush of Evadne's face was from the bite in the air and not overexertion.

The afternoon was cold and crisp with the arrival of the harvest. She and her family had been working from dawn to dusk collecting and pressing the olives. And when night arrived, they gathered in the common room, breaking bread and sharing stories and singing choruses.

It had been four moons since Evadne had left Mithra. Four moons since Evadne had returned to Isaura. And she had finally begun to sing again.

In the distance, they heard the gate bell ring.

"Agh, who could that be?" Gregor said.

"Probably the herald, Uncle Gregor," Maia said as she joined Evadne in raking.

"He was just here a few days ago, though." Aunt Lydia scowled as she dumped an apron full of olives into the wagon.

"I will go and see what he wants," Lysander swiftly volunteered, as if it were a chore to leave behind his rake. He jumped down from his ladder, where he had been harvesting at the top of the tree, and ran up the path, disappearing around the edge of the villa.

Evadne did not break her work. She was eager to focus on the branches, on the olives, on the motions of her rake. The work dulled her mind and her thoughts, made her sleep heavy at night, and she was grateful for it.

"My gods!" Aunt Lydia suddenly cried, and all of them looked up at the path.

Evadne saw Halcyon striding toward them, her bronze armor spangled with light, her smile broad, her strides eager.

Everyone rushed to her, and Halcyon embraced them all, saving Evadne for last. Evadne saw a gleam in her sister's eye, a gleam that she had not seen in a long time.

"We were not expecting you until Ari's holy day," Phaedra said, and they abandoned work to walk with Halcyon back to the villa.

Indeed, Halcyon had been in Abacus, preoccupied with work. Evadne had not allowed herself to hope to see Halcyon for a while.

The legion needed her sister more, ever since Straton's death.

"I took a hiatus," Halcyon said as they entered the courtyard. "I want to help with the harvest."

Evadne could see how her father was all but bursting with pride over that statement.

"It has been a while since you raked olives, Sprout."

Halcyon laughed. She had left her horse in the courtyard, and she walked to the mare, unknotting her saddlebag. "Yes, Father. But do not worry: I remember how."

Lysander offered to take Halcyon's horse to the stable, and Halcyon cradled her saddle pack in her arms, like something precious was hidden within it. She was looking at Evadne again, and Evadne cocked her brow, as if to say, *What is it?*

"I did come home to help with the harvest," Halcyon confessed, reaching into her leather bag. "But there is another reason . . ." She withdrew something bulky, wrapped snug in a linen sack. "I also have a delivery for Evadne."

Halcyon held it out to her sister, and at first all Evadne could do was stare at it.

"Here, Sister. Take it."

Evadne took the heavy linen sack in her arms. A leather string was bound about it, and a piece of parchment hung from the string.

For Evadne's eyes only, the parchment declared, in horrible handwriting.

Maia, who had crept up to Evadne's side, scrunched her nose as she tried to read it. "Divines, that is some terrible handwriting! How can you even read it?"

Evadne's breath caught. She felt the weight of the sack and she knew exactly what it held, knew exactly whose hand had written that crooked message. She met Halcyon's gaze. Halcyon who only smiled, her eyes thrilled.

Without a word, Evadne turned and rushed into the villa.

"Eva? *Eva!*" Her mother called after her.

"Let her go, Phaedra," Gregor said, and then he added to Halcyon, "You are certain you have no inkling as to what is in that bag?"

"Not even a smudge of an inkling, Father."

Evadne ascended the stairs, ignoring the jar of her ankle, and flew into her bedchamber, all but slamming the door. Her heart was wild; her breaths were uneven. She slowly walked to her bed and set the bundle down, suddenly afraid to open it.

For Evadne's eyes only.

Her hands shook as she opened the linen sack. She drew forth two different scrolls, and she recognized them both. One was thick and beautiful, its handles gilded. The other was slender and simpler, with smooth ashwood handles.

She traced them. It felt like reuniting with two long-lost friends, even though she had never held or written in these scrolls. But Damon had. To her greatest marvel and curiosity.

She took up the square of parchment and saw there was more written on the other side.

Start with the gilded scroll, he instructed.

Evadne crawled onto her bed and took the gilded scroll into her lap. It was thick, heavy, and she took a deep breath as she opened it.

His handwriting greeted her, crooked and ridden with ink blots. These were all of his right-handed words. And she began to read them.

11th Day of Storm Moon

Today I graduated from the Destry. This, Professor Zosime tells me, will be my breaking point. Anything after this day—after my finger takes the ring—will be lost should I run my magic dry. Should I break.

She told me to keep a journal. All wise mages do, even the most powerful of ones. Professor Zosime says I should record everything that means something to me, even if it is simple things, daily things that most take for granted.

"Would you be sad to lose it?" she posed the question to me. "If the answer is yes, record it down before the sun sets."

"But how?" I asked her. "I cannot write with my left hand, and I can hardly write legibly with my right."

She only raised her brow at me, and I know that look. I am to figure out a way, whether that is to strengthen my right hand or hire a scribe to record my daily experiences or take the risk of loss. But why would I want a scribe to hear all my inner thoughts? These pieces of my life that I want to ensure do not break from my mind?

Anyway, today is the breaking point. And my hand is already tired and I am frustrated—will I even be able to read all of this, if I am misfortunate enough to break?—and so I will write more tomorrow.

12th Day of Storm Moon

The worst and best thing about graduating from the Destry is putting your hand in the fire. For eight years, I have a been a student, studying and learning spells, eager to make my own someday. For eight years, I thought that my magical well would be as deep as my aunt's. My father thought this, too.

I set my hand into the magical fire, before all of my professors and fellow classmates, before all of our families, and I waited for my ring to form, to reveal how powerful I am.

The fire did not burn me. But I felt the ring take shape, welding to my finger.

When I drew my left hand back from the flames, there was the ring. Silver as the moon. Gleaming on my middle finger.

Average. I am average.

I am not strong. I am not weak. I am in the middle.

And I felt such envy to see a mage like Macarius come up behind me, set his hand in the fire, and come away with a deeper well, with more power than me.

And I could not bear to look at my father's face. All of his hope had been resting on me for our mission, and now it is waning, and I know he will not think I am capable, strong enough.

Why am I even writing this down?

Perhaps, though, to write it down is to find release. To find some catharsis.

And so I press this memory to papyrus and hope it will soon become iron, something to sharpen me.

This scroll was not at *all* what Evadne had thought it would be. And she continued to read his journal, knowing this was the path he had forged for himself, the path he would take to remember. He had an entry for every day. He always wrote about what had happened that day, even if it was something small, insignificant. And her heart started to pound as she drew closer to their meeting, knowing what was coming . . .

9th Day of Archer's Moon

My brother is dead.
My brother is dead, and I am coming undone.

11th Day of Archer's Moon

My brother is dead. And my father is missing. And I do not know what happened.
I do not have the strength to endure this.

19th Day of Archer's Moon

Halcyon killed Xander. I can hardly fathom this. My father finally sent word and has informed us that we must travel to Abacus at once.

Evadne had to stop reading. To stand and walk about her room. She lit her lamp, for evening had come. Eventually, she sat on her bed again and cried as she continued reading his entries of the hard days, the painful days when the truth came together and Halcyon had to take the fall.

And then she came to these lines: *I did not know that Halcyon had a younger sister. She sat across the assembly hall from me. I watched her for a moment before she noticed, and then she met my gaze directly. As if she could see through me. And suddenly, I found it difficult to be so angry, to be so bitter at Halcyon. Because I saw Evadne's pain as she listened to the trial unfold. I saw her pain as if it were a reflection of my own.*

Gradually, Damon began to write more and more of her. Evadne drank his words, felt them stir her heart. She could hardly breathe as she read by firelight, and she held these certain entries close. She felt her stray pieces begin to come back together:

I swore to Halcyon I would watch over her sister, and yet the first night of travel, Evadne tries to get herself killed. By none other than one of Ivina's phantoms. In the shadow of Euthymius. I want to rend my clothes with the irony of it all!

I should not care that Evadne is scrubbing our floors. I tell myself not to care, and yet I cannot sleep, thinking about her hands being cracked and broken by the lye. I asked Lyra to make a healing salve. My sister looked at me dubiously, like she knew exactly who it was for, and I am a fool, and I should guard myself. But Lyra made the salve, and I had it delivered to Evadne's room, and despite it all, I still cannot sleep.

I want to ask Evadne to be my scribe. And yet I am terrified. She will undoubtedly turn me down.

She has agreed and I can hardly believe it. Now I need to tell her the truth of the mission, and yet how? How is the best way for me to do this? Why do I feel so vulnerable in her presence?

Evadne moved on to the second scroll. This one began with his entry of Mount Euthymius, and Evadne knew Damon had purchased this scroll in Abacus, just before he joined up with his father's legion. Because the gilded scroll was still in Mithra, and Damon could not risk losing these memories.

In the utter darkness of the mountain's heart, I almost perished. I should have perished, and yet there was a girl, a girl made of secret wings, who carried me, brought me down gently in her arms.

His last entry was the night Evadne had seen him writing in the tent. He wrote of Halcyon's triumphant return to the legion. He wrote about his worries of breaking and running his magic dry, and yet despite the risk, how he did not want to be afraid.

She has strengthened me. When I hear her sing, all of my fears and all of my doubts drift away. If I must break, then I will. I can live without the magic. But I cannot live without—

That was it.

His last entry. He had not even completed his sentence. *What?*

Evadne wanted to breathe to him. *What can you not live without, Damon?*

She sat there, stunned. It was long past midnight. Halcyon had never come to their bedchamber, granting Evadne the privacy she needed.

Evadne made to close the scroll until she saw something. The tip of a feather, peeking from the right roll of the papyrus, as if beckoning her to open it, just a little more.

She did and found a falcon feather, resting above one more entry. The final entry, inked only four days ago. And as she read his words, Evadne knew. She knew he had found his way back to her.

7th Day of Olive Moon

Evadne, my heart. My chorus. I would sing with you until the end of days. I would sing with you until my bones turned to dust.

❧ XXXVIII ❧

Evadne

"Y ou are raking them all wrong, Hal."

Halcyon paused on her ladder, staring at the branch she had been harvesting from. "What do you mean?"

"You are supposed to rake in the *other* direction," Lysander said from below, but he burst into laughter and Halcyon pelted him with an olive.

"I told you I remember how to rake olives," she said, resuming her work with feigned indifference.

Evadne sat on the ground plucking stray leaves from the harvest, a mountain of olives spread on her shawl. It was just the three of them working on this side of the grove. The sun was setting; soon their mothers would call for them to return to the villa for dinner.

In the distance, the gate bell rang.

And it would almost seem that Halcyon was expecting it,

because she dropped from the ladder and said, "I'll get it!" before the bell had even finished clanging.

Lysander was on her heels, as if opening the gate required two people.

Evadne merely watched the two of them race up the path, Halcyon leaving Lysander in her dust. And then it was quiet, and Evadne leaned her head back against the olive trunk and closed her eyes, listening to the sounds of the grove.

It was cold, and she shivered, her arms bare. She should carry her shawl and the olives up the path to the wagon, but she delayed, reveling in the quiet dusk.

She heard footsteps approaching, soft on the grass.

She thought it was Halcyon and drawled, "And what news did the herald bring now?"

A pause. She felt the prompting of a gaze, but Evadne kept her eyes closed.

"He says that it is miraculous he remembered how to find this place."

The voice was deep and mirthful, with a bite of gravel in it.

A voice Evadne had longed to hear for moons.

She opened her eyes to see Damon standing a few paces away. For a moment, she could not breathe, and it seemed he could not, either. And then he smiled, and Evadne rose to her feet, suddenly embarrassed that her chiton was stained with dirt and grass, and her hair was loose and wild, and she smelled of olives.

Not once in his recordings had he described her appearance. He would not remember what she looked like, and now . . . he was finally seeing her for the first time, this girl he had written about in his journal. This girl he had come to love.

"I was not expecting you," she said, discreetly attempting to brush the wrinkles from her clothes.

"You received my delivery?" He took a step closer to her.

"I did. But I . . ." She let her voice trail. It had only been last night that she had read his journal. And his final entry had been inked only days before. She should have surmised he would come within days. She should have known he and her sister had coordinated this. "I did not know you would come so soon."

Damon stopped. He was so close to her. So close she could smell the sun and wind in his clothes, see the sheen of golden dust on his sandals.

"I should have waited another day."

"No. I am glad you are here."

Damon was quiet for a breath, drinking her in. His eyes drifted to her shoulders, where her bronze wings caught the sunset. He would not remember them, she knew. He would not remember that he'd had made them for her, because he had never written about them. And yet something stirred in his eyes. As if he was realizing a dream had not just been a dream.

"I read every word," she said.

"Then you know that there are a few things that I have forgotten," he replied.

"I will help you remember," she whispered.

He drew in a deep breath and she shivered, from the cold and his beauty and his nearness.

A wry smile danced on his face. "Are you cold, Evadne?"

Ah, he had written about that night in his scroll. The night when they had been traveling to Euthymius. When they had lain back-to-back. It had taken him forever to fall asleep because he could not cease thinking about her.

"I am freezing, Damon." She dared to reach out and touch him, uncertain until his arms came about her as if he had been waiting, dreaming of this moment. He held her close, and she felt his breath stir her hair, his hands touch her back where her wings had once beaten.

"My magic is gone, Evadne," he said, mournful. Evadne drew back so she could look at him.

"Then we shall have to make our own." She kissed him, soft and gentle, until he opened his mouth beneath hers.

The stars had begun to emerge, gleaming through the boughs of the olive tree, and Damon finally broke their kiss to whisper against her lips, "You have kissed me before, haven't you?"

Evadne laughed, a pure, sweet sound. She found his right hand—his left was still bandaged—and she wove their fingers together and began to lead him on the path.

"You must be hungry. Let us go and eat with my family, before my father begins to worry and comes hunting for me."

"Gods forbid," Damon said, and Evadne smiled, tightening her hold on his hand.

They walked in the quiet starlight, the nightingales crooning above them, the grass and clover fragrant beneath them.

Gregor's villa came into view, a house brimming with light and voices.

Evadne paused, soaking in the sight of home. She cast her eyes to Damon and saw he was regarding it, too.

"Sing with me tonight?" she invited.

Damon met her gaze and smiled. She saw the stars in his eyes, a slow awakening of joy in his face.

"I would like that," he said.

He followed her into the villa, into the laughter and the firelight.

⇀ACKNOWLEDGMENTS⇀

It's hard to believe I now have three books out in the wild. Some days, it feels like I only just began this journey, and when I reflect on how each of my stories came to be, on all the people who have been instrumental in their creation and publication, I am deeply humbled.

First, to my husband, Ben. It's about time I dedicated a book to you. Although I think my love for you is woven into every one of my stories. Thank you for all of the support and early-morning prayers, the encouragement and wisdom, the laughter and tears and love you have shared with me on this journey. For listening to me plot and dream and scheme, and for taking me out to dinner when I was too preoccupied with drafting and revising to cook. And for coming up with the nicknames Pupa and Sprout.

To my pup, Sierra. I can't resist putting you in every book, too. Thank you for inspiring Arcalos. I'm always glad for your reminders to go for walks and get sunshine.

To my parents, Tim and Beth. For always encouraging me to

dream. I would not be the writer I am today without your love and support. To my siblings, who I love and would absolutely offer to take half of your punishment in a trial (although let's not test this, okay?): Caleb, Gabe, Ruth, Mary, and Luke. To my grandparents, who are my constant inspiration, and my in-laws, Ted and Joy Ross, and the entire Ross clan, who have loved me so well. To all of my extended family—aunts and uncles and cousins. Thank you for supporting me.

To the kindred spirits who continue to inspire so much of my characters: Kaylin, Deanna, Aly. You are my shield sisters and I love each of you dearly.

To Kristen Ciccarelli, Mindee Arnett, Adrienne Young, and Elly Blake—for your beautiful and generous words about this story. Your books, in turn, have inspired and filled my creative well.

To my lovely CP, Heather Lyons, who read an early draft of this book and has given me so much encouragement and insight. To Isabel Ibañez, who is the wind in my sails and can always make me laugh when I need it the most. To Taylor at the bookish ballad, for all of your love and support and excitement for my books. I am so happy you and I met at Comic Con, and I hope to see your own book on the shelf soon!

To Suzie. Agent Extraordinaire. You have been my rock and my champion, and I am eternally thankful for you and your passion for my stories. I know I say this time and time again and you always laugh when I do, but truly, I could not do this without you. Thank you for giving my dream the wings to take flight.

To Dani, for being so wonderful and helping me in all things. To the inimitable team at New Leaf: Joanna, Mia, Veronica, Kathleen, Cassandra, Pouya, and Hilary. I could not do this without each and every one of you. Thank you for making my dreams come true.

To my editor, Karen Chaplin. I'm so thankful I've had you for three whole books! If not for you, this would still only be Eva's story, and I would have never written from Hal's perspective. Which has, indeed, made this book so much fiercer. Thank you for all the hours and insight you have given to my characters and worlds.

To Rosemary Brosnan and the splendid team at HarperTeen. What a journey this has been, and I continue to be honored and humbled that I got to share it with all of you. From editorial to design to production to marketing to publicity and sales—I am thankful for all the many hands and eyes that have shared a part in the making of this book, and for the countless hours the team has given to me to make this story shine.

To the wonderful Epic Reads—I am so thankful for all of your posts and pictures and enthusiasm. You are the best.

To Kate O'Hara, who created the beautiful map and cover. It is everything I dreamt of for this book. To Molly Fehr, whose hand lettering is divine and who brought such vision together for my cover—thank you a hundred times over.

To R. G. Grant and his volume *Warrior*, for granting me insight into hoplite armor and weapons and their battle tactics.

To my incredible and passionate Street Team, who has gone

above and beyond. I am immensely thankful for each and every one of you for joining the Legion, for helping me spread the word and celebrate the release of this book alongside me. I am simply awed and humbled by you, and can never thank you enough for your love and support.

To my readers and fans, in the United States and overseas, for all of your sweet messages and posts and reviews. For always believing in me. Thank you, *thank you*.

And to my Heavenly Father. I stand amazed.

Soli Deo Gloria.

1

September's new moon waited for the sun to set, and I found myself trapped in Mazarine's library, drawing her twelfth portrait by candlelight. For as long as I had known her, she had never left her house during the day, and she kept her curtains closed while the sun reigned. She liked to summon me every few months for various things, the foremost to commit her face to paper with my charcoal stick as if she forgot what she looked like, the second to read to her from one of her leather-bound books. I was eager to do both because she paid me well, and I liked the stories I could sometimes coax from her. Stories that came from the mountains. Stories that were nearly forgotten, turning into dust.

"Do I look the same as I did the last time you drew me?" she asked from where she sat in a chair, its armrests carved as roaring lions. She was wearing her usual raiment: an elegant velvet gown the shade of blood with a diamond necklace anchored at her neck.

The stone caught the firelight every time she breathed, winking with secrets.

"You look unchanged," I replied, thinking that I'd drawn her only three months ago, and I continued with my sketch of her.

She was proud, even with her multitude of wrinkles and her age spots and her strange beady eyes. I liked her confidence, and I drew it in the tilt of her chin, the hint of her knowing smile, and the waves of her long quicksilver hair. I wondered how old she was, but I didn't dare ask.

Sometimes I feared her, although I couldn't explain why. She was ancient. I had rarely seen her move from the furniture scattered about this gilded, shadowed room. And yet something pulsed from her. Something I couldn't identify but all the same cautioned me to keep my eyes open in her presence.

"Your father does not like when I summon you here," she drawled in a smoky voice. "He does not like you alone with me, does he?"

Her words unsettled me, but I concealed my feelings. The dimness of the room was like a cloak, and while it seemed impossible to draw a portrait in such poor light, I did it well.

"My father simply needs me home on time today," I said, and she knew what I implied.

"Ah, a new moon awaits you tonight," said Mazarine. "Tell me, Clementine . . . have you read one of my nightmares recorded in your father's book?"

I had not, because there were no recordings of her nightmares in the book my father filled and guarded. I didn't want to confess such to her, for fear it might upset her.

And so I lied.

"My father doesn't let me read all his recordings. I'm only an apprentice, Ms. Thimble."

"Ah," she said, drinking from a sparkling glass of wine. "You are an apprentice, but you wage war beside him on new moon nights. And you are just as strong and skilled as him. I have watched you fight in the streets on the darkest nights. You will surpass him, Clementine. Your magic shines brighter than his."

I finished with her portrait at last. Partly because her words fed a hungry spirit within me that I strove to keep hidden.

"Your portrait is done." I set down my charcoal, wiped my fingers on my skirt, and walked the paper to her. She studied it by the candlelight that burned from iron stands around her, wax dripping like stalactites.

She was quiet for a long moment. A bead of perspiration began to trace my back, and I felt anxious until she grinned, her yellow teeth gleaming in the firelight.

"Yes, I am unchanged. What a relief." She laughed, but the sound was far from reassuring.

My blood hummed with warning.

I gathered my supplies, tucking them into my leather satchel, eager to be gone. I couldn't judge the time of day, since Mazarine had the curtains drawn, but I sensed that afternoon was waning.

I needed to get home.

"A magician and an artist," Mazarine mused, admiring my sketch of her. "An artist and a magician. Which one do you desire to be more? Or perhaps you dream of learning *deviah* magic and combining the two. I would indeed like to see an enchanted drawing of yours someday, Clementine."

I hefted the satchel strap onto my shoulder, standing halfway between her chair and the double doors. I didn't want to say that she was right, but she had an uncanny sense of reading people. She had also watched me grow up in this town.

Since I was eight, my father had instructed me in *avertana* magic, a defensive magic that lent its strength to spars and duels. We often faced spells bent by malicious intent, which made for dangerous and unpredictable situations, such as the new moon nights. And I liked *avertana* more for those things, but I also had started thinking of the other two studies of magic, *metamara* and *deviah*—but *deviah* in particular. To take one's skill and create an enchanted object was no simple feat, and I had read of magicians who had devoted decades of their lives to reach such achievement.

I needed more time. More time to hone my craft of art before I tried to layer magic within it. I had taught myself how to draw and had gradually become proficient with charcoal, as art supplies were hard to come by in this rustic town, but I knew my experience was lacking, and there were many other branches of art, waiting for me to explore.

"Perhaps one day," I replied.

"Hmm" was all Mazarine said.

Rachel G. White

Rebecca Ross received her bachelor's degree in English from the University of Georgia. In the past, she has worked at a Colorado dude ranch, as a school librarian, and as a live-time captionist for a college. She resides in northeast Georgia with her husband and her dog. She is the author of *The Queen's Rising* and *The Queen's Resistance*. This is her third novel. Visit her on the web at www.rebeccarossauthor.com, on Instagram @beccajross, or on Twitter @_RebeccaRoss.

FIND REBECCA ROSS ON

Also available as an ebook and as a
downloadable audio.

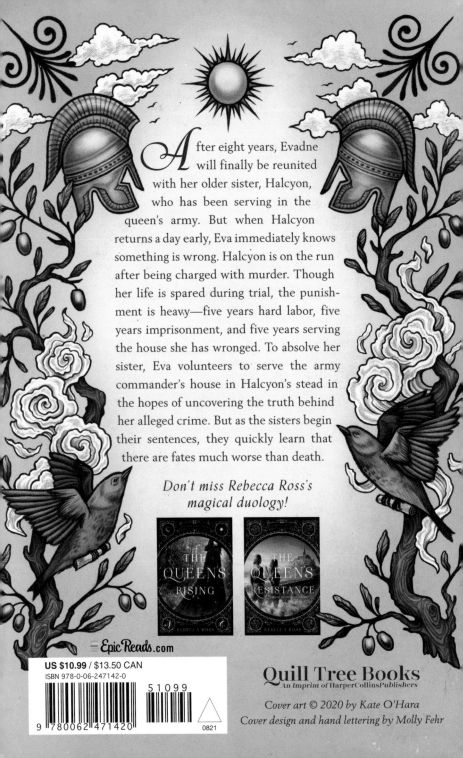

After eight years, Evadne will finally be reunited with her older sister, Halcyon, who has been serving in the queen's army. But when Halcyon returns a day early, Eva immediately knows something is wrong. Halcyon is on the run after being charged with murder. Though her life is spared during trial, the punishment is heavy—five years hard labor, five years imprisonment, and five years serving the house she has wronged. To absolve her sister, Eva volunteers to serve the army commander's house in Halcyon's stead in the hopes of uncovering the truth behind her alleged crime. But as the sisters begin their sentences, they quickly learn that there are fates much worse than death.

Don't miss Rebecca Ross's magical duology!

THE QUEEN'S RISING

THE QUEEN'S RESISTANCE

Quill Tree Books
An Imprint of HarperCollins Publishers

Cover art © 2020 by Kate O'Hara
Cover design and hand lettering by Molly Fehr

US $10.99 / $13.50 CAN
ISBN 978-0-06-247142-0

51099

9 780062 471420

0821